THE DEMON OF SICILY

Gothic Classics

THE
DEMON OF SICILY

A ROMANCE

FOUR VOLUMES IN ONE

Edward Montague

Foreword by Jo Beverley

Be thou a spirit of health, or goblin damn'd?
Bring'st with thee airs from Heaven, or blasts from Hell?
Be thy intents wicked or charitable,
Thou com'st in such a questionable shape
That I will speak to thee.

SHAKESPEARE.

Kansas City:
VALANCOURT BOOKS
2007

The Demon of Sicily by Edward Montague.
First published by J. F. Hughes in 1807
First Valancourt Books edition, August 2007

Library of Congress Cataloguing-in-Publication Data

Montague, Edward, fl. 1806-1808.
 The demon of Sicily : a romance / Edward Montague ;
foreword by Jo Beverley. — 1st Valancourt Books ed.
 p. cm. — (Gothic classics)
"Four volumes in one."
 Originally published in 4 v.: London : J. F. Hughes, 1807.
ISBN 978-1-934555-11-8
I. Title.
PR5029.M787D46 2007
823'.7--dc22
2007016237

Published by Valancourt Books
Kansas City, Missouri

Composition by James D. Jenkins
Set in Dante MT

10 9 8 7 6 5 4 3 2 1

CONTENTS

Preface by Jo Beverley	vii
Editor's Note	xiii
The Demon of Sicily	I
Volume I	3
Volume II	79
Volume III	139
Volume IV	222

FOREWORD

JANE AUSTEN has a lot to answer for. In addition to some wonderful novels she has left behind the idea that most people in the late eighteenth and early nineteenth centuries were only reading the likes of *Emma* and *Pride and Prejudice*.

Not so. In truth, they were consuming by the cartload novels with titles such as *Miraculous Nuptials, Husband Hunters!!!* (yes, with the three exclamation marks,) and *The Demon of Sicily*. Some of the novels were set in the readers' own world, more or less, but many took the reader to foreign lands where the extreme, the bizarre, and the paranormal were so much more believable.

After all, the English have always known foreigners are weird.

A similar factor still exists today in the long-running and extremely popular Harlequin Presents line of novels from Harlequin/Mills and Boon publishers with titles such as *At the Greek Boss's Bidding*, *The Mediterranean Millionaire's Mistress*, and *Sicilian Husband, Blackmailed Bride*.

Ah-ha! Sicily, you see. Things can still happen in Sicily that wouldn't be believed back in good old England. Or in America, for that matter, where the Presents books are equally popular.

The Presents romances are set in contemporary times, but the regency popular novels were often historical, and frequently medieval because this more easily permits unreality and settings for dark drama such as castles, dungeons, and torture chambers.

Medieval weapons were more direct than the gun in use from the late eighteenth century on. Is there any significance to the fact that historical fiction emerged and rose in popularity just when civilian gentlemen ceased wearing a sword?

Europe and a medieval setting also brings Roman Catholicism. To Protestant readers in particular, Catholicism was fertile grounds for extremes. The enforced chastity of monks and nuns was to them the perfect context for an active devil and vile sexual urges, as we see in *The Demon of Sicily*. Just the ticket for rampant bestsellerdom. There's a similar impetus behind *The Da Vinci Code*.

This type of novel was very popular, and Austen's *Northanger*

Abbey is a spoof as her heroine, Catherine Morland, creeps around Northanger Abbey both fearing and hoping for mysteries and murders. Read without the context of the bestsellers of the time, however, it loses much of its impact on the modern reader.

Even *Pride and Prejudice*, whose romance dynamic has great staying power, loses something if the modern reader fails to understand the economic realities of the early nineteenth century gentlewoman. For more on this, see my essay, "Gold Diggers of 1813", in *Flirting With Pride and Prejudice* (Benbella Books, 2005).

From my earliest days writing romance novels set in the English Regency (1811-1820) I needed to become familiar with the everyday lives of real people of the time. There are all levels of research, but I have gained most from primary sources—the letters, diaries, magazines and newspapers of the time. I have also explored their plays and novels, going beyond the ones that have been endorsed by time to the equally or more popular ones that wowed them back then.

In my early days as a published author, finding these obscure works of the past was hard, but now I can read some online, for which I thank Project Gutenberg, Google Books, and various university libraries. More! More! It's also wonderful that Valancourt Books is creating lovely editions that can be read as the stories were meant to be, from paper.

In the late eighties, when I was rewriting *An Arranged Marriage* (I'd created the first draft in 1977) I didn't have much access to the more ephemeral novels of 1814. Through a university library, I did learn some titles, however, and that is how I came to toss in a throwaway detail that my heroine chooses *Miraculous Nuptials* and *The Demon of Sicily* from the shelves. It was this chance occurrence that caused the editor at Valancourt Books to contact me about doing this foreword.

The title choices weren't completely random picks. Eleanor has recently made a strange marriage that could almost be called miraculous, and the lurking evil implicit in *The Demon of Sicily* surely fits with a mind still struggling with betrayal and a drugged rape that opens the book. It's a shame I didn't have the chance to read *The Demon of Sicily* back then because Eleanor could have thought about some elements of the story as she and Nicholas fight their way through and free of the coils of evil.

Once I was aware of the popular reading of the time, it was natural to include some reference to them in my Regency-set novels, but sometimes they have become significant.

In the second *Company of Rogues* novel (the first being *An Arranged Marriage*), Beth is a bluestocking schoolteacher and follower of Mary Wollstonecraft, author of *The Rights of Women*, which also plays a significant part in the novel. She is suitably shocked and horrified to be forced into a marriage with the Marquess of Arden, heir of the Duke of Belcraven. For the rationale and outcome, you'll have to read *An Unwilling Bride*.

A novel of the time came into the book because Eleanor would no more travel without a book to read than I would. I chose a novel rather than a more serious work because I liked the reflection of the passage from scholarly life to one of frivolous luxury—as she sees it. I made the choice believable by having her mentor ask her to evaluate the novel's suitability for their pupils.

This time I picked a novel I could read, Mary Brunton's *Self Control*, mainly because I was intrigued by the title. I admit it, I'm a sucker for titles. *Self Control* has survived with some respect, perhaps because it is set in the author's time and is thus seen as more realistic.

Jane Austen, however, it is not. In fact, it should be prescribed reading for all students to show how superior Austen was to most of her contemporaries. Austen herself was kind to the novel's technique (see below.) I am not. *Self Control* is an absurdly plotted, tediously paced, preachy tirade against any succumbing to emotions, especially those of love.

Brunton uses the novel as a moral battering ram, a crime itself in my opinion, attempting to point out the folly of any lady believing the wild protestations of love from any man. Decent men, says the novel, don't behave like that. The real lives of humans through the ages shows us that yes, they do. Science shows us that temporary insanity is a natural part of the human bonding process. (See Helen Fisher, *Why We Love*, paperback from Owl Books, 2004.)

Laura Montreville could have rejected her suitor on the

grounds that he is not her type; that his wealthy lifestyle and self-indulgence were not something she wanted to share. Instead, she demands that he prove his love by changing to suit her pattern card of the ideal man. This is the classic folly in the human mating dance and also rises out of an unpleasant certainty of moral superiority. He tries, the effort proves too much for him, and his turn into a stalking would-be rapist causes Laura to flee, even so far as North America, which is where *Self Control* finally loses all control on reality.

However, the novel provides an interesting context for Beth Armitage, also the victim of compulsion, though that is based on cold practicality, not emotion. To begin with she's inclined to agree with the message of the book — that virtuous people should, and should be able to, control all impulses and emotion and act solely on reason. She identifies with Laura, pressured and emotionally assaulted by a man. As she experiences the complexities of reality, however, and comes to understand the natures and motives of the alien others she now lives among, her certainties waver and she loses a sense of moral superiority. Laura becomes less and less reasonable and believable every day.

In that, she's in agreement with Jane Austen herself, who wrote, "I am looking over *Self Control* again, and my opinion is confirmed of it being an excellently-meant, elegantly-written work, without anything of nature or probability in it. I declare, I do not know whether Laura's passage down the American river is not the most natural, possible, everyday thing she ever does." As that adventure involves paddling herself in a canoe and going over a waterfall, Austen's comment says a lot.

My interest in the popular novels of the time was present in my first published novel, *Lord Wraybourne's Betrothed*. My research then had thrown up the fascinating Minerva Press, owned by William Lane. It was a highly successful publishing house, putting out a large number of novels, mostly written by women for women. Jane, who is Lord Wraybourne's betrothed, is introduced to the forbidden delights of Minerva novels by her future sister-in-law and is thrilled to meet Mr. Lane at a literary gathering at the Lambs' house.

The main purpose of the novels in that book is to show Jane's movement from her restricted, religious upbringing into more liberal and fashionable delights, but such novels play significant parts in two of my works.

One is a novella called *Forbidden Affections* (in the anthology *Spring Bouquet*.) *Forbidden Affections* does apply to the love that develops between a sixteen-year-old schoolgirl and the thirty-year-old rake next door, but it is also the title of the imaginary gothic novel that starts the trouble.

Forbidden Affections had been the last work of Mrs. Jamison, Anna Featherstone's favorite author. When Anna's family travels to London and she ends up in a bedroom that is an exact replica of the one in the novel, even to the skulls for drawer knobs, what's a girl to do other than test whether the fireplace is actually a secret door.

Anna is truly shocked when the portal opens, but it opens not into a rat-infested castle, but into the house next door, home of the wicked Earl of Carne who fled the country years ago after falling under suspicion for murdering his lover. Given that the house is unoccupied, it wouldn't hurt to look around a little, would it?

The novel, the novelist, and the history of the room weave together to create this story of a love that should never be.

The other example is in *To Rescue A Rogue.*

Lord Darius Debenham has returned from the battle of Waterloo addicted to the opium given him because of his wounds. His childhood friend, Lady Mara St. Bride, sets out to drag him out of his moody isolation and help him heal. She recruits him to escort her to a lending library to pick up some novels simply as an excuse to be in his company, but that excursion starts a powerful thread in the book.

She picks up the novel waiting for her, Sarah Burney's *Tales of Fancy* in three volumes, then looks over the shelves for other treats. She can't resist *Husband Hunters!!!*. It's Dare who's attracted to the more darkly gothic *Barozzi, or The Venetian Sorceress*. (A ripping good yarn, also available in a Valancourt edition.) From there, they begin the game of creating a gothic novel, originally called *The Captive Corpse of Castle Cruel*. This soon it turns into a novel in rhyme in this passage.

"Despite the delicious sound of the word 'corpse'," Mara said, scraping up the last of the cream on her plate, "it makes no sense to hold a corpse captive. Unless it rises to haunt."

"Ah-ha! *The Ghastly Ghoul of Castle Cruel*. A rhyme, begad, to boot."

"He moans and groans and trails his drool/He is the dread Canute!"

Thus, they're off on a zany adventure of the imagination that Mara uses to spend time with Dare and to drag him back from the darker brinks. It also, however, reflects their own story as Juliet Whyte seeks to free her Canute Ornottocanute from dark entrapment and Mara helps Dare fight free of addiction.

What was the particular appeal of these novels at this time, for they are just as typical of the time as an Adams interior, or the subdued elegance brought into men's fashion by Beau Brummell. I think the appeal lay in the increasing safety and stability of the times. The industrial and agricultural revolutions, despite their many problems, were creating greater prosperity and security for more people. Various improvements in health and hygiene were reducing child mortality and extending life. Due to tolls and technology, roads were generally in good condition and safe; a traveler no longer feared highwaymen within sight of Hyde Park.

When daily life becomes calm, becomes the world of Jane Austen, many enjoy wild adventures of the imagination, especially when they take place safely in a far off land and in another era. Such stories, in fact, enhance the feeling of comfort in one's own situation.

So enjoy *The Demon of Sicily* in the spirit of its times, perhaps at a book party, taking turns to read out loud by the light of a fire and candles. Then perhaps you, too, like Catherine Morland, will be looking around nervously for headless ladies and mad monks as you creep off to bed, but sure deep down that it will not happen to you.

Jo Beverley

More information about Jo Beverley's fiction can be found at www.jobev.com.

EDITOR'S NOTE

This 200th Anniversary Edition of *The Demon of Sicily* is based on the first edition published at London by J. F. Hughes in four volumes in 1807. The first edition is extremely rare, with copies recorded at only two libraries: UCLA and the Bodleian Library at Oxford; a third copy currently listed for sale by Robert Temple Booksellers of London is priced at £4,200 ($8,300).

A second edition appeared in "penny dreadful" format in 1839,[1] issued in twenty parts by the notorious publisher William Dugdale. Dugdale was known as a publisher of "pornography" and was prosecuted under the Obscene Publications Act, although apparently not for *The Demon of Sicily*. The Dugdale edition survives in two known copies, one at the Cleveland Public Library, and the other at the British Library. This odd edition was published in double column format and included lurid illustrations. The illustrations in the present edition are taken from the Cleveland Public Library's copy.

In this edition, obvious spelling errors have been corrected (e.g., "ecchoes", "appaling", "yeild", "visper", and far too many others to list). When Montague calls a character by the wrong name, as when he calls Ricardo "Rodrigo", these errors have been corrected for the sake of clarity. Dozens of errors of sloppy typography have been silently corrected as well, such as "clock" for "cloak", "piered" for "pierced", "hould" for "should", "whdt" for "what", and semi-colons and commas inserted in nonsensical positions. One error of bizarre proportions deserves to be singled out: on pp. 86-87 of Volume IV of the first edition, the text reads, "He watched the gentle features alternately; her dark eyebrows and long silken eye-lashes, the glow of health which dwelt in her cheeks; and her lips, which invited the kiss, contributed to rage the monk to the completion of the horrible design for which heavings of her bosom, and her lovely toe Demon had conveyed him

---

[1] The British Library gives the publication date of this undated reprint as 1841; however, it is advertised in *The Fly: A Literary and Pictorial Miscellany for 1839* as "Now Publishing in Weekly Numbers."

there." This utterly unintelligible sentence appears in Dugdale's edition without the words "heavings of her bosom, and her lovely toe", and I have followed Dugdale's approach.

However, in keeping with Valancourt Books' policy of editorial restraint, archaic and idiosyncratic spellings and usages (e.g., "ought" for "aught", "corridore" for "corridor", "chear" for "cheer", "skreen" for "screen", etc.) have been retained. I have also retained the overwhelming majority of Montague's grammatical mistakes ("each others eyes", "thou shall", subject/verb agreement problems with "was" and "were", etc.)

In short, I have tried to balance competing interests, namely, the desire to produce a book that is intelligible and does not appear to be marred with dozens of obvious errors, with the need to preserve the original text, including its flaws and shortcomings.

For information on the author, Edward Montague, I refer the reader to the Valancourt Books edition of Montague's first novel, *The Castle of Berry Pomeroy* (1806), in which I set out the few pieces of information available on this elusive figure.

I would like to acknowledge the staff of the Cleveland Public Library, who were kind enough to allow me to photocopy the illustrations from their rare edition.

James D. Jenkins
Kansas City

May 31, 2007

THE

DEMON OF SICILY.

A ROMANCE,

IN FOUR VOLUMES,

BY

EDWARD MONTAGUE ESQ.

Author of Legends of a Nunnery, the Castle of Berry
Pomeroy, &c. &c. &c.

Be thou a spirit of health, or goblin damn'd?
Bring'st with thee airs from Heaven, or blasts from Hell?
Be thy intents wicked or charitable,
Thou com'st in such a questionable shape
That I will speak to thee.
                              SHAKESPEARE.

VOLUME THE FIRST.

LONDON:

PRINTED FOR J. F. HUGHES, WIGMORE.
STREET, CAVENDISH SQUARE.

1807.

Facsimile of the title page of the first edition (1807)

The Demon of Sicily

THE
DEMON OF SICILY.

CHAPTER I.

THE clock of the monastery had told in iron notes the midnight hour; loudly it reverberated through the long corridors of the edifice and lofty aisles of the chapel, at length, dying away in sullen tones. Padre Bernardo started at the sound. Till then his eyes had been intently fix'd on a painting of the Saint to whom the religious pile was dedicated, the Santa Catherina; it was the master-piece of the first Italian painter of those times. A pleasing melancholy dwelt in the beautiful features; the mild blue eyes were raised in seeming adoration to Heaven; her golden locks flowed on her ivory neck, and the swelling charms of her bosom were perhaps too well represented for the gaze of the secluded inhabitants of a monastery, where whatever tends to excite the passions should studiously be avoided. The monk had been intently viewing this painting till he was roused from his meditations by the tolling of the bell; his lamp but faintly glimmered; he trimmed it, and again resumed the train of his thoughts. The light now gleamed brightly on the painting, the monk fixed his large black eyes, shaded by his bushy eye brows, on the beautiful representation.

What a lovely face! said he mentally, what expression! tis surely such as glows in the countenance of the angel of Mercy when receiving commission from on high to bring tidings of forgiveness to the world! Sure no earthly woman can possess such charms; if they did, passion would overcome reason, and steep in forgetfulness the cold vows of seclusion. But what am I saying? Lovely painting, how hast thou caused my mind to stray, my passions too—But why were such feelings given us, if they are not to be indulged? I repent me of my vows.

At this moment a low noise was heard in the cell. The monk looked around, the taper dimly illumined the nearer objects with its uncertain rays, beyond them all was enveloped in murky obscurity, and in the dismal gloom uncertain shapes and appearances seemed to flit along.

A strange sensation shook the soul of the monk; he stretched out his tremulous hand to aid the lamp's expiring beams, when, as he fearfully glared around him, he saw close by his side an unusually tall figure in a monastic habit, the close drawn cowl of which completely enveloped the features from view; the arms were folded, and the head bent toward the ground.

Scarcely could Bernardo collect sufficient fortitude to demand the cause of such an unusual visit, when the mystic form thus addressed him. Hollow, deep, and harsh was his voice; it was such as awed the monk into a strict silence.

"I know, Bernardo, what thou wouldest now say to me; thy other thoughts are also in the page of my remembrance. Thou art right, Padre, man was not formed to live alone, to whine out his solitary hours in useless meditations and regrets. Padre, thou hast not seen the world; these walls and a few musty volumes contain the extent of thy knowledge, yet hast thy thoughts soared beyond them, thou hast dared to meditate on the most seducing objects in nature. Knowest thou, Bernardo, to what I allude? It now dawns in thy breast—'tis woman! Padre, you think that woman cannot be so beautiful as that painting. Know that it is a faint attempt at the true representation of their charms. Wouldst thou see one, monk?"

Bernardo had in some degree recovered from his astonishment during the speech of the stranger. Attentively he had listened to it; each word sunk deep in his recollection, his curiosity was roused, he had never seen other women than the veiled Nuns of the convent which was contiguous to the monastery of Santa Catherina, and his ideas of their features were only formed from the painting of the Saint which was suspended in his cell. A sudden emotion seized his mind, unlike what he had ever before experienced; he turned himself around; and though he could not avoid a secret dread stealing over his soul as he surveyed the tall figure beside him, he replied,

"It has long been the wish of my wakeful hours to survey

the master-piece of Nature. The more we see of its wonders, the more we are disposed to adore the Author of them."

Saying these words, he again raised his head to try if he could observe the countenance of the mysterious figure. The cowl had been misplaced, he saw a smile on the dark features, it was a smile of contempt; dreadful was the expression of the lower part of the terrible visage, the upper part was still concealed by the cowl, but a slight motion made by the figure shewed to the monk one of the eyes, which appeared to him like a glowing flame. He started from his seat, and with ideas too terrible for utterance, he covered his face with his hand, lest he should again behold such an horrible appearance.

At this moment the bell of the monastery tolled *one!*

"Bernardo!" said the harsh voice, "expect me here to-morrow at midnight. Let not these vain fears prevent thee from profiting by my condescension."

The monk heard the words, but unable to reply, he remained in his present posture some time; at length he ventured to look around him. The lamp was nearly expiring, but as well as he could judge by its dim rays, he was alone, yet no opening or closing door had announced the departure of his visitor; whom the monk now conjectured was no inhabitant of the convent or even of the earth, but some demon, who, taking advantage of his wandering thoughts, had, watchful of the too fit opportunity, endeavoured to alienate him from his duty. He had promised to be there the next night in order to prosecute his further plans; there, however, thought the monk, he will fail; no more will I listen to his specious arguments.

Such were the ruminations of Bernardo after the departure of the terrible nocturnal intruder. Taking the lamp in his hand he traversed his cell, looking fearfully around him lest in some dark recess should still lurk the horrid figure.

His fears, however, were vain; for at the tolling of the first hour of morn he became the solitary trembling inhabitant of his cell. A mystic awful silence reigned throughout the pile; and the monk, as he paced his chamber, softly trod the floor, for he started at the sound of his own steps, and feared to behold the attendant shadow of his tall figure gliding along the wall.

He placed the lamp on the table, and advanced to the casement, which he opened. Chilly blew the blast of morning.

The moon shone on the waving branches of the trees, which thickly tenanted the garden belonging to the monastery, and brightened the gray walls of the building with her silvery beams.

The soul of the monk, disturbed by the occurrence of the night, took no pleasure from the tranquil scene which lay before him. In his bosom there yet remained not only a chaos of contending terrors, but also of contending passions. In the moment of his fears his resolutions had been good, but in proportion as they abated, so faded away his resolves to resist the temptations which he conceived about to be thrown in his way.

At any rate, thought he, I will again see this mysterious person, who it appears wishes to enlarge my thoughts, to make me acquainted with the world, from which I have been hitherto excluded. It still lies with me to baffle his evil designs: in struggling with temptations lies the sole proof of virtue.—It is surely no proof of goodness to act well when we cannot do otherwise, when the will has nothing to do with our actions.

Instead, therefore, of being doubtful of himself, he placed confidence in his virtue; he conceived himself able to resist, and therefore no longer thought of flying from temptation—Fatal reliance.

Having staid indulging his reverie some time at the casement, chilled by the cold air, he at length returned from it, and sat down by the table on which was the lamp. The painting which had so greatly fascinated him was again the subject of his meditation, and he recalled to his mind what the nocturnal visitant had said respecting it. Little trouble was there in bringing those words to his remembrance; deeply were they rooted in his breast.

"If that" said he "is but a faint attempt to represent their charms, what must they be in reality? How anxious I feel for the appointed hour, when I shall judge myself the truth of that assertion."

The matin bell roused the monk from meditations so unfit to

be held within the walls of a monastery; and by one, too, who at the altar had sworn a solemn and irrevocable oath, registered in Heaven, to dedicate his life, his soul and body, to the worship of Him who dwells far above mortal ken, and is far beyond mortal comprehension.

Reluctantly he joined the train of the holy fathers, and entered the lofty aisles of the chapel, at the same time that the nuns and boarders of the convent preceded by the Lady Abbess, took their accustomed seats within the gilded skreen that separated the part they occupied from that appropriated for the monks.

The service began—but the thoughts of the monk wandered from the avocations of the hour; he joined in the responses but his heart that morning had no share in the words of his mouth.

His eyes were fixed on the nuns and boarders, if haply he could get a glimpse of their features; there, however, he was disappointed; he listened to their melodious strains with rapture, but it was not the rapture which devotion yields to her pure votaries; it was a rapture sullied with thoughts which the midnight occurrences had awakened in his mind.

He was glad when the service ceased, for conscience told him he was acting wrong in letting his imagination rove on subjects contrary to what ought to have so entirely occupied them as to exclude all worldly ideas; but the arch enemy of man had seized on his fluctuating soul while it lingered in its election of heavenly blessings or earthly pleasures, and, like a wary foe, noticed the breach, and entered the weak bulwark which had so feebly opposed him.

Slowly wore away the tedious hours; often did the monk look to the Heavens, where glowed in meridian splendor the regent of day. At length he began to decline, and the shadows of the larches and tall pines encreased on the earth; slowly he sunk beneath the hilly boundary of the western horizon, but not at the moment that he illumined other worlds was his total departure manifest, for the clouds still retained their borrowed radiance, and the face of nature glowed with their golden reflection.

The vesper bell then tolled. Again was the monk obliged to

attend in the chapel, but his ideas were still more distant from what was then passing than in the morning.

Soon, thought he as he surveyed the nuns, soon I shall behold one of your sex. This night is to present to my view the fairest of Nature's works; but how it is to be effected I know not. Much I have heard of the potency of magic, but surely it must be powerless within these consecrated walls. He, however, who knew my thoughts ere my lips had given them utterance, is surely able to effect his promise.

After the hour of repast was over, the monk retired to his cell; he fastened the door to prevent any intrusion. And having carefully examined every part, he sat down, and with anxious expectancy awaited the arrival of the promised visitor.

On the table lay a volume of monastic tales, such as might be supposed to originate from the superstitious and ill-informed minds of those who lived in a still ruder era than when these imperfect records were traced by the hand that now no longer grasps the descriptive pen. The monk had yet two hours to wear away ere his ear would be greeted by the long-sounding hour of midnight, and he sought to pass the time in the perusal of some of the pages of the ancient volume.

He read a little—he started, and looked around him; he had opened the book where began a gloomy relation which was increased by his expectations of the probable events of the night. Still a kind of anxious curiosity to know the rest of the tale made him again turn his attention to the pages, which in a short time completely engaged it.

The clock now tolled eleven—the Padre counted the reverberating strokes of the ponderous hammer. Another hour, thought he, in the perusal of this tale will soon pass.

He then trimmed his lamp, looked for some moments anxiously at the painting before him, then gazed around the gloomy chamber, and again fixed his attention on the book.

The legend which had so greatly excited his attention he finished ere half the period of time that remained to the appointed hour was elapsed. Bernardo yawned, he closed the book, his senses were fatigued, the last night he had not slept, and during the day the agitation of his mind made him wish not for repose; he leaned back in his chair, drew his cowl over his face, and soon the somniferous deity weighed heavy on his eyelids. Thus we will leave him while we relate the tale that had engaged his attention.

———

Leonardi de Vicensio and the Fair Isabella.

Furiously flashed the red lightnings, and dreadfully roared the peals of thunder on the bleak mountains!—But what was the lightning, or what the thunder to Ugo De Tracy? Little recked he either; not so his terrified steed that starting and stumbling continually, forced him to alight. Long had De Tracy wandered through the dark folds of night, uncertain of his course; till the lofty walls of a castle appeared to his searching eyes as the lightning, darting from the black bosom of the low-hung clouds, illumined the dreary waste.

The building appeared ruinous and uninhabited, but as the jaded steed was unable to proceed farther, the Signor determined to seek a shelter for him beneath the ruin during the storm.

Entering the large hall he tied him to a pillar, and a blue glimmering light which seemed slowly to wave in the air at some distance, attracting his notice, he drew forth his trusty faulchion, and advanced toward it.

With some difficulty, however, he effected this, as the roof laid in heaps on the pavement in many places, and the fragments of the huge columns crossed his path; when at length he had advanced to the further extremity of the hall, he saw that the blue flames whose slow-waving motion had caught his eye proceeded from a lamp, carried by a form that appeared to have been some time claimed by the relentless angel of death: the face was ghastly pale, the eye deep sunk in the socket, and the disgusting traces of putrefaction were visible on the countenance.

Confounded at this horrible appearance, which bore the resemblance of a female, De Tracy stopped, when a hollow voice said "De Tracy, dost thou not know me? dost thou not know thy Isabella?"

"Gracious powers! what mean you by these words! Isabella De Tracy lives not here."

"This is her tomb," again said the spectre seemingly fixing her rayless eyes on him, "follow me!"

Ugo knew not fear; resolutely he replied, "I will walk in the shadow of thy steps, mysterious being, who hast mentioned the name of that much-loved wife, under circumstances which overwhelm my soul with a terrible dread. Heaven forbid that any sinister event should have befallen her."

The spectre sighed deeply, and turning round, seemed to look sorrowfully at Ugo De Tracy; it then passed on to a pair of folding doors, which, at its approach, flew wide on their massy hinges.

———

Ugo De Tracy, had just returned to Sicily from a pilgrimage to the Lady of Loretto, and was going to the southern parts of it, where arose his stately castle, when being benighted, he met with the extraordinary and melancholy adventure which is recorded in these pages by Bartolo, one of the first monks who resided in the holy walls of Santa Catherina, which building is erected on the same site as that whereon the ruinous castle formerly stood.

———

Ugo followed the spectre through the corridore. Arrived at the extremity, part of the wainscoting which was pannelled gave way, and disclosed a dark flight of steps. Aided by the feeble gleams of the blue light, which the terrible form carried, he followed it down an almost dismantled staircase for some time, till at length Ugo observing that the steps were cut out of the solid rock, and that they were descending into the bowels of the earth far beneath the foundations of the Castle, suddenly stopped, and thus questioned the spectre:—"Whither wouldst thou lead me?

what can be your object in bringing me here? I will proceed no further."

The spectre replied not, slowly it raised its hand to its throat, and a deep sigh echoed through the dull, gloomy place.

The soul of De Tracy, disdaining the impulses of fear, now determined to follow the form, which having slowly descended to the bottom of the steps, turned into a small chamber, or rather dungeon, where what was De Tracy's horror at beholding the headless trunk of a female lying on the ground!

The spectre stood by the side of it. A hollow voice which seemed to fill the dungeon, slowly said "revenge the deed!" Ugo started; till now his eyes had been fixed on the mangled form at his feet, when suddenly the blue light died away, and he was left in the black horrors of impenetrable darkness.

———

Isabella was lovely as the rose when first it unfolds its beauties to the morning beams; eight months had she been the happy wife of De Tracy, when Superstition with her ominous voice bade him bend his knee at the shrine of the Lady of Loretto.

Ugo with many sighs embraced his wife, and she beheld his departure with the frequent tear of unavailing sorrow; she took her station on the topmost turret of her castle, and while she saw his loved form winding along the valley which it overlooked, she still retained sufficient fortitude to restrain the tide of grief which swelled her sad heart; but when distance had rendered him almost invisible, and an intervening hill obscured him from her anxious sight, then it was, that, dissolved in tears and uttering deep and heartfelt sighs, she sunk almost bereft of animation into the supporting arm of her attendants, who conveyed her from the towering turret to her now cheerless chamber.

Daily, however, did she revisit the turret, daily cast her eyes toward the place where she had last beheld her loved De Tracy, while her sighs would increase the zephyr, and her tears trickle down her lovely cheeks.

One evening as seated on the turret, she leaned her beauteous head on her snowy arm and was pensively contemplating the splendor of the setting sun as he was sinking in the watery wave, the clash of arms drew her attention toward the place from whence the hostile sounds proceeded; when near the entrance of a wood whose leafy tenantry overshaded a large track of land, she beheld a Knight engaged in furious contest with four seemingly well appointed ruffians; a dart pierced his breast, and he fell from his horse. Isabella shrieked at the sight; she arose from her seat, and summoning her attendants, bade them fly to the succour of the wounded Knight, and offer him an apartment in her castle, if the breath of life lingered in his veins.

Hastily the domestics obeyed the commands of their Lady. From her turret she still surveyed the deeds of the banditti; they were now proceeding to strip off the armor of the Knight, who still lay on the earth. The dart had not been the messenger of death; his sword was still in his hand; rage strung his nerves, and indignant at the new insult offered him, the Knight raised his glaive, and with a sudden thrust made a passage for the current of life in the breast of one of the ruffians, who fell to the blood-stained earth; the others with terrible execrations were on the point of avenging the death of their comrade; already had they upraised their swords, thirsting for blood, when the approach of the domestics of the Lady Isabella put them to sudden flight.

The wounded Knight was placed on a litter, and borne to the castle, where he was attended by the surgeon of the household. Speedily he recovered, a few days saw him able to take his departure, and he desired to be brought to the Signora Isabella to thank her for being the preserver of his life.

He was conducted into her presence; when, struck with astonishment at the blaze of beauteous charms which concentered in that lovely female, he remained like one amazed; and, unknowing of his actions, with difficulty at length he stammered out his thanks to the Signora for her kind conduct toward him; while his dark expressive eyes rolled unceasing over the beauteous form of Isabella.

Leonardi di Vicensio was the name of the Knight. He was of gigantic stature, like the hero's of other years, his face was gloomy as the dark lowering clouds of night when the thunder is heard and the lightnings play around the arch of Heaven; his bushy eyebrows protruded far over his darkly rolling eyes; his cheek bones were high; his nose was long and aquiline; a dark smile played at times on his lips, but it was like the ocean, which puts on a serene look just before the storms raise its angry billows to the skies.

Such was Leonardi di Vicensio; who, when he had left the presence of the peaceless Isabella began to meditate on the means to get her to consent to gratify the base passions which her charms had raised in his bosom.

All night he slept not; he arose ere the lark yet awoke in his downy nest, or ere the breeze of morning had dispersed the unwholesome vapors of night.

Restless was the soul of Leonardi as he strode through the halls of the Castle of De Tracy, revolving in his mind dark and horrible deeds.

Passing by the portals which led to the chapel, he thought he heard a voice within; he listened again; the voice sweetly sounded in his ear, it was like music to the bite of the deadly tarantula, it charmed his senses to a forgetfulness of all beside, for it was that of Isabella.

On her knees before the altar he beheld the lovely wife of De Tracy; with impatience and dissatisfaction he heard her petition the saints for his safe return. At that moment he stood by her side, she turned around, and overcome by a sudden emotion of fear, she shrieked aloud.

Echo alone heard her. Thrice she repeated the exclamation along the vaulted roofs and dreary corridores where she held her reign; but it reached not the ears of other mortal than those of the gloomy Leonardi.

On the step of the altar, seizing the trembling hand of Isabella, he bent his knee, while through his grated visor, by the light of the bright clouds which tinged with the glories of the sun, who was then fast retiring from other worlds, cast a crimson radiance into the chapel through the twisted panes of the large altar window, she beheld his darkly-rolling eyes.

"Fair Isabella," said the Knight, "why petition Heaven to bring thee thy husband? Listen to the suit of Leonardi; he loves, he adores thee; thy beauties dwell in his heart; all night he has thought on them; behold him a suppliant who never knelt before."

"And of little use, Sir Knight," said the fear-struck Isabella, "is that lowly posture now. Suffer me, Signor Leonardi, to use my own discretion in retiring from this place, nor longer detain my hand."

"Say not so, beauteous Isabella, suffer me to hope that time and my unceasing attentions may"—

"May what, Signor?" said Isabella, her lofty soul swelling high with indignation. "Know you not that I am the wife of Ugo De Tracy, who, if he were here, would well chastise thee for this insolence. Like him, I spurn whatever is base and dishonorable, and such I hold the Signor Leonardi."

The Knight rose from his bended knee, in a transport of rage he flung from his grasp the arm of Isabella; he laid his hand on his faulchion, suddenly he withdrew, while he gnashed his teeth, and inwardly muttered curses deep and horrid.

Isabella, with a dignified firmness walked toward the portals of the chapel. Soon her elegant form was lost to the view of the deep-plotting Vicensio; who, when he heard the closing of the distant portals, laid his right hand on the altar, and solemnly swore to be revenged of Isabella De Tracy.

The statue of the Holy Mother started at his horrid oath, while from each marble tomb in the chapel burst a melancholy groan, which deep sounded in the ears of Leonardi.

"Groan on, and start," he furiously exclaimed, "portents and prodigies are lost on me, use your arts, ye mouldering bones, and you, inanimate representative of the immaculate Virgin, may raise your arms again, and look with horror on me, I fear not all that you can do."

Dark grew the chapel; a murky cloud hung before the large casement; but by the still small glimmering of light Leonardi beheld himself surrounded by tall skeletons, who waved their fleshless arms for him to depart.

"The skeletons waved their fleshless arms."

It was then that cold drops of water stood on the forehead of Leonardi—"Tremble!" said a voice over the altar. He raised his eyes, the statue of the Virgin again appeared animated; its gaze was fixed on him.

Leonardi fled, he was unable to endure the horror of the moment. With him fled the shadow of night, the murky cloud disappeared, and the frail remains of mortality sought their silent tombs.

Hastily he proceeded to the stables, where snorted his coal-black steed; quickly he saddled him, and vaulting on his back, was soon far from the ken of the tower of De Tracy's castle.

In the bosom of a dark forest, where the beams of day in their meridian lustre faintly glimmered, Leonardi reined in his steed; there he alighted; and there his memory recalled the horrible prodigies he had witnessed; but his memory likewise retained the charms of Isabella, his dreadful oath, and her insulting expressions.

"And I will be revenged," said he, as unlacing his helmet shaded with black plumes he cast it on the verdant grass; "let but the sun descend, let but the gloomy shade of night be unfurled from the battlements of Heaven, and I will bear away the haughty, lovely Isabella."

———

Ryno, the black steed of the savage Vicensio, was cropping the herbage, while the Knight, with arms folded, leaned against the stem of a large tree. The increasing shade shewed the sun to be declining from his meridian altitude. Gloomy was his soul, and far more black his thoughts than the fabled river which rolls its sable waves into the vast Tartarean gulph.

The Knight prepared to depart: he stooped to take from the ground his helmet, when he hastily drew back on perceiving that a snake had made it his abode.

He had not as yet armed his hands with the ponderous gauntlet. Sullenly he drew them on. Approaching the snake which had twisted its scaly folds in the hollow of his casque, he suddenly seized on its head which rested in the midst.

The poisonous reptile twisted its speckled form round the body of the Knight, but its efforts were vain, for the head was soon crushed in the gauntlet, and it for ever ceased to dart its deadly tongue.

Leonardi smiled horribly. "What other men," said he, "would have converted into an omen of bad import, I construe into success. Scaly wretch, thou shall adorn my helm with the bright colors of thy variegated skin."

This said, he bound around his casque the long body of the snake, unmindful of the black gore which dropped from the lacerated head, and then called to Ryno his steed.

The sable courser at the well-known voice of his master threw up his head in the air, and neighed aloud. In an instant he came up to the place where stood the vindictive Knight.

Leonardi was on his saddle in a moment; the steed measured back his swift paces, and soon arrived at the skirts of the forest.

A gloomy horror presided over Nature. The sun had sunk to other worlds; the crimson of the clouds had disappeared; a misty vapor enveloped the face of creation; a mournful silence reigned around, save that at a distance was heard the unceasing roaring of Etna in her fiery caverns.

Leonardi looked toward the place where the mountain rose, but the flames were obscured by the gloomy vapor.

This opaque mist, thought Leonardi, favors my design; under its kind covert I can, unseen, approach the castle of the peerless Isabella, and, if fortune will befriend me, bear her away.

He now drew near its lofty walls. Ryno he placed in the concealing recess of a buttress while he strode into the hall with cautious pace, his hand grasping his glaive.

Unseen he crossed it; and entering the chapel, leaned against the column which was nearest to the portals, for his soul had not yet forgot the terrific omens of the morning.

The storm that had been long gathering in the gloomy clouds now burst forth in awful fury, blue lightnings darted around the chapel which vibrated at the tremendous peals of thunder that roared unceasing in the arch of Heaven. The rain poured down in torrents, and, driven by the blast, dashed against the painted casements of the chapel. At times he heard the wild shrieks of the spirits of the mountains between the pauses of the angry gusts of wind; but he derided the utmost fury of the storm, and waited impatiently in the hope of seeing Isabella enter the chapel.

Nor long did he hope in vain; the unfortunate wife of De Tracy, alarmed by the storm, left her chamber to supplicate at the altar for the safety of her husband.

With a cautious, trembling hand, she opened the portal; she raised her lamp to illuminate the dusky aisle, but its feeble rays pierced the surrounding gloom but a few paces before her.

Leonardi concealed his gigantic form behind a column, and as the Signora advanced he rushed forward, and caught her in his arms.

She rent the air with her shrieks, but her exclamations were lost in the wild howling of the storm; and soon her senses forsook her, and she lay inanimate in his iron grasp.

Hastily he bore her through the hall, and coming to the buttress looked in vain for Ryno; scared by the peals of thunder and vivid flashes of lightning, he had wandered from the place. Loudly he called on him, and soon the faithful steed appeared through the dull gloom.

The sound of his voice awoke the hapless Isabella from her insensate state to a knowledge of the extent of her misery. She was placed on the steed; Leonardi held her in one arm, while the other grasped the reins; and swiftly as the arrow from the bow of the hunter they darted through the stormy vapors which clustered around.

———

Their course lay by the base of Etna: as they approached toward it, the flames lighted them on their way. Isabella trembled when she beheld the fiery torrents which descended the mountain sides, but she trembled more at being in the power of the unprincipled Leonardi.

Swiftly the steed proceeded obedient to his master's will the whole of that night. When gloomily the morning dawned the turrets of a dismantled castle rose to view.

At the decayed bridge Leonardi alighted, he conducted the trembling form of Isabella through the broken portals. Well knew the Knight the subterraneous recesses of the castle; within its tottering walls his own arm had perpetrated dark deeds of horror.

Down many a step which seemed to be a passage to the bowels of the earth, he forced the wretched Isabella, till at length they entered a dungeon.

"Now, lady," said he in harsh accents, "'tis like thou mayest repent of the deep insult you have offered me. No longer a suitor, I command thee to yield to my wishes; dreadful indeed will be the punishment of disobedience, for my soul yet burns with the remembrance of the injury I have received."

The soul of Isabella rose above the horrors of her situation; she seized the dagger that glittered in the girdle of the gloomy Leonardi.

"Barbarian," said she, "I fear thee not; in a moment I can put myself beyond thy infamous design. Powers of mercy, receive my soul!"

The dagger she had directed to her bosom here interrupted her; she fell to the ground, her pure blood dyed her garments.

Furious grew Leonardi at being disappointed of his expected prey; he looked blackly on the prostrate Isabella; she still lived, for the wound was not mortal.

"Since not my desires, I can however yet satiate my revenge; the pangs of death from my hand shall torture thee."

Thus said, he drew his glaive; he divided the lovely head of Isabella from the convulsed body; he caught it by the beautiful long black tresses, and strode away with it to another chamber; he set it on a piece of a broken column, and contemplated with a demoniac satisfaction the features once so lovely, so interesting, but now ghastly with the agonies of death. "Those eyes," said he "will no longer look indignant on me; neither will that mouth further insult me. Would I could have increased the torture of death; gladly would I have done it; for her groans were comfort to my soul."

Some days he continued indulging his black revenge; at length a new thought struck him; "I will go" said he, "to the cell where

Vicensio's Revenge on the Body of Isabella.

her body lies, and take from it her proud heart; I shall find pleasure in trampling on it."

He was going; when strange terrors shook his soul; on a sudden his imagination hears the complaining spectre of the murdered Isabella groan, his hair stiffens, he starts, the headless shade seems to pursue him through the gloom—his blood chilled, he stood leaning on his faulchion, while with a pale, disordered countenance, he questioned thus himself:

"What! shall Leonardi become the slave of superstitious terrors? shall his mighty soul yield to the fever of imagination? perish the thought, perish myself first! No, I am resolved I will tear out the heart of Isabella!"

Mournful was the soul of Ugo de Tracy when the supernatural appearance faded from his view; and the blue light ceasing to illumine the dreary cell left him in the murky shades of night; left him too with the murdered, headless body which he was told was that of his beloved Isabella.

Suddenly he heard a heavy step sounding through the subterraneous caverns of the castle; the clank of armor accompanied the echoing paces.

Bearing a torch, entered a gigantic figure clothed in sable armor; round his helmet, shaded with black plumes, was twisted a large snake, the poisonous head hung loosely in the air; in his left hand he bore the head of a female, as appeared by the dark flowing locks, in his right an unsheathed faulchion and the torch.

His vizor was up. Dark as the shades of night when the lightnings fly and thunder is heard, was his countenance. His eyes rolled gloomily dreadful.

De Tracy, anxious to know the purport of his coming, drew back into the gloom of the cell. Nor long staid he there.

"Thus," said the sable, black-hearted Knight, "do I seek my last revenge. I will find that heart, that proud, vaunting heart of Isabella, which made her defy me, which made her resist the desires of my bosom."

Thus having spoke, he flung to the earth the head; it rolled toward De Tracy, the light of the torch gleamed on the sunken features, he beheld in them the mortal remains of his adored wife. Rage, bloody rage, strung his nerves; he drew his glaive, and as the Knight was tearing away the garments that once concealed the swelling beauties of Isabella's bosom, he strode from his murky recess.

"Fiend of Hell!" in accents hoarse with rage he exclaimed, "my eyes have seen thy deed, my ears have heard thy speech, look up, before thee stands Ugo de Tracy!"

Leonardi stopped his dreadful employment; he rolled his eyes on Ugo.

"Thou, then," said he "art the husband of that Isabella who lies between us. There lies her head, this sword separated it from her body; it has the like office to perform on thee."

Furiously rushed the knights to combat. Leonardi flung his torch to the earth; dreadful was the contest, for the fierce power of just passion swelled the soul of Ugo de Tracy, black malice and revenge the heart of Leonardi de Vicensio.

The combat long hung in doubtful balance, till at length Ugo pierced the throat of his dire opponent; dreadful he fell, the clash of his armor rung through the vaulted caverns of the castle, a black torrent of blood rolled out his soul, the attendant fiends of hell in anxious expectation stood awaiting its escape from its mortal coil, they seized it in their sharp talons, grinning horribly they darted through the bosom of rifted earth, and plunged it deep in red oceans of unextinguishable flames.

Sadly mourned Ugo de Tracy over the body of his beloved Isabella; he kissed the wan lips, he raised the earth over the once so much adored form; but the body of her savage murderer he left uncovered.

Such was the fate of the fair Isabella; such was the punishment of Leonardi de Vicensio. The avenging Deity who surveys the sinful actions of men at last brought on him the retributive arm of justice.

Pray for his soul, ye who read these pages, for it endures horrible torments. His bones yet lay embruised, the left wing of the monastery covers the dragon's cell, where it is said his spectre on

the first of every moon is compelled to come and view them whitening through time, while the attendant furies lash him with their
whips formed of scorpions' deadly stings. Such is the punishment
destined for the murderer, and which Leonardi de Vicensio will
endure to the end of time.

Such was the tale which the Padre Bernardo perused while
awaiting the arrival of the Demon. It was sad, it was horrible.
Bartolo, the monk whose hand had traced the descriptive characters, had increased the gloom of the tale; perhaps his soul was
as melancholy as his writing, for the breasts of the inhabitants
of a monastery, shut out from the enlivening intercourses of the
world, are too frequently the receptacles of superstition; which
heightened by the monastic gloom which pervades around them,
produce nothing but ideas of horror and images of woe.

CHAPTER II.

NEAR the town of Pollizzi, in a beautiful valley stood the ancient
residence of the noble family of Carlentini. Nobility of birth was
indeed all that the Marchese had to boast of, for the dissipation
of his ancestors had only left to him the estate on which he resided, the late Marchese having, in order to raise a sum of money,
disposed of it, under a particular restriction that it should be the
property of his son during his life time; by this he thought he had
amply fulfilled his duty as a parent; and he had also provided for
himself the means to continue in his career of dissipation.

Such was the limited state of the pecuniary resources of
Ricardo de Carlentini, the present Marchese, when, in consequence of the death of his father, he came to the estate and title;
but, though poor in his purse, he was rich in love, for the beautiful
Louisa de Bononi returned his sincere passion.

During the life time of his father his solicitude was great lest
his attachment to his adored Louisa should come to his knowl-

edge; for well he knew how greatly he should incur his anger, as the object of his passion resided with her mother, who was possessed of a trifling independency on the estate of the Marchese, whither she had retired with her daughter on receiving the afflicting intelligence of the death of her husband, a Sicilian officer who had fallen in one of the contests which so often disturbed the Italian states.

To see Louisa and not to admire her were impossible, but to be acquainted with her, to enjoy the charms of her conversation, to behold those nameless excellencies she possessed, and not to love, to adore her, were equally so.

Ricardo returning from the chase beheld this lovely female sitting on a bank shaded by the myrtle and jessamine beside her neat but lowly residence. She had not put on her veil as the weather was very warm, that the gentle zephyrs, no longer heated by the rays of the ardent sun, might the better refresh her, being languid from the heat of the day.

Her dark brown hair, braided after the Sicilian mode, and adorned with a few simple flowers, the beauties of her interesting countenance, and her harmonious voice, which accompanied the soft notes of a lute, made Ricardo start with astonishment, and an expression of admiration proceeded from his lips.

Surprized at his voice, the enchanting musician raised her lovely eyes, and when she saw the Signor standing at the low paling which separated the garden from the road, she instantly ceased to charm the listening inhabitants of the groves with her voice, or touch the trembling strings of her lute; she blushed deeply, but it was the pure blush of innocence unacquainted with the ways of the world, and, in the already enamoured eyes of Ricardo it added to her resistless charms.

Ricardo would not add to her confusion by his longer stay, but saluting her respectfully, rode toward the Castello.

Louisa gracefully returned his salute, for she knew him to be the son of the Marchese to whom the domain belonged, and had often before seen him pass her humble residence. She had admired his graceful form, and his countenance, which now leaving the uncertain features of youth, were assuming a manly expression. Among the Sicilian nobility who sometimes visited the Castle she had seen no one so interesting as Ricardo, and no one occupied her thoughts so much as he did.

She felt for him an indefinable sensation, pure as the morning zephyr, when, rushing from ambrosial caves, it first touches the summit of the western waves.

Her bosom was the blissful seat of innocence; it was like the heart of the rose before it opens to the sun; it was the residence of unadulterated sweets. Hitherto, whatever were her thoughts she disclosed them to her beloved mother, but now she kept secret her growing friendship for Ricardo.

Strange it is that she should feel such a sensation for one whom she had never spoken to; but what mortal can account for the sensations of our hearts? A pleasing exterior at all times commands attention. Ricardo was the most graceful Louisa had ever seen; she thought too that his heart must be endued with equal attractions as his person; she thought that where the Deity had stamped a godlike form, he had endowed it with godlike attributes. Such, indeed, is sometimes the case; and in the judgment Louisa had formed of Ricardo she had not erred.

When Ricardo rode from the cottage where he had seen the lovely Louisa, his whole soul dwelt on her melodious voice and her fascinating beauties. Often he looked back, his eyes wandered around the cottage, but the little arbor hid from his view the lovely form that rose with such strong emotions to his imagination.

The Castello was situated on the gentle rising of a verdant hill. It was an irregular fabric of considerable extent, and seemed formed for the abode of a numerous train, such as in those days were necessary, either for the purpose of ostentatious magnificence, or as a residence for the troops which sometimes it was requisite to entertain in the turbulent times, which often witnessed the destruction of the efforts of the peasants, the ensanguined field, and drew the tear of misery from the aching eye of the widow and orphan.

The present inhabitants occupied little more than one wing of the extensive building, the other parts were desolate and gloomy. The Marchese had neither the wish nor the ability to restore the place to its ancient splendor; indeed he was not often at his estate himself, for he resided almost constantly at Palermo, the gaiety and dissipation of which place agreed more with his ideas than the retirement of his Castello. Seldom were any inquiries made by him concerning its inhabitants, who in its silent courts and melancholy halls passed their monotonous hours.

During a few of the hottest weeks in the year the Marchese would repair to his estate, attended by some of his dissipated companions, and consume the hours in wild revelry and debauchery.

For his son he shewed little if any affection. His wife was said to have died suddenly before Ricardo had attained his fourth year; but there were strange reports concerning her sudden dissolution; and whether it was the solitary situation of the Castle which excited the idea, or that the fearful fancies of the domestics had been acted upon by some of those almost unaccountable sounds which are heard in ruinous places, is not certain; but it was reported, and generally believed by the peasantry, that the spirit of the Lady haunted the apartments of the Southern Angle Tower, and that the rays of a lamp had been frequently seen at night gleaming through the apertures that were made in the wall to give light to the circular steps which led to the chambers.

The situation of the tower made it the more likely to be fixed on by the domestics as the residence of an unquiet spirit, for it reared its frowning black walls at the extremity of a dilapidated pile of buildings which had not been inhabited in the memory of any of the present inhabitants of the Castle.

Ricardo could not feel much love for a father who seemed to have so very little for him, and he rather rejoiced than otherwise when he saw the day arrive on which the Marchese and his riotous companions returned to Palermo.

The only companion he had in the castle was Father Grimaldi, a monk who had been many years confessor to its inhabitants. He was a man of gloomy deportment, and stern exterior, his manners were particularly forbidding and unpleasant to the young Ricardo, who from his infancy was disgusted with whatever seemed to wear the semblance of disguise and mystery.

Yet strange to relate, this monk, repugnant as he appeared

in his manners and behaviour to the inhabitants of the Castle, was the constant companion of the Marchese in his retired hours. Whether it was that the monk unbent the austerity of his demeanour before the Marchese, or that the advice of the father was necessary to him in some of his schemes, remains to be developed. Certain it is that he appeared to have great sway over the Marchese.

It was on the evening of the day succeeding that on which Ricardo first beheld the lovely Louisa, that, having made himself acquainted with her name, he alighted at the door of the Cottage, and desired the female attendant who appeared to acquaint the Signora Bononi that he was come to pay his respects to her.

Though she wished to remain perfectly secluded from visitors during her necessary retirement, yet it was impossible to refuse the attention which the son of the Marchese seemed disposed to pay to her.

Louisa blushed when she heard of the arrival of Ricardo; his earnest gaze, his respectful salute, and his frequent examination of the cottage as he retired, immediately recurred to her. Studious to escape the eye of her mother, she turned aside, and seemed to be busily employed in arranging some flowers in a vase when Ricardo entered.

Hastily his eyes were rivetted on the magnet which had attracted him to that place; he beheld her far more enchanting than he had at first conceived; and from that moment love entered his heart.

But it was not the love of the voluptuary, it was not the base passion which inflames the breast of the seducer; it was that pure flame which animates pure hearts; it was such as may be conceived to exist in disembodied souls.

His agreeable and respectful deportment soon made his visit productive of pleasure to the Signora Bononi. Louisa too never passed so happy an hour; the moments flew unheeded by on the downy pinions of young loves.

She sighed when he departed; Ricardo sighed too. He felt that in leaving Louisa he left all that was dear to him, all that could charm the rugged path of life, and make it appear bedecked with roses.

To be united to her, what happiness! what ecstacy! to be always with her, to sit beside her on the margin of the murmuring rivulet, to listen to her converse, to ascend the lofty enclosure of the valley, to mark the beauties of the rising or the setting sun, to view the variegated beauties of indulgent Nature, to view herself, the greatest charm of the creation! to anticipate her wishes, to possess her love, oh! that were indeed to possess Paradise.

Such were Ricardo's thoughts as he pursued his way toward the Castle. How dull, how gloomy it seemed, as he entered it; he almost was astonished to think how he could possibly have existed so many years in it; while the cottage where dwelt Louisa seemed decked with all that could charm the senses. He recollected the little bower, the green lattices, the simple vases filled with flowers gathered by her hand; there, whatever he saw gave him pleasure; here, all around filled him with disgust.

Horror seemed to sit brooding over the time-dismantled turrets of the Castle; she had spread around her sable wings, which added an additional gloom to the scene.

Hastily Ricardo crossed the dull hall, and entered his chamber; he sat down by the casement, and leaning his arm on the stone frame-work, remained deeply absorbed in meditation.

It is easy to divine that the fair Louisa was the bright subject of his thoughts; and remained so till his attendant, entering the chamber with a light, for awhile stopped the train of his ideas.

"The Padre, Signor," said the man, "awaits you, at the supper table."

"Tell him, Carlo, that I am not well enough to attend."

The domestic bowed, and Ricardo was left by himself. At no time did he like the company of the father, but at the present moment his dislike of the monk's forbidding manners was greatly increased by the remembrance of the delightful society in which he had passed that evening.

Weary at length with indulging the long train of thoughts which crowded into his mind, he threw himself on his couch.

In his slumber, fancy brought him back to the cottage where

Louisa was; again he conversed with her, again he sighed, again he suffered the pain of parting from her. At that moment he awoke, he started at the unusual glare of light which appeared in his chamber, but soon perceived that it was the silver radiance of the Queen of Night, who threw her bright beams through his casement; he watched her through the Heavens in cloudless majesty; perhaps, thought he, bright planet, thou dost likewise illumine the chamber of Louisa, perhaps she too views thee with emotions of wonder and rapture.

In the morning Ricardo arose; he went to the casement, and looked toward the valley, but his apartments being in the northern angle, but a small part of it could be seen.

Leaving his room, he passed through the long corridore which conducted him to the grand staircase that led to the North Hall, whose lofty roof, supported by triple rows of black marble columns, and the partial light that entered from the casement, tinted with armorial bearings, made it appear gloomy, even in the bright meridian glare. Hastily he crossed the hall, and wound round the Castle till he came to that part which commanded a view of the side of the valley, where he saw rising amidst the almost unbowing shrubs the white walls of the cottage where Louisa dwelt.

He was now standing nearly opposite the Southern Angle Tower, and he immediately formed a wish to have his apartments in it; from thence he thought he should at times behold the lovely Louisa, and he could always gaze on the spot where she resided.

From that moment the lovely situation of the tower and the various reports concerning it were thought of no longer, and he determined to ask leave to reside there from the Padre Grimaldi, who ordered every thing in the Castle during the absence of the Marchese.

Having staid some time with his eyes fixed on the distant walls of Louisa's residence, he retraced his steps, delighted in the idea of at least living where he could gratify his sight at pleasure.

When he entered the Castle he found that the hour for the morning repast was not arrived, and that the Padre had not yet left his chamber, he was therefore obliged to exercise his patience, and employ his thoughts in forming plans of frequently visiting his new acquaintance, and of disclosing to the lovely cause the tender passion which gathered strength with the revolving moments.

At length when the Castle bell proclaimed the hour for the morning repast Padre Grimaldi appeared in the hall; he saluted Ricardo in his usual austere manner, which he returned with more than his accustomed courtesy.

"Father," said Ricardo, "the beauty of the morning has made me an early riser. Among the many enchanting views which the Castle commands, I know of none that has more extent and variety than that which is seen from the Southern Angle Tower."

The Padre started; for a moment he raised his dark eyes with a deep penetrating look on Ricardo, while an inward chill blanched his cheeks; said not a word, but seemed immediately after to have fallen into a reverie, which, from the effect it had on his frame, was on no pleasing subject.

Ricardo observed the agitation of Grimaldi with great surprise; he, however, affected not to notice it, but after a short pause continued his speech.

"I should feel obliged, father, by your allowing me to have the keys, that I may see that part of the Castle; and, if you have no objection, I should like to reside in the tower."

"To reside in the tower?" said Grimaldi, in a deep voice, rendered almost inarticulate by the apparent emotions of his mind; "Signor Ricardo, you know not what you ask."

Suddenly the Padre arose from his seat, he strode about the hall in a gloomy silence, his actions increased Ricardo's desire to be acquainted with the mystery that he saw clearly was connected with the tower.

After awhile the monk resumed his seat; he seemed to have recovered from the agitation the request of Ricardo had plunged him into.

"Have you," said he, looking steadfastly at him, "have you any particular reasons for wishing to see that tower? for as to residing in it, you must be well aware that its ruinous state will render that impossible."

"It was the wish of living there, father," replied Ricardo, "that made me ask to have the keys to procure an entrance."

"Probably," said Grimaldi, with a scrutinizing glance, "you wish to look for the supernatural beings who are said to haunt it, and to endeavour to raise your fame in the opinion of the vassals as being daring enough to perform so desperate an enterprize."

"The idea," replied Ricardo, "never entered my mind; the beauty of the scenery delighted me; neither am I superstitious enough to believe that there is any truth in the report of the peasantry."

"No!" replied the father, in a deeper voice, after some moments of reflection. "I was once of your opinion, but I have witnessed a sight there—horrible indeed it was."

Here he ceased to speak, for the thoughts that then seemed to rush to his memory denied him the power. Again he traversed the hall, sometimes stopping and looking on the ground, then casting a side-glance at Ricardo, who, greatly amazed, sat with his eyes intently fixed on him.

"The recalling of past terrors," said Grimaldi, stopping opposite to Ricardo, "sometimes shocks as much as if the scenes were but then acting. It is always so with me; but my sufferings the night I entered that tower were such as will in future teach me the folly of incredulity." Here the monk paused awhile, and then said, "If after what I have advanced you wish to visit that ruin, I will give you the keys, and this night you may commence your search."

"And why not by day, father?" said Ricardo, somewhat amazed.

"What, so soon afraid, Signor?" said Grimaldi. "You have heard, no doubt, that the unquiet spirits who haunt that place appear only at midnight, and therefore would wisely shun a possibility of meeting with them by going there in the morning; this is indeed a rare proof of courage."

Ricardo felt angry at the words of the father, and as his curiosity was roused by what he had said concerning the Southern Tower, he immediately replied that it was not fear which made him desire to inspect that part of the Castle by daylight; and that

if the father pleased, he would at midnight explore the long deserted recesses of that building.

To this Grimaldi assented, and promised to deliver him the
keys which opened the gates of the court-yard, and of the folding
portals of the South Hall, from which there was a communication with the tower. He then left the hall, and Ricardo to his own
reflection; on the singular behaviour of the Padre Grimaldi, and
permitting him to explore a place where, according to his own
account, he had witnessed a terrible sight; and indeed it was very
apparent from his agitation at the mention of the South Angle
Tower that some dark mystery was connected with that building,
which however Ricardo hinted the coming night would fully develop.

A gloomy reserve sat on the features of Grimaldi when
Ricardo met him in the hall; at the hour of dinner he seemed to
be revolving somewhat of dark purport in his mind, for a frown
dwelt on his forehead, and his eyes glared fiercely beneath his
bushy brows. He ate little, and spoke not to Ricardo, whose mind
was too intently employed in thinking of the beauties of Louisa,
to feel a desire to interrupt a silence which corresponded with his
wishes.

When the repast was concluded, the father arose from his
seat. Ricardo was on the point of demanding the promised keys,
but was prevented by Grimaldi's saying,

"When the bell tolls eleven, Signor, I shall await you in the
hall."

"Do you then mean to accompany me father?" demanded
Ricardo.

"By no means!" replied the Padre; "reflect on what I said this
morning; after that, you will find it not likely that I should wish to
seek to renew the horrors I have endured."

Saying this, he left the hall; and Ricardo walked on the verdant lawn which gently descended to the valley. He soon found
himself winding along the margin of a beautiful stream of water,
which fertilized the plains around. He continued advancing immersed in thought, till suddenly raising his eyes, the neat habita-
tion of the Signora Bononi appeared before him. The temptation

was irresistible; and he was proceeding toward it when he saw before him that Signora and the lovely Louisa.

The heart of Ricardo beat high with emotions of delight at the unexpected pleasure. He soon joined them, and entered into conversation with the Signora Bononi, now and then casting an enamoured glance at her charming daughter.

When at length, Ricardo bid the Signora Bononi adieu, he tenderly gazed on Louisa, her eyes were at that moment fixed on him; blushing deeply she turned aside, and so great was her confusion, that she omitted the common forms of parting.

Ricardo noticed her conduct. Good Heavens! thought he, if the lovely Louisa should survey me with the eyes of affection, what happiness!

Indulging the pleasing reflections excited by the behaviour of Louisa, Ricardo found himself near the Castle.

Somewhat fatigued with his long walk, he sat down on the trunk of a fallen tree, and continued musing till the Castle bell reminded him that it wanted but one hour to his appointment with Grimaldi.

It was now completely dark, the moon had not yet peeped over the eastern hills, and the deep shades of night prevailed. Ricardo was seated nearly opposite the ruinous part of the Castle, and as he looked toward its grey walls his attention was suddenly rivetted by a faint gleam of light which appeared at one of the broken casements of the southern buildings. It was however soon removed, and all again was enveloped in darkness; when a few minutes after he plainly discovered a figure bearing a lamp slowly pass along the hall.

This was then a proof that the reports concerning that part of the Castle were not without foundation, and Ricardo was somewhat shaken from his intention of exploring those mysterious chambers.

He arose from his seat and directed his steps to the hall, pondering in his mind on what he had seen. At length however, his curiosity surmounted his fears, and he was determined to ascertain whether aerial or corporeal beings made those chambers their residence.

It was near eleven when he entered the hall; a few lamps hung against the black pillars served to shew the extent of the place, and to add to the gloomy horrors which always seemed to reside in it.

A distant pace made Ricardo look forward, and he soon recognised the father Grimaldi; at that instant the bell tolled.

"You look pale, Ricardo," said the Padre, fixing his dark gaze on him, "do you repent your undertaking?"

"No, father," said Ricardo, "on the contrary, I feel most anxious to commence my intended search."

"But that must not take place before twelve; the moon will then assist you," replied the father; "recollect that when you have opened the portals of the hall, you continue straight forward, the door at the opposite end leads through a narrow passage to the Southern Angle Tower. Do you take any arms?"

"Most assuredly" replied Ricardo, who was almost on the point of relating what he had seen that night, but suddenly stopped through fear of being prevented going; "I shall take my sword and a trombone."

"Your sword will do without the trombone," said Grimaldi; "the report, should you be tempted to fire it, might endanger your life in bringing down some of the old walls of the buildings. Besides a sword is surely a sufficient security against ghosts; I should certainly advise you not to trouble yourself with a trombone."

Ricardo consented to take only his sword with him; and having received the keys from Grimaldi, he went to his apartment to make the necessary preparations for his bold undertaking.

He concealed his lamp and sword beneath his cloak, and waiting till the clock had tolled twelve, when, assisted by the light of the moon, which shone brightly on the castle walls, he crossed several passages of the castle, till his progress was stopped by a large iron gate which led into the southern courtyard.

The rusty wards of the lock made it extremely difficult to turn the key in it; but at length Ricardo forced back the bolt, and pushing against the gate, it slowly yielded to his efforts, harshly creaking on the time-worn hinges.

The court-yard was choaked up by rank grass and weeds, through which Ricardo with some trouble forced his way; and had it not been for the moon, he would have been perplexed to have discovered the door of the South Hall. Its beams however rested on it, and Ricardo searching for the key forced it into the large lock.

At that moment a dismal clank was heard in the hall, which echo repeated in various gradations of melancholy sound that smote chilly on the senses of Ricardo.

He started back, leaving the key in the lock, and awaited in dismal expectancy the result. The noise, however, died away in sullen murmurs, and at length all was hushed. Ricardo endeavoured to compose his agitation; and again advancing to the portals, threw them open; he drew his sword, and raising his lamp surveyed with caution the dusky recess. All seemed silent within; and the beam of the moon streaming through some of the further casements, served to shew the great extent of the hall.

At length he entered. The sound of his steps ran in loud whispers around the place. At first he paused, and looked about, for the echo had so often repeated his steps that he thought there must be more than his.

He now continued on in a direct line, according to the instructions of Grimaldi, in order to find the door that opened to the passages leading to the Angle Tower, stopping, however, at intervals, for the continual echo of his steps grew painful and ever dangerous, as they might conceal the approach of an enemy, who could unseen advance toward him though the gloom that reigned around.

In one of those places he was conscious that he heard another pace, though at some distance. This circumstance, combined with what he had already witnessed in that hall but a short time before, almost made him resolve on turning back.

Something laying in a heap before him, at the foot of a column, at this moment attracted his attention. It was a heap of old armour that had fallen from its station on the column, and in all likelihood was what occasioned the noise that he had heard when he stood at the outside of the hall portals.

In the moment of terror the being able to account for any one circumstance of alarm that occurs often composes the mind. Such was the case with Ricardo; he smiled at the fears which had seized him when he heard the clanking sound of armour against the marble floor of the hall, and began to think the footstep he had heard might be nothing more than a continued reverberation of his own.

The door he sought was half open; he could just discover it by the aid of his lamp; and his fears being greatly abated by the view of the fallen armour, he at length advanced softly toward it.

When he came within a few paces, and just as he was going to stretch out his arm to push it back, it was suddenly closed against him with a thundering noise, and a low hollow groan assailed his ears.

Ricardo staggered back to a column against which he leant with his eyes fixed on the door, expecting every moment to see some spectre issue from it, which busy fancy soon depicted with a horrible and soul-appalling form.

When at length Ricardo was able to think, various ideas crowded on his mind. At one time he determined to stay where he was till the morning, but then he feared his lamp would not last so long; and to be in the dark, in the lonely hour of night, in such a place, would be more than his spirits, considerably weakened by the shock he had received, could support. Had there been any wind that night he would willingly attribute to that the sudden closing of the door, and even the dreadful moan he had heard; but not a breath of wind was abroad; even the zephyr slept in distant caves.

After remaining near half an hour in ruminating on what he had heard and seen, Ricardo left the column, and advanced toward the door, curious to know whether it had been fastened or not; but the door yielding to his slight pressure, opened, and the rays of the lamp gleamed on the walls of a corridore.

Half determined to proceed, and prepared to turn back on the slightest alarm, Ricardo crossed the threshold. In the corridore he felt more secure than he did in the hall, for his lamp gave a better light than it could in that extensive place.

Still irresolute, he slowly advanced, at times looking behind him on the door, and then before him, half expecting to see some dreadful form in the distant shades.

Hardly had he proceeded many paces, when a hollow voice said, "Stop!" and to the astonished eyes of Ricardo a bloody sword and arm seemed thrust out of the solid wall, and which, waving furiously in the air, prevented his further advance. At the same moment deep and dismal groans, and now and then a shriek, with a dreadful discordant laugh, was heard. These repeated by the attentive echos became a thousand times more dreadful than even the noise itself.

Ricardo hastily retreated; he crossed the hall, and rushed out of the portals, then passed the court-yard, and, locking the iron gate, began to breathe.

He now repented of his temerity in persisting in his visit to the ruins after the hints thrown out by Grimaldi of what he had witnessed in them; and when he was able, retraced his way, and soon arrived in the North Hall, from whence he proceeded to his chamber.

Having closed the door, he laid his sword and lamp on the table; and throwing himself into a seat, endeavoured to compose the agitations of his mind, which shook his frame to a dreadful degree.

His mind resembled a chaos of half-formed ideas, which it was totally impossible to reduce to order; his brain became confused, and, at length, in hopes of enjoying a slumber which would compose his disturbed faculties, he laid down on his couch without taking off his cloaths.

After some time he closed his eyes in sleep; but his distempered fancy tortured him with a repetition of the horrors of the night, adding thereto whatever extravagant forms inventive airborn fancy could produce. Still however Ricardo slumbered; but it was a slumber that, far from composing his faculties, plunged them deeper in wild disturbance.

At length the beams of the morning robbed sleep of its influence on his eyelids; he started as he awoke, and wildly looked around the chamber. On the table he saw the keys, the sword, and

"A bloody sword and arm seemed thrust out of the solid wall."

the lamp. "Tis all true then," said he; "would it had been but a dream."

His brain seemed on fire; an acute pain throbbed in his temples; he arose from the couch and threw open the casement. Morning was just arising in the east, the rays of the sun feebly penetrated the mist of night, the grass yet bent beneath the dew, the hedges glittered with the transparent drops of water that were suspended from their branches, the sheep were heard bleating in the valley and on the verdant hills, and the birds of the forest gaily hailed the lovely approach of day.

Ricardo for a time surveyed the peaceful scene before him; it composed his mind, the gentle gale that slowly winded through the valley cooled the burning heat of his forehead, and now the idea of Louisa, with all her lovely charms, recurred to his memory. Intent on the pleasing ideas which he permitted his thoughts to revel in, the transactions of the night grew dim on his recollection.

Thus his mind became more composed; and when the hour arrived for the morning repast, the traces of the terrors of the night were but faintly visible on his countenance.

Father Grimaldi seemed to be awaiting the entrance of Ricardo in the hall. When he entered he raised his eyes on him, and a momentary surprise seemed to dwell in his countenance.

"Your curiosity, Signor," said he at length, "is no doubt satisfied."

Ricardo came prepared to answer the interrogations of the Padre, and therefore told him what he had heard and seen, and that his progress being stopped by the bloody sword, he had not been able to enter the Angle Tower.

The monk heard the whole relation of Ricardo without interrupting him. When he had concluded, he said, "you have doubtless now, Signor, given up all idea of visiting or residing in apartments where you must be well convinced supernatural beings have taken their abode."

Ricardo could not help owning that he had; "yet still," said he, "I could wish, with you, father, and some attendants, to endeavour to penetrate into those mysteries."

The Padre was silent some minutes; at length he said, "have you brought back the keys, Signor?"

"I have, all but the one which opens the portal of the South Hall; it is in the lock."

"After what I have witnessed there," said Grimaldi, "and what you have yourself seen, I do not deem it proper for any one to disturb those mysterious places. Should my lord the Marchese, when he comes, think proper to listen to your request, I will give up the keys, but till then I will not part with them."

The determined air with which he spoke those words rendered it needless for Ricardo to say more, for he well knew that the Padre Grimaldi was not of a disposition to be moved by any entreaty. In silence they now concluded the repast, and the father immediately rose from the table, and requested Ricardo would send him the keys, which he instantly complied with, and now calmly brought to his remembrance the event of the night, which however served to involve him in a mist of tormenting and fruitless ideas.

CHAPTER III.

PADRE BERNARDO was awoke from his slumbers by the bell of the monastery tolling twelve. Scarcely had the last tones died away in distance, when the supernatural visitant made his appearance; he was habited in the same manner as on the last night, and carried a wand in his hand; his features were carefully concealed.

The monk, whose memory still dwelt on the pages of the volume, and whose mind, from his being just awakened from sleep, had not resumed its natural strength, trembled with an internal horror as in discordant tones the following words grated harshly on his ears:

"Padre, I am come to make my promise good, if thou art willing; but I must first attain thy assenting signature to this scroll, for without the wish of its members I may not act within these walls."

"And who is there that can restrain thee, whose power appears so great?" demanded the monk in an inquiring tone.

"Those who are too curious sometimes pass unanswered," replied the mysterious voice.

"Of what nature is the contents of the schedule to which I am to give my assent? surely that may not be conceived an improper question?"

"No;" replied the voice, "but it shows that baneful suspicion lurks in your breast. Your thoughts, during the day, when other subjects occupied your mind, ill agree with this cautious mode; you then longed anxiously for the night that would bring to your view a woman far lovelier than that inanimate representation before you; and you now consume the time by idle questions. What view, Padre, can I have but your pleasure? is not man master of his own actions, in every sense a free agent? can I guide the secret workings of his soul from the channel into which it is his will they should flow? as easy could I force you to repose on the bosom of the invisible gale, as form your ideas contrary to your own consent.—In thee I am disappointed; I thought you possessed a mind restless and cautious; I knew you were without the means of attaining perhaps even the smallest of your desires, I pitied your situation; you know the rest. From what passed in your heart I knew you wished to see me, I obeyed even thoughts to which you had not given utterance. Where is there one of the Saints you worship who would do the like? thou mayest call on them, I defy them to attend thy invocation."

The monk was going to reply, and even to sign the scroll without any further delay, when loud claps of thunder burst in tremendous peals over the monastery.

"The Saints protect me!" said the terrified monk, starting from his seat, and holding to a rude pillar to support his agitated frame, for the earth was convulsed, and the cell rocked with the dreadful visitations of nature, when on a sudden a bright blaze illumined its dusky sides. The monk turned his gaze toward his visitant; tremblingly he stood in the spot where he had first beheld him; and in proportion as the brightness increased around, his gigantic form dissolved, till at length, like the uncertain vision of the night-born fancy, it existed but in idea.

Another object, far more pleasing, now attracted the attention of the monk. Soft and harmonious melodies sounded throughout the chamber, which was perfumed with aromatic odors. The monk cast his eyes upwards; the roof of the cell no longer was there, and a dazzling bright cloud, in which was reclined a still brighter form, slowly descended to the floor; the radiant mist separated, and Bernardo beheld, from the known expression of the features, the Santa Catherina.

The Saint surveyed Bernardo with a mild but sorrowful look; while the monk, lost in sensations of ecstasy, gazed on her lovely form; her golden locks, enriched by a *tiara* of brilliants, waved in captivating ringlets on her bosom; the rose of youth sported in her lovely cheeks; but how shall the pen of man describe the beauties of a Saint?—vain presumptuous effort!

"Padre," said the lovely Saint, in a voice in which was con-centered the melody of a thousand harps, "what form was that which faded away on my approach? Who hast thou suffered to gain entrance within walls devoted to my service?"

Abashed the monk held down his head, but yet beneath his overhanging brows his dark eyes gazed on the Saint.

"I know him not, celestial visitant; neither gave I him entrance here; he came unsought, unasked, unwished."

"Say not so, misguided mortal, 'tis like thou didst not invoke his presence, but by indulging wicked thoughts, Bernardo, you permitted him to enter; and after you had once seen him, after you had heard him ridicule the religion to which you belong, you again wished to see him. Thou seest how superior is my power to his; how like a guilty wretch he slunk away, even at the reflection of the radiance which surrounds me. Listen to him, Bernardo, and dreadful will be the state of your soul when death has done his office on your corporeal form. But repent of your faulty con-duct, amend your future life, and by tears, fasting, and penitence, render yourself worthy to become an inhabitant of the blissful regions of Paradise. Behold now, Bernardo, the fate of those who are impious in this world!"

This said, a chasm yawned hideously in the earth at the feet of the monk, who when at length his eyes had wandered down the dreadful profundity, beheld a sea of liquid fire, like the me-tallic ore which the alchymist melts in his crucibles in order to pour into the mould to receive its destined form. Of boundless extent appeared this horrid ocean, which raised its fiery waves in lofty ridges; deep plunged in this abyss of misery inexpressible appeared thousands of forms, whose screams deep and soul-felt rushed to the ears of the terrified monk; groups of fiends at times amused themselves by taking the burning wretches from the fiery sea and plunging them in rivers whose water appeared stagnant with intense cold; dreadful was the change, dreadful the torture to the sufferers, but to the fiends it afforded delight, manifested by their hideous, discordant yells of merriment.

Slow stalking over the burning sea appeared a figure of unusual size; his form was noble; a beautiful symmetry dwelt in his limbs, but his countenance bore the marks of regret, disappointed ambition, and inveterate malice; dark and dreadful passions had marked his features with their gloomy hue, and by his eyes of fire the monk recognized in him his nocturnal visitant.

Terrified and horror-struck, Bernardo hid his face with his hands, and shook with the agitation of his mind.

The lovely eyes of the Saint were fixed on him; but she who could read the dark volumes of futurity, to whom the deeds of other years, and what is to occur in the boundless tide of eternity appeared without a shade before her, sighed deeply.

"Lift up thy view now, Bernardo, and weigh well the difference in the existence of the immortal soul after a life virtuously employed."

The monk obeyed; but so many dazzling glories met his view, that his eyes shrunk from the transcendent effulgence; again he ventured to raise his eyelids, the horrid chasm at his feet was closed, and the roar from those regions of horror no longer appalling his soul, made him the more freely indulge in the blissful scene of Paradise.

Myriads of bright forms, seated on thrones of silver canopied by golden clouds, unceasing in grateful adorations tuned their harps to hymns of praise. Beauty dwelt around, each of the celestial inhabitants appeared to have just attained the age when the loves and graces unite to bring to perfection the human frame, no cares, no sorrows seemed to dwell among the heavenly host; all was joy in its most perfect state.

After the astonishment of the monk had in some degree ceased, he began to contemplate the scene before him with the eye of the voluptuary: here were no envious veils to conceal the lovely beatific charms of the radiant host; little attire suited their beauteous forms, for guiltless were their minds. A zone of immortal make pressed to their taper waists the transparent robes that gently floated on the fragrant wing of the zephyrs. Deeply sighed the monk, greatly he panted to be amongst those lovely forms, when the Santa Catherina, shocked to see so much depravity inhabit a human being, closed the view from his unhallowed gaze.

Discontented the monk turned his eyes on her who thus addressed him:

"Now, Bernardo, I leave you to make your election; you have seen the result of a wicked and of a well-spent life, conduct yourself piously, and I will be your friend; act the reverse, and I leave you to the common enemy of mankind, who will fawn before you to accomplish his dark designs, and finally rejoice over you when writhing in unutterable agonies such as you have but seen the guilty suffer, you toss on unfathomable boundless oceans of liquid fire."

Slowly the bright cloud united in front of the Saint, who directing her beauteous eyes to Heaven, slowly ascended toward those exalted regions of bliss. The cell grew dark, the monk lost in thought, leaned against a pillar, revolving in his mind what he had heard and seen; at length turning round, he beheld the table, the volume, the lamp and the chair, in the same position as when he left them; he advanced with faltering steps, and taking the lamp, held it up to the painting, but what had before given him so much pleasure, now disgusted him. "How feeble," said he, "are the efforts of the painter to afford even a single idea of the angelic charms of the Santa Catherina."

The monk threw himself into his seat, deeply ruminating on the past, or rather on the beauties he had beheld, and which entirely obliterated from his mind the regions of despair and horror which had been open to his view. His soul was far gone in guilty thoughts and wishes. "If" said he, "the women of this world are as lovely as those in the next, methinks I could tear down these my prison walls, to enjoy their enchanting converse."—

Suddenly a means arose in his mind by which there was a

slight possibility of gratifying his curiosity; 'tis true the greatest danger attended it, and therefore the attempt would call forth all his art, skill, and dexterity; he reflected on it with sensations of pleasure, and though at that moment he meditated no real crime, yet he knew not that by it he threw himself into temptations to him irresistible.

The near approach of the morning beams rendered it impossible for him to make the attempt at that time, he was therefore obliged to defer it till the next night; he then lay down on his pallet, and endeavoured to court a short repose ere the matin bell should call him to the duties of the day.

Rest however awaited him not there; he turned from side to side, but in no posture would calm sleep steep in forgetfulness the agitation of his mind. He arose, and leaving his cell, walked into the gardens belonging to the monastery as the bell tolled four. Ascending an eminence which commanded an extensive view there, he beheld the sun rising in radiant majesty from the calm waves of the sea; first he threw his broad beams on the aspiring summit of Mount Etna, then emitting volumes of black smoke, which ascending became condensed in the air till driven abroad by the western breeze, which rolled them toward the Ionian Sea.

The monastery and convent of Santa Catherina was erected on the side of one of the lofty hills which form the well-known Val de Demone, which lays in the north-east part of the island of Sicily. To the north it commanded a view of the Mediterranean sea and the isles of Lipare; to the west it overlooked a vast extent of country interspersed with several castles and large towns, particularly those of Randasso and Lingua Crossa.

From the eminence which the restless mind of the monk had made him desirous to ascend was seen a part of the convent gardens which were separated from those belonging to the monastery by a lofty wall. Eagerly did Bernardo gaze toward that place; and it was evident that not the wish of seeing the sun arise from other worlds to perform his daily course over this hemisphere, or to survey the beauties of the lovely prospect which now so sweetly opened to the view, drew the monk to that elevated spot; some dark, some deep design, evidently was on the anvil of his mind, and which as it appeared, shunned the inquiring face of day, as he had fixed on the coming night to accomplish his purpose, whatever it might be.

Well it might be supposed that the events which had so strongly marked the past night would have obliterated from his mind all ideas of doing any thing that was not consistent with the rule of right; but the monk now remembered the whole but as a baseless vision, excepting, indeed, the remembrance that he cherished of the heavenly charms he had beheld, and which acted as a powerful stimulant to urge him to the completion of his intentions; so hard is it to turn the current of evil thoughts when virtue holds but a doubtful sway over the mind.

Bent on the accomplishment of his wishes, he had sullenly listened to the voice of the immaculate Santa Catherina, who had so graciously evinced her solicitude for the welfare of his soul by condescending to be herself his monitor.

The dreadful view which she had disclosed of the regions of eternal horrors suited not the religious tenets of the monk, who looked only to a short duration in purgatory for a remission of all worldly offences, should the abbot refuse to grant him absolution before death; neither did he approve of acts of mortification and penance, for the Padre Bernardo was well affected toward the indulgence of his appetites, and he almost began to believe the whole brought about through the means of the mysterious visitant, in order to prove whether he was worthy of his efforts to serve him. In this disposition he thought of him no longer with terror, and he determined that, as he meant to make some attempt to satisfy his curiosity that night, the next should be the one when he would see the supernatural being and comply with his requests, on condition, that he should perform whatever was required of him.

In such a melancholy determination as this the sound of the matin bell broke on the silence of the morning, and the Padre Bernardo hasted from the eminence in the garden of the monastery to join the train, and in the chapel to appear as an assistant in what was so far distant from his thoughts, which now grew each hour darker, and more pregnant with evil designs.

CHAPTER IV.

LOUISA's breast, unknown almost to herself, cherished the most pure love for Ricardo. She thought it was really the sensations of friendship and esteem that made her continually ruminate on that Signor, but the subtle deity of hearts had made her completely his vassal ere she was conscious of it. She began to feel a distaste to whatever before had attracted her attention and had given her pleasure; her flowers were sometimes neglected for whole days, the jessamine which wantoned round her favorite bower wanted her attentive hand; she often sighed without being conscious of it; and whenever a horseman passed the cottage, she would raise her eyes to see if it was not Ricardo, while a sudden suffusion crimsoned her lovely countenance.

In the mean time various emotions possessed the soul of the Signor. He found it impossible to drive from his mind the mysterious events of the past night. The noises he had heard at the time the sword was waved against him, increased by the attendant echo, were such as might be supposed to proceed from the dark bosom of the bottomless pit where the souls of the wicked are continually undergoing a new series of tortures and horrors.

Neither that day nor the next did he stir from the Castle. Grimaldi, whom he only saw at the hour of repast, never turned the conversation to the ruins; he seemed, indeed, either to have forgotten what had so lately taken place in them, or to wish to do so, and his general conversation was on the expected arrival of the Marchese, a courier having been dispatched from Palermo bearing intelligence to that effect.

Ricardo then determined to visit Louisa, for he was fearful that when the Marchese arrived he should not have many opportunities of doing so unobserved. On the evening of the third day he approached the cottage, and when he entered it, to his inexpressible delight found the lovely Louisa sitting by herself; the Signora Bononi having gone to a neighbouring cottage to assist a poor woman who was unwell.

The innate modesty of Louisa made her blush deeply as Ricardo entered the apartment. Secluded as she had hitherto been from society, it was the first time she was ever alone with a stranger. Some other emotions which it is likely she also felt, contributed to increase her confusion.

Such an opportunity of declaring the sentiments of his breast was eagerly seized by Ricardo; he threw himself at the feet of the trembling and almost alarmed Louisa, he poured forth his soul to her.

"Beautiful Louisa! the first moment that gave thy lovely form to my eyes my heart no longer owned my sway, but when I became acquainted with your virtues and the numberless and nameless graces that adorn you, my whole soul became yours. Do not conceive, most amiable Louisa, that I am guided by other motives than those of honor and virtue. Oh! Louisa, avert not that sweet face from me; let me gaze on those beauties I must ever adore."

"Rise, Signor," said Louisa; "the lowly posture you have taken distresses me; you forget yourself, or the son of the Marchese de Carlentini would not surely thus address himself to the humble Louisa."

"Love, dearest maid of my heart," replied Ricardo, "love levels all distinctions; but were I possessed of a crown, I should lay it at Louisa's feet. Suffer me," continued he, taking hold of her hand, "suffer me to hope that the attentions, the adoration, of Ricardo, will one day be blessed with a return from the divine object of them."

"Signor," said Louisa, "whatever were the sentiments of my heart, they could be of no import to you; the future Marchese de Carlentini must look to one of equal rank with himself as his wife."

"By the powers of love I swear, if Louisa listens not to my vows of adoration, never to wed; the thought of other than you is torture to my soul. O Louisa! lovely! dearest Louisa, let not my heart burst with agony. Perhaps, oh! heavens, perhaps another has your love. O envied mortal! speak, my Louisa, tell me my fate, but be merciful."

Here his speech failed, his eyes suffused in tears were fixed on the pallid Louisa, who, affected at his emotions, sought to comfort him.

"Signor, if the assurance that the humble Louisa has no other acquaintance than yourself, (if I may be allowed the honor of ranking you as such,) is of any importance to your comfort, I should be wrong not to mention it. I am yet too young even to dream of love; but if the friendship, the esteem of Louisa, are worth acceptance, no one possesses them more than the Signor Ricardo."

In ecstacy at this speech, which freed the bosom of Ricardo from an insupportable burthen, he kissed the tender hand he held, nor did the now blushing Louisa seek to prevent him. At her solicitation he arose from his suppliant posture, while Hope with her golden pinions fluttered around him, and sweetly whispered in his ear that Louisa would be his.

Scarcely had she time to compose the agitation of her mind, when her mother entered the apartment. She seemed surprised to find her daughter alone with Ricardo, and an air of gravity prevailed over her features. He instantly observed it; and, elated with the reception he had met with from Louisa, determined no longer to conceal from her his sentiments concerning her daughter; he therefore took an opportunity when Louisa was out of the apartment to commence the interesting conversation.

All attempts on the part of the Signora Bononi to convince him that an union with her daughter would be little short of madness, were in vain; and with difficulty she obtained a promise from him not to mention to the Marchese his wild project, for she well knew that both herself and the innocent Louisa would become the immediate objects of his persecution. And she had also the welfare of her daughter too much in view not secretly to rejoice at the attachment of Ricardo, particularly as she had every reason to believe it mutual.

With his breast lightened of an oppressive load, and hopes of future days of halcyon joy, Ricardo quitted the cottage where dwelt his only comfort, the bright star which was to lead him to the flowery paths of domestic bliss.

When he entered the Castle, he found some of the servants

of the Marchese already arrived, and making preparations for his reception and the Signors who usually accompanied him. The gloom that had so long reigned within its lofty walls now began to be dispersed, the apartments were furnished in a sumptuous style, and the long tables were once more laid in the centre of the hall.

The next day the merry trumpeters announced the approach of the Marchese, and Ricardo, with the Padre Grimaldi, staid in the North Hall to meet and welcome him to his residence. He was accompanied by three Signors, and a numerous train of domestics followed them. He slightly embraced his son as he entered, and having presented him to the Signors who were with him, he passed on to father Grimaldi to whom he spoke for some time, but in such low tones, that Ricardo, who was engaged in conversation with the companions of the Marchese, could not hear a word. The steward now attended to shew the strangers their apartments, and the Marchese quitted the hall with Grimaldi.

Ricardo thus left alone, had leisure to reflect on the companions of his father. In the Count Altona, he saw a combination of the most repulsive manners that, according to his ideas, could possibly exist in one person; dissimulation, pride, and envy, formed the leading traits of his disposition. The Signor Roderigo de Romanzo appeared little better than the captain of a banditti, his person was gigantic, his face almost covered by a pair of enormous whiskers, a long Roman nose, and black piercing eyes, glared beneath his overhanging brows, while his whole countenance was shaded by a large plume of black feathers, which he wore in his military hat, and which added to the sombre appearance of his features. The third person was the young Count de Leoni, in whom Ricardo saw one who perhaps possessed a congenial disposition with his own thoughts. At the first interview, it was almost impossible to judge, but each seemed to be pleased with the other, and to feel a desire to cultivate his friendship.

An elegant entertainment was prepared in the North Hall, of which the Marchese and his three companions, with Grimaldi and Ricardo, partook; and Ricardo found, that when the enlivening flask had gone briskly round, and each character began to develop itself, that he was not mistaken in the opinion he had formed of the haughty Count Altona, and the ferocious looking Signor Roderigo de Romanzo. All of them seemed to pay the greatest attention to the Count de Leoni, Grimaldi excepted, who still retained his usual repulsive manners, notwithstanding the evident exertions of the Marchese to induce him to unbend from his stern deportment.

When at length they retired from the banquet, the company proceeded to the apartments of the Marchese, where they sat down to play. Ricardo was astonished at the vast sums which were staked, and concerned to see that the Count de Leoni, and the Signor Roderigo de Romanzo, who were opposed to the Marchese and the Count Altona, lost to a considerable amount.

He at length retired from the apartment, and in the solitude of his own reflected on his beloved Louisa; but his reflections occasioned both joy and sorrow; joy, that she seemed to regard him in a favourable light; and sorrow, that it would be impossible to be united to her during the life-time of his father.

In such reflections the hours wore sadly away, when the stillness which hitherto had reigned around was interrupted by sudden bursts of laughter and merriment, which appeared to come from the North Hall.

Ricardo now for the first time reflected that it was long past the hour of supper, which had sounded unobserved during his meditations. He, however, felt curious to know what it was that occasioned such noisy merriments, and for that purpose leaving his chamber, proceeded to the extremity of the corridore, where a small portal opened on a gallery which ran round the hall.

From thence he perceived the Marchese and his companions, who appeared in a state of inebriation. Their exclamations were loud, and their conversation disgusting to the ear of Ricardo, who rejoiced that his absence of mind had prevented him from joining such a dissipated crew.

At one side of the table sat the father Grimaldi; who alone partook not of the general festivity. He appeared to be indulging his usual gloomy ideas, even in the midst of such a licentious scene.

Surely, thought Ricardo, that man must have committed some horrible act which seems unceasingly to embitter his existence, and renders him a burden to himself and unpleasant to every one around.

Weary with viewing the scene which presented itself to his sight, Ricardo left the gallery and returned to his couch, where sleep awaited to close his eyes, and the powers of fancy to bring to his imagination his beloved Louisa.

In a few days, Ricardo having found an opportunity to speak to the Marchese, informed him of the events that had taken place in the southern wing of the Castle, and requested to be permitted to search them with a party of domestics.

The Marchese listened to him with impatience, and when Ricardo had concluded, thus addressed him:

"From Father Grimaldi I have already been informed of your adventures in the ruins, and I cannot conceive the reason of your wish to explore them. Tell me, Ricardo," continued the Marchese, fixing his eyes steadfastly on him, "is it not in consequence of some idle reports which I understand exist among the peasants and domestics? Have you been so weak as to listen to them? It must be so, or your curiosity could never have been so greatly roused. Answer me truly."

Ricardo ingenuously owned that his first wish was to reside in the Southern Angle Tower, as it commanded so beautiful and extensive a prospect, and that afterwards the appearance of the figure bearing the lamp excited his curiosity to examine the deserted chamber.

"Idle chimeras of the brain," replied the Marchese, whom Ricardo could not help observing turned pale at the mention of the South Angle Tower; "henceforth Ricardo, let me hear no more on this subject, thou wilt infect all the inhabitants with thy fears, which I am sorry to say can only exist in a weak and uninformed mind. Or supposing that what you have asserted were true, is it possible, think you, to drive away aerial beings? Reflect on the absurdity only for a moment, and recollect too that I charge you never to attempt to enter those ruins, and never to make them the subject of your conversation as you fear my displeasure."

Such was the result of Ricardo's conversation with the haughty Marchese, who immediately left the hall and joined the Count Altona and Signor Romanzo who were walking on the lawn; while Ricardo, somewhat confused at the stern comportment of his father, retired to his chamber; and leaning over the stone frame of the casement, gave way to the reflections his conduct had excited.

While he was thus employed a low murmur of voices made him look on the terrace below, where he saw the Marchese in earnest conversation with his two companions; he heard them once or twice pronounce the name of the Count de Leoni, from which circumstance it was evident he was the subject of their discourse.

"It ought to be shared equally amongst us," said Romanzo, in a tone loud enough to be heard by Ricardo.

To this the Marchese replied, and a long conversation ensued, the result of which was the departure of Romanzo in evident anger from the Marchese and Altona, who still continued to converse together long after the enraged Romanzo had quitted the terrace.

The Count Altona then departed, and the Marchese continued slowly pacing the terrace, at times leaning over the wall and betraying tokens of suspence and anxiety; at length, however, Altona appeared with Romanzo; the Marchese hastily advanced toward him; and, by their gestures, the difference that had taken place seemed to be amicably adjusted.

They then left the terrace, and Ricardo to his reflections on their conduct, which indeed was little in favor of the rectitude of their intentions toward the Count de Leoni; and he shuddered at the horrid surmises which he could not prevent entering his mind.

At times he almost felt inclined to disclose his suspicions to the Count himself; but the idea of the foul light in which he must represent his father obliged him to be silent.

He had improved his acquaintance with Leoni, and used to ride out with him about the estate, which was extensive and beautifully diversified with the luxuriant productions of Nature, and he observed with regret that the features of the Count at times bore an air of deep melancholy, and which seemed to increase upon him.

The cause was unknown to Ricardo, who now never mixed in the evening parties of the Marchese, but generally used after the banquet to turn his steps to the dwelling of Louisa, where his hours passed in sweet converse with the beloved of his heart.

She at length blessed him with an avowal of a mutual affection, and on the downy pinions of delight happily passed the fleeting hours; blessing and blessed they looked to each other for happiness, and found it in the endearing smile and tender pressure, warm with the emotions of pure and sincere affection.

Such is the happiness attendant on virtuous love; each moment increases the dear charm, each moment it becomes more interwoven with existence itself. It is like the pure flame which the Virgins of the Sun attend, and which never expires.

Deeply impressed with sentiments sacred to love, the happy pair indulged without reserve in transports known only to those whose bosoms have felt the sweet influence, but in which the most rigid attention to modesty was never violated.

Happy lover, recollect what your emotions were when you learned that the soul of her you adored was free, peaceful, and unconquered, and that you might aspire to the supreme felicity of teaching it to love; recollect too the ravishing delight which seized your soul, when the sweet confession of a mutual affection slowly proceeded from the coral lips of the beauty of your heart; were not those moments of ecstatic bliss? Recollect what you then felt, and confess that the delights of that moment were worth ages of pain.

Such happiness did Ricardo enjoy; and which would have been without alloy were it not for the constant fear he was in lest the Marchese should come to the knowledge of his attachment.

One morning when he had just taken leave of Louisa, at the gate which opened to the road, he was suddenly accosted by the Count Altona, who, it seems was at that moment riding past. He saluted Ricardo, and after a short conversation, invited him to join him in the ride.

Ricardo, although vexed that he had been seen at the cottage, comforted himself with the idea that Louisa could hardly have been observed by the Count, and in order to find out if she had, readily consented to the invitation, and accompanied him through the extensive and beautiful valley; but the Count was silent respecting Louisa, and Ricardo felt assured that his secret was safe.

He saw with the greatest concern the increasing melancholy that marked the features of the Count de Leoni; when that day they had assembled in the Hall at the banquet he drank frequently, and evidently appeared to endeavour to drown obtruding thoughts in the inebriating juice of the grape. When the repast was concluded, they repaired as usual to the apartments of the Marchese, and Ricardo to his own chamber, for he was fearful of going that evening to the residence of Louisa.

The misty shades of night were advancing with rapid strides, for the sun had long ceased to illumine the valley, and was pursuing his bright journey to other worlds, who were now rejoicing at his gladdening approach.

A hasty step on the terrace made Ricardo lean over the lower frame of the casement, and to his astonishment he beheld the Count de Leoni. His gestures betrayed the anguish of his mind, and as he passed under the casement, Ricardo heard him speak in disordered accents the following words.—"Oh Heavens! wretch that I am not sooner to see the snare that was laid for me! Ruined—utterly ruined! Accursed walls," said he, looking at the Castle, "why did you not fall and overwhelm the vile crew ye shelter ere my destruction was completed?" Thrice he smote his forehead, then looking over the wall and seeing some of his domestics, he ordered them to bring his horse directly, and then quitted the terrace.

The astonishment of Ricardo, the shame he felt, rendered him incapable of action; to be the son of a man who was guilty of so much baseness, afflicted him more than the weak pen can describe. He still staid at the casement, and in a few minutes beheld the unfortunate Count gallop furiously across the lawn, and disappear in the surrounding shades.

The Castle bell soon after announced the hour of supper, and Ricardo determined to station himself in the gallery, to see what would pass between the Marchese and his companions on hearing of the absence of the Count. Accordingly he took his station in a place where he could not be seen, and when the Marchese and his associates met, he perceived they were in unusual spirits; when the domestics announced the Count de Leoni, a smile was visible on their features, and they gaily sat down to the repast.

Their conversation, while the domestics were in the room, was on general topics; but when they were away, the Marchese thus addressed his companions:—

"Count Altona, I am sorry to be obliged to renew the subject in which the Signor Romanzo appeared to conceive himself unfairly dealt with. You know," said he, lowering his voice, "that the terms of our agreement with the Signor was to allow him one thousand gold ducats, on condition of his introducing to us the Count de Leoni."

"You will do well, Marchese," sullenly replied the Signor Romanzo, "to recollect the conversation I held with you before we came to the Castle, and also the promise you made before the Count Altona, that I was to share with you equally the pillage of Leoni."

"We did that," replied the Count, "in order to keep you quiet; the Marchese and myself are willing to conform to our first promise. What pretensions, Signor Romanzo, can you possibly have to such a partition? Content yourself with the thousand ducats; the next time you shall have more."

"The Saints curse me if I do!" furiously replied the Signor Romanzo; "give me one third, or by the Virgin I will expose you at Palermo.—Marchese, I address myself to you; it was with you my agreement was made."

"You know my resolves," said the Marchese, "nor am I to be intimidated by the threats of Signor Romanzo, whom I have honored by permitting to reside beneath my roof."

"I am resolved to have my right," said Romanzo, "or"—

"Or what?" replied the Marchese.

"Or dispute it with my sword."

"Your sword," said the Marchese, "will do little for you. No one fears it here. There are your ducats," continued he, throwing a large purse on the table.

"Marchese," said the furious Romanzo, rising up and unsheathing his sword, "hear me—you are a villain."

"That word shall be your last," said the angry Marchese, and instantly drawing, attacked Romanzo.

Ricardo rushed from his place of concealment in the gallery, and flew toward the Hall; he had, however, arrived too late, for the Marchese was wounded and lay on the floor weltering in his blood.

"Count Altona," exclaimed Romanzo "'tis your turn now."

"No, villain!" exclaimed Ricardo, snatching from the hand of his dying father the sword which had been of so little use, "first you must fight with me."

Romanzo, eyeing him contemptuously, aimed a furious blow at his head. Ricardo avoided the stroke, and at the same instant pierced his unguarded side. The sword reached his heart; and the gigantic Romanzo with a hideous groan fell lifeless on the marble pavement.

The domestics, alarmed by the clashing of swords, had rushed into the Hall. They instantly conveyed the Marchese to his couch, and Grimaldi, who was skilled in surgery, dressed his wound.

But the feeble efforts of man wanted power to assist the Marchese; life was ebbing fast; the sword had pierced some of the vital parts, and the wound was mortal.

Ricardo was standing mournfully by the side of the couch, when the Marchese opening his eyes, thus with difficulty addressed him:—

"Thou hast done well, my son, to revenge the wound I have received by the death of Romanzo. I feel the lamp of life is near expiring, and ere it is quite extinguished, I would unburthen my conscience of a dreadful secret which weighs heavy on my soul."

Father Grimaldi, who was in the chamber, now hastily came to the side of the couch; his countenance was pale and agitated.

"Signor Ricardo," said he, suddenly interrupting the speech of the Marchese, "may I request your absence for a few minutes;

The sword reached his heart!

the mind of the Marchese seems disordered, and needs, while he is able to receive it, the holy rites of the church."

Ricardo reluctantly, and greatly surprised at the earnest request of the father, withdrew, and left him alone with the Marchese. It was, however, but a short time before Grimaldi came to inform him he might again enter the chamber, which he instantly did.

The countenance of Grimaldi had recovered its usual composure, but that of the Marchese seemed dreadfully agitated. The sharp pangs of death assailed him; his eyes rolled about with a dreadful meaning, while the crimson flush on his cheek indicated the fever that was preying on his vitals.

"Why am I thus surrounded," said he, looking wildly about him; "did not I tell you how it happened; ask Grimaldi, it was his fault."

Again the confessor approached the bed.

"Marchese," said he, "recollect yourself; there are none in the chamber but your son and myself."

"Grimaldi, deny it not; it was your fault," said the Marchese. "Oh! how the recollection tortures me. Now would I could recal that hour. How the demons stare at me—they are waiting for my soul—oh! Ricardo, hold me; let me not go; they will tear me to pieces—mercy—oh, mercy!—Heaven have mercy on my"—

"Soul!" he would have said, but death for ever stopped his further speech. A groan of long and horrible continuance announced the departure of the breath of life. Now he lay motionless; his countenance blackened and distorted by his struggles with the relentless power and the pangs of his body, and what was far worse, his conscience, for Ricardo too plainly perceived that there was some dreadful secret which he wished to unfold, but was prevented either by Grimaldi or the pangs he endured.

Ricardo now left the chamber, and Grimaldi being left alone, approached the breathless form of the Marchese; he gazed at it while he said in a low voice "had but a few minutes more of existence been allowed thee, thou wouldst have betrayed me to the world. Now I am secure, save from that avenging Power which doubtless now hovers over me grasping the retributive sword of justice. Would I could fly from conscience; would I could fly from death! Oh! what tortures must be mine in that awful moment when the soul is leaving its mortal coil and going to give an account of its deeds before the dreadful throne of judgment.—But let me not think of it, lest I hasten my dissolution; let me steel my heart and resist the attacks of conscience, which renders my existence one scene of horror."

Such were the words of Grimaldi, who now left the side of the couch, and summoned the attendants to perform the last offices to the body of the Marchese de Carlentini.

Ricardo mourned with filial affection the loss of his father, though he had so little demeaned himself as one. Yet he forgot all the instances of his unkindness, and remembered only those few moments in which he had shewn the most trifling marks of affection for him.

On the evening of the second day a train of monks arrived from a neighbouring monastery, which was near the town of Pollizzi, and the body of the late Marchese was conveyed into the chapel, which was hung with black, and lit by the torches carried by the domestics. Ricardo attended the awful ceremony. The deep voices of the Fathers chaunting the Requiem was alone heard; the solemn sounds floated in the air, and Echo, with all her busy train, increased the mournful harmony. At length the mortal remains were consigned to the peaceful tomb; and the service being concluded, the procession left the chapel.

The superior of the monastery remained some time with Ricardo, in order to pour into his bosom the consolation of religious discourse; and when the ebullitions of Ricardo's sorrow had in some degree subsided, he left him, and proceeded to his peaceful abode.

The Count Altona had, the day after the death of the Marchese, sent a message of condolence to Ricardo, and had departed with his people from the Castle, as had also the domestics of the unfortunate Count de Leoni in search of their master; and the people belonging to the Signor Romanzo with his breathless remains.

Such was the termination of the dreadful events which an unprincipled motive of ruining an unwary and unfortunate youth gave rise to. Associates in a bad cause never long agree; if Justice does not overtake them, they generally inflict it on themselves.

No longer in fear of his attachment to Louisa being known, Ricardo sent a messenger to her with earnest inquiries after her health, and that of the Signora Bononi.

The answer of Louisa was long; she condoled with him on the late unfortunate events at the Castle, and represented her mother and herself as being perfectly well; but there was an air of melancholy diffused throughout the letter which greatly distressed Ricardo. It seemed written as if she was labouring under some calamity, and which she wished not to divulge, but which had taken such hold on her faculties that she was unable to avoid almost expressing it by her style of writing.

The recent events at the Castle rendered it improper for Ricardo to leave it; and his respect for his father was such as to make him rigidly conform to the rules which custom had rendered unavoidable.

In searching among the papers of his late father, in order to ascertain whether he had left any will, he found a large packet, which on inspection he found to contain the writings relative to the estates of the Count de Leoni.

Delighted beyond measure at an opportunity of rendering justice to the unfortunate Count, he instantly despatched messengers after him, to acquaint him with the circumstances that had taken place at the Castle, and that if he would repair there, he would be informed of a circumstance of the utmost importance to him.

Having done this his mind became more composed, and he waited with much anxiety for the return of his messengers, in the fond hope of making the Count de Leoni every satisfaction for the wrongs which he had received from his father and his agents.

But the people returned after having been to Palermo, and to the estates which the Count had possessed, without being able to gain the least intelligence where the Count was; and Ricardo, when he recollected the despair and distraction which was but too apparent in his actions on the evening he had left the Castle, at times greatly feared that he had, in one of his fits of desperation, laid violent hands on himself.

The father Grimaldi seldom appeared in the presence of Ricardo; he was almost always shut up in his apartment, and sometimes, either very early in the morning, or when the shades of evening enveloped in their dusky mantle all around, he would walk on the lawn, and seek to find relief from the evident disturbance which reigned within his breast; his face grew meagre; his eyes and cheeks were hollow, and it was evident he was labouring under some dreadful evil which was fast hurrying him to "that bourne from whence no traveller e'er returned."

At length he entirely confined himself to his apartment, and soon after to his bed; a fever preyed on his vitals, and reduced him to the dreary brink of the grave.

In this extremity he sent for Ricardo, who immediately complied with his request, and came to his apartment. He was greatly shocked to see the dreadful change that had taken place in so short a time, and that even now the hand of death was on the mysterious Grimaldi.

After motioning to his domestic to quit the chamber, he thus addressed Ricardo:—

"My hour is at length arrived. I already feel the cold chill of dissolution anticipate the dreadful moment of my departure from this world; dreadful indeed to me, whose evil deeds weigh down my soul! No gleam of comfort animates me; hope is extinct; deeply have I sinned; dreadful must be my atonement. But there is mercy; and my long repentance may perhaps at last be considered as some alleviation of my crime. Thou wilt, ere long, Signor, know the mystery of the South Angle Tower.—These papers will inform you with the extent of my guilt; but I entreat with my dying breath that you will not break the seal 'till I am in my grave; and if it be possible, do not curse me, for misery and despair have been my portion since I committed the dreadful deed.—Surely"—

At that moment a pang sharp and heartfelt, the harbinger of death, distorted the countenance of the monk; he groaned dreadfully, and turned up his eyes to Heaven with an expression of contrition which seemed to come from a heart almost hopeless of mercy.

Ricardo wished to speak to him words of comfort, but was unable; he was ignorant of the crime he had committed; but from the continual torture he seemed to endure, and the last words of his father, which vibrated in his ears, he was convinced it was an offence dark and dreadful, and which concerned himself.

He promised that he would not break the enclosure of the packet till the time he had mentioned; and Grimaldi, who had now become a little composed by the discontinuance of the pangs of death, in a faint voice continued:—

"Surely the torments I have endured in this world will be considered. Nor peace, nor comfort, have I known for many years. Oh! had virtue ever been the constant attendant on my actions, how widely different would this awful hour appear to me. On the brink of eternity, stained with the blackest crime that human nature can be capable of! O earth, swallow me up, nor let my soul escape; imprison it deep, deep in thy dark bowels; let it not ascend to give an account of my offences; let it not descend to endure the torments it merits. Ah! now are fast opening the gates of Eternal life—have mercy Heaven!—have mercy on the soul of a murderer!"

Ricardo started at the dreadful word, which was the last that Grimaldi spoke in this world; the angel of death had claimed him as his prey, and his soul had fled to those dreaded regions above to give an account of the dreadful crimes it had been guilty of.

Ricardo pensively left the chamber with the packet given him by Grimaldi in his hand, deposited it his cabinet, and perceiving that the moon was breaking over the eastern horizon, which now glowed with the near approach of the radiant regent of day, he determined to stay an hour in his chamber; and then to see Louisa, as he was anxious to know if his suspicions respecting the state of her mind when she wrote to him were right.

The recent events crowded so thick upon his mind that more than an hour passed ere he was aware of it; he now descended from his chamber, and hastily, with the fond impatience of an anxious love, proceeded to the residence of Louisa. But dreadful was the intelligence that awaited him there; he entered the cottage, and not seeing any one in the apartment where the Signora Bononi and her daughter used to sit, he was proceeding into the garden; when the sound of lamentation assailed his ears; hastily he flew, directed by them, into a chamber, where he saw the Signora Bononi and her domestic gagged and bound with cords in such a manner, as to render them unable to stir. He immediately released them, and in reply to his almost distracted inquiries concerning Louisa, was informed by the Signora Bononi that late the preceding evening, three men in masks had entered the cottage, and after having confined herself and servant in the manner he had found them, had carried off Louisa.

CHAPTER V.

WHEN the Padre Bernardo left the rest of the monks he went to his cell, and having replenished his lamp with oil, he repaired to the chapel.

Darkness and silence reigned in the long-drawn aisles. Often the monk started at the echoes of his slow paces as they reverberated along the vaulted roof.

At length he stopped at the gilded screen which divided the part allotted to the nuns of the convent. With scrupulous attention he examined the fastenings of the folding gates, and applied several keys to the lock, but without success.

Though doomed to meet a disappointment at this place, he did not despair; but turning from the screen, he crossed the aisle, and opening a large door, proceeded down several steps, taking care to shroud his lamp from the blasts that rushed in melancholy moans through the dreary subterraneous repositories for the departed monks of Santa Catherina: for it was the cemetery of the monastery that Bernardo was now in.

He often looked around to see if his steps were followed; but no human sound broke on his ear. The ground he was now traversing rose in many small hillocks terminated by a cross, which marked the spot where lay the mouldering remains of the Monks.

Strange ideas disturbed the mind of Bernardo which was naturally superstitious, his terrors increased every moment; that beings who belonged not to this world were allowed to visit it he was well assured of, and he each moment expected to see the graves burst open, and their inmates rise from their silent recesses and stop his further progress.—In fancy he saw them stalking around him. The bell now tolled eleven.

The monk collecting his courage proceeded rather quicker

than before; and leaving the cemetery, advanced into another cavern, which he crossed.

This place was of great extent, and the roof was supported by a number of rude pillars; it was immediately beneath the chapel; and Bernardo, after he had noticed every part of the opposite wall, hastily returned to the cemetery, and taking from thence the implements with which the graves were made, began to open the ground in a retired corner, where it was not likely the most prying eye would discover his operations.

In a short time he effected his purpose, for the stones which composed the wall fell down deprived of their support; and the monk crossing through the aperture he had made, found himself, to his great delight, in the cemetery of the convent.

Eagerly he proceeded forward, holding his lamp up to enable him to discover what course he should pursue, when suddenly a deep sigh met his affrighted ear, and as he looked toward the place where the sound proceeded, he saw a figure seemingly rise out of one of the graves, and, with a lanthorn in its hold, proceeded slowly and mournfully from the place.

The terrified monk staggered back to the wall, against which he leant almost deprived of reason; his large eyes were fixed intently on the figure which was crossing the cemetery, and shortly after ascended some steps on which the lamp gleamed. Soon it arrived to the summit, and the light of the lamp was lost. A closing door then assured the monk that he was rid of the object that had so greatly alarmed him.

He hesitated for some time to proceed; however at length he slowly went forward, glancing his eyes around in every direction. He looked with particular attention toward the spot from whence he had beheld the figure rise, and saw a grave which appeared by the freshness of the earth to have been made the preceding day. While he was looking on it he heard a groan as if beneath his feet, and these words faintly uttered:—

"Help!—Oh! mercy!—I shall die!"

These words Bernardo was confident came from the new-made grave.

"Good Heaven!" said he; "a human being, a female too, has been interred alive."

Hastily he ran for his spade, and threw aside the earth that scantily covered the coffin, the lid of which he tore open, and beheld in it a nun clothed in the habiliments of the grave.

Wildly she arose from her dreary abode, and gazed silently for some time on the monk. "For what horrible purpose," said she at length, "was I here enclosed? Oh! too well I am convinced this was the work of sister Agatha."

During her speech the monk surveyed her features; they were interesting, but a languid, pallid hue, like that of death, prevailed over them.

He now was struck with the danger he ran of being discovered, and was greatly perplexed what he should do with the nun, who, exhausted with the efforts she had made to release herself from the grave, was sitting down on the coffin of which she had been so lately the tenant.

Nothing short of the attendant circumstances could have prevented the monk, who now for the first time was alone with a woman, from taking advantage of her defenceless situation. It was at this moment that the Demon, darting his watchful eyes through the centre of the terraqueous globe, beheld the monk, and knew the dark passions which assailed his breast; he smiled with a malignant satisfaction, and felt assured he should succeed in his designs, and add another victim to his numerous bands.

The monk would willingly have bore the nun to his cell, but his fears of a discovery alone forced him to relinquish that idea; he therefore thus addressed her:—

"Whatever was my motive in visiting these vaults, to you, at least, they have proved fortunate, since ere a few more moments had elapsed you would have been annihilated. You must now take a solemn oath not to mention the means by which you escaped, or that you saw here a monk of Santa Catherina."

The nun acquiesced with the wishes of Padre Bernardo, and swore on the cross which had been raised at the head of her grave not to divulge the circumstances of her wonderful escape.

Bernardo then assisted her to the steps which he had observed the figure that had so greatly alarmed him ascend, and throwing open the door found himself in that part of the chapel which was behind the screen, and appropriated solely for the convent. He then bade his wan companion sit down on the steps of the altar, and there await the coming dawn.

Vexed at the interruptions which had attended him, he then retraced his steps, and having replaced his tools, and closed the passage he had made with the loose stones, he cautiously entered his cell, fully determined to return to the convent the next night.

He threw himself on the pallet and lay ruminating on the past events, when the tolling of the convent bell made him start up, and proceed to the casement which commanded a view of its grey walls.

Light gleamed momentarily from many of the casements, and his eye caught the forms of the nuns proceeding hastily past them. Soon the bell ceased, and all was silent.

The monk then returned to his couch ruminating on the probable cause of the disturbance in the convent, which at length he attributed to its right source, namely, the appearance of the nun whom he had rescued from the grave.

The abbot of Santa Catherina, disturbed by the bell at that unusual hour, arose, and throwing on his garments proceeded to the parlour of the convent, where he saw the venerable abbess, who related to him the wonderful event that had taken place respecting sister Marianne, who, after she had been interred in the cemetery, had returned again to a mortal existence.

A deep and inexplicable mystery seemed to attend the transaction; the nun was also mysterious in her answers, and it appeared necessary that the abbot should exert his authority in order to make her declare how she had effected her escape from the grave, from which she had emerged without assistance.

Such was the relation which Bernardo heard among the fathers of Santa Catherina. Greatly did he tremble lest the nun should not pay a strict observance to her oath.

But when he heard that she had confessed that she was bound by a solemn promise not to disclose the manner of her regaining her liberty from the grave, and that the abbot had sent to the

Pope for authority to absolve her from that oath, his bosom then became the seat of a thousand fears lest it should be discovered that he had dared to seek an entrance within the forbidden walls of the convent.

The rules of the monastery were particularly severe with respect to women, who were excluded from attending divine service in the chapel, except on the celebration of the festival of the Santa Catherina, which took place but twice in a century. As that period was now near at hand, many of those monks who had been placed there from their infancy, and which was the case with the Padre Bernardo, had not seen the face of a woman, the forms of the nuns of the convent, with their long black veil seen through the chapel screen, was all they had to form their ideas from respecting that fascinating sex. But the monk Bernardo in the conversation of the Padre Pietro was made acquainted with what happy had it been for his soul he had never known. His passions were rouzed by the ill-judged relations of Pietro, and daily and nightly did he gaze and sigh at the inanimate representation of the tutelary Saint of the monastery, as the reader has already seen in the first pages of these records.

The soul of the monk chilled with fear when he reflected on the danger he ran of being discovered in his nocturnal attempt to enter the convent. In a few days the messenger would return from Rome with the necessary indulgence from the Pope to absolve the nun from all guilt in divulging the circumstances she had sworn to conceal.

He was fearful of putting his design in practice the next night, which he passed in his cell in a state of agitation which deprived him of rest. Often was he going to invoke the presence of the Demon, but as often was he deterred by the feeble voice of virtue, which in some small degree restrained him in his rapid advances to vice.

In the midst of these meditations the passing bell of the Convent tolled. All the monks were roused from their pallets, and attended in the chapel to pray for the repose of the departing soul.

High was raised the soft harmonious melody of the nuns;

mixed with the deep voices of the monks, the sounds floated along the vaulted roof; and borne on the breeze of night, ascended toward the heavens.

Soon the ceasing of the bell told the dissolution of the frail mortal whose soul was now winging its rapid flight through the vast aerial space toward the dreadful tribunal, to give an account of the offences it committed while it animated its mortal coil.

Slowly the monks left the chapel. Bernardo spoke not to any of the fathers, but wrapt in gloomy meditations, retired to his cell.

A heavy slumber stole on his eyelids; when the dreadful visions of the night clustered around him, and appeared to his wakeful imagination.

He thought he beheld a woman, fairer if possible, than any of the radiant groups which the Santa Catherina had displayed to his view; eagerly he ran toward her, when suddenly the earth yawned between them; he now thought he saw the Demon advancing toward him, who at his request made the earth unite. In ecstacies of delight he conducted the fair to the verdant banks of a rivulet, where they sat down on the grassy slope beneath the shade of a wide spreading larch. He then thought he drew near to embrace her; his arms encircled her lovely waist; when suddenly the beauteous form faded to his view, the flesh deserted the bones, and a hideous skull was before him. Forth from the eyeless sockets rushed two snakes, who instantly twined around his shuddering limbs their scaly folds; hastily he dropped the loathsome skeleton, the bones rattled as they fell to the ground.

The face of Nature, so beautiful before, now suddenly changed; the verdant bank, the shady tree, the sparkling rivulet vanished, and Bernardo thought himself on a huge ridge of aspiring Etna. On one side he saw a dreadful abyss, on the other he beheld the fiery bowels of the mountain casting forth volumes of flames and smoke. He dared not move, for he conceived himself so nicely poised on the ridge that the least inclination one way or the other must either cause him to be dashed to pieces down the steep, or to perish in the fiery caverns of the mountain.

In this state of dreadful agitation he awoke; cold drops of

sweat stood on his pallid face; for some time he thought what he had seen was a dreadful reality, and he feared almost to move in his bed from a recollection of his imaginary situation. At length he started from his pallet, and having opened his casement, the bright beams of the morning illumined his chamber. By degrees his senses became more composed, and ere the matin bell had warned him to the chapel, the effect of pale fears and deep terror were banished his countenance.

When in the refectory, he learned that the nun who had made her escape from the grave in so wonderful a manner, had been re-called to it, and that it was her for whom the bell had tolled during the night.

Joy illumined the countenance of the monk at this so un-looked-for escape from his worst fears, and he scarcely listened to the many surmises which escaped the fathers on a circumstance so mysterious; but when some of them expressed their apprehen-sion that sister Marianne had not been fairly dealt with, that part of their conversation struck Bernardo and recalled to his mind that at the moment of the nun coming to the use of her reason and speech, she had accused sister Agatha as being the author of her then melancholy situation.

In the delight occasioned by the intelligence, the remem-brance of the night faded on his recollection.

Thinking there was now no danger in putting his designs into execution, he determined that night, if no sinister event took place, to visit the convent, he knew that according to custom, the body of the nun would not be interred till the next morning, and he thought if he did not go then, that some person might be ap-pointed to watch the grave; he therefore resolved to take advan-tage of the present time, as the next night his attempt might be attended with the danger of a discovery.

Having thus formed his resolves, he waited anxiously till the descending shades of night should render it safe for him to put his design into execution, for the monk was wary and cautious to a great degree, as he well knew the dreadful punishment that would be his portion should his proceeding be discovered, for the disposition of the abbot was haughty, cruel, and vindictive, and hapless was the life of him who displeased the stern superior.

At length the shades of night gradually prevailed, and the gay scenes of mid-day splendor gave place to the solemnity of twilight; the peaceful moon with captivating majesty rose slowly to the height of Heaven.

But the silence of night, which encreases the harmony of the feelings of those whose unaccusing conscience produce nothing but anticipation of happiness, ill agreed with the restless soul of the monk, who was preparing to turn his cautious steps toward the convent, when a fear of being discovered made him pause; his dream too returned to his recollection with the dreadful sensations he had endured, but at the same time it brought to his imagination the visionary charms of the female; passion and curiosity impelled him to advance, while fear kept him back.

"The mysterious visitant," said he, gloomily, "might advise me—would I could see him, but it wants near an hour of midnight. I will stay till then, perhaps he may come here."

Seated on an ebon throne, high raised over the burning sea, the Demon darting his piercing eyes through the regions of night and horror which surrounded his dreadful dominions, saw the monk, and though deep plunged in the centre of the globe, he heard his request, and determined at the hour when he was permitted to visit the earth to accede to the wishes of the wretched monk, whose soul he sanguinely hoped would be added to the number of those, who, tortured with intolerable torments, vexed the murky regions of contaminated vapours which hung around his horrific regions with their dreadful unavailing plaints.

Having formed his wish, fatally pregnant with future horrors, the monk threw himself into a seat; his eyes glared about the chamber, the baneful passions which existed in his bosom darkened his sallow visage, he folded his arms, sunk his head on his breast, and waited with impatience till the tedious moments should bring on the midnight hour.

Slowly, as if anticipating the miseries it would produce, sounded the long-toned bell of midnight; and as echo ceased to reverberate the sullen sounds, and the breeze had borne them afar to other parts, the Demon appeared before the monk.

Though anticipating his presence, though wishing to see him, yet the monk trembled, and the half-formed sentence died away ere he could give it utterance.

"You wished to see me, Padre; you wished my advice; behold me ready to serve you. You need not," continued he, "tell me your purpose, I know your thoughts as soon as they are formed; this night there will be danger in going to the convent; had you attempted it, you would have been discovered, and to-morrow would have seen you shut out from the society of man, the inhabitant, perhaps for life, of a gloomy dungeon."

The monk trembled, "but your power doubtless," said he, "could have emancipated me."

"Yes," replied the Demon, "even if mountains had been piled upon thee, easily could I upraise them."

Security glowed in the countenance of Bernardo; he now feared not human power, since he could so easily escape its thralls; and in proportion as those fears died away, his reliance on the Demon increased. Alas! he little knew that he was forging the fetters that were to bind his soul for ever to him.

"As it would not be prudent," said the arch Demon, "to visit the convent this night; suffer me to bring you to a place where you may behold the greatest beauty in Sicily."

"How?" said the monk astonished; "I go? I cannot climb the lofty walls."

The Demon smiled ghastly. "Did I not tell thee," said he, "that were mountains thrown on thy trembling form, I could hurl them off? and thinkest thou that these walls are in my eye as any restraint? To me they seem formed of passive air; the strongest embattled ramparts give way to my approach, and I can dive into the bowels of the earth as easily as the bird wings his fleet course on the zephyrs of day. Say then, monk, wilt thou trust thy self with me for a short space of time? for ere the clock has tolled the coming hour thou wilt be in thy present place."

Eagerly the monk consented. At that moment a strong grasp seized his arm, the walls of the cell divided to let him pass, and he was instantly elevated in the regions of air. The Demon spread two broad black pinions to the wind that shadowed the plains below, and in a moment of time, even ere the fears which his novel situation might well occasion had taken any hold on his frame, he found himself in a large garden opposite the folding doors of a pavilion which was illumined with tapers.

"We are both," said the Demon, "invisible to mortal sight. In that pavilion is the lovely female I wish you to see; she now awaits the arrival of her lover; we will enter and observe their meeting."

They now entered the pavilion. Powers of love! what a sight met the eyes of the monk. Reclined on a superb couch lay the most elegant female, such as even the strong powers of fancy would fail in ability to raise to the imagination. Beautifully arched eyebrows, eyes sparkling with lustre, cheeks where the rose appeared but newly blown, and a mouth breathing ambrosial sweetness around; her bosom partially covered with a thin gauze, that by the slight concealment of her panting orbs permitted the imagination to revel in ideal charms.—Her lovely dark hair flowed on her ivory neck in glossy ringlets, part sported over her polished forehead, and part was confined by strings of pearls, whose whiteness improved the beauty of her tresses.

This lovely female was leaning on her arm and looking toward the door when the monk entered. The idea of being invisible was new, and for a moment he thought he was discovered; he drew back confused, but the Demon bade him enter. The lovely Signora knew not what dangerous spirits were now so near her; she was in anxious expectation of the promised arrival of her lover.

Scarcely could the monk restrain himself from rushing toward her; his passions at the sight of so lovely an object were wound up to the highest pitch of frenzy. The Demon smiled at his emotions; he meant to raise them still more, he meant too to make him feel other sensations, which would more completely bring about the dark designs he was forming, and make the monk irrevocably his.

A hasty step was now heard; the lovely Signora raised herself on the sofa, the door flew open, and a young cavalier of extraordinary beauty rushed to her arms.

The Monk and the Devil beholding the happiness of true love.

What a sight was this for the monk; his bosom burned with rage, his breath grew convulsed, his eyes rolled on the intruder with expressions of the blackest revenge and hatred. The Demon knew what was passing in the mind of the monk, but restrained him from darting on the Signor by his iron grasp.

"Wait yet a little while," said he to the Padre, "you shall have your wishes; I read your thoughts, my friend, I will serve you."

Somewhat comforted by this, the monk again fixed his impassioned gaze on the lovely countenance of the Signora, who, as she lifted her eyes to the cavalier, which seemed by turns animated with lively passion, by turns melting with the softest languor, seemed now more beautiful than ever. The presence of the beloved object of her affections restored to her countenance the rose which expectation had made pale on her cheek; her fair bosom trembled to her sighs—sighs which increased the force of every charm, and expiring on her ruby lips invited the kiss.

Her dress was of light thin gauze, on which the wanton zephyrs played, whose balmy breath was the fragrance of the new-blown rose.

The monk listened to their soft expressions of mutual love; love which constitutes the perfection of earthly happiness; he saw too that as enamoured they conversed the fire of love concentred in their eyes.

The pavilion was beautifully ornamented with whatever could charm the senses; lovely paintings, done by the ablest Italian masters, decorated the walls; curtains of the richest silk flowed in profusion before the casements; Etruscan vases, supported on silver tripods, held the lamps that illumined the chamber, which was perfumed by aromatic flowers, which richly breathed their fragrance around. The enchanting place seemed animated by a spirit of tenderness; a soft languor seized the soul of the monk—how did every snare of voluptuousness encircle him.

Philomel sweetly tuned her plaintive strains in the adjoining grove; she chaunted in weak notes, yielding to the sorrows of her heart.

The moon was seen sweetly gleaming on the waving outline of the trees from a casement which was inclosed; a sweet tranquillity pervaded each scene; the monk felt the influence of the place, and his eyes expressed it; but at times, when the raging fever of jealousy pervaded his soul, his countenance grew dark as the stormy clouds of night, and the flash of rage and anger from his eyes was as the lightning gleaming through the shades; while his whole frame would shake with the new-born emotions of his soul.

Delicious to the lovers was the reciprocal tale of love; sweet was to them the love-inspiring look, the gentle pressure of the hand, and the fond expressions of their eyes, which seemed to dart to each others soul.

At times they mentioned the approaching festival which was to take place at the monastery of Santa Catherina, as the period which would render them truly happy.

The eyes of the monk were never weary of gazing at the lovely female; the raging passion, now first known, and under such a powerful incitement, pervaded his whole frame; but the Demon, who saw that the purpose for which he brought the monk there shewed every prospect of success, now told him that the morning hour would in a few minutes arrive, and that he must convey him back to the monastery.

"Let me stay, mysterious being; let me stay here, I conjure you; can I leave that divinity, leave her too with that man? O torture! torture!—give me but a dagger, I feel myself capable of any act, however atrocious. I will murder him, and then with your assistance I shall prevail, I shall be truly happy. What concession would I not make to you for so great an indulgence."

However willing the Demon might be to accord with the desires of Bernardo, and thereby add to his long black list another hapless soul, yet it was not in his power to grant his request. As to what respected the ruin of that Signora, he had no power over a virtuous mind, but the moment it made a false step, then his influence began.

"I would," said he, "willingly grant what you ask, but the time will not permit; you reflect not, Padre, that you are now near twenty leagues from the monastery of Santa Catherina; wait with patience, you will have the beautiful Signora in your power, that I can promise you."

Ere the monk could reply, and while yet his gaze lingered on the lovely form before him, he felt himself rising from the place whereon he stood; the roof of the pavilion divided to let him pass, he heard the wide flapping of the black pinions which the Demon spread to the breeze of night, and cleaving the air a thousand degrees swifter than the arrow from the bow of the hunter, in a few moments the monk was in his cell.

"To-morrow night," said the Demon, "thou mayest enter the

convent; there is a female there whose charms, though not equal to those thou hast gazed on this night, are nevertheless such as boast many attractions. I will dispose her heart to thee; but be not precipitate, thou must be cautious, and reflect on the dangers attendant on a discovery."

The bell of the monastery now tolled one; the monk, whose gaze was fixed on the form of the Demon, saw it gradually dissolving into air, and vanish from his sight ere echo had ceased to reverberate the sound through the vast pile.

The monk trimmed the dim lamp, and throwing himself into a seat, reflected on the events of the last hour. The Demon had promised him that he should have the lovely Signora in his power; that promise alone was his comfort in his absence; but though he thought almost unceasingly of her, yet the words of the Demon respecting the female in the convent escaped not his recollection. But how, thought he, shall I discover her among so many? to me it appears impossible to be effected; but doubtless he who seems to possess such power will throw her in my way.

The nun who had escaped from the grave, and who had so strangely ceased to exist, had been again committed to the silent repository for the dead, and the past morning had witnessed the solemn ceremony, therefore he did not fear being disturbed in his nocturnal visit on that account.

Other ideas now crowded on his mind. The festival of Santa Catherina drew near, and the Signora and her lover had mentioned it as the period which would render them happy; from that he conceived that they meant to be united there. That, thought he, if I have any interest with the Demon, shall never take place. No, I would terminate his existence at the very altar itself ere he should be the possessor of so much loveliness.

The remembrance that the Demon had promised he should have that lovely woman in his power now again recurred to him, and soothed the rising tempest of his soul; while the new prospect which was opening to his view of the nun, a boarder of the convent, whom he should see the next night, served to assuage the disquietude of his mind, and to make him long for the hour when he was to enter those forbidden walls.

Amidst his various meditations the sombrous deity of slumber weighed heavy on his senses; he retired to his couch, where sleep closed his eye-lids, while his restless and perturbed imagination brought to his view the lovely female, whom he oft essayed, but in vain, to clasp in his embrace, for as often as he opened his arms, the visionary form eluded his purpose.

The summons for matin service awoke him from his deep slumbers, and the Padre Bernardo rising from his couch, entered the chapel, where his ideas wandered to what he had beheld in the pavilion, and to the adventure he was that night to have in the convent, while the devotional duties of the morning were neglected and were unthought of.

END OF VOLUME ONE

THE

DEMON OF SICILY.

CHAPTER VI.

DISTRACTION seized the mind of Ricardo when he heard that his beloved Louisa had been carried off. For some moments in speechless agony he gazed on the equally distressed Signora Bononi, then having informed himself of the time she was taken, he rushed swiftly out of the cottage, and vowing he would seek her in every part of the island, proceeded as swiftly as his limbs trembling with horror, consternation, and despair, could carry him.

Arrived at his castle, he ordered the fleetest horses to be saddled, and, attended by some of his domestics, set out on his journey. From the peasants who resided near the residence of the Signora Bononi he learnt that a lady was observed to ride by very early in the morning, and that there were some horsemen with her.

As there was no doubt but that the person described by the peasants must be Louisa, Ricardo pursued his course along the road they informed him she had gone; and, animated with the hope of soon reaching her, and revenging himself on the ruffians who had bore her away, he soon crossed the hills that closed in the valley, and darted into the black bosom of a forest through which lay the road they had taken.

The forest extended some leagues, and sheltered them by its umbrageous recesses from the burning heat of the mid-day sun. Toward the evening, Ricardo was obliged to stop, to rest the wearied steeds, and to allow his people to refresh themselves; for himself, his mind was too miserable to permit him to think of food, and each moment was an age that delayed his pursuit of Louisa.

His people were soon mounted on their horses, and leaving the forest, they now began to wind over a mountainous tract of country.

Ricardo reached the summit of the last of the chain of hills just as the clouds, tinged with the radiant beams of the setting sun, were losing their borrowed lustre. Before him lay for many leagues a flat country, and as swiftly his eyes surveyed the windings of the road, he caught a glimpse of some horsemen, who were soon hid from his sight by the grey livery of evening. One of his servants at the same instant declared that he had observed something white before one of the men, and Ricardo cheered himself with the hopes of soon overtaking Louisa.

His horses, however, being jaded with the fatigues of the day, proceeded but slowly, and the night closed on them soon after they had left the lofty hills, and were proceeding on the plains below.

The east wind now began to rush mournfully along the face of the country, while its attendant vapours became every moment more dense. Ricardo oft cast a supplicating look toward the heavens, in hopes of seeing the moon brightly rising in the vaulted arch, but he looked in vain, for the clouds darkly clustered around, and the distant thunder rolled mournfully above.

Thus situated, and unable at times to discern the road, the party wandered far out of its beaten tract ere they had observed their error, to rectify which became impossible, and every moment increased their difficulties and the agitation of Ricardo. All hope of continuing his journey that night was at an end, and he had only to pray that the same weather which detained him would do the like to the party who were carrying off his adored Louisa.

The domestics now alighted from their wearied horses and waited for the coming dawn, when a horn was distinctly heard to wind amongst the far distant hills, and a response was shortly after made to it in still fainter sounds.

Ricardo sprung on his horse, and bidding his domestics do the same, without being able to see whither they were going, save when the flashes of lightning darting through the vapours partially illumined the scene around them, and was their only guide over an unknown tract of country.

Ricardo often listened in hope of hearing the horn again, but all was silent; he however still continued in the direction of the sound till the horses were hardly able to proceed; for in addition to their fatigue, the ground they were now passing over was an uncultivated heath, and the briars and long trailing brambles entangled their feet. Ricardo was at length on the point of reining in his steed, when the waving of a torch and the sound of a horn, which appeared not far off, made him determine to proceed; fearful, however, of meeting with banditti, which in those wild secluded and desert regions was not improbable, he ordered his people to preserve the strictest silence.

A light gleaming from a casement, which from its height apparently belonged to a large edifice, directed Ricardo to the portals of what appeared to be an ancient castle. He took hold of the horn which hung by their side, but ere he applied it to his mouth, he deliberated on the step he was going to take, for he considered that the inmates of that building might be banditti.

At this idea the horn was dropping from his hand, when he suddenly reflected that his adored Louisa might be in their hands. Without hesitation, and confiding in the number of his attendants, he blew the horn. A hoarse voice from above demanded "if that was Gomelli?"

"No," replied Ricardo looking up to a small turret window which rose on one side of the gates, and from whence the voice proceeded; "Having had the misfortune to be benighted with my attendants, I have to request you will grant me and them a shelter for a few hours."

"I don't think we can," replied the voice; "however wait there, and I will ask our Capitano, I mean the Signor of the Castello."

Some voices in conversation were then heard, and presently another man demanded how many there were, as he was afraid there would not be room for them.

Ricardo having satisfied him on that head he departed from the casement, and after waiting some time, they heard the paces of people on the other side of the gates, which were soon after thrown open.

The aspects of the men who appeared in the court of the edifice, and who held torches in their hands to dispel the gloomy shades of night, were such as by no means were calculated to give a favourable opinion either of them or their profession. They were of gigantic stature, each wearing on his head a casque of iron on which was fixed a large lock of horse-hair. Their coun-tenances were dark and ferocious; and they were all armed with long swords.

As soon as Ricardo and his people had entered the court yard, the men closed the gates, and conducted them to a large hall, where the remains of a fire yet blazed. One of them threw several faggots upon it, and in a few minutes the walls were illumined by the cheerful light.

The men then departed promising to acquaint the Signor of the Castello with his arrival; and Ricardo, who had now every reason to believe that he had unfortunately got amongst a horde of banditti, acquainted his people with his suspicions, and desired them to be on their guard, and by no means to separate.

The sounds of many voices, which appeared to come from a passage, the door of which was open, made Ricardo advance toward it, to endeavour to learn what was going forwards. Hardly had he gained the entrance of the passage when the sounds ceased, and a manly voice sung a beautiful Sicilian ariette.

"Bravo, Capitano," said a number of voices when it was con-cluded, and the conversation was now resumed. The voice he had heard greatly interested Ricardo; it was familiar to his ear, and he had some hopes that he had little to fear for his personal safety.

Approaching footsteps made him retire from the entrance of the passage, and shortly after a man approached and informed him that the Signor of the Castello was coming.

When he entered the hall what was the astonishment of Ricardo to behold in him the unfortunate Count de Leoni.

He started at seeing Ricardo; his countenance betrayed to-kens of pleasure, but that satisfaction appeared clouded with an uneasiness too apparent to escape Ricardo's notice.

"Good heavens!" said he at length, "what fortunate event brought you here?"

"No fortunate event," replied Ricardo; "you see me, Count, the most miserable of men. A lady whom I tenderly loved, has been forced from her abode by some villains, and in seeking her I was benighted with my attendants and"—

"I know the whole, Signor," said the Count impatiently, "follow me."

Greatly astonished, Ricardo accompanied the Count, preceded by an attendant with a torch.

"Lead to the suit of chambers next the North Hall."

The man bowed, and in silence they crossed through several passages, till at length the man stopped at a door, which the Count de Leoni throwing open, Ricardo once more beheld his adored Louisa.

Great was the delight which they shewed at this so unlooked-for meeting; and after some time passed in mutual expressions of their happiness, looked on the Count for an explanation of his meeting there with Louisa.

The Count, who was pacing the chamber with folded arms and a melancholy deep fixed in his countenance, understood what he meant.

"You cannot be astonished at my situation here, Signor Ricardo, if you will recal to your mind the cruel and base artifices made use of by your father to deprive me of my property."

"Too well I know it, "said Ricardo, "but that act, Count, was the cause of his death, and also of one of his associates, Roderigo de Romanzo."

"Just Heaven!" exclaimed the Count, "are they both dead?"

"Yes," replied Ricardo, "the night after you left the Castle saw my father slain by Romanzo, who himself fell by my arm."—

"And the Count Altona! this night fell by mine," said Leoni.

"The Count Altona!" exclaimed Ricardo.

"It was he who carried off that Signora from her home."

Ricardo's eyes gleamed darkly and dissatisfied when he heard that the persecutor of his Louisa had fallen by other hands than his.

"I was returning to this place," continued the Count, "with some of my people, when I heard the voice of a female seemingly in great distress. I hastened instantly to the spot, and beheld the Signora in the arms of Altona, who was placing her before him on his steed. My people immediately by a signal surrounded his party, while, instigated by a just resentment for his base conduct toward me, and also to rescue the lady, I challenged him to the combat. We fought and Altona fell. In answer to my questions the Signora disclosed to me who she was, and her knowledge of you. The blushes which appeared in her cheeks as she mentioned your name avowed her sentiments for you, and to-morrow I should have had the pleasure of conducting her home. Your fortunate arrival here has taken that duty from me, and I rejoice in having been the instrument of protecting your Louisa."

Count Leoni rescuing the beautiful Louisa from Count Altona.

Ricardo flew into his arms, and embraced him with the deepest sensations of gratitude.

"One favour, Count, I have to request," said he, "that you will accompany me back. I entreat you not to refuse me; I have circumstances of great importance to your comfort to disclose to you."

The Count de Leoni assented to the wishes of Ricardo, who shortly now returned to Louisa and during their conversation was informed by her of the circumstances that preceded the daring outrage of the Count Altona.

It has been stated that the Count, the day after the death of the Marchese de Carlentini, left the Castello with his attendants; he had, however, on the day he unfortunately had met Ricardo at the residence of Louisa, beheld that lovely female, and then resolved on forcing her away to his own residence.

He went not far from her abode and concealed himself in a peasant's cottage for a few days with two of his men; he then left it, and lurked about the abode of Louisa in order to find an opportunity of effecting his designs.

That evening she was taking a solitary walk on the banks of the stream that meandered through the valley, when she perceived three men swiftly following her. Terrified at this, and alarmed at the lateness of the hour, (for ruminating on Ricardo the minutes had passed insensibly by,) she exerted all her speed in order to avoid the men who were evidently pursuing her; but her attempts were of little avail. Breathless with terror she had sunk insensibly on the ground, and the steps of the ruffians sounded close to her ear, when a party of peasants who had been cutting timber in the forest happily came up, at the sight of whom the men who had given her so much alarm slunk away, and under covert of the grey mantle of evening escaped.

It was under the influence of the terrors excited by this circumstance that she betrayed such evident tokens of the melancholy that pervaded her breast in the letter she wrote to Ricardo, which, however, she forbore mentioning to him, as she felt unwilling to increase the distress he then endured for the loss of his father.

Some evenings after, just as she was retiring to her couch, the door of the cottage was suddenly burst open, and a party of men entered, who seized her, and having placed a handkerchief to her mouth to prevent her cries being heard, and taken the same precaution with her mother and the domestic, whom they also cruelly bound with cords, they placed her on a horse, which the Count mounted, and then swiftly proceeded to their place of destination; but the watchful eye of Providence was on the actions of Altona, and he paid for his violent outrage and base intentions against the peace and honor of Louisa with his life.

Such was the detail which Louisa gave to Ricardo of her adventures; and when she had concluded he again embraced her, and again gratefully expressed his sense of the obligations he was under to the Count de Leoni; obligations which he felt happy he should be able to make some small return for.

The grey dawn now began to glimmer through the casement of the apartment they were in, and soon Aurora tinged the eastern clouds with a roseate hue. The Count judging of the impatience of Louisa to quiet the distractions of her unhappy mother by her presence, ordered fresh horses for Ricardo and his attendants, and when the beams of the morning smiled on the turrets of the castle and the waving summits of an adjacent forest, the party, late so melancholy, but now anticipating future years of joy and happiness, set out on their journey, accompanied by the Count, who, however, had not recovered the tranquillity of his mind, and whose frequent sighs bespoke the agitation of his breast.

Well acquainted with that part of the country, the Count led the party a much shorter road than that Ricardo had traversed, and about noon they stopped to rest themselves and the steeds in the refreshing shades of the extensive forest.

Here he took an opportunity of acquainting Ricardo with the events that had taken place since he left the Castle on that fatal evening which placed all his property in the possession of the late Marchese, his associates the Count Altona, and the savage Roderigo di Romanzo.

"To describe to you the distraction of my mind when I found myself stripped of all my prospects is impossible. A thousand times I formed resolutions of terminating my existence, but, the Saints be praised, they failed; I however determined on leaving the Castle, for I well knew that, having exhausted every resource, I should be regarded with contempt by my undoers.

"I travelled on, careless whither I went, and only anxious to extend the distance between me and your Castle. About the dawn of the next morning I found myself in this wood. Its gloomy shades were congenial to my feelings, and I remained here the greater part of the day. At length the calls of hunger forced me to seek a cottage, in order to procure some food, and after a long and tedious search, I discovered a wood-cutter's cabin, where I procured some fruit and bread.

"I staid there that night, and early the next morning I pursued my way along the road we have just passed, driven almost to madness to think of my blindness and folly in allowing myself to be made a dupe of, and in consequence turned out on the world to endure the extremes of wretchedness and poverty.

"In this temper of mind I was attacked by a banditti, and almost glad of an opportunity of reeking my passions on some one, and careless about my own safety, I fought with their leader, whom I killed, and severely wounded two others. Numbers then overpowered me, I was disarmed, and keeping gloomy silence; I entered the building where you found me.

"The actions I performed, which, though seemingly the result of bravery, were only the rash attempts of a man weary of life, and incensed against his fellow creatures, were regarded with astonishment by the banditti. They saw I did not fear to die, and that carelessness of my personal safety preserved my life. Their troop was now without a leader, and, strange to tell, they pitched on me to supply his place.

"The offer was made me. What was I to do? I had no home to go to, beggary must have been my lot. To be brief, I accepted the situation. Thus, through a cursed desire for gambling, the Count de Leoni became the chief of a band of robbers."

Here the Count paused. The thoughts of what he once, and what he *now* was, crowded to his memory, and grief sat heavy on his heart. Ricardo, respecting his feelings, and acutely suffering for the cruel and base conduct of his parent, was silent. At length the Count broke a silence so painful to Ricardo, and thus concluded his relation:—

"I had not been long with these men before I perceived that many of them under their ruffian forms had hearts which with a little culture might become the residence of humanity. Now I had it in my power to revenge myself on my fellow creatures my nature began to relent, and I employed my time in tutoring my savage troops, and in weaning them from their dreadful propensity to shed guiltless blood. With many I have succeeded; but there are still some wretches among them whose savage bosoms the gentle dew of mercy will never penetrate."

Thus did the unfortunate Count de Leoni conclude his tale; and now Louisa, who almost fainting with the fatigues she had undergone had laid her head on the soft turf, and for a short time gladly courted the refreshing influence of sleep, awoke from her slumbers, which with the returning composure of her mind had greatly contributed to refresh her, and the domestics bringing up their horses, they hastened to leave the forest ere the gloom of evening should render their journey difficult.

The dark mantle of night was swiftly descending on the earth when Ricardo and his party entered the valley. The hapless Signora Bononi was standing at the gate of her little garden, anxiously awaiting the return of Ricardo, when her bosom was gladdened by the tender and long-continued embrace of her daughter, who was so happily restored to her arms.

Ricardo participated in the happiness which dwelt at the cottage; mindful, however, of the duty he was so anxious to perform respecting the possessions of the Count de Leoni, he reluctantly tore himself away from what he so dearly prized, the company of his Louisa; and leaving two trusty domestics there, lest any attempts should be made by other persons, he departed, after having promised to be there early in the morning.

The hope of future days of unalloyed delight now fondly fluttered around Ricardo, who mounting his horse, accompanied by the unhappy Count, still ruminating on the melancholy situation to which he was reduced, soon beheld the dark battlements of the

Castle of Carlentini, and alighted at the gates of the court-yard that led to the Northern Hall.

Ricardo looking toward the long casement of the chapel, saw that it was illuminated, and on inquiring the reason, learnt that Father Grimaldi was then about to be committed to the silent bosom of the grave.

The solemn strains of the monks were now heard. Ricardo and the Count entered the chapel; the same hangings were up as had covered the walls at the interment of his father, and notwithstanding the happy events of the day, a tear stole from either eye, and a deep sigh issued from his breast when, by means of the solemn scene he now witnessed, the memory of his parent became fresh in his recollection.

When the service was concluded the Abbot advanced to Ricardo, who, delighted to see a man for whom he felt the greatest esteem, willingly protracted the conversation, till the train of monks being ready, he was obliged to depart. The abbot informed him that he was going to leave the monastery he now presided over for another, the name and situation of which he minutely described to Ricardo, and concluded with expressing an earnest wish to see him there should either pleasure or business bring him near the place.

Ricardo now requested the Count de Leoni would follow him to the interior of the Castle; he conducted him to the chamber of the late Marchese; when taking out the packet from the cabinet he thus addressed him:—

"Count Leoni, I am happy that I can make you amends for the injustice, (not to call it by a harsher title) of my father. This packet contains the whole, as far as I know, of the titles of your estates, and I hope you will consider it as a trifling mark of gratitude for your preservation of my Louisa."

So unlooked-for a circumstance almost deprived the Count of the power to express his thanks to Ricardo; he embraced him, and, when he could speak, overwhelmed him with protestations of his gratitude. Ricardo, who knew that he had done no more than his duty, hastened to prevent the ebullitions of the Count's grateful heart by quitting with him the chamber, and descending to the hall, where the evening repast awaited them.

Being both greatly fatigued, they soon after retired, and Ricardo, amid the pleasing reflection of having his Louisa restored to him, and the happiness of the Count de Leoni, fell asleep, while visions of bliss hasted to appear before his wakeful imagination.

In the morning the Count de Leoni took his leave, after promising to be at the Castle again in the course of a few days; and Ricardo hasted to his beloved Louisa.

Never in his eyes did she appear so beautiful as this morning; the healing powers of sleep had freed her from her late alarms.

The happy Ricardo now made the lovely Louisa an offer of his hand; and anxious to be possessed of such an inestimable treasure as she appeared in his eyes, he entreated her to name the day, when at the altar he should be united to her.

Louisa's blushes told the emotions of her bosom, and at length Ricardo drew from her a consent that that day week should unite their destinies.

Seldom absent from Louisa, unless at the hour of repose, and when he was employed in the necessary preparations for the approaching nuptials, the hours sweetly glided by, and at length brought on that which was to be so productive of bliss to Ricardo.

On that morning all was joy and gaiety at the Castle, the mourning habits for the late Marchese were thrown aside, and Ricardo at the head of his numerous domestics left his residence to proceed to that of Louisa, to conduct her and the Signora Bononi to their future abode.

The tenantry and peasants, dressed in their best apparel, crowded on the lawn in front of the Northern Towers to welcome their approach, and as Ricardo, leading Louisa, passed through their opened ranks, prayers for their happiness proceeded from every mouth.

At the portals of the North Hall they were met by the abbot of the neighbouring monastery, who not having yet departed to his new situation, had, at the request of Ricardo, attended to perform the nuptial ceremony.

Ricardo was agreeably surprised on entering the hall to see the Count de Leoni, who had arrived there during his absence, anxious to be present at the ceremony which was to produce happiness to his generous friend. He was attended by a numerous train of his vassals, all superbly arrayed, and increased the grandeur and festivity of the scene. The centre of the hall was covered with rich tapestry, as were also the corridores which led to the chapel, and on each side of the hall; behind the triple row of columns which supported the lofty roof, were bands of musicians, who filled the air with their pleasing melodies.

Preceded by the abbot, Ricardo and Louisa, followed by the Signora Bononi, the Count de Leoni, and the principal attendants, entered the chapel, and at the altar were united in the indissoluble bonds of matrimony—their hearts were united before.

A splendid banquet awaited them in the hall, and numerous tables were laid out on the lawn fronting the Castello, where the peasantry were regaled, those loud acclamations when they heard that their lord was united to his Louisa were borne on the wings of the breeze to the neighbouring hills, where echo reverberated the sounds which long dwelt amongst their verdant recesses.

When the banquet was over, the abbot was going to take his leave; but Ricardo rising up requested to have a few moments discourse with him, to which the venerable father consenting, they retired to an apartment, from whence after they had remained there some time, the abbot retired to his monastery, and Ricardo resumed his seat by the side of the lovely Marchesa de Carlentini; he, however, was silent on the subject of his conversation with the abbot.

In the evening the hall was brilliantly illuminated; the dulcet sounds of the musicians floated in the air; the peasants on the lawn, whose canopy was the beautiful Sicilian sky, whose light the silver beams of the moon, aided by myriads of bright stars, danced away the sportive hours to the gay and airy Sicilian measures which resounded on all sides.

Thus concluded the happy day of the nuptials of Ricardo Marchese de Carlentini, who now had the felicity to behold irrevocably his own the sweet beauty whose form had captivated and whose mental accomplishments had so entirely enveloped him in the soft bondage of love, rendered the height of human bliss by its being mutual.

The Count de Leoni, when he left Ricardo, proceeded immediately to his estates, where he was joyfully received by his vassals and domestics, who had fruitlessly endeavoured to trace his steps when in all the agony of despair he had left the Castello di Carlentini; having then arranged whatever was requisite he repaired to the solitary residence of the banditti at the foot of the lofty mountains, which form the Vale di Demone; they were delighted to see him return, but their joy was turned to grief when they understood he was going to leave them. He selected amongst them such as he knew would form good members of society, and then proposed to allow them a certain tract of land on his estate, which they might cultivate and leave off their present desperate trade, which sooner or later would bring them under the iron grasp of Justice.

Joyfully his offer was accepted, and leaving to those who still determined to carry on this trade of blood and rapine all their ill-got treasures, they bent their steps to the Count's estate, little regretted by the rest, who, in consequence of their departure, found themselves in possession of an immense booty.

The Count then returned to his estate, where, as he was allotting his new vassals their promised lands, one of them who had been in conversation with the Count's domestics came up, much agitated, and requested to speak in private to him.

The Count consented to grant the man's request, who begged he would inform him if it was true that the Marchese de Carlentini was dead, as in that case he had something of consequence to impart.

Somewhat surprized, the Count satisfied him on that head, and the man continued:—

"About fifteen years ago, my Lord, I resided at Palermo, and was connected with a set of bravos. My circumstances were such as drove me to the dreadful trade of blood. I had nothing to depend on for subsistence but my stiletto. One evening as I was walking along the Strado Nuovo, at the back of the church of San

Nicolo, I was accosted by a cavalier, whom I afterwards found to be the Marchese de Carlentini.

"It seems that I had been pointed out to him as one who would perform the business he wished to have done, as he entered on that subject immediately, which was an offer of forty ducats if I would assassinate a Signor.

"I accepted his offer without hesitation, and followed him to the end of the strada; where, after waiting some time opposite to a house, he pointed out to me a man who was approaching it, and having informed me that he was the person against whom my stiletto was to be used, told me where he resided, and left me.

"It was then almost dark. I drew my cloak over my face, and advancing toward the person, prepared to execute what I had undertaken to perform, but was prevented by the approach of some people; and while they were passing my victim entered the house.

"I staid some time in the passage without hearing any one move about the house, and concluding from that circumstance that there were no domestics in it, I determined to enter it at midnight; and marking the place, went away. In order to be certain if my suspicions were right, I stopped at a little shop where ices were vended, and there learnt that the house was inhabited only by a cavalier and one female domestic.

"At midnight I entered it, having a lamp concealed beneath my cloak. After some trouble I discovered the chamber where the Signor slept, and moving the curtains of the bed aside, I let a ray of light fall on the countenance of the sleeper, but started on beholding the features of Signor Valvano, who had saved my life; for but a few evenings before, being ignorant of my horrid profession, he had assisted me against the attacks of two cavaliers, one of whom I had attempted to kill.

"I found it totally impossible," continued the man, "to raise my dagger against the Signor; a thought, however, instantly arose in my mind, that I might obtain the forty ducats and preserve the life of Valvano. There were some difficulties in my project, but I was in need of the money, and I could not spill the blood of one who had saved my life.

"Without hesitation I awoke the Signor Valvano, and bid him arise and dress himself. Unarmed as he was, resistance was useless, and the glittering steel of my dagger told him the fate that awaited his non-compliance with my orders.

"At that hour I had little fear of meeting with any one to interrupt my purposes; and after I had passed through a few stradas, I left the city, and wound along the sea shore.

"Signor Valvano's terrors increased at seeing himself in the power of a man on the beach at the solitary hour of midnight, and in accents of the highest distress frequently entreated me not to murder him.

"Had your life been my object, Signor, (said I,) I could have accomplished my purpose when you were asleep.

"This seemed to comfort him, and at length, after walking a considerable time, I came to the residence of my associates, which was in a lone house on the beach, more than a league from Palermo. It was here I determined to keep the Signor Valvano; for though the remembrance of the service he had rendered me made me resolve not to deprive him of life, yet I had no scruples in confining him, even though that confinement were to last as long as I lived.

"In the lower parts of the house were many secure places well adapted to my purpose, and in one of them I left the unfortunate Valvano.

"The next morning I waited on the Marchese de Carlentini. 'Well, Ugo,' said he, 'have you been successful?' Yes my lord, I replied, his body is now food for fishes.

"He seemed not to approve of what I pretended I had done with the remains of Valvano; I however invented as the reason a tale of his having fled from me toward the sea shore, into which, after having stabbed, I had cast him. He then gave me the forty ducats, and I retired well pleased with the success that had attended my proceedings.

"The unfortunate Signor Valvano remained for some time in confinement; during which period I continued to obtain further sums of money from the Marchese de Carlentini, threatening him, in case of refusal, to publish to the world his having employed me to murder the Signor.

"Thus passed away near five years, when our retreat being discovered, and learning that the officers of Justice were proceeding to apprehend us, we escaped in a vessel which was always in readiness for such an emergency.

"The Signor Valvano was taken with us, and as we were connected with the banditti at the foot of the solitary castello near the Val di Demone, we hasted thither, and from that period made it our residence.

"The Signor Valvano was forced by me to take an oath never to attempt to leave the Castello, on which condition he was not again confined in a dungeon, while I still at different times found an opportunity of importuning the Marchese for money, which he, through fear, never refused me. As he is now dead, the Signor Valvano is freed from his oath, and I trust, my Lord, that you will take the proper means to restore him to the world."

The man, who was called Ugo, thus concluded his long story; and the Count de Leoni immediately sent to the Castello to request the release of Signor Valvano.

The Count related these circumstances to Ricardo the day after his marriage with Louisa; he was greatly shocked to hear of this horrible instance of his father's depraved and wicked conduct, and sent a party to escort the Signor Valvano to his residence, that he might endeavour by his attention to him to make him forget the wrongs he had received from his parent.

Ugo had not made known to Valvano by whom he was instigated in his conduct toward him; Ricardo had therefore a painful task to perform, and he looked forward with anxiety to the moment when he should be obliged to develop the dark designs of the late Marchese against his life.

The second day the attendants returned, bringing with them the much-wronged Signor Valvano. Ricardo on beholding his form wasted with his long confinement, his pallid cheeks, and the infirm state to which he was reduced, could not command his feelings, and was obliged to retire to endeavour to recover from his agitation. When he had in some measure fitted himself for the interview, he requested the presence of the Signor Valvano in his apartment, where he related to him the substance of Ugo's story, though not without several interruptions from the acuteness of his sensations in thus being obliged to expose the base conduct of a father.

However enraged the Signor Valvano might be at the conduct of the late Marchese de Carlentini, yet he could not but feel interested for Ricardo, whose grief he endeavoured to assuage by assuring him that as his enemy was no more he would endeavour to forget the wrongs he had received, and then embraced Ricardo as a further proof that against him he had no cause of complaint, as he was far from revenging the wrongs he had received from the father on his innocent son; he however requested to be left alone that day, and promised on the next he would have the pleasure of being introduced to the Marchesa, and of reassuring Ricardo of his perfect amity with him.

Ricardo was greatly consoled by the conduct of the Signor Valvano, and in the society of Louisa he found a charm that drove from his mind all unpleasant thoughts. She was to him every thing that he could wish, and there was now but one circumstance that gave him the least uneasiness, and that was how to provide for his children should he have any. It was on this head that he had held so long a conversation with the venerable abbot before he took his departure from the Castello on the day of his nuptials, and though the abbot had in some measure relieved his mind on that head, yet still there were circumstances attendant on the steps he should be obliged to take that hurt the feelings of Ricardo. Fearful of creating a moment's uneasiness in the breast of Louisa, he had not said a word to her on the subject, and awaited the time when it would be necessary to explain to her his situation, well knowing how important it is in this sublunary state to seize every moment of happiness, and to forbear to cast a shade sooner than occasion required on the happiness his Louisa seemed to enjoy.

The next morning Ricardo had the pleasure of introducing the Signor Valvano to the Marchesa; he seemed struck with her beauty, and complimented Ricardo on his taste. He was perfectly silent on the treatment he had received from the late Marchese, and Ricardo felt happy that the subject so unpleasant to his feelings was not renewed.

The hours now rapidly passed in the round of amusement which Ricardo prepared, solicitous to amuse his Louisa, and to prevent the Signor Valvano from ruminating on the injurious treatment he had received. Sometimes they would embark in his gondola on the stream which flowed through the valley, and land at a pavillion which was erected in a spot enriched by the beauties of Nature and exertions of Art. There they would partake of a refreshment, while the soft Sicilian harmony from the musicians who were placed in a retired glen floated on the air, and seemed like the effect of enchantment.

Some days now passed, and the Signor Valvano was obliged to depart for Palermo, in order to regain his possessions, which on supposition of his death had fallen into the hands of his nearest relative. He took leave of the Marchese and Marchesa, and promised, as soon as his affairs would allow him, to return to the Castello.

The Count de Leoni still remained, and Ricardo found in him whatever he had anticipated on their first meeting. He was gratitude itself for the kindness he had received from Ricardo, and took every opportunity that presented of manifesting it; he seemed to be entirely weaned from his fatal propensity to gambling, of which he had seen the dreadful effects. He staid a week after the departure of the Signor Valvano, and then with much regret left the happy pair at the Castello.

Ricardo in the conversation of Louisa and the Signora Bononi felt not a wish for other society; he daily grew more and more attached to the Marchesa, and hourly did he bless the day that made her his.

He employed some of his time in directing various alterations to be made in the north wing of the Castello, and banished the gloom which had so long reigned in the Hall by making large casements, which descended to the floor and opened on the lawn, where sometimes he permitted his happy vassals to assemble, and with Louisa would delight to see them enjoy their innocent sports by the light of the nocturnal luminary, which in that climate almost equalled the brightness of day.

Amid the various occurrences that had taken place since the decease of the Padre Grimaldi, he had entirely forgot to peruse the packet which he gave into his hands but a few minutes before his death.

That circumstance, however, now occurred to his recollection, and he determined to dedicate the following morning to the examination of those papers; in which, unfortunately, he had to learn more of the dark conduct of the late Marchese his father, and the circumstance that had so long spread a gloom over the countenance of Grimaldi; which had often made Ricardo conjecture was occasioned by remorse for some horrible act he had committed.

The next morning Ricardo entered the apartment where the cabinet was in which he had deposited the papers, and securing himself from interruption, unfolded them, and read the following lines:—

CHAPTER VII.

TO RICARDO MARCHESE DE CARLENTINI

"At length the long-dreaded hour is fast approaching; life will soon cease to flow in my veins, my heart beats with a slow and languid motion, my body is emaciated, and my strength begins to fail. Fatal symptoms of dissolution! Oh! how my soul recoils with terror at the idea that when the link is broken which connects me to the world, when my soul wings its rapid flight, and trembling and confused stands before the tribunal of justice, what will it offer in extenuation of the dreadful crime it will be charged with? alas! what excuse can be made for a murderer?

"How often at the hour of midnight have I started from my restless couch, how often has my disturbed imagination made me think I beheld, slow stalking through my chamber, the blood streaming from the side, the murdered form of——

"As yet I am not able to name the victim of that accursed hour when I first embrued my hands in innocent blood. Marchese de Carlentini, thou wilt hear it too soon; let my body rest in the tomb, do not in thy just indignation leave it to be consumed by the scorching rays of the sun or the ravenous beasts of prey.

"Short is my tale, yet 'tis long ere I can summon resolution to begin it. I wish to supplicate for pardon ere I confess my guilt; I wish to tell what have been my sufferings, in order to raise some pity, even in the breasts of those I have injured.

"Conscience with her endless sting has deep pierced my heart, the agonizing pangs prevent the influence of slumber on my aching eyes, society has long been a torment to me, for surely every one must read my guilt in my perturbed looks.

———

"A day has elapsed since I wrote the above; I am unable to continue this intended exposition of my deeds of horror without renewing in all the bitterness of recollection my guilty acts; but I must do it; I must commence the recital while my trembling hand is able to guide my pen.

"Oh! ye who peruse these lines, reflect that the hand that traced them is no more endued with vital motion, that the heart which suggested the deed of horror contained in these pages is returning to its original dust, and that the soul of Grimaldi is suffering for the guilty acts done in his days of life.

"Marchese de Carlentini, thou art gone before me; repentance never entered thy bosom; with all thy load of dark and deadly crimes thou hast left this world. Soon we shall meet; but oh! the horrors of that meeting! Let me not ruminate on it, lest it bewilder my senses, and incapacitate me from my present purpose.

"About twenty years ago, when only the experience of thirty years had dawned on my mind, I was appointed confessor to the castle. The family of the Marchese consisted of his wife, the amiable Theodora, and you, Ricardo, whose infant tongue had just learned to express the first endearing words of childhood.

"Two years glided away in domestic tranquillity; the Marchese appeared to be greatly attached to Theodora, whose whole happiness seemed to be centered in him and yourself. The Marchese at the expiration of that time went to Palermo. That journey was fatal to the peace of Theodora, and was the consequence of plunging me into a horrible abyss of guilt.

"When the Marchese returned his conduct was entirely changed, he became gloomy and morose; he no longer took any pleasure in the society of Theodora, on the contrary, he diligently avoided being near her, and I often used to behold him on the hills walking with folded arms, apparently deeply ruminating on the subject that caused his change of conduct.

"It was from accidentally overhearing the conversation of some of the domestics who had attended him to Palermo that I began to have a suspicion of the cause that agitated the bosom of the Marchese.

"It appeared that he had lost while at Palermo vast sums of money at the gambling table, and that he was obliged to dispose of a considerable part of his estate to discharge them.

"His conduct to the Marchesa became harsh, and even cruel; frequently have I surprised her when she had been giving vent to her sorrows by floods of tears; my heart sympathized with her unfortunate situation. Would to Heaven it had ever done so; what horror, what distress, what torturous pangs of an accusing conscience should I have avoided.

"One evening the Marchese sent to my apartment, to desire me to meet him on the North Terrace. Well I recollect that, without knowing why, a sudden chill seized my frame at the message. It was a sad presentiment of dreadful consequences which resulted from it.

"As soon as I appeared on the terrace he motioned me to follow him; I obeyed; and leaving the Castle, we entered into the valley.

"'This is a pleasant evening, father Grimaldi,' said the Marchese.

"'It is, my Lord,' I replied; for the first time raising my eyes on his countenance, which was pale and agitated. 'Such an evening as this, my Lord,' I continued, 'sooths the mind, even when labouring under heavy calamities; it breathes peace and serenity to the woe-worn breast.'

"'To light sorrows it may, father; but where grief is deep seated, the tempestuous fury of the elements is more composing than the mild serene weather which only tortures by presenting a scene of tranquillity to the view which is foreign to the thought. I speak as I feel, father.'

"'I am truly concerned for it, my Lord,' I replied; 'indeed I have of late noticed that some deep seated melancholy oppresses you.'

"The Marchese did not make any answer, but seemed to be deeply reflecting on some important subject. I could observe that his countenance grew dark, and an expression of determined resolution pervaded his countenance. I walked by his side till we entered into the forest, wrapt in wonder as to what would be the consequence of this meeting.

"The Marchese struck into an unfrequented path, he looked once or twice cautiously around him, and then addressed me in words to this effect:—

"'Is it not hard, father, to be surrounded with what the world calls friends, and yet not to be able to select from them one in whom it would be safe to confide?'

"'It is, certainly, my Lord, a matter of concern,' I replied, anxious to know whither this conversation would tend.

"'And yet, Grimaldi, that is my case, and is the cause of my melancholy. Father, it lays in your power to restore peace to my breast.'

"'In mine, my Lord?' said I, 'name what it is you would have me perform; great indeed would be my happiness if it is in my power to be of service to you.'

"'Grimaldi, I must first impose on you an oath of secresy.'

"'I was somewhat disturbed at this, as it seemed to infer that what he had in view was of a nature that shunned the light.

"'You hesitate, father; 'tis enough; I shall drop the subject.' He then turned about.

"'No, my Lord,' I exclaimed, 'you shall not have it to say that you have no one in whom you can place confidence. I will take the oath,' said I, holding up my crucifix; 'by this I swear never to reveal, during your life-time, what you shall think fit to repose in my bosom.'

"'I am satisfied, Grimaldi, thou art now my friend,' replied the Marchese, ''tis concerning the Marchesa I would speak to you. You have yet to learn that I married her in hopes that her uncle would on his demise settle on her his immense possessions. On my arrival at Palermo I unfortunately fell in with a set of villains, who took advantage of my propensity for gambling. In fine, I lost all my property save this estate. In this exigency I turned my thoughts to the Marchesa's uncle. From his well known attachment to his money I well knew he would not assist me with any; and in hopes he had made his will, I hired a ruffian to destroy him. He succeeded.'

"Here the Marchese stopped, seeing the horror which was depicted in my countenance at his relation.

"'Grimaldi,' said he with a severe look, 'recollect your oath and protestations. Am I yet to look for a friend?'

"He said these last words in a tone of voice which seemed to supplicate me not to desert him; at least I felt them so, and I replied—

"'No, my Lord, you have a faithful servant before you. I pray you to proceed.'

"'I was, however, rightly punished,' continued the Marchese, 'for my precipitate conduct; for Theodora's uncle had not made any will, consequently, the whole of his property went to another relation. Money I must have, or never more shew myself at Palermo. Now, Grimaldi, I was thinking of a second marriage.'

"'A second marriage, my Lord,' said I, 'you surely forget that the Marchesa Theodora'—

"'Still lives, you would add, Grimaldi,' said the Marchese interrupting me. 'Ah father, it is there I want your friendship, your assistance.'

"'My Lord', said I, growing pale with horror, 'you would not surely'—

"'I do not mean to hurt Theodora,' said the Marchese; 'do not, Grimaldi, anticipate what I have no idea of. I have formed my plan, but without your concurrence it is of no avail. Will you assist me, Grimaldi?'

"'In any thing short of the destruction of the Marchesa,' I replied, 'you may command me, my Lord.'

"'Grimaldi, I shall look on you as my preserver, nay more, as the preserver of the young Ricardo from future penury, my gratitude will be unbounded.'

"He then proceeded to inform me of his intention, which was, to confine the Marchesa in some part of the Castello, the size of which, and the number of deserted chambers it contained, rendered it an easy matter to keep perfectly secure from all observation the hapless object of his persecution. Meantime the world was to be deceived by a report of her death; in order that he might be able to enter into an alliance with some lady whose rich possessions would make amends for his losses and disappointments.

"Unfortunate Theodora! I who ought to have been thy protector, and exerted the authority of the church in thy behalf, was unhappily influenced by thy most bitter enemy to assist him in his horrible unprincipled schemes against thy peace and liberty; and, as it afterwards fatally proved, against thy life.

"I must now lay down my pen; the pains I endure would be dreadful, even to the innocent, who look forward to an hereafter, as seamen in a storm, to the peaceful haven. What then must they be to me, joined to the anguish of a guilty conscience, and anticipating the punishment allotted to the murderer.

"When the Marchese had informed me of his plans, we returned from the shades of the forest and proceeded toward the Castello. The deserted and lonely situation of the South Angle Tower caught his attention, and he determined, if it was not in too ruinous a condition, to make it the prison of the Marchesa. We lost no time, for he was impatient to commence his cruel and unmerited persecution of the gentle Theodora, and taking a lamp, examined the place. In the tower we found an apartment which seemed to have been formerly a place of confinement, as the casements were all boarded up, except one, which looked into a solitary court, and which gave light to the place. Here security seemed to reign, and here it was resolved Theodora should be brought.

"The next day, purposely to expedite his plans, the Marchese had some words with Theodora, and the result was his ordering the door that led to her suit of apartments to be locked, and no one admitted to her but her own domestic. This step was only preparatory to others more violent, for he soon after forbade the servant to attend her lady, and brought her provisions into the outer chamber every day himself.

"Her unmerited confinement, and the unkindness of the Marchese, afflicted Theodora so much that she fell ill, and I was ordered to attend her. The dew of sensibility was not yet scorched up by the fervor of my wishes to serve the Marchese, and I could not behold her sufferings without commiserating them; knowing too as I did the fate that awaited her. The impatience of the Marchese increasing, by his desire I prepared a potion for the unfortunate Theodora which had the power of arresting for a time the vital motion, making the taker appear as if dead. With a trembling hand I gave her the fatal draught, which the hapless victim to a barbarous husband unconsciously drank.

"As soon as it had taken effect, and the Marchesa lay motionless on her couch, I acquainted the household with her death. Great was the grief of all the domestics, who had every reason to love her. They rushed in crowds to her chamber, and loudly lamented her loss.

"Under the idea that the disorder she died of was infectious, I restrained the eagerness of the servants, who wished to kiss her hand as the last proof of their affection, and would not permit any of them to advance nearer than the door of the chamber.

"Preparations were made instantly for the interment, and the inanimate Marchesa was placed in the coffin, the lid of which I pretended to fasten myself.

"The funeral ceremony was to take place at midnight; and about two hours before that period, assisted by the Marchese, I removed her from her dreary abode, and carried her along the silent halls and corridors which led to the South Angle Tower, leaving her on a couch which had been previously brought there;

and locking the door of her future prison, we proceeded to her former apartments; when having put into the coffin a weight equal to her body, I fastened it up, and at the time appointed it was carried into the chapel, and laid in the tomb prepared for it with the same solemnity as if it had been the mortal remains of Theodora.

"The Marchese for some time confined himself to his chamber, and appeared greatly to lament the loss of the Marchesa; but he rejoiced in private at the success of his well-concerted plans, and loaded me with presents and expressions of gratitude that drove away all compunction from my bosom, and I became hardened against all emotion of pity for the Marchesa.

"The next night I went to the tower; I unlocked the door, and as the gleams of my lamp penetrated the gloom that reigned in the apartment, I beheld, setting by the side of her couch, the unfortunate Theodora.

"I will not attempt to describe my feelings at the sight of her; I evidently slunk from the penetrating glances of her eyes. She noticed my emotion.

"'You start, father, at beholding me; tell me what is the reason of my being in this dismal chamber? Sure you have no design against my life. Oh! father, do I then—can it be possible; that I see in you an agent of the Marchese?'

"'Your life is safe, Marchesa,' I replied, 'ask no more questions, as they will not be answered. These are your provisions; to-morrow at this hour I will bring you more;' so saying I departed, and left the hapless Theodora to bewail her sad fate.

"The next night I entered her chamber. She besought me to take pity on her, to restore her to liberty, to bring her little Ricardo to her. She even threw herself on her knees before me, and laying hold of my habit, with her eyes streaming with tears of heartfelt woe, entreated me to let her know what were the designs of the Marchese respecting her.

"I tore myself from her grasp, she fell to the floor with a dreadful groan, having greatly hurt herself, and I rushed out of the chamber without assisting her.

"The Marchese in a short time went to Palermo, leaving me,

as usual, at the Castello. You, Ricardo, were then near five years of age. You had already forgot your mother, who still existed in her dreary confinement, whither I constantly brought her provisions once in every three days; for a report prevailed among the peasants that the southern chambers of the Castle were haunted; and one man affirmed, that passing by the Angle Tower at a late hour one night, he had heard deep groans, and had seen a light gleam from the shattered casements of the tower.

"I was greatly shocked to hear the reports that went about, knowing them partly to be founded in truth. I however affected to disbelieve them, and endeavoured to silence the propagators of the tales; for I feared lest by some means it might lead to an examination of the Southern Chamber, when the Marchesa would be discovered.

"The Marchese soon after arrived from Palermo. The first question he asked me was concerning Theodora. When he heard that she was well, he looked disappointed, and the relation of the account concerning the tower, and the increasing terrors of the domestics, (for none of them would now on any account approach the ruins after sun-set) did not appear to contribute to his repose. He looked at me with an expression in his countenance which told the dark designs which he was planning before he gave them utterance.

"'Father,' said he, 'self-preservation is the first law of nature; it is no sin in such a cause to commit any act, however unpleasant to the feelings or repugnant to laws made in the cool moments of reflection. If we see a venomous reptile it becomes a duty to destroy it, not only on account of our own safety, but also to prevent it doing an injury to another. Doubtless, father, your opinion wanders not far from mine in this instance.'

"'There certainly are cases, my Lord,' I replied, 'where it is no sin to conduct ourselves as you mention; but what would you infer from your question? which, pardon me, is so foreign from the subject we were conversing about.'

"'No, father,' replied the Marchese, 'it is not so foreign from that subject as you seem to think. I am glad to find you of the same sentiments as myself. Now, father, what if I were to tell you

that the envenomed serpent I but now hinted at is—your prisoner.'

"I started at his words, and in an instant clearly comprehend-
ed his meaning.

"'Listen to me, Grimaldi. Should Theodora escape; should
any person, curious to know the reason of the lights that have
been seen and the noises that have been heard in the Angle Tower,
invade its privacy, and release the Marchesa, think you that she
will be silent? No, she will represent my conduct to the King; and
your's, father, in assisting me, will doubtless be laid before the
Pope. If you see as you ought your danger and mine, Grimaldi,
you will not hesitate. In the dead of night, a single blow will release us from all fears. Take this,' said he, drawing a dagger from
the folds of his vest, 'and do away the cause of our disquietude.'

"Hardly conscious of what I did, I grasped the fatal instrument. My blood chilled with the sensations that pervaded my
frame, while the Marchese continued:—

"'I repeat again, father, the necessity of this step. Our danger
is great, and great must be the effort to preserve ourselves.'

"By such conversation did he gain me over to his horrid purposes. I thought I saw the danger he described, and even grew
impatient to perpetrate the crime that has embittered my existence.

"The Marchese left me not that day; he would not allow me
an opportunity to ponder on the deed I was going to perform; he
parted not from me till the midnight hour had tolled.

"Surely if I had but for a moment reflected I never could
have committed the dreadful act; and this, in all probability, the
Marchese was fully aware of.

"Grasping the dagger in my hand, I hasted to the Angle
Tower. My hapless victim started at the sight of me; the rays of
the lamp gleamed on the dagger; she shrieked with the dreadful
apprehensions that arose in her mind.

"That shriek was her last!

"When I saw the blood-stained form of the Marchesa lying
on the floor, bereft of animation, what sensations of horror arose
in my bosom. Alas! the deed was perpetrated. Hastily I left the

The Monk murdering the Marchesa.

chamber; I fled along the dreary corridores, thinking I was pursued by avenging furies, urged on by the blood-stained spectre of
Theodora.

"Once I ventured as I crossed the hall to turn round, when
slow pacing amongst the columns appeared her form; the garments were dyed in blood, in her hand she bore a pale burning
lamp which illumined her features, that were marked with the
agonies of death; struck with horror, I rushed into the apartment
of the Marchese, pale and haggard with the dreadful emotions
excited by my fears and the deed I had perpetrated.

"'Is it done?' said the Marchese.

"Yes, I replied, and I am condemned to be a wretch for ever. Oh! that I could recal the past hour.

"'Consider, my friend,' replied the Marchese, 'that this step was necessary to our peace; nay more, to our safety. Now we are secure. The dead tell no tales.'

"No? Marchese; think you not the soul of Theodora is now supplicating for justice at the throne of retribution against her murderer? and she will obtain it!

"The Marchese endeavoured to soothe the perturbation of my mind; but from that hour never have I had one moment's peace; my life has been one scene of horror and misery; yet I clung to existence, fearful of worse torments when my mortal frame had returned to its original dust.

"From that time I never had courage to enter the southern chambers; and the remains of Theodora have lain in the Tower more than fifteen years.

"You, no doubt, Ricardo, observed the agitation I endured when you declared your wish of inhabiting the South Angle Tower; the place where your mother was murdered, and where her remains still lie.

"Greatly alarmed lest you should find some means to enter the place, and discover the horrid deed, I suddenly formed the resolution of letting you have the keys, determined to alarm you in such a manner as to prevent your entering that part of the Castle again. You know what followed. From fears of my personal safety I dissuaded you from taking a trombone, and before the time that you were to receive the keys I entered the South Hall, and made what little preparations were necessary. Although so many years had elapsed since the commission of the horrible crime which the privacy of the tower concealed, yet it is impossible to describe my agitation on again entering that part of the Castle.

"I hastily retired from the place, and met you in the North Hall. The sound and appearances which alarmed you so much were caused by me. When I found you seemingly resolved to enter the passage which led to the fatal tower, I determined to prevent you, and thrusting my arm through a hole in the partition which separated a small chamber I was in from the corridore, brandished a large sword, at the same time uttering those dismal sounds which, increased by the echo, almost alarmed myself. My plan succeeded, and you fled.

"Confident that the Marchese would not allow you to examine that part of the Castle, I referred you to him. You know the rest.

"Thus at length have I concluded my tale of horror. At the throne of the Most High I shall soon give an account of my offences, and receive the punishment that awaits such crimes.

"I feel the chilly grasp of death seizing on my frame. Is there no avoiding dissolution? Oh! would I could hide myself in some dark cave where the searching eyes of the sun never penetrated, where the breeze of morning or the zephyrs of evening never wandered; but in vain do I wish to avoid what all mortals must at one time or other meet.

"Ricardo, pity my sufferings! do not heap curses on my guilty head!"

———

Ricardo sighed deeply as he finished the perusal of Grimaldi's confession; the sad fate of his mother dwelt heavy at his heart, and the groan of filial commiseration oft burst from his agonized breast.

"Oh! my sainted mother," he exclaimed, "and do your precious remains lie unentombed in the dreary prison where the fell assassin pierced your innocent heart? This moment will I go and water them with my tears: dreadful indeed is the mystery contained in the gloomy recesses of the Tower."

He arose from his seat with an intention of exploring the dungeon where the remains of the Marchesa lay, but on looking at the declining shadow of the sun, he found the day was too far spent to admit of his carrying his design into effect, in the present disturbed state of his mind; he was not sorry at being prevented going, and he determined to employ the intervening hours between the present and the melancholy spectacle that he well knew would meet his eyes of the sad remains of a murdered mother, in composing the agitation of his bosom, to render him able to endure the sad scene.

It was a gleam of comfort to his soul to know that his father was not guilty, as he supposed he was, of the murder of Signor Valvano; and the hour of repast drawing nigh, he endeavoured to compose himself as much as possible, in order to conceal from Louisa the grief that oppressed his bosom.

But her anxious gaze when she saw him enter the hall pale and agitated, soon rendered his endeavours useless; and when with fond solicitude she inquired the cause of the evident melancholy that oppressed him, he found himself unable to frame any other reason for it than the true one, which he then related to her.

The gentle heart of Louisa swelled at the sad recital, and sorrowfully passed away the time devoted to the banquet; when it was concluded, Ricardo returned to the privacy of his chamber, and passed the hours in painful reflections on the dark deed, which had deprived him of a mother.

The sun had long withdrawn his beams, and the moon now began to shew her bright form above the summit of the hills that bounded the horizon, when Ricardo, leaving his chamber walked pensively on the lawn; raising his eyes, he beheld the rugged walls of the South Angle Tower illumined by the silver beams of the nocturnal lamp. Sadly he gazed on them, while the dreadful act that had been performed in its gloomy interior returned to his recollection with increasing grief.

Unable to support the painful emotions that arose in his breast, he slowly returned to the Castello, to seek in his Louisa's converse that comfort he was so much in need of; determined, that ere another night covered with its shades the face of the creation, that the remains of his mother should be consigned with all holy rites and ceremonies of the church, to the tomb; that done, he hoped that time would soften the acuteness of the sorrow he then endured.

Some of his domestics were ordered to attend him at an early hour in the morning with the steward of the Castello, in order to assist him in his intended examination of the Angle Tower, whose dreary walls for fifteen years had never reverberated to the voice of man.

CHAPTER VIII.

IT wanted one hour of midnight when the Padre Bernardo left his cell. Entering the chapel he was surprised to observe, near the skreen that divided it, a light; and curious to know who it could be that at that lonely hour visited the chapel, he shrouded his lamp, and slowly and cautiously proceeded forward. He now heard a low whispering, and soon after, saw a man enveloped in a cloak in converse with a nun, who had thrown off her veil. The beams of her lamp shone bright on her countenance, which rivetted the attention of the monk. Large expressive dark eyes, with eye-brows beautifully arched; her cheeks the residence of the blushing rose, and her coral lips inviting the rapturous kiss.

This nun, thought the monk, must surely be the one mentioned to me by the Demon; true it is she is not quite so enchanting as the lovely female I beheld in the pavillion, yet her beauties interest me, and the flames of love arise in my breast.

The monk now started at beholding the nun unlock the gate of the skreen, and the man enter and follow her toward the portal that led to the interior of the convent.

He now determined to watch them; and passing through the gate, which was left open, he cautiously advanced along a passage, and ascending a broad flight of stairs that appeared at the end, entered a corridore, where observing a light streaming from a door that was not closed he approached it, and saw the man who having laid aside his cloak, was seated by the side of the nun, with whom he appeared in earnest conversation.

Bernardo now beheld a sight which filled him with rage. The Signor leant toward the nun, and throwing his arm around her neck, joined his lips to hers.

The monk was ready to burst into the chamber and separate the fond pair, but a better plan was formed by his ready invention; he took his sandals off his feet, and uttering a deep hollow groan threw back the door, and hastily running to the extremity of the passage, shrouded his lamp, and awaited with impatience the result of his scheme.

After some time the monk beheld the Signor come to the door and cautiously look around him; he then went back, and soon after appeared with the nun. Hastily they left the corridore, and descending the stairs, the monk, who followed them at a distance, saw the nun open the gate in the skreen, and when her lover was gone she locked it, and tremblingly retraced her steps toward her cell.

At the foot of the stairs that led to the chambers belonging to the sisters of Santa Catherina stood the monk. Agatha, when she beheld his tall figure, and found that her guilty acts were discovered, trembled with sudden horror as the leaf of the aspen to the restless breeze of night. She uttered a faint scream, and was sinking on the floor, when Bernardo hastily rushed forward, and caught her in his arms.

He threw back the veil which covered her countenance, and as the rays of the lamp shone on it he gazed with unsated delight on her lovely features, while a flush crimsoned his cheeks, and his heart beat with increasing violence against his side.

He however checked the emotions he felt, though with great difficulty, while he thus questioned the nun:—

"Daughter, who was it that but now I saw in company with thee?"

The nun tremblingly raised her eyes on the monk, who now held her arm. She beheld herself irrevocably lost if she could not cause a sensation of pity for her to arise in his breast; and in a supplicating voice she replied:—

"Holy father, have mercy on me. I acknowledge my crime. Forced within these walls by the cruel order of a father, because my heart was susceptible of the passions of love, I did not conceive myself bound to obey the rigid rules of a convent. As yet too the last ceremony has not been performed. My lover has contrived to obtain an entrance to the chapel, and I have admitted him into the convent; but, father, if ever your heart felt the soft passion of love, if ever you knew the pangs of parting with the object you held dearest on earth, I conjure you, by the remembrance of those emotions, to pity my situation."

The monk from the violence of his feelings was silent; his cowl he had thrown back, and Agatha raising her supplicating eyes to his countenance, read there that he not only forgave, but that the beauties of her person had excited his admiration.

The terror which had agitated her by degrees subsided, and a softer sensation assumed their place; the pallid hue which usually overspread the cheeks of the monk had given way to a crimson tint, his eyes were fixed on her, there was a languishing expression in them, his other features were handsome, and his years seemed not greatly to exceed her own.

"What," said the monk in a softened voice, "what if I were to conceal the knowledge I have obtained of thy proceedings out of pity for your situation. I demand but one thing in return."

"Name it, father; what is there I would not do to shew my gratitude?"

"Thou must then promise not to see the cavalier more," said the monk.

"I will sacrifice every thing to your wishes," blushingly replied Agatha; "I will not allow him again entrance in the convent."

The Demon from his gloomy abode beheld the meeting of Bernardo and the nun, who long had been the votary of vice, whose soul confessed his sway; he saw in her a fit tool to further his designs against the monk, he made her breast glow with the base passion of sensual love, and caused the fevered languishment of desire to rage without control through her frame. He did not, however, intend that the monk should so easily attain his ends; and he determined to prevent him from fulfilling his wishes that night.

The monk, satisfied with the promise made by Agatha, that she would no more admit her lover, by a sudden motion of which he was almost ignorant gently pressed her hand. The soft pressure was returned—he looked at the nun—their eyes glowed with passion—he gently drew her toward him—he put his arm around her slender waist—he bent his head till his face came near hers—he felt he inhaled her breath, sweet as the fragrance of the zephyrs impregnated with the odors of May—their lips joined—what ecstacy did it impart to the monk!—a mist swam before his eyes—his whole frame was convulsed as he pressed Agatha yet more closely to his bosom........

Just at that moment a distant pace was heard. The monk hastily looked around, as did also the nun, and beheld advancing through the gloom the form of the abbess.

The monk shrouded his lamp, and muttering a curse at thus being disappointed, in having the cup of bliss dashed from his lips at the moment he was going to take its delicious contents, begged Agatha to be the next night at eleven in the convent cemetery, where he would meet her; he then hastily retreated toward the chapel, and Agatha flew to her cell.

But what they had supposed to be the abbess was nothing more than a delusive form, raised by the Demon to part them ere the languor of satiety had seized on the monk.

Bernardo retracing his steps arrived in his cell, where gloomily he threw himself on his pallet. Sleep, however, rested not on his eye-lids; but while he regretted his disappointment, he comforted himself with the idea that the next night would be more propitious to his wishes.

Agatha had not been in the convent of Santa Catherina more than a year; the ceremony of her taking the vows of seclusion was reserved to grace the approaching festival of the Santa Catherina. Whatever was the occasion of her being obliged to reside in a place so ill suited to her disposition, she gave great proof of her being an adept in all manner of vice, since she had been within those holy walls; but her actions being hitherto clouded by an impenetrable veil, which she had the art to throw over them, hitherto escaped detection, and even suspicion. Early on the same morning she entered the convent her conductors had stopped the carriage at a village in order to procure some refreshment; she was ushered into a small chamber, where a table was spread with the coarse fare the cottage afforded, but the heart of Agatha was the abode of sorrow at being obliged to leave the pleasures of the world; she neglected to partake of the morning repast, and absorbed in melancholy reflections which caused the frequent tear to steal down her lovely cheeks, passed the moments leaning on her white arm at the small casement which was not far from the ground.

A cavalier passing by on horseback observed her grief; he was struck too with her beauty, and he advanced to the casement.

"Fair Signora," said he, "I grieve to see the distress you so apparently labor under; can I be of any service to you?"

"Alas! Signor," said the weeping Agatha, "I am against my will doomed to reside in a convent; that is the cause of my tears; in a few hours I shall be inclosed in those hated walls."

"Cruel fate," said the cavalier, "that you, Signora, possessing such charms, so fitted to adorn the world, should be secluded from it. Sure," continued he, in a low voice, "you could easily descend from the casement; and if you would permit me to place you on my steed, you would in a short time be far from hence. The moments are precious; will you trust yourself with me?"

Agatha hesitated, not in her reply. "I will willingly do it," she replied. "The Saints grant me success."

She then arose from her seat, and was attempting to descend from the casement when her conductors came out of the cottage. Terrified at the sight of them, she hastily drew back, and the cavalier, disappointed of his lovely prize, rode away.

He however watched the men who had the care of the handsome Agatha, and saw them soon after conduct her to the carriage, which he followed for some time, till it stopped at the entrance of the convent of Santa Catherina.

He passed by at the moment that Agatha was entering its holy walls; she turned round at the noise of his horse's feet, and eyed him with a look so hopeless and sorrowful that he determined if possible to effect her deliverance from her sad destiny.

He stopped at a village which was near the convent, and in the evening attended the vespers in the chapel. He placed himself near the skreen, and observed Agatha, who raised her veil on purpose to make herself known.

Her beauties had interested him, and he saw that could he by any means liberate her, that there was little doubt but that he should be amply repaid for the danger he might encounter.

After the service was concluded he left the chapel, and by the light of the moon examined the lofty walls that inclosed the extensive pile of building. No where, however, could he perceive the least likelihood of succeeding in any attempt to scale them; and he repaired to the village despairing of being able to effect his purpose.

The next morning he renewed his endeavours, but still he was unsuccessful; and not wishing to be seen by any of the inhabitants of the monastery, he concealed himself in the shade of an extensive forest, which was on the south side of the building.

Here as he wandered his attention was caught by some ruins which appeared to have been formerly a small chapel; it was of great antiquity, covered with ivy, and part of the roof which had fallen was almost hid by the long waving grass. Solitary and deserted was the spot; "the thistle shook there its lonely head, the moss whistled to the wind."

As he was examining the place he found a flight of rough steps which appeared to lead to some place beneath, probably to a cemetery. He cautiously descended them, and found himself when arrived at the bottom in a vaulted chamber. It, however, had not been appropriated to the purpose of a burial place, and the cavalier was on the point of quitting it, when he discovered a door in the wall.

As the only light which entered was from the aperture above, the cavalier did not think proper to attempt to open that door without having a lamp with him; and as he felt curious to know what place it concealed, he determined to return there in the afternoon with implements for procuring a light. Leaving the place he then proceeded to the village, and as he passed by the walls of the convent cast many an anxious look at them, for within their lofty boundaries was the beautiful Agatha.

Toward the evening he again repaired to the ruins of the chapel in the forest, and when he was in the vaulted chamber he lit a lamp, and advanced to the door, which was strengthened by plates of iron, and appeared to be strongly fastened on the other side. Time, however, had for a series of years been busily employed on the massy bolts and hinges; and when the cavalier endeavoured to burst it open, the door gave way to his efforts, and fell into a narrow passage.

Taking up his lamp, the cavalier passed over the fallen door, and proceeded along the passage some time, often stopping to trim his lamp, which burnt dimly surrounded by the foul air which had probably for more than a century been pent up in that subterraneous place.

The passage often varied in its width and length; in some places it seemed formed by Nature, and in others was evidently made by Art; the great length of it fatigued the cavalier who sat down on some of the fragments of the side wall which had given way, in order to rest himself. The cold damp chill, however, warned him to keep in motion, and he arose and proceeded forward, till at length he came to a flight of steps, which having ascended, he plainly heard to his great delight the voices of the monks chanting the vesper service.

The reader will recollect in the pages which the monk perused of the volume written by Bartolo, which contained the melancholy tale of the fair Isabella de Tracy, and of her savage destroyer Leonardi de Vicensio, it was mentioned that the monastery was partly erected over the place where the Castello, the scene of those dreadful events recorded by him, formerly stood. And the cavalier had happened to find out a passage which led from the Castello to the chapel in the forest; and which had served as a means of retreat in times of danger to the inhabitants.

At the top of the steps was a door, which the cavalier was fearful of attempting to open while the monks were in the chapel, for by the sound of their voices he was convinced he was not far from it. The fastenings of the door were on the inside, and consisted of large bolts which ran far into the stone frame; and the cavalier rightly conjectured that it was so secured to prevent the egress of the inhabitants of the monastic pile.

He sat down on the steps, awaiting the conclusion of the service, revolving in his mind the probable consequences of his daring enterprize. Should the passage he was in, open to the convent, it would be easy to carry his schemes into effect; but should it communicate with the monastery, and which he had every reason to believe from the nearness of the voices of the monks, he was as far from the object of his wishes as ever; unless, indeed, he could find out the communication with it and the convent, but that was a thing which seemed almost impossible.

In the midst of his rumination the service was concluded, and he heard the departing steps of the monks so plainly as to leave it no longer a doubt where the passage would lead him to. He now waited till silence had resumed her reign, when he essayed to draw back the bolts that secured the portal.

This was a work attended with some difficulty, for the bolts were so rusted in their holds, that without much trouble they would not move. At length however, all of them were drawn out of the stone work, and the cavalier listened if any sounds of approaching paces should meet his ear.

All, however, was silent; and from the time he had been in unfastening the door, it was probable that the monks had retired to their cells; and consequently there was no danger in his emerging from the subterraneous passage.

The door slowly moved to the efforts of the cavalier with a harsh grating sound, which often made him stop lest the noise should alarm the attention of the monks. And at length he entered a small chamber; this he crossed, and opening a door on the opposite side, found himself in a lofty vaulted corridore.

Recollecting the direction of the sounds of the monks' voices when performing the evening service, he advanced that way, and opening a large folding portal, entered the well-known chapel of the monastery.

He advanced toward the skreen, and looked anxiously about for some way by which he might enter the convent; but his search was fruitless. He, however, determined on taking some method to let Agatha know the discovery he had made, and to request her to be in the chapel at an appointed hour the next night in order to consult on the means of her escape.

As he found it would not be possible to make any further attempts till he had seen her, he now retraced his steps, carefully fastening the door by which he had gained admittance into the monastery, and traversing the long subterraneous passage at length found himself in the ruins of the chapel.

The next morning he attended the service, and stationed himself near the skreen; he however found it impossible to effect his purpose without fear of a discovery. He saw Agatha, who was the last of the long train of nuns, and who often turned her head as she was leaving the chapel to gaze on the cavalier.

In the evening, however, he was more fortunate, the increasing gloom made his actions less liable to be observed, and as Agatha was leaving the place, he contrived to throw a paper toward her through the grating of the skreen, and which falling near her feet she unobserved stooped down and picking it up concealed it in her bosom. The cavalier then, greatly pleased at his success, retired.

From the moment that Agatha had entered the convent she had abandoned herself to all the bitterness of grief; and far from repenting of her sinful actions, for which it appeared but too probable she had been sent to that place, which was one of the most rigid orders in Sicily, she continually lamented her deprivation of those enjoyments which had constituted the happiness of her life.

She often thought too with sensations which ill became the heart of one now devoted to a life of religious seclusion, of the animated countenance of the cavalier, his regret for her hapless state, his instant offer of assisting her, and the distress that appeared to overwhelm him when he found it impossible to rescue her. A ray of hope beamed on her breast, when she saw him in the chapel, and served in some small degree to lighten the heavy burthen of despair which had began to oppress her almost beyond a possibility of endurance.

When she had, as already is mentioned, possessed herself of the paper, she thought each moment an age till she could retire to her chamber and peruse its contents. She was, however, obliged to wait till the nuns were dismissed by the abbess, when she perceived it to contain the following words.

"BEAUTIFUL SIGNORA,

"The Deity of love, and kind fortune, have in some measure favored my attempts to preserve you from the cruel fate that awaits you within these walls, and to restore to an admiring world a jewel so sweetly formed to adorn it. If you have a wish to know how far I have succeeded, be at midnight in the chapel, where you will see your ever devoted

"FERDINANDO."

Agatha kissed the lines, which afforded her real delight; she counted the tardy moments as they slowly passed by; and when at length the appointed period arrived, she descended from the chamber, and entered the chapel.

The Signor Ferdinando was not there; and anxiously waiting his coming, she leaned against the skreen, leaving her lamp at some distance on the steps of the altar. Soon, however, she heard the echoes of hasty paces, and a man, muffled up in a cloak carrying a lamp approached the skreen. When he came near it, he let fall his garment, and Agatha beheld her expected friend.

"Lovely Signora," said he, "thus far have I penetrated into this gloomy abode of superstition and horror, so unfit a residence for you. But alas! no way can I find to enter the convent. This cruel skreen divides us. Could I force the iron gate, even at this moment you might escape. Perhaps you may find some means to open it."

"Alas! Signor," said Agatha, "I know of none; but fortune, which hitherto has attended you, may not desert us. I will, however, make every effort to procure my wished-for enlargement from this dreary place. My gratitude, Signor, to you is indeed great; your disinterested goodness must ever claim my warmest thanks."

"And does not the beautiful Agatha," said Ferdinando, "perceive that it is love the most ardent which impels me? From the first moment I saw you, I devoted myself to your service. Continually have I lamented your cruel destiny, and continually have I endeavoured to seek to alter it."

The countenance of Agatha, covered with blushes, shewed that the declaration of Ferdinando was not unpleasant to her ears. She raised her eyes on him—they met his enamoured gaze—they spoke more than the tongue could ever express—the fire of love was in them.

Ferdinando with rapturous sensations rivetted his eyes on her beauties. A silence ensued, but it was a silence which expressed the sentiments of Agatha, and the unspeakable sensations of Ferdinando, who at length interrupted it by declarations of the tenderest attachment to that lovely female.

Thus passed away the now fleeting hours, and at length the Signor Ferdinando seeing the grey dawn peeping through the casements of the chapel, was obliged to depart; but not before he had imprinted on the white hand of Agatha, which she held out to him through the grating, a thousand kisses, and swore on it an eternal adoration.

Slowly they withdrew, often turning back to gaze on each other, for the passion that reigned in the breast of one existed with equal strength in the bosom of the other; but it was that passion which ceases to exist the moment it has attained its object.

As Agatha had much to perform, and the Signor Ferdinando had some affairs to arrange at Lingua Crossa, a city near the base of the fiery Etna, their next meeting was fixed for the seventh night from that period, and Agatha in the interim was busily engaged in ruminating on the means by which she might obtain the key of the gate, and so effect her deliverance from the convent.

The Demon, whose searching eyes penetrated the dark womb of futurity, and who had long looked on Agatha as his own, resolved to aid her in her present purpose; foreseeing that by it he should plunge her still farther in guilt, and that she would commit an act, at which human nature recoils, but which to him was the height of happiness to glut his gaze with.

She had on the fourth night from that on which she had parted with Ferdinando retired to her couch rather earlier than usual; she felt little inclined to sleep, but lay looking at the moon which

Ferdinando taking leave of Agatha.

was gliding along the heavens, and threw her silver radiance into the chamber of Agatha.

As the tones of the clock proclaiming the midnight hour broke on the silence around, she felt a sudden drowsiness seize her, and yielding to its influence was soon enwrapped in a deep slumber.

At that moment the Demon took his station by the side of her couch; on his blasted form the beams of the regent of night refused to shine, and she retired to the welcome covert of a dark cloud.

The arch enemy of man by his powerful arts caused visionary scenes to appear to the wakeful imagination of Agatha, in order to prepare her for what was to follow.

He brought to her view the form of Ferdinando, whose countenance, beaming with smiles of delight, and irradiated with the fire of love, appeared more captivating than ever. She thought he was sitting by her side breathing in her ear the delusive expressions which proceed from the ardour of the moment, but which to her misled ideas appeared to be the dictates of a heart truly devoted to her. As such she heard them, as such they gave her the greatest delight.

She thought that they were sitting in an arbor formed of various odoriferous flowers; the beams of the moon trembled on the gently agitated waters of a stream that rolled its transparent waves not far from the spot where they were; while a distant waterfall and the plaintive notes of the nightingale sweetly broke on the silence around.

The rays of the silver lamp of night found their way through the variegated foliage of the arbor, and gave sufficient light to enable her to see the interesting features of Ferdinando; whose gaze was fixed on her, whilst his arm fondly attempted to encircle her slender waist, but from which he was prevented by some invisible power.

Suddenly the form of a monk seemed to stand before them, his face was concealed by his cowl, in his hand he held a key, and Agatha thought she heard him speak these words.

"Lovers, I come to break the spell that prevents your happiness, this key will be the means of bringing you to each others arms, and of enjoying those delights which those who love like you can only be conscious of."

Agatha hastily stretched forth her hand to receive the key, its coldness made her start, she awoke, and at that moment by the returning light of the moon beheld a form receding from her sight; and soon became sensible that part of her dream was realized, for in her hand was the key.

Terrified, she let it drop from her hand, and raised her head to see if there was any one in the chamber, but the beams of the moon enlightened every part, and nothing met her view that could alarm her.

Hardly expecting to see it, and conceiving that the strength of her imagination operating on her senses had made her think that she in reality had a key in her hand, when she awoke she looked amongst the cloaths and to her astonishment found it. It was a large key, of an uncommon construction, and similar to one she had seen hanging up in a corner of the parlor belonging to the Abbess.

The singular way in which it had been conveyed to her made her almost fearful of touching it. She again considered her dream; what, said she, if this key should open the grate of the skreen— yes, it must be so; it is the means of escape, which some kind deity has thus conveyed to me.

In her impatience to know the fact, she was on the point of getting up and descending to the chapel, but lay down again on reflecting that she had no light, and that the moon could not assist her, as the chapel casements were on another side of the edifice.

She laid the key beside her, and long tried, but in vain, to compose her senses to sleep. Toward the morning, however, she closed her eyes, and when she awoke, the remembrance of the strange occurrences of the past night crowded to her recollection. Hastily she looked for the key, which she beheld in the same place as she had left it.

Agatha now arose, and having placed it in the corner of a deep recess which was in her chamber, she sat ruminating on Ferdinando, and enjoying the fond idea that, now she probably had it in her power to leave the convent with him. She looked forward with anxiety to the next night, when she should know whether she had been feeding herself with delusive hopes, respecting her deliverance or not. And she also reflected, that on the third night, if Ferdinando recollected his promise, she should have the happiness of again seeing him, and perhaps of having her dream sweetly realized.

According to custom the Abbess after the morning service sent for Agatha and the other noviciates, and read to them a pious exhortation, in which was set forth the happiness of a conventual life; and the certainty of future bliss that awaited its votaries.

Agatha paid little attention to the words of the Abbess, her thoughts were intently fixed on Ferdinando, and her dream of the preceding night. She once raised her eyes to the place where she had observed the singularly constructed key to hang, but it was no longer there.

The supernatural means by which it had been conveyed to her, while it made her shudder with sensations of terror, yet afforded her real delight, since she conceived that some kind power was interested in what she thought was her welfare.

The discourse of the Abbess was insupportably tedious, and when at length Agatha was dismissed, she retired to her chamber, where she could ruminate at leisure on the prospect of happiness that was now opening to her view.

Night, that shares with day the empire of the world, at length threw her shadowy veil over the face of nature; and Agatha, who had long watched from her casement the increasing gloom, arose, and taking the key and a lamp in her hand, softly left her chamber, and descending the stairs at the extremity of the corridore, entered the passage that led to the chapel.

With an agitated pace she advanced toward the gate and tried the key in the lock, the bolt flew back, and Agatha trembled with excess of delight at beholding the gate open, and the only seeming impediment that had existed against her gaining her liberty removed.

Having carefully locked the gate she returned to her chamber, and placing the key in its secret repository retired to her couch, where she long lay awake enjoying the pleasing idea of speedy emancipation.

At length to the delighted view of Agatha, the sun sinking behind the western hills left to the pale nocturnal lamp her wonted empire over the silent face of creation, on the night when she expected Ferdinando. With majestic splendor the silvery orb attended by myriads of bright satellites rising from the dark waving summit of an extensive forest, threw over them her radiant beams, and tipped with silver the heads of the tall mountains. Not a cloud obscured the azure arch of Heaven from the wondering gaze of silent contemplation. But no celestial meditations existed in the bosom of Agatha, there were only nurtured the worst of human passions; and her bosom panted not with the sensations of the rapt enthusiast when beholding the sublime works of an incomprehensible Being, but with the fond expectation of leaving her present seclusion, and of sating the unruly tumult of sensual ideas that the captivating form of Ferdinando had raised in her distempered imagination.

The hour appointed for her meeting with that Signor was now proclaimed from the highest turret of the monastic pile, and as the sounds retreated on the bosom of the nocturnal breeze, Agatha arose, and taking the key, descended to the chapel.

Punctual to his promise, Ferdinando in the tenderest language of love, which sweetly sounded in the pleased ears of Agatha, hailed her as she approached to the gate; but when he saw her hand, which trembling with the various emotions that agitated her bosom, long time essayed in vain to turn back the bolt of the lock, his sensation of expectation and astonishment, of hope and fear, kept him silent. At length the gate opened, and he held to his bosom the panting form of the lovely Agatha.

The most impressive language that ever the fervent lover poured forth to the sweet idol of his heart would be inadequate to describe the sensations of Agatha and Ferdinando, when in mutual embrace they beheld themselves free from the cruel restraint imposed on them by the grating. They were silent, but that silence how expressive! their eyes wandered over each other, they seemed to read in each others souls the sweet expressions which their agitated sensations rendered it in vain for them to utter.

But those sensations how unworthy to hold a place in minds endued with reason; how did they prove the degeneracy of human nature? and sink it almost to a level with the brute creation.

A smile of pleasure sat on the features of the Demon, who from his horrific abode piercing the gloomy condensing volumes of smoke which rose from the eternal flames of divine wrath, beheld the pair embracing each other in the chapel of Santa Catherina. The pollution of a place dedicated to the worship of

Saints afforded him the greatest satisfaction, and for a while made him forgetful of his fallen state, since he beheld his empire extending around, and vice increasing in her dreadful sway over the hearts of mankind.

Let a veil be drawn over the actions of that night which proved how great is the influence of the passions over those minds who have once deviated from the paths of virtue. The chapel of Santa Catherina beheld the guilty pair wantoning in the fulfilment of their wishes till the grey dawn made their long untrimmed lamps almost useless.

They now saw their error in not leaving the convent when they met. It was now too late; in another hour Agatha's flight would be discovered; Ferdinando was therefore compelled to defer till the next night the liberation of the nun; and then hastily left the companion of his deeds of darkness ere the morning sun should reveal them to the world.

Agatha retired to her chamber; the powers of reflection weakened by the frequency of her guilty acts, prevented not the influence of sleep, on her weary eyes; and it was not until the bell had summoned the inhabitants of the convent to the chapel that the somniferous deity left her to proceed to another hemisphere, where other worlds awaited his welcome approach.

Borne on the tedious wings of time passed the lengthening hours of day, and when at length the pale luminary of night held her silent reign, attended by myriads of scintillating orbs, Agatha hailed her approach as the harbinger of her emancipation, and her mind began to anticipate the first scenes of voluptuous dissipation that would await her when again restored to the world.

At the appointed time she entered the chapel. The beams of the moon streaming through the casements shone full on the statue of the Virgin; it attracted the notice of Agatha, and as she gazed on the lovely countenance, the remembrance of the deeds of the past night rushed full upon her mind.

It was then that pallid fear drove away the roses of pleasure from her countenance. She trembled as she lightly paced the centre aisle of the chapel, for a consciousness of the guilt of her past conduct, of her dreadful profanation of the purposes to which that edifice was erected, made her feel sensations of remorse, though steeled as her breast had long been against the sting of conscience.

She went to the gate, and leaning against a column long waited for the coming of Ferdinando, anxiously listening for the welcome echo of his paces. But the gloomy silence remained undisturbed; and the long sounding hour of midnight arrived without bringing with it the expected Signor.

The breast of Agatha grew every moment more agitated; she unlocked the gate, and advanced to the portal of the chapel which communicated with the monastery. There she stood bending forward in the passage, and holding her lamp high up in order that its rays might penetrate further into the gloom, and shew her the wished-for form of Ferdinando when he should approach.

The clock of the monastery now struck one, and still Ferdinando came not; the breeze of morn made her tremble under its chilly influence. Sighing she left the portal and retraced her slow melancholy steps to the gate of the skreen, while words of self-reproach proceeded from her pale lips.

"Fool that I was to yield to the impetuous dictates of passion; but for that I might have been now blessed with my liberty. Ferdinando has gained his object, and he has now deserted me. Was I to learn that enjoyment which increases the love of woman totally estranges it from the heart of man? Silly Agatha, thou at least hadst no occasion for further experience; thou hast then thyself only to blame. While the raging flames of unsated desire pervaded his frame, what would he not have dared to have gained my emancipation? But now he no longer thinks on me; or if he does, a smile of exultation marks his countenance at my folly in believing his vows, and consequent acquiescence to his wishes."

Thus through the tedious night did Agatha repine at what was now too late to alter; and at length she beheld the grey dawning of morn, and the dark folds of night departing to hold their reign in other worlds. She then locked the gate, cast one more despairing look down the grand aisle, and sorrowfully departed to her chamber, which with increasing agony of mind she paced till warned to attend the matin service in the chapel.

When she entered her eyes were immediately directed to the skreen, but no Ferdinando was there. She opened not her mouth during the service, she was unconscious of what was passing about her; her hopes of escaping from a life so odious to her now began to decrease, and as that tranquillizer of the bosoms of the unhappy fled, despair and horror filled the dreary void.

The coming night she again visited the chapel; she stood listening to the melancholy tones of the clock as it proclaimed the departing hours; but no other sounds broke on the silence that reigned in undisturbed horror in the gloomy and extensive chapel of the monastery and convent of Santa Catherina. All hopes of Ferdinando's coming now entirely deserted her, and she formed the dangerous resolution of endeavouring to find out the way by which he had entered the monastery, determined to make her escape by it.

Entering the aisle she proceeded to the portals; which having cautiously opened, she lightly trod the marble pavement of the lofty corridor, almost afraid, yet urged to proceed by her new-born hopes of escape. She advanced nearly to the extremity of the passage, examining the several doors which were on each side of it, but did not dare to open them, lest they should belong to the chambers of the monks.

At the extremity of the corridore which opened into a large hall rose a magnificent flight of stairs which communicated with a large gallery that was raised round it. As she was going to enter the hall Agatha suddenly stopped, and then hastily retreated, for she plainly heard several footsteps in the gallery above, and a light flashed on the sides of the hall; terrified at this, and finding the paces increasing and the sounds of several voices above, she flew with dreadful apprehension of being discovered toward the chapel, and as she was proceeding down the aisle the grand bell of the convent began to toll. Agatha's trembling hands could hardly lock the gate, and scarcely had she entered her chamber when she heard the steps of the nuns, who, alarmed at the unusual tolling of the bell, were hastening to the chapel whither it warned them.

CHAPTER IX.

WHEN the first beams of the morning shot over the eastern mountains the Marchese de Carlentini arose, and, attended by the steward of the Castello and two domestics, proceeded toward the South Angle Tower.

Crossing the grass-grown court-yard that led to that wing, the portals of the South Hall being thrown open, disclosed a structure so spacious and gloomy that the heart of Ricardo, already saddened with the anticipation of what would meet his view in the Tower, was doubly sensible of the silent horror that seemed to reign in these deserted walls.

The centre of the hall was of great width and height; the vaulted roof was supported by lofty columns that rose in majestic grandeur on each side; long casements, which formerly served to admit the cheering beams of the sun, were above the galleries, which were likewise supported by columns; beneath them were another range of casements, which once gave light to the lower, as those above did to the upper parts of the hall, but now the ivy wound about the broken panes, and the diligent spider wove there his snareful web. The columns were adorned with spoils of the contested field, and the torn banners waved mournfully to the blast that rushing through the broken casements sighed along the galleries.

Ricardo paused as he passed through the hall to contemplate the ravages of the destructive hand of Time. Many of the rafters which supported the roof had fallen on the marble pavement, and some seemed just deserting their hold, and only awaiting the next blast to increase the ruins below.

The armour which had so greatly alarmed him on that memorable night when he first entered the hall was still lying in a heap at the foot of the column, and he directed his people to replace it in its former situation.

That done, he went on to the passage where Grimaldi had so successfully alarmed him. Arrived at the extremity, a winding stair-case met his view, which he descended, and found it led to a large corridore, of which nothing but the walls remained; with some difficulty he passed over the crumbling ruins of the roof, but no door or outlet met their search. Ricardo with the assistance of some fallen rafters raised himself sufficiently high to look out of a dismantled casement, and saw beneath him a court wild and grass-grown, and the well-known black rugged walls of the Angle Tower rearing aloft their threatening heads, its embattled turrets far o'er-hanging the base, and were crowned with long rank weeds that mournfully rustled when agitated by the wind.

From its situation Ricardo became convinced that the corridore must have some communication with the Tower, and directing his people to clear away a heap of rubbish which had fallen against the end wall, after some time and trouble found a small door, which having opened, the party cautiously passed along a narrow passage, for the bending rafters of the floor threatened to give way and precipitate them to the chambers below. They now gained a narrow flight of stone steps, and Ricardo shuddered to think that he was within the walls of the Tower where his mother's blood had been shed. A dreadful execration at the remembrance of Grimaldi's acts arose in his breast and had nearly escaped his lips, but he checked the rising tempest of his soul, for Grimaldi was now doubtless suffering for his guilty acts.

The steps were lighted by long narrow apertures which were made in the wall, and enabled Ricardo and his party to find their way. At length they came to a door, which, from Grimaldi's description, must belong to the chamber where the hapless Theodora met her fate. Ricardo trembled, and when the steward had opened it, hardly dared to examine the dusky interior. The men likewise stopped, and an awful pause took place.

Ricardo at length looked forward, but the objects in the chamber were involved in obscurity; all the casements save one were closed, and that faintly admitted the beams of day.

One of the men slowly entering went to the casement, which he opened, and tore down the ivy that had clung to the stone divisions. Ricardo now saw an old dirty couch, covered with damps and mildew, in one corner of the chamber; he looked on it with a steadfast tearful gaze, expecting to see the bones of his mother. Such a spectacle was, however, spared him; the couch contained them not; other parts of the chamber were examined, but the remains of Theodora were not to be found.

Ricardo was now lost in wonder. From the description which Grimaldi gave him in the papers of the prison of the Marchesa, it was perfectly evident that the one he was now in must have been that where he gave vent to the vital current of her existence.

He then looked on the floor, but it was covered so thick with the accumulated dust of fifteen years that the boards could not be seen. On removing it, however, Ricardo clearly discovered the traces of blood on some of them, and the melancholy evidence, while it made him certain he was in the room where his mother was confined and murdered, increased his astonishment, for he was certain that Grimaldi had not consigned her remains to the tomb; and from the behaviour of the Marchese, when he solicited permission to examine the tower, it was also evident that he had not concealed them. Indeed the keys that led to the Tower being always in the possession of Grimaldi, he could not have interred the remains of his wife without Grimaldi's knowledge; he was therefore bewildered in a maze of conjectures which increased every moment.

In the idea, however, that there might be a similar chamber, Ricardo proceeded by a long passage to the opposite side, but he became convinced, on examining the different rooms, the one he first entered was that alluded to by Grimaldi.

He again narrowly examined every part of the chamber, and at length retired, perfectly convinced that the object of his search was not there.

In crossing the South Hall, having observed on one side two large folding portals, curiosity made him approach them, and having caused them to be opened, he beheld a chapel, whose spacious dimensions caused an involuntary exclamation of surprize to escape his lips.

It appeared evident to him that the southern parts of the Castello had been erected many years before the north, and that this chapel contained the remains of the ancient founders of the extensive pile.

He lightly trod the long-drawn aisle while awful reflections sunk deep into his soul. The monuments of his ancestors rose thickly around him; the figures recumbent on the tombs engaged his attention, they were for the most part formed of brass, and grey marble; that which appeared to be the effigy of the long in-urned body of the founder of the ancient pile was the representation of a knight, formed of black marble, resting on a magnificent tomb of the same materials in his coat armor; a stone slab supported by four emblematic figures served as a canopy to the tomb, and on it was laid the rusty remains of the armor worn by the knight.

Ricardo endeavoured to read the inscription, but time had defaced the letters, and his curiosity remained unsatisfied. He looked around him, but the other tombs were far inferior in magnificence, and only attracted his momentary gaze.

Ah! thought he, how vain is the pageantry that is displayed here, how humble is now your pride, the poorest menial occupies as much room as the remains of him on whose nod he submissively attended; the form that once was clothed in that cumbrous armor is now a heap of dust, the leavings of the loathsome worm.

This train of reflections, however, did not long inhabit the mind of Ricardo, a mystery yet seemed to be connected with the Angle Tower which now appeared to be inexplicable, for only Grimaldi could explain it, and he was no more.

He left the chapel, and having examined all the apartments which communicated with the hall, ordered the portals to be closed, and hastened to relate to Louisa the event of his researches.

She was greatly astonished at the account, and found herself unable to say any thing that could serve to allay the astonishment and rouse from his meditations the Marchese de Carlentini.

Weeks and months now rolled on, and Ricardo began to emerge from his train of melancholy ideas respecting the unfortunate Theodora in the contemplation of an event which was the bar to his perfect felicity in his union with Louisa. In a few weeks she would become a mother to an infant who after his decease would have no means of existence, as the estate would then pass into other hands; he was, however, determined not to mention this circumstance to Louisa till she was able to bear it without affecting her health, which now began to be very delicate.

Louisa, who little expected the impending blow which would strike at the root of her happiness, hailed with the greatest delight the moment that made her a mother; she kissed and bedewed with tears of joy the rosy cheeks of a lovely infant, the pledge of her tender affection for Ricardo, and the pen is not adequate to express her delight when she saw him embracing his boy, who greatly resembled them both in the interesting beauties which dwelt in his countenance.

But the happiness of Louisa lasted not long; two months had elapsed, and Ricardo, trembling with anxiety for the result, began to prepare the mind of Louisa for what must take place.

He informed her of the state of his pecuniary affairs, and as no provision could be made sufficient for the young Ricardo to support the elevated rank to which he must attain on his decease, the church was the only place which held out her fostering arms for him, and slightly hinted that the sooner he was taken from them, the less would be their affliction, for every day their love for their dear offspring increased, and, in consequence, so would their affliction at parting with him.

Great was the grief of Louisa as she clasped the little infant to her maternal bosom, and looked at Ricardo with a countenance so full of melancholy, that, unable to bear the sight, he hastily left the apartment and wandered on the dark recesses of the neighbouring forest, and for the first time reflected with some asperity on the inconsiderate conduct of his father, who had by his dreadful propensity for gambling and dissipation deprived his son of the means of supporting his family.

He saw that it would be almost necessary, to prevent the increasing fondness of Louisa for her infant, to send him from the Castello, and accordingly when he returned to it he wrote to the abbot of whom mention has already been made, informing him

of the birth of his son, and claiming the performance of his promise respecting him; he ordered a man to carry his letter the next
morning to the monastery where the venerable father presided,
and then endeavoured, with the joint efforts of the tender Signora
Bononi, to comfort his afflicted Louisa, and prepare her for the
approaching separation.

On the third day the messenger arrived from the abbot with a
packet for Ricardo, who having broke the seal, read the following
lines:—

"My son, I have perused your letter, and with the assistance
of the blessed Saints will perform my promise. I will take an active
interest in your behalf, for I feel for your situation. Your child may
be brought up in the village near the monastery, I will see that
all due attention be paid to his tender years, and should mine be
permitted to increase, he shall be instructed by me and the holy
fathers to the extent of our poor abilities. Farewell, my son; may
the Saints take you and yours in their holy keeping. The blessings
of the church attend you."

The next morning the little Ricardo, attended by his nurse,
left the Castello. Great was the misery of Louisa, but she was
obliged to give way to imperious necessity, and also to endeavour
to appear composed, that she might not add to the distress of her
fond husband.

The child when it arrived at the monastery was solemnly dedicated at the grand altar to the service of the church, and when
that ceremony was performed, was sent to the village, where,
under the auspices of the good abbot, he was to remain till of a
proper age to enter the holy walls of the monastery, where he was
to pass the future years of his existence.

In order that no future regret might disturb the happiness of
his life, the Marchese requested of the abbot that the name of his
son should be changed, and that he should remain in ignorance of
the rank he was entitled to by his birth.

Time with his lenient hand in some degree softened the sorrows that had long reigned in the bosom of the Marchese and
Louisa on account of their son, who now devoted to the service
of the church, was entirely lost to them, when intelligence was

received of the death of the Signor Valvano, and which was shortly after followed by the arrival of a messenger with his will, in
which he had bequeathed a large portion of his immense wealth
to Ricardo.

At first the news increased their grief, since what unhappiness
might they not have prevented if they had not been so hasty in
parting with their infant, but this was in some measure alleviated
from the circumstance of Louisa's being likely to produce another pledge of her love for her lord, which now, in consequence of
Valvano's legacy, would remain with them.

The bequest of Valvano not only enabled the Marchese to
redeem his estate, but also to make various alterations in the
Castello, and take from it that ruinous appearance which rendered it an unfit residence for a nobleman of his rank.

In process of time the Marchesa was delivered of a daughter,
which was named Angelina, in compliment to the Conte Angelo,
a distant relation of Ricardo's. Great was the joy both within and
without the Castello, for the peasants partook of the happiness
of their lord, whose kind conduct toward them was rewarded by
their ardent prayers which they unceasingly offered up to Heaven
in his favour, and its blessings which they each moment called
down on him.

The Count de Leoni on receiving the pleasing information
of his friend's increase of fortune, repaired to the Castello to con-
gratulate him upon it, and happily passed the hours in the enjoyment and anticipation of future days and years of increasing
comfort. One circumstance only clouded the bosom of Ricardo,
and that was the mystery that hung over the fate of his mother.
Nothing had occurred since his search that could tend to throw
the smallest light on the dark transactions of the Padre Grimaldi.
At times many hopes would arise in his bosom, but they were
soon dissipated by the perusal of the papers which that monk had
committed to his hands.

Louisa had now to endure the severe loss of an affectionate
mother; for some time her health had been declining, and it was
now evident to all that she was fast hastening to the period of her
existence. She was prepared for it, and awaited the awful moment

with a calm composure, in the pleasing hope that her blameless life would be rewarded with eternal happiness.

"Do not weep, my beloved Louisa," were her last words, "a few short years, and we shall meet again in Heaven. I leave you in the highest state of human felicity, in the possession of innocence and virtue, and blessed with a husband who loves you. Should any adversities assail you, be not dismayed, resist them with a steady fortitude, and in every situation of life fail not to keep a firm reliance on Him who is all powerful. My soul longs for eternity; it is anxious to quit this earthly receptacle, to wing its rapid flight to the footstool of its Creator, and join in eternal hymns of praise with the celestial myriads who throng to offer up the grateful tribute of their adoration. Heavenly father," she continued, after a pause occasioned by the pains of dissolution, raised her languid eyes toward the heavens, "bless, I humbly beseech thee, with the choicest of thy gifts a virtuous and contented mind, my Louisa and her Ricardo, and may we meet, when it shall please thee, in the bright regions of eternity."

Death now hasted on with rapid strides, and stopped the further current of her speech; she looked at Louisa, gently pressed her hand, and for ever left the world.

Over the griefs of Ricardo and Louisa we will draw a veil; both, indeed, deeply regretted her loss, but the sorrows of Louisa far exceeded those of Ricardo, for the tenderest and most affectionate of mothers was to her the lamented Signora Bononi.

END OF VOLUME TWO.

THE
DEMON OF SICILY.

CHAPTER X.

DEATH with his restless sable pinions now hovered over the monastery of Santa Catherina; his intended victim was the venerable Abbot, who, now on the verge of immortality, was going to reap the reward of a well-spent life. Feeling the near approach of the relentless power who sooner or later pays his chilling visitation to all human beings, he signified his wish to be conveyed to the altar, that he might there breathe forth his last prayer while yet he retained the power of speech.

The great bell of the monastery announced to the inhabitants the situation of the Abbot, for on such an occasion only was it tolled; and the monks immediately arose to attend their superior, and supplicate by their prayers for the happy reception of his soul in the blissful regions of Paradise.

On this solemn occasion the Abbess, with her long train of nuns and boarders, entered with a slow and solemn pace into the chapel. Among them was Agatha, yet trembling with the terror she had endured of being discovered, and suffering the most dreadful despondency of mind, for even Hope, that consoler of the wretched, had fled far from her.

A strain of heavenly harmony now floated on the air; the notes were plaintive; it was the service for the dying; it was a supplication to the Almighty to pardon the sins of the departing soul, and to permit its reception in the regions of eternal bliss.

The venerable Abbot lay in a litter on the marble steps of the high altar; on his breast was a crucifix, and in his now almost nerveless hand lay his rosary. His eyes, dim with the shades of death, were fixed on the statue of the Virgin; he regarded it with pleasure; he essayed to speak, but the powers of utterance were no more. His moving lips spoke him engaged in prayer; a slight tremor now seized his aged frame, and on the gale that bore the harmonious strains that then filled the chapel to the heavens, ascended the spotless soul of the Abbot.

An awful pause succeeded, which was only interrupted by deep sighs; every one lamented the loss of the good Abbot, who for more than twenty years had presided over the monastery.

Again did the solemn harmony, which was increased by the tremulous tones of the afflicted monks, break on the melancholy silence; and when the service was concluded, the pale remains of the Abbot were borne back to his chamber, and the nuns retired from the awful scene.

Padre Ignazio succeeded to the elevated station of Abbot of Santa Catherina. He was a man of a stern and unbending disposition, of austere and repulsive manners, and the nuns and monks, in the various new regulations he subjected them to, found they had daily fresh cause to regret the mild sway of the late venerable Abbot.

Thus the situation of Agatha became every day more irksome. Formed as her ideas were for sensual and voluptuous gratifications, how miserable must be her life in the gloomy seclusions of a cloister.

Several nights she had passed in the chapel, but still no Ferdinando came; and at length she desisted from her nocturnal visits, and frequently in all the agonies of hopeless grief would pace the narrow confines of her chamber, while the earth was under the silent dominion of night and sleep.

Days, weeks, and months rolled on, each minute of which witnessed the sorrows of Agatha. The festival of Santa Catherina was near approaching, and at that time she was to take the irrevocable vows of seclusion from the world.

One evening when the service in the chapel was nearly concluded, Agatha beheld the form of a man enveloped in a mantle approach the skreen; her heart beat with increasing agitation, and she fixed her gaze on him; when removing his cloak, she saw with the greatest delight the well-remembered countenance of Ferdinando. But his cheeks were no longer the abode of rosy health, they were pale and hollow, his eyes had lost all their fire, and his form was greatly emaciated.

Agatha turned pale on observing the change that had taken place in Ferdinando. She was, however, pleased with seeing him once more; and Hope, which had so long deserted her, again enlivened her heart with her cheering rays.

The service being concluded, the Abbess was returning to the convent, and Agatha lingered behind the train that she might attract the notice of Ferdinando: he knew her notwithstanding her veil; and as she was passing near the skreen, he took a paper from beneath his mantle and endeavoured to throw it toward her; it however unfortunately fell at the feet of another nun, who immediately picked it up, and looking at Agatha, for whom she saw it was designed, put it into her bosom and walked on.

Words are inadequate to describe the feelings of Agatha and Ferdinando, who also witnessed the untoward circumstance; he retired hastily from the chapel, and Agatha continued in the train, though her agitation was so great as almost to deprive her of the power of motion.

It cannot be supposed that such a disposition as Agatha's could have procured her any friends in the convent; on the contrary, her haughty bearing caused her many enemies; and sister Marianne, who had so unfortunately picked up the packet destined for her, had great reason, amongst many others, to rejoice in having it in her power to draw on her the severe reproof and punishment which the superior would not fail to inflict when apprized of her actions.

The moment the Abbess had dismissed them, Marianne hastened to her chamber to peruse the contents of the letter; which she found to be as follows:—

"LOVELY AGATHA,

"Misfortunes crowding on each other have hitherto pursued me; yet do not imagine, beloved idol of my heart, that your sweet beauties have ever been absent from my memory. With gratitude do I remember that night which gave to my arms the only woman I can ever adore. To-night let me see you; let me

again hold you to my heart, and consult with you on the subject
of your release from the gloomy seclusion you have so long endured.

"FERDINANDO."

The nun shrunk with horror from the view of the epistle
which disclosed such a sinful transaction, and determined to acquaint the abbess the next morning with Agatha's wicked deeds.
She then devoutly crossed herself, and kneeling before her crucifix thanked the Saints for having preserved her from such deeds of
horror.

Meantime dreadful were the sensations which agitated the
bosom of Agatha; she was ignorant of the contents of the billet,
and feared the worst that could befal her; namely, the exposition
of the acts of that guilty night when she last saw Ferdinando, and
her consequent punishment, which would probably extend to her
life. She was not able to descend to the refectory that evening,
but agitated with a chaos of distracting thoughts, remained in her
chamber in an agony of mind which baffles description.

Weary at length with walking about, she threw herself into a
seat, and giving way to her sad ruminations and dreadful anticipations of what she would suffer on the morrow, the clock of the
monastery unnoticed sounded the lengthening hours.

Favorable was the situation of Agatha's mind for the dreadful
deeds which the Demon wished to make her perpetrate; and at
that hour when he was permitted to visit the world he entered her
chamber. Agatha started at beholding the tall figure of a monk
stand before her, and she was on the point of uttering an exclamation of affright, when he thus addressed her:—

"Agatha, do not give way to needless alarm. Behold when you
least expected it, but when you are most in need, a friend ready to
assist you with such counsel as will ease you of your present fears
and keep the knowledge of your crimes a secret."

"Father," replied the trembling Agatha, "such a friend is indeed invaluable. But say, how did you come to the knowledge of
these acts which thou hast hinted at? Has Marianne disclosed her
having received a paper intended for me?"

"Agatha, some time ago thou mayest recollect having received the key of the gate in the skreen. Call to thy remembrance the dream that attended that circumstance. Thou hast seen me before."

The nun trembled at the idea that now arose to her mind that the person before her was a supernatural being. The Demon well knew her thoughts, and hasted to hinder her fears from protracting the time till he should be obliged to return to his chaotic abode of eternal horrors.

"Thou hast rightly thought, Agatha; I am a being possessed of great power, and though subject to Him who resides in the Heavens, yet numberless as the stars which glitter on its surface are the beings who bend before me. I took pity on you, I brought you the key, which from its situation you could never have obtained. You are now on the brink of danger, and I come to save you from the impending ruin that tottering at its base will soon overwhelm you."

"And can you indeed save me?" replied the delighted, astonished Agatha. "Ah! name the means—let me hear them, let me rejoice in my security, my sufferings have been dreadful; haste to relieve me of the insupportable burthen."

"It can only be effected by the death of Marianne," replied the Demon.

Agatha started; pale horrors shook her frame, she had indeed been guilty of many sinful acts, but murder was new to her.

"Is there no other way," said she as soon as she was able to speak, "to save me than by her death? Dreadful thought! I cannot reconcile myself to be accessary to such a deed."

"And where is the harm," said the Demon with a malicious smile; "in the exposition that she will make to the abbess to-morrow will not Marianne seek your life? If attacked by your own species, is there any harm, think you, in saving yourself by their destruction? Self-preservation is the first law of Nature, and in terminating the existence of Marianne you do but obey its dictates."

Agatha shook her head; she was still irresolute.

"Listen thou to your fate," said the Demon. "By this time to-morrow you will be confined in a dungeon far beneath the surface of the earth, the abode of loathsome animals and fœtid vapours; there chained to the earth in utter darkness, you will be barely kept alive by bread black and mouldy, and water taken from the green mantled pool. Soon your shrunken form will

The Demon appearing to Agatha.

shew the bones ready to start from beneath their enclosure; but you will still cling to existence, and will languish many a month in the endurance of all the torturous sensations that ever found a place in the minds of mortals. And when at length the last gasp of breath has departed your skeleton form, your bones will become the sport of venomous reptiles, and in your hollow skull will the viper and toad reside."

This speech had no sooner passed the lips of the Demon than Agatha, overcome by the dreadful picture he had drawn of her sufferings, determined to commit any deed, however horrible, rather than subject herself to them.

"You have prevailed," said she to the Demon in a tremulous tone; "but how shall Marianne die without incurring suspicion?"

The Demon was pleased to find Agatha willing to commit the crime of murder, than which nothing could afford him such real pleasure; his joy at beholding the murderer in the commission of that act still was as great as when for the first time he saw the earth stained with blood, and the smoke of it ascending to Heaven in damning evidence against the homicide.

"Sister Ursula," he replied, "is skilled in medicinal knowledge; the chamber next to her is appropriated to the purpose of containing the various inventions of the laboratory; repair there this night, and in the corner at the right side you will see a green phial; its contents are of such a nature as will instantly arrest the vital powers; the blood will cease to circulate, and hang curdled in the veins: a small portion will be sufficient for your purpose, and when at the morning repast contrive to mix it with the drink of Marianne; you will then be secure. The billet of Ferdinando you must however be careful to possess yourself of; you will find it in her bosom; you will see him on the following night. Be resolute, or you will endure the horrid torments I have but now foretold you of."

This said, the Demon, satisfied that he had sufficiently persuaded the hapless Agatha to the commission of the horrible act, suddenly receded from her sight, and in an instant of time was at the entrance of the straights which connect the Mediterranean and Atlantic oceans, where he stirred up the bloody-minded Moors to murder and unheard of acts of barbarous revenge against each other. Seated on the highest pinnacle of the aspiring rock of Gibraltar he glutted his pleased sight with the dreadful scenes produced by him and his infernal agents.

Agatha, when she saw the misty form vanish from her sight,

sunk almost insensible into her chair, where she long remained enduring those agonies which disturb the mind between the resolution of performing and the perpetration of deeds of blood and horror. She found that either Marianne or herself must perish. Struck with this truth she at length arose, and taking her dim untrimmed lamp found out the chamber described by the Demon. The door was not fastened; she entered and looking around saw the fatal phial; a sudden chill pervaded her frame as she stretched out her arm and took it down, her countenance was blanched with her internal agitations, and she hastily left the chamber, and entering her own sat down, to recover if possible from the horrors she endured.

The rosy-fingered morn, unconscious of the dark crimes that would sully the day she was now producing to the world, brightly gleamed in the eastern horizon with streaks of golden hue; the light and airy clouds that here and there floated in the vast ethereal expanse soon were irradiated with the bright rays of the glowing luminary of Heaven, who rising above the covert of the mountains, threw his broad beams over the gladdened face of Nature.

The convent bell now tolled for the matin prayer: every stroke of the ponderous hammer sadly reverberated on the soul of Agatha; she looked on them as the funeral knell of Marianne; she however endeavoured to dismiss sensations which would incapacitate her for what she was going to perform.

She took the phial, and concealing it in the folds of her garments, left her chamber, and descended to the chapel, while busy fancy made her suppose every eye fixed on her as seeing the dark intents of her soul. Marianne and Agatha mutually endeavoured to avoid each other; Marianne from the horror she had conceived of the guilty acts of Agatha, and she from the force of sensations occasioned by her dreadful designs against the existence of the nun.

The service being concluded, it now approached the moment of action. The nuns were assembling in the refectory, when Agatha, pressing forward, contrived, as she passed by the seat of Marianne, to pour some of the contents of the phial into the glass which contained her beverage. As the nuns had not taken their places at the table, she was unobserved, and she soon after beheld her victim drink the fatal draught.

In the course of a short space of time the effect took place; Marianne complained of being unwell, and soon after fell senseless on the floor. Agatha hastily ran to assist her, and contrived during the confusion to take away the billet of Ferdinando, which she found in her bosom, according to the information she had received from the Demon.

Marianne was now carried to her chamber, where every exertion was made by sister Ursula to recover her; but no motion, no feeble pulsation gave proof that the breath of life yet lingered in her pale form, and preparations were made for her interment in the convent cemetery.

Claudina, a nun of Santa Catherina, was the bosom-friend of the unfortunate Marianne. She wept unceasingly for her loss, nor could she be prevailed on to quit for a moment the pallid remains.

When the sable investiture of night descended from the heavens, Marianne was borne to the gloomy regions of death. Sobs and tears bespoke the feelings of the sisterhood, but Claudina in silent anguish beheld the earth heaped over the friend of her heart.

Conscience, how deeply didst thou dart into the panting bosom of Agatha thy torturous sting; no herb, no power is there in medicine to allay the fever of the mind. Often did her senses appear ready to desert her, but the fears of being discovered alone made her able to support the trying moment. When the remains of Marianne were laid in the cold bosom of the tomb, gladly she retired from the sad scene, and hastening to her chamber, sought, by thinking of her present security, to calm the emotions which tormented her.

She had perused the billet of Ferdinando, and sighed to think that he had in vain waited for her the past night; conceiving, however, that it was probable he would enter the chapel that night, she determined to go there and attend his arrival, which would serve to relieve her mind from the anguish it endured; and she hoped too that she should soon be far from the convent, which was now become insupportable to her.

Claudina remained in the cemetery; seated on the grave of Marianne, she poured forth the sorrows of her heart.

"Beloved friend," said she, "how great is the distance between our souls, which once vibrated with delight at the sound of each others voice. No more shall I enjoy the dear pleasure of seeing you; no more hear those accents, those declarations of friendship, so sincere, so disinterested. Oh, Marianne! you, you are alive to happiness; 'tis I that am dead to comfort, to all that can make existence supportable. Did I not know that your pure soul is now in the presence of its Creator, and insensate to the griefs of Claudina, I should call it unkind that it did not assume the earthly form which once pleased my delighted gaze, and hover over me, to give me some consolation, to inspire me with fortitude to bear thy loss."

Here floods of tears rendered Claudina incapable of speech; the lamp, which she placed near her on the earth became every minute more dim, its weak rays now glanced on the nearest hill-ocks beneath which rested the mouldering remains of the nuns of Santa Catherina. Suddenly the powers of speech and of recollection were renewed, and Claudina exclaimed:

"Yes; it was the morning of this day, when Nature awoke to fresh animation, that Marianne was alive. She greeted me in her usual manner, embraced me as she was wont to do. What a change! Beneath this new-raised earth, in the cold womb of the tomb, she now lies, her form is for ever hid from my view. To-morrow will come, and I shall not see her; days, months, and years will roll on, but they will not bring Marianne to me."

Thus mourned the disconsolate Claudina, her tears frequently interrupting her sad speech; at length she sunk insensible on the grave, and in that state continued some hours; but when the returning powers of animation enabled her to arise, she took up her lamp, and turning her tearful gaze on the grave, sighed deeply; and slowly leaving the cemetery, passed through the chapel to her chamber in the convent.

It was at the moment she sighed that the monk Bernardo had

effected an entrance, for purposes known only to himself, into the cemetery of the convent and it was her figure which had so greatly alarmed him as to make him abandon his evil projects.

Agatha, after the interment of Marianne, had immediately proceeded to her chamber, where she remained till it was near midnight, the time that Ferdinando usually arrived in the chapel; she then went to the gate, where she found him waiting.

"Dearest Agatha," said he, "at last am I blest with your presence. Great as have been my sufferings since I saw you, the sweet pleasure I enjoy this moment overpays me; but what did I not endure when I beheld the failure of the billet I endeavoured to throw toward you. Tell me, dearest Agatha, was it perused by the nun, or did you contrive to get it from her?"

The countenance of Agatha was as the lily cut down by the bleak blast of night; a deadly paleness overspread her features, she trembled, and was silent, for she reflected that but a short time before she had seen that hapless nun laid in the silent grave.

Ferdinando beheld her emotions; he knew not what to ascribe them to; he hasted to support her, for she seemed sinking on the marble floor of the chapel, while her eyes rolled about with the wild unsettled gaze of delirium.

"I got it from her," she replied at length in a low voice, rendered almost inarticulate by the inexpressible emotions of her breast; "question me no further about it. Was I not advised to do it? Yes. I am safe; she cannot betray me—her voice is silent. . . . Hark! did I not hear her? See! see! her pale form now flits before me, half veiled in the shades of night."

"Agatha, my love," said Ferdinando, "recollect yourself. Your senses wander. Why do you thus wildly roll your eyes about, and utter such unconnected sentences?"

Agatha now began to rouse herself from the horrible imaginings of a guilty conscience, and fearing that the dreadful secret of her heart had escaped her in the distracted ravings of the moment, she endeavoured to recover herself, and to learn whether Ferdinando had come to the knowledge of the deed which the Demon of darkness had stirred her up to perform.

She soon, however, was convinced that he was as yet ignorant

of the extent of her guilt; and as soon as she was able, she endeavoured to account for the great perturbation of her mind, alledging as a reason the affliction she had endured at his long absence,
and the consequent total failure of her hopes of escaping from
her detested situation.

Ferdinando endeavoured to comfort her: he drew her toward
him, and tenderly embracing her, renewed his protestations of
love for her, and his intention of effecting her escape. "But at
present, dear Agatha," said he, "from the very weak state of my
almost exhausted frame, you will yourself easily judge it impossible for me to be able to undertake so important a circumstance,
which will call forth every exertion; for, to elude the pursuit that
would instantly take place, we must travel many hours ere security will await us. An opportunity which is likely to be a favourable one will, I understand, soon occur. At the approaching festival, occupied with the pomp and pageantry of the ceremonies,
your absence will not be known for some time, and the number
of people who will be travelling on the roads will make us the
less noticed:—Tomorrow night, dearest Agatha," continued he, "I
will come again at an early hour, and relate to you the adventures
which have detained me so long from the sweet idol of my heart."
This said he took his leave, and Agatha in the expectation of her
release, and of enjoying the pleasures of the world, retired to her
pallet, where, however, her rest was soon disturbed, for the bell of
the convent summoned its inhabitants to witness an unexpected
and almost unheard-of circumstance.

The powers of life had been only suspended in the bosom of
Marianne by the mixture she had taken, for Agatha, owing to her
fears of being observed, had poured so small a quantity of the
contents of her phial into her beverage, that, although it affected
her in the manner described, and she appeared to the nurse as
if dead, yet the vital spark was not extinct; and when time had
robbed the poison of some of its potency, blood began slowly to
circulate through her veins, and her heart to resume its motion.
But what was her horror when her senses returned to find herself
inclosed in the narrow bounds of a coffin, and that, her respira-
tion becoming every moment more difficult, she must perish. It

was at this awful instant that, exerting herself, she gave utterance to those words, which the Padre Bernardo hearing, (as the reader is already informed in the fifth chapter of these records) released her from the opened jaws of destruction.

When she was able to stand, the monk led her to the chapel; and, leaving her seated on the steps of the altar, he departed. Marianne, however, staid not long there; exerting her yet remaining strength, she slowly proceeded toward the well-known apartment of the sorrowing Claudina.—She entered the chamber; all was still; Claudina had just before closed her aching eyes, and a disturbed slumber lay lightly on her grieved senses.

"Claudina!" tremblingly uttered Marianne as, fainting with excess of bodily anguish, for the poison had not lost all its power, she sunk insensible on her couch.

The sound of her voice awakened Claudina. She started up, and looked around her, but all was enveloped in the shady mantle of night, for the pale moon was obscured by a cloud which was borne on the gentle zephyrs of the approaching morn.

Claudina now became sensible that something heavy was lying at the foot of her couch; she hastily arose, and, laying her hand upon it, found that it was the form of a woman. Her astonishment increased, and she stood for some minutes unable to move, when all her faculties were bound up in horror, for she again heard her name faintly pronounced, and the tone of the voice was that of Marianne.

The idea that the departed spirit of her friend was now hovering about her, the form recumbent on the couch, and the gloomy darkness that prevailed in the chamber, affected the senses of Claudina to such a degree that with a wild shriek of affright she essayed to leave the apartment; but being unable to find the door; and to bear up against the panic that had seized her mind, she fainted, and fell on the floor.

Her scream awoke some of the sisters whose chambers were contiguous to hers, who, wishing to know the cause of it, procured a light, and entering her chamber beheld Claudina lying on the floor, and the pallid form of Marianne in the dreary habiliments of the grave sitting on the couch.

Affrighted at the sight they rushed out of the chamber, and immediately went to the door of the apartment of the Abbess, whom they acquainted with what they had witnessed with the addition of a multitude of fear-formed exaggerations.

The Abbess ordering the convent bell to be tolled to call up its inhabitants, prepared to investigate the truth of the incredible reports of the nuns, and soon proceeded, attended by them, to the chamber of Claudina.

To describe the horror, the astonishment, and the fears of Agatha when she beheld her victim returned from the grave, would far exceed the limited powers of the pen; her only consolation was that Marianne seemed almost unable to speak, and that she had not the hand writing of Ferdinando to produce as a positive evidence of what she might make known to the Abbess of her guilty deeds.

Claudina by the attentive care of sister Ursula was at length brought to her recollection, and during the time that she remained in a state of insensibility the Abbess put several questions to the almost inanimate Marianne; her answers, however, were such as served to increase the astonishment of the Abbess, and the mysterious silence which she observed as to the way in which she was liberated from the grave incensed her, and she determined to acquaint Padre Ignazio the abbot, with her conduct, in the hopes that he might be able to wrest the secret from her. All however he could obtain was, that she was bound by an oath not to reveal that circumstance.

Anxious to be acquainted with the whole of this most unaccountable transaction, the Abbot, in order completely to do away all objections on the part of the nun, sent to the Pope a detail of these strange events, and requested that he would absolve the nun from her oath.

Agatha meanwhile remained in her chamber, a prey to the liveliest sensations of terror; every noise, every step she heard, alarmed her, lest it should be occasioned by the bearer of an order from the Abbess, to appear before her. Marianne, however, was too ill to enter on the subject of her suspicions, and Agatha determined if possible to prevent her from ever doing so.

She examined the phial, and seeing how small a part of its contents were gone, easily divined the reason of the reanimation of the nun. She put the fatal mixture in the folds of her garment, and leaving her chamber anxiously looked for an opportunity of administering a second potion to Marianne.

It was then evening, the dusky livery of approaching night prevented the agitation that resided in the countenance of Marianne being observed; she was walking about the refectory when an unexpected opportunity offered of putting her evil design into execution, for Ursula requested her to carry to Marianne's chamber a medicine she had prepared in order to assuage the violent pains that hapless nun complained of.

Agatha hastily took the vessel from the hands of Ursula, and when she had left the refectory immediately poured into it as much of the contents of the phial as she thought would quiet all her fears of being discovered, if Marianne had not already divulged what she knew of her.

Still however conscience slept not, and the agitation of her mind became so great when she had poisoned the drink that was prepared for Marianne, that she was obliged to lean against the side of the corridore, in order to support her trembling frame.

One of the nuns coming by, demanded if she was unwell, and Agatha replying in the affirmative, she took the vessel from her hand, and carried it herself to Marianne.

Claudina, from the moment that she had recovered, had remained with her loved friend, and sitting by the side of her couch watched over her with the tenderest anxiety.

When the nun entered with the fatal mixture, Claudina took it from her and gave it to Marianne, who drank deeply of the deadly draught.

In all probability the medicine which Ursula had prepared was of such a nature as to prevent the sudden effects of the poison, for it was not till near midnight that the watchful Claudina seeing the symptoms of approaching dissolution in the convulsed features of Marianne, sent to acquaint the Abbess therewith, who directed the passing bell to be tolled, and proceeded to the chapel with the nuns and boarders where the service was performed for the dying.

Agatha was amongst the number; but she had now steeled her bosom against all sensations of pity, and black and horrible were the emotions of her soul; but guilt is never free from alarm, and when the death of Marianne was announced, still Agatha feared that she had disclosed her deeds either to the Abbess or Claudina.

Miserable indeed was that hapless nun, and alive only to grief, she held for a long period in her embrace the cold body of Marianne; and when at length she was with difficulty separated from it, became so long insensible that her soul seemed to have joined that of her loved friend in its passage to regions of eternal happiness.

Agatha waited impatiently for the hour when she might expect to see Ferdinando. She felt curious to know what had been the circumstances which had so long detained him from carrying into effect her much wished emancipation, and at the time when she might expect him in the chapel she left her apartment.

She had not, however, proceeded more than half way down the flight of stairs when she observed one of the nuns who attended on Claudina on the point of ascending them, having been to procure some medicine for that unfortunate friend of the deceased Marianne.

Alarmed lest she should be discovered to be up at that time of night, Agatha instantly extinguished her lamp, and turning back hastened along the corridore in which was the door of her apartment; she was, however, fearful of entering it, lest the nun might observe her, but continued along the passage, and turning to the right when she had arrived at the extremity stopped to listen if the nun was coming that way. Presently the light of her lamp flashed on the opposite wall, and Agatha, confused and hardly conscious of what she was doing, gently pushed open a door near which she stood, and entering a chamber closed it, and there waited till the nun should pass by. Soon she was delivered from her fears, for the nun hastened on, and the echo of her steps grew every moment more indistinct.

Agatha then ventured to look around her. The moon darting through the casement her silver beams, which shone full on a pallet, disclosed to the distended eye-balls of Agatha, which almost deserted their sockets, the wan corpse of Marianne.

Agatha's horror on discovering the corpse of her victim.

Dreadful Deity of retribution, what a sight was this for the murderess. Who shall pretend to describe the sensations of agony, remorse, and horror, which thou thinkest proper to inflict on the guilty? Vain and presumptuous must be such efforts. The body of Agatha shook with the dreadful workings of her mind; chaos on chaos of miseries raged in horrible tumult in her breast; she tried to close her eyes, but her efforts were in vain; she essayed to cover them with her hands, but she possessed not sufficient strength to raise them to her face.

In this awful situation she thought she heard a voice say, "Agatha, the multitude of thy crimes begins to overtop the brink of the huge measure; view the stiff corse which but for thee had yet inhaled the breath of life, the gift of the Almighty torn from it by thy accursed deeds. Thy name appears frequent in the dreadful register of the accusing angel; endeavour to blot out some of thy guilty acts by future days of repentance; remember how short, how uncertain is thy existence, and that perhaps between thee and a dreadful immortality only a few hours, nay, moments may intervene. The blood of thy pale victim is now crying aloud for that vengeance which is its due!"

Agatha either heard, or her guilty imagination made her conceive she heard, these words. By an effort of desperation she acquired sufficient strength to open the door, and as fast as her terrors would permit her, moved along the passage; but before she could bring her mind to the least knowledge of the actions of her trembling frame, she had proceeded into the chapel, where her senses, unable to sustain the warring horrors of her bosom, deserted her, and she sank down by the grate insensate to the torments of conscience and never-ending remorse.

CHAPTER XI.

NOTHING of moment sufficient to deserve a place in these records occurred in the family of the Marchese de Carlentini for some years, the little Angelina daily improved in beauty; she possessed the united graces of her parents, and promised to be a pattern of loveliness both in her mind as well as person. The Conte Angelo had a daughter a few years older than Angelina, called Laurentina, who became a visitor at the Castello in consequence of the Conte, who was a widower, being obliged to take a journey to Naples on business of moment.

Far different was the disposition of Laurentina from that of the lovely Angelina, owing perhaps to the want of the attentive care of maternal affection. Her passions oft-times overcame her reason; the Marchesa saw and endeavoured to check as much as was in her power her intemperate disposition, but in vain; her bad habits had taken deep root in her mind, and finally became a part of herself. She sighed for the pleasures of the world. She longed to see crowds of prostrate adorers offering up the tributary incense which she conceived was due to her charms. As yet, however, her thoughts had only strayed, her actions had not been swayed by them.

Many of the young Sicilian nobility frequented the Castello de Carlentini, but none of them was more indebted to Nature for a prepossessing exterior than the Count Cavini; he saw, and seeing, admired the attractive charms of Laurentina; he knew well the various sensations that existed in the mind of that Signora, for he had ever been an attentive observer of the human heart; he saw that the language of flattery was pleasing to her ears, and with the assistance of that powerful nurse, lulled to sleep the few principles of rectitude which yet bore some sway in her bosom.

The syren voice of adulation, the tremor of affected love, the deceptive tale of sufferings which Cavini well knew how to employ to advantage, aided too by his graceful external appearance, sunk deep into the heart of Laurentina. When the sun illumined the earth, or when the veil of night overshadowed the creation, his image was present in her imagination, and the dulcet expressions of his adoration and love lived in her pleased remembrance.

Such was the dangerous situation of Laurentina, when the dark regent of the bottomless abyss commissioned one of his infernal agents to hover over her, and with delusive dreams to heat her imagination till her ideas, vitiated by them, should be such as would suit with the wicked deeds which to seduce unwary mortals to perpetrate, constituted his greatest happiness.

Oh! woman, lovely woman last formed of animated beings, the master-piece of the whole, when the divine artist crowned his work with producing thee, he did indeed shew the magnitude of his power; Man, solitary and unhappy felt the want of thy cheering converse ere yet his tongue could find expressions for the wishes of his bosom, and the divinity to make him truly happy then created thee to be his comfort in affliction, to partake of his joys, to live in the bosom of his affections, to be to him an adored self. Man, whom he destined to hold the sovereign sway, he endued with greater strength of mind to bear up against the various ills of life. He meant him to be as the elm, and the woman as the clustering vine, which embraces and ornaments with her leafy arms her stately support; thus she needed not that firmness of mind which is the characteristic of man; and this want well knows the Demon, who too often takes a fatal advantage of it.

Unhappy sex, your beauty, your charms, expose you to the snares of man who basely profits by your too great credulity and reliance on his deceitful asseverations of love and constancy; surely if you act wrong the crime originates with him.

Listen not, then, to the alluring voice of flattery, for know that no greater charm exists than the possession of virtue; respect, esteem, pure unsophisticated love, is the result.

Cavini had been breathing the soft tale in the attentive ears of Laurentina while wandering in the umbrageous recesses of the grove near the Castello, when at length the moon, rising in resplendent majesty over the waving summits of the tall trees, warned her to return, lest notice should be taken of her long absence.

At the portals of the North Hall she parted with her lover, who kneeling on the marble steps gracefully kissed her lily hand, and took his leave, after having entreated that she would favor him with an interview in the same place the next evening, which, with averted face and mantling blushes, she granted.

She passed through the hall, and from thence to her chamber, her thoughts full of the tender expressions of Cavini, and her bosom full of love for him.

She retired to repose, a ready slumber closed her eyes caused by the powerful arts of the agent of the Demon in obedience to his will, who taking on himself the form of a being in the first bloom of youth, attired in radiant vestments of celestial blue, appeared to her in a dream.

"Sleepest thou, fair maid?" said the spirit; "dost thou close up those radiant eyes in slumbers which delight the admiring world? the glorious orb of night gazes enamoured on thy beauties, myself, while I look on them, cannot but acknowledge their pre-eminence even over the bright host of heaven. Love, fair maid, has bound in his golden toils thy tender heart, it pants after unknown enjoyments, why delay to indulge in those dear gratifications of which Nature, anxious to fulfil great and wise purposes, has deeply implanted a wish for in the breasts of mortals—Cavini loves thee, his happiness is dependent on thee, and wilt thou refuse to make him a return for his tender affection? Perish the frigid dictates of mundane laws! let Love, almighty love, be the guide of thy actions; 'tis Nature commands you to love, and she will be obeyed.—Too often in the formal tie of marriage the sweet emotions of the soul, the ineffable delights of existence, the charms of love are for ever lost—risque not then the future happiness of thy life on so uncertain a foundation; follow the flowery courses of Pleasure's votaries, and taste of all the delights of the world while thy youth and peerless beauty enable thee so to do."

With such artful converse did the Spirit address the sleeping Laurentina—His words sunk deep in her remembrance—and now she thought herself reclined by the side of the elegant Cavini on a bank of fresh-blown roses—Cavini slumbered—the glow of health rested on his manly cheek, his lips appeared like two opening rose-buds when they unfold their beauties to the morning sun. Laurentina in thought hung over him enamoured; she felt his palpitating heart, and inhaled his breath; her lips touched his, and, with the strength of the new-born sensation of her bosom she awoke—

The Spirit succeeded in his mission; Laurentina slumbered no more that night, her thoughts were entirely occupied by her dreams, and the tumult of unruly passions raged in her breast.

Thus it is when the Demon of darkness sees that virtue is fading in the breasts of mortals that he endeavours by his infernal arts and specious arguments to delude the unwary till his dark purposes are accomplished. In proportion as the mind grows weak in virtue, he strengthens the vicious habits, till finally they predominate with a despotic sway over the heart.

Knowing then the watchful sentinel we have over our actions, how careful should we be to exclude with persevering vigilance all thoughts derogatory to the self-approving principles of a virtuous mind.

With anxious expectancy did Laurentina await the hour of appointment with the fascinating Conte. The moon rose with a pallid face in the East, while the declining rays of the sun ceased to illumine the valleys, and soon sunk from the view beneath the bosom of the western waters. It was then that Laurentina descended from her apartment, and leaving the Castello, directed her steps to the shady recesses of the grove, where Cavini waited in expectation of her arrival.

The musical notes of the feathered creation had ceased; in their downy nests they sunk to rest, and dreamt of the blythe carols of the past day; the moon in all her silver majesty brightly rolled along the heavens. It was an evening suited to the pleasing reveries of silent solemn meditation. It was an evening too, which, lulling the senses by the tranquillity that exists around, leaves them in a state to receive the fond tale of love, and to believe the impassioned expressions of its seducing language.

Cavini hastened to meet the beautiful Laurentina, and in elegant terms expressed his gratitude for her condescension.

"Lovely Laurentina," said he "since I saw you time seems to have slept. When I parted from you last evening, I sought again that seat where I had the bliss of telling you how greatly how fondly I adore you. Alas! the melody of thy voice no longer sounded in my ravished ears; silence reigned around; the streams flowed on in its devious course unconscious of my sighs, which increasing proceeded from that bosom so fondly devoted to thee."

Such was the language of Cavini, and to which Laurentina listened with delight. He led her to the banks of the stream; the glittering radiance of the moon-beams played on its undulating waters. Resting on a mossy seat he spoke of his passion, he kissed her hand which now trembled in his, she remembered her dream; well had the evil spirit performed the commission of the Demon. Her eyes melted in soft languor—she breathed slowly a sigh—she looked at Cavini—his dark eyes irradiated with the fire of love were fixed on her interesting countenance. The emotions she had felt in the vision of the past night again recurred to her bosom!! . . . . All around was favorable to raise the tender sensations of her heart. The soft light of the moon displayed in perhaps a more alluring view the seducing features of Cavini. The gentle vibration of the branches of the surrounding trees discovered and concealed at intervals the animation of his eyes, fixed on her in all the tender adoration of love, mingled with the fire of unruly longings. The delicious fragrance of the wild flowers which thickly adorned the banks of the stream was exhaled around on the wings of the gentle zephyr, and now the melodious nightingale broke on the silence which reigned in the aerial regions with her voluptuous notes, and seemed to invite the animated creation to the enjoyments of love.

Cavini saw how favorable was the present moment; he looked entreatingly on Laurentina. She was silent, and returned his gaze—he took her hand, and advancing nearer, pressed his lips to hers. . . . .

Her dream was thus realized; and the sensations of the moment were beyond utterance—Cavini triumphed and Laurentina was undone.—

Such is the language of the world. Cruel triumph! but it was not Cavini that triumphed! it was the Demon, who beheld the success of his schemes, and rejoiced in the sway he held over the heart of the Conte, who had confessed it by the commission of a crime which leads into all the horrible mazes of vice, the unfortunate unthinking female.

The wild inhabitants of the forest prey not on their own species, man alone who is endued with reason, and reflection, marks out his own kind for destruction.

Prudence obliged the lovers to notice the movements of time, they at length separated and Laurentina retired to her chamber, "to think on what was past and sigh alone."

Those satisfactory reflections with which conscience disturbs the rest of the guilty, were however soon banished her bosom. She soon ceased to regret the loss of her honor, and anticipated the delight attendant on her next meeting with Cavini.

The sensations of Cavini after his successful attempts on the honor of Laurentina were such as exist in the bosom of the libertine. It was now no longer in her power to give him pleasure; the moment of gratification was past, his bosom was incapable of love, it was only a base lustful passion that occupied his breast; even that had now forsaken it, and he thought no more of the female who had given to him the greatest proof how much she loved, by confiding to his keeping that invaluable jewel her honor.

This fatal truth Laurentina had to experience; Cavini's conduct was no longer the same, his attentions to her became evidently forced; till at length he left her.

Laurentina, who really loved him was almost inconsolable; frequently did she at midnight, when every eye was closed, pace the long corridores and halls of the Castello, and sigh forth the name of her faithless lover, while tears of bitter agony coursed each other down her pallid cheek.

Her pride, however, at length enabled her to surmount the grief of her bosom; and perhaps too the attentions of the Signor Marino contributed not a little to compose its perturbation; she listened to his protestations of love, and Cavini was forgot.

Meantime the youthful Angelina advanced in years, beauty, and accomplishments; the Marchese beheld her with delight, and the amiable Louisa, her mother, neglected nothing that could tend to enlarge her ideas and increase her love for virtue. The Count de Leoni, whose health, owing to his former dissipated life, had long been in a precarious state, at this time ceased to exist; by his will Ricardo became possessed of his estates, and in consequence he now found himself enabled to live in a style suited to his rank, and to make on his Angelina a settlement which would not be rejected by the first nobility of the kingdom of Sicily. Happiness seemed now to have made the Castello de Carlentini her fixed abode; eighteen years had witnessed the domestic comfort of Ricardo and his amiable Louisa; their lovely daughter Angelina had completed her sixteenth year, rich in virtue, beauty, and every accomplishment that adorns the female. But the days of the Marchese were numbered; the Angel of Death sent that dread summons which man cannot disobey, and Ricardo patiently submitted to the awful moment which consigned to eternity the divine spark of immortality, which flew on the glad pinions of delight to adore its Maker.

Louisa had watched with unceasing solicitude the sick couch of her fond husband, every sigh that pain or the thought of leaving her forced from his bosom, was echoed by one from Louisa. Long did she cherish the fond delusions of hope, but when they were banished her bosom, existence had no charms for her; the attenuated chord of life, stretched to the utmost, at length broke, and the pure soul of Louisa accompanied her Ricardo's to regions of celestial bliss.

With a distended tearless gaze Angelina viewed the inanimate forms of her parents; hers was no sorrow that words could express. The fever of her mind at length preyed on her intellects, and a melancholy delirium seized them. "Lead me," she exclaimed one day to her sorrowing domestics, "lead me to the grave where sleep my parents. I know they will awake at my call, for they always delighted in whatever gave me pleasure. Why do ye hesitate to obey me? I will go," she continued, rising from her seat, and supporting her trembling form on the arm of an attendant, "I will see, and once more be fondly embraced by them."

The attendants gazed on each other as if irresolute what to do, when Margueretta, who formerly was the favorite attendant of the hapless Theodora, desired them to comply with the wishes of Angelina.

With some difficulty they supported her to the chapel, and stopped at the marble monument which contained the remains of her parents, on the top of which were their sculptured representations.

Angelina long gazed with a vacant stare at the tomb, till at length the power of recollection dawned on her, and a flood of tears relieved her bursting heart.

"Here lie," said Margueretta, wishing still more to increase the salutary stream of sorrow which flowed down her pale cheeks, "here lie the bodies of your father and mother; their memory is fresh in the hearts of all who knew them; deeply regretted did they die, for they delighted in acts of virtue and goodness. Ah! Signora, you may indeed weep for their loss, but they are now receiving the blessed rewards of a well-spent life."

Touched with the renewed recollection of the virtues of their late superiors, the attendants could not forbear weeping; and Margueretta, perceiving her speech had the wished-for effect on Angelina, was silent, while her aged eyes told the emotions of her bosom.

From that period her delirium ceased, and the tide of sorrow, which hitherto had overflowed the boundary, began to roll with less impetuosity, and she endeavoured to stem the torrent of her grief, in order to receive the Conte Angelo, who it appeared by the will of her father was appointed the guardian of herself and estates until such time as she should be married, or attain the age of maturity.

As the Conte will form a conspicuous part in the succeeding pages, it will be necessary to acquaint the reader with his character, and the sordid longings of his bosom, which actuated him to those acts of violence which we have now to record to posterity.

It is pleasing to guide the pen in giving descriptions of the votaries of virtue, and their good acts; but when obliged to pourtray deeds actuated by the Demon of darkness, it slowly passes over the page; it however proceeds as anxious to endeavour to show to the world the wide contrast between virtue and vice, the happiness attendant on the one, and the eternal misery and horrors which invariably follow the other.

The Conte Angelo, whom the late Marchese appointed to be the guardian of the Signora Angelina, was of a ferocious disposition, possessed of a great share of cunning and duplicity by which he endeavoured to veil the traits of his real disposition; he was revengeful and avaricious, and little recked the means, so as he attained the accomplishment of any favorite project.

When he heard of the death of the Marchese de Carlentini, and that he had appointed him the guardian of his daughter and her estates; a secret pleasure filled his soul; and he hasted to the Castello; where his presence would be necessary, and where he determined to take up his residence during the minority of his lovely ward.

That beauteous plant, though now somewhat faded by the bleak blasts of sorrow, yet retained the native gracefulness of its form; and the Conte, who had not seen Angelina for some years, was struck with her appearance, and immediately began to form various plans and designs in his breast which he meant to unfold at a convenient season.

Laurentina, during the illness of the Marchese, and the subsequent calamitous events, had frequent opportunities of receiving the attentions of her new admirer, the Signor Marino, without fear of being discovered, since the domestics of the Castello were too much engaged to notice them and Angelina was always in the apartment with her parents while they yet lived.

Her father, the Conte Angelo's, arrival, however, obliged her to be more circumspect in her conduct; and instead of meeting Marino as she used to do in her own apartments, or the adjoining grove, she was obliged to go at midnight into the Southern Hall, where Marino, who had found means to effect a secret entrance to that part of the Castello, used to await her coming.

Thus was Laurentina, through her own depravity and the artifices of the subtle Demon, totally divested of all female delicacy, and sought only to sate the turbulent desires of her guilty bosom.

It was not long after the arrival of her father that proceeding, according to her usual custom, in her nocturnal visitation, just as she had passed the corridore that led to the North Hall, that she was astonished to hear some paces in it. Bending forward at the open portal she observed by the light of a lamp which was suspended from the lofty roof, Lupo, the confidential domestic of her father, in earnest converse with him; frequently they stopped, and appeared by their actions to be debating on a matter of great moment.

Having observed them for some time with much astonishment, she continued as they were proceeding down one of the side aisles formed by the triple row of columns that supported the roof, to cross the hall at the further extremity, veiling her lamp lest its rays should cause her to be observed.

She soon gained the well-known passage that led to the court-yard which fronted the portals of the Southern Hall, when she thought she heard a noise; terrified, she stopped and listened, but all was silent; and collecting her natural courage, she crossed the court-yard and entered the South Hall.

It was no longer in the ruinous condition in which the late Marchese had found it when seeking the remains of his murdered parent, the hapless Theodora, for he had repaired the ravages which Time had made in the Castello, when by means of the munificent bequest of the Signor Valvano he became possessed of the ability to do it.

On one side of the Hall was a suite of chambers which were adorned with the best part of the ancient cumbrous furniture that from time immemorial had been used in this part of the Castello. There it was that Marino when he had met her in the Hall, would conduct her; and it was also there that, abandoned by every idea of delicacy, and studious only to gratify her passions, she passed the hours of midnight in shameful and sinful intercourse with him.

Marino on this eventful night received her as usual when she entered the portal of the Hall; they then proceeded to the well-known chamber. Laurentina mentioned to him the uncommon noise she had heard, which had somewhat blanched the roses on her cheek, when Marino smiling at her fears, endeavoured by his caresses to restore her to her wonted gaiety. He frequently kissed her, and now the fire of love mounting from their hearts concentred in their eyes, when at that moment the door burst open, and to the terror-struck gaze of Laurentina appeared her father, the Conte Angelo, with Lupo by his side, both with their swords drawn.

Enormous rage distended the features of his face as he rushed toward the unarmed Marino; and ere he could extricate himself from the fainting Laurentina, who clung to him for protection, the sword of the Conte had pierced his body, and the sanguine stream of life flowed over her now senseless form.

"Take this, and this," said the savage Angelo, as he replunged the sword into the dying Marino; "'tis thus I would wipe out the stain my honor has received."

Marino uttered not a word, but with a deep groan fell on the floor, and by his side lay the blood-stained form of Laurentina motionless as the mouldering inmate of the tomb.

Count Angelo Stabbing the Paramour of his Daughter.

"Lupo," said the Conte, "bear to her chamber that female whom I no longer call daughter: to-morrow will see her far from these walls."

Lupo did as he was desired; and Angelo, casting a look of satisfaction at the still bleeding body of Marino, followed his domestic, who bore in his arms the pale insensate form of Laurentina.

The most extensive imagination cannot form an idea of the horrible sensation which assailed the mind of Laurentina. When returning to her senses she found herself in the ruffian grasp of Lupo, and saw her father preceding her with a lamp, still holding the bloody unsheathed sword which had pierced the body of her lover. The dread of instant death, aggravated by the tortures, which she conceived the revengeful fury of her father would cause him to inflict on her, almost caused a second suspension of her vital powers.

In gloomy horrific silence she was borne through spacious passages and halls to her apartments, where Lupo laid her on her couch, and retired with the Conte, who locked the portal of her chamber.

The sound of the bolts as they were shot into the side-beam of the door-frame, vibrated with agonizing sensations on the soul of Laurentina. She had nothing to hope; the passions of her father were roused to their highest pitch; she knew his remorseless nature; he had witnessed the depravity of her conduct, and her punishment she was well convinced would be great and terrible.

Through the long dark melancholy night she listened in fearful expectancy of his return; each gust of wind as it sighed along the passage, or agitated the leafy summit of the grove, made her heart palpitate with terror lest the sounds should be caused by the approach of her father.

The morning chearless dawned in the east. The rosy tints of the rising sun glowed on the casements of the Castello; Laurentina arose and opened hers to admit the early zephyrs to refresh her. Exhausted by the poignancy of her sensations, she had not been long there when the noise of horses in the courtyard caught her attention; and looking down, she beheld some of the domestics of the Castello busied in making preparations for a journey. A carriage was standing at the portal of the North Hall, and the gigantic figure of Lupo was amongst the crowd, giving the men directions.

The white garments of Laurentina as she was crossing the Southern Hall had caught the eye of the Conte Angelo as he was communing with his confidential Lupo on some dark and deep designs. Curious to know whither she was going at that silent hour, he cautiously followed her steps, and at length beheld her in the arms of Marino.

His passion being in some degree allayed by the bloody revenge he had taken in murdering that Signor, left him in possession of a moment's thought with respect to his daughter, and that it was which prevented him from completing the tragic scene by her destruction.

It would be difficult to describe the various conflicts of warring passions which raged by turns in his bosom; his hopes respecting his daughter being married to a Sicilian nobleman of high rank were entirely destroyed, and in her depravity his honor had received a wound. On mature consideration he determined to send her to a convent, where she should remain for life. Such was the result of his intentions, and Lupo had orders to put them in execution.

Early in the morning the Conte advanced along the corridore that led to the chamber of Laurentina. At the well-known sound of his steps she started, but unable to rise from her seat, she listened to the noise occasioned by the receding bolts which secured the portal, while busy fancy made them appear to be the knell that preceded her death.

The Conte entered. With a stern ferocious air and contracted brows he gazed on the fear-struck Laurentina. "Foul stain to my peace," said he, "instantly prepare to depart. The world shall no longer know that thou art in existence. In the gloomy cloister thou shalt wear out thy wretched life; a small punishment, for by the Saints, I could this instant foul my hands with thy blood, and scatter thy dismembered limbs to the ravenous beasts of prey."

The passions of Angelo were mounting to their highest pitch. One moment his countenance was red with rage; the next, deep and deadly malicious revenge would blanch his cheeks. Laurentina saw the furious tempest of his wrath, but silently; for she well knew that a word from her would fire the deadly mass of his resentment, which like the resistless composition that give wing to the murderous ball, would bear down all before it.

Tremblingly she arose; and with a downcast and averted face put on her veil; and her attendant entering made the necessary preparations for her departure, while the Conte with a disordered pace traversed the chamber.

When she was ready, the Conte looking out of the casement called to Lupo, to whom, when he entered the apartment, he delivered a packet, charging him to give it to the abbess of the convent of Santa Catherina, whither he was to conduct the Signora Laurentina, whom he now ordered to depart.

With a dejected pace she followed her savage conductor, who, assisting her to enter the carriage, mounted his horse, and, with two attendants, left the courtyard of the Castello.

The unhappy Laurentina, when she felt the motion of the vehicle which was to convey her from the delights of the world, unable to support her miserable sensations, sunk into a state of insensibility, in which she continued some hours.

The reader will perhaps not be surprised to find that Agatha, of whom so much mention has been made in these records, was no other than the Signora Laurentina; the Abbess, in compliance to the wishes of the Conte, having directed her to bear that name on her admission into the convent.

The Conte Angelo, when he had in some degree calmed the dreadful perturbations of his mind, again returned to the rumination of his designs respecting the Signora Angelina; but the period for putting them in execution was not yet arrived, as she mourned almost incessantly the loss of her parents.

CHAPTER XII.

THE Signor Ferdinando, when he came according to his promise to the skreen of the convent chapel, was struck with horror at beholding stretched on the marble pavement the senseless form of Agatha. To approach her to render her any assistance was impossible, as the gate was locked, and Ferdinando for more than an hour remained with his eyes steadfastly fixed on the prostrate motionless nun.

At length, however, a feeble movement of the limbs announced the return of animation; and Ferdinando endeavoured to forward the exertions of nature by calling on her name, to bring back her recollection. "Agatha! my love," said he, "how miserable is thy situation, which precludes the possibility of my affording you any assistance. I stand here like the distracted lover on the shores of the ocean, when he sees the bark which holds the adored of his heart dashed against the rocks without the possibility of aiding her in that horrible moment. Agatha! speak to me, my love, my Agatha!"

"Who calls the wretched Agatha?" said the nun, with a tremulous voice, "is it the shade of Marianne? What wouldst thou with me? Speak thy purpose, nor harrow up my senses further than their bearing, lest wild delirium should crack the attenuated thread that connects them!"

"Dear Agatha, it is Ferdinando that speaks to you."

"Ferdinando! I know that name, who utters it? would I had never heard it! My heart so deeply stained with crimes of blackest hue, would at least have been free of that which was against all laws, human and divine."

"My lovely Agatha, recollect your Ferdinando's voice. Oh! heavens! what a miserable situation is this that I am not able to approach you to endeavour to calm the agitation which doubtless the solitude and gloom of the place have caused in your tender bosom."

Agatha at length turned her gaze on Ferdinando, and recognized his well-known features. With some difficulty she took the key of the gate from its place of concealment in the folds of her garment, and reached it to Ferdinando, who having opened it, raised her prostrate form, and after some time succeeded in calming the wild tempest that disturbed her senses.

Although greatly surprised at the incoherent sentences which she had uttered, and which caused various surmises to arise in his breast, Ferdinando would not ask any questions of Agatha of the reason of them, lest he should awaken the sensations they seemed to be occasioned by more forcibly in her recollection; he therefore discoursed on a subject he well knew would not fail to please, and that was her emancipation from the convent.

Agatha by degrees forgot her terrors in the tender embrace of her lover, and the still more tender expressions which he made use of to restore her wonted spirits; but she looked on his features with anxiety, for the brilliant expression which once animated his dark eyes, and the colour which glowed in his cheeks, were gone. He observed her pitying gaze, and in order to account for his wan looks, as well as to perform the promise he made her the last night, he thus began the tale of his adventures.

"You no doubt, beloved Agatha, well recollect my promise of endeavouring to release you from these walls soon after you had entered them. It is perhaps necessary, in order to elucidate the various occurrences which since that time befel me, to commence my recital from an early period of my life.

"On the death of the old Marchese de Cavini, his son came to reside with my father, the Marchese de Montalino; for some time our friendships increased; we were about the same age, and apparently of similar dispositions. Two years had passed which had witnessed an uninterrupted scene of comfort at our mansion, when my sister Palmyra came from the convent where she had been educated.

"To the finest of forms in Palmyra was added a heart endued with the greatest sensibility. Cavini possessed uncommon attractions, and that descriptive language which is pleasing to the ears of females, because they are inclined to believe what they wish to be true."

Here Agatha sighed; well she recollected the fascinating Cavini, and how by the syren voice of flattery and affected adulation, he had seduced her from the sweet paths of virtue; and which was finally the cause of her plunging into the most dreadful of all crimes—that of murder.

"The credulous Palmyra paid attention to the soft sighings of Cavini. I saw plainly the growing attachment. Immersed in state affairs, my father could pay but little attention to his family, and I determined to question Cavini myself on the subject.

"The rank of my father was equal to that of Cavini, but their possessions were not so; the old Marchese had left to his son great store of wealth, while my father, in consequence of his former dissipation, found it difficult to keep up appearances suitable to his rank in life.

"For the first time Cavini seemed confused, when I requested he would accompany me to my apartments, as I had something of consequence to discourse with him about.

"When I told him that I thought it the duty of a fond brother to be anxiously interested concerning the welfare of his sister, and that having observed he had paid of late great attention to Palmyra, I wished to know, if he had any design to honor my family with an alliance with it; he replied that 'twas true that the charms of my sister had interested him, and that he hoped when he was of an age to act for himself, that she would condescend to bless him with her hand.

"I was satisfied with his answer, and looked with impatience to the time when he would become possessed of his estates and I should embrace him as my brother.

"But alas! ere that period arrived, Palmyra was undone; and the cruel Cavini forgot the vows which had induced her to listen to his fascinating converse.

"In the melancholy looks of Palmyra, I read what had taken place, and when I questioned her, she threw her arms about my neck and acknowledged her weakness.

"Full of rage against Cavini, I challenged him to meet me in the field on the following morning. He haughtily accepted it, and we left each other with a look of stern defiance.

"That evening I passed in my chamber; and being fully determined that either Cavini or myself should fall, I passed some of the hours of night in arranging my affairs; and at length, somewhat fatigued, retired to rest.

"Hardly had I closed my eyes when an assassin hired by the treacherous, base Cavini, sheathed twice his trusty dagger in my body, and left me weltering in my blood.

"My groans were heard by some of the domestics, who, rushing to my assistance, the bravo was taken, and confessed at whose instigation he had attempted to murder me.

"The Marchese, my father, would have reeked his vengeance on Cavini, but he had left the Castello.

"My wounds were not mortal, but the loss of blood ere they could be bound up was very great; and the gates of Death appeared to be open to receive me. After some time, I began slowly to recover, but the injury I had received remained deep fixed in my bosom; and I determined to be revenged on Cavini whom I intended to seek as soon as my health would permit me.

"My rage was still further increased by the death of the unfortunate Palmyra; grief at her own indiscretion and my situation stopped the current of life. And thus, through the villainy of Cavini she found an early tomb.

"As soon as I was able, I commenced my search. Having learnt that Cavini was at the Castello of the Marchese de Carlentini, I repaired there, and to my great disappointment I was informed that he had left it; and it was on my return from that inquiry that I first had the happiness of seeing the lovely Agatha.

"You know," continued Ferdinando, "that from this place I repaired to Lingua Crossa; my journey there was in order to find out Cavini, but I did not succeed; and according to my promise, I immediately returned.

"On leaving you in order to prepare horses for our intended flight, as I wound up the steps which led to the ruined chapel in the wood, I thought I heard a noise as of a hasty footstep. Somewhat alarmed lest the privacy of the place should have made it a resort for banditti, I stopped; and drawing my sword, attentively listened for some moments. Nothing, however, disturbed the silence of the hour. And at length, concluding that it might have been the attendant echo of my own paces I ascended the remainder of the steps. When as I was leaving the chapel I was suddenly attacked by several armed men. Concluding that they had a design against my life, I resolved to sell it as dearly as possible, but a dreadful wound which I received in my head soon rendered me incapable of resistance, and I sunk insensible on the earth.

"How long I was in this situation I am ignorant; but when

my senses returned I found myself in a small vessel, in company with two fierce-looking wretches. The wound in my head had been bound up, and the bleeding had stopped. I was silent; for I well knew that my entreaties or invectives could little avail with the men who were with me, whose countenances too plainly bespoke their savage natures.

"I perceived that we were steering for one of the isles of Lipari, and in the evening the boat came to an anchor at the mouth of a small creek in the island of Stromboli. The men assisted me to go on shore, for I was still faint and weak with the loss of blood.

"By the time we had reached the shore the shades of Night had completely enveloped the face of Nature in her dark investiture. Patrono, one of the men, held a torch, while his comrade Lupoli seizing my arm in his nervous grasp, hurried me along the beach. We ascended the steep side of a rock, and when we had arrived at the summit, Patrono, laying down his torch, rolled away a large stone which concealed an aperture. It would be difficult to form an idea of my sensations when Lupoli fastened some cords round my arms, and told me that I must descend into the dark interior of the place whose approach seemed to be so well concealed. The horrible idea that I was to be entombed alive made me exert my small remains of strength in order to prevent the completion of the dreadful fate that awaited me. Wounded and weak, my efforts only served to irritate my conductors, who thrust me into the hole, and lowered me down till my feet reached the bottom of the cave; they then desired I would take the ropes from my body, and on my persisting in my refusal to comply with their request, they threw down the part they held, and rolled the stone over the mouth of the cave. For some time I sat on the damp earth, while the most dreadful ideas occupied my mind. Not the smallest glimpse of light was perceptible, and the silence of the place was as undisturbed as that which reigns in the grave. At times I conjectured that my entrance into the monastery had been discovered, and that the monks had thus effectually prevented me from troubling them again; and I was the more easily tempted to be of this opinion, because I could not fix my suspicions elsewhere, being unconscious of having an enemy.

"In these ruminations passed the hours of night, and in all likelihood a great portion of the next day. No food had been given to me, and my thoughts became every moment more gloomy and desponding, when a noise above, and a sudden stream of light which illumined that part of the cave in which I was, made me look up. The stone was removed, and a basket was let down at my feet, and the voice of Patrono directed me to take out the contents.

"While I was thus employed I heard voices in conversation above. One in particular engaged my attention, which, trembling with rage, I well recollected to be that of Cavini. How did my bosom swell with anger; in an instant I forgot the anguish of my wound and the weak state of my exhausted frame, and in accents of the highest indignation I reproached that base wretch for his conduct, but my words, almost lost in the vast expanse of the cavern, but slightly reached the ear of my persecutor, who derided my threats, and laughed in the contemplation of his supposed security from the effects of my just indignation.

"The stone was again rolled over the cavern, and darkness and silence resumed their mournful dominion in it; I partook of the provisions which had been let down to me in the basket, and ruminated only on revenge. From the quantity of food which was brought, I conjectured that I should not be visited for some days, and I determined to examine, as well as I was able, the extent of my dungeon, in the hopes of finding some outlet to escape.

"One consideration made me long deliberate what to do ere I entered on this undertaking, and that was the fear lest I should not be able to discover the place where my provisions lay after I had left them.

"The ropes with which I had been lowered into the cavern were still about my arms; I took them off, and, having unravelled them, tied the pieces together, and the end to the pitcher which held my allowance of water; with this clue I set forward, and carefully felt a part of the rugged inclosure of my abode, but no where could I discover any means of escape: the cavern was of such great extent that my clue would not permit me to search round it, but which, however, I effected at another period, when, through long residence, I had become used to my miserable prison.

"My provisions were regularly lowered down to me every fourth day, as I was afterwards informed; for in those regions of night and horror the day and night were alike enveloped in opaque gloom.

"I had long given over all hopes of ever being able to effect my escape, and in all probability should there have terminated my miserable existence, but for a circumstance which, though attended with horrors inconceivable, brought about the means of my deliverance.

"It was a terrible convulsion of nature; the igneous particles of combustible matter which had long been maturing in the fertile bosom of the earth, at length exploded; the ground heaved and rocked beneath me; unable to stand, I fell on it, and every moment expected to be swallowed up in the opened clefts, and to be crushed to atoms in them when they closed. I heard the dreadful roaring of the thunder, and, after a terrible concussion the large stone that covered the hole above was removed from it; then the lightning, at times, illumined my cavern, and by shewing me my situation, increased the horrors that reigned in my mind. A gulph, deep and wide, was opened on one side of the dungeon, and my aching eyes, whenever the lightning darted into my abode, were strained in vain to discover its depth. After some time the trembling earth began to subside, and at length all was quiet. I looked up, and saw the clouds tinged with the bright radiance of the morning sun, and for the first time since my miserable confinement, a gleam of hope dawned in my mind that I might perhaps find some way to effect my escape; I looked anxiously at the aperture in the roof, but to raise myself up to it was impossible. A stream of air made me hastily remove my gaze, in order to find out from whence it proceeded, and a faint glimmer of light from the further extremity of the cave made me start forward to examine it. The motion of the earth had made a small fissure in the side of the rock, but so narrow that I was not able to force my body through it. The hopes of deliverance from my dreary prison gave me sufficient strength to enable me to pull down a large piece of rock, which, however, had almost annihilated me in its fall.

"While thus engaged, I heard a voice calling to me from the aperture in the roof: it was Patrono, who came to see if I had survived the earthquake. My agitation was so great lest he should discover the opening in the rock, that I could scarcely answer his inquiries; great indeed therefore was my satisfaction when he returned the stone to its former place, and left me to proceed in my exertions for my liberty.

"With great difficulty I forced my body through the fissure, and looked out to find whither it led; but to my sorrow I saw rolling beneath me the billows of the ocean, and that there appeared no way for me to escape, without precipitating myself into the sea.

"My resolution was soon formed; I returned to the cave, and taking up the ropes, twisted them together till I judged them sufficiently strong to bear the weight of my body; I then went to the fissure, and tying the end round a projecting rock, lowered myself down. Fortune favored my attempt; the water was not deep at the place where I descended, and I gained the beach in safety.

"As it was still light, I was fearful of being seen, and until Night had spread her shadowy veil over the face of creation, I remained in a recess formed in the rock in whose hollow womb I had passed so many days and nights of misery.

"When at length I emerged from the rocks, I wound along the beach, uncertain where to go, and anxiously looking out for a hut where I could stay till an opportunity offered to leave the island.

"The noise of oars on the water now broke on the nocturnal silence, and at length I perceived a boat approach that part of the shore where I was; fearing that it might be some of the ruffians whom Cavini had employed against me, I quickly retired, and, seeing a light among the rocks at no great distance from me, repaired toward it.

"Without any means of defence or resistance, you will hardly be able to judge of my agonies when, on advancing to the light, I found it proceeded from the mouth of a cave in which there was a fire, and as the blazes illumined the place I plainly discovered standing by it Patrono and Lupoli, and at the same instant heard behind me the paces of the party who had arrived in the boat. To have fled from the place would have occasioned instant discovery, and my only resource was to lie down on the rock, and trust to Fortune and the darkness of the night for my protection.

"As the party approached how did my bosom burn with rage when I plainly distinguished among the voices that of Cavini; they all passed without discovering me, and entered the cave, when Cavini inquired of Patrono concerning his prisoner.

"Patrono replied, that thinking it probable I might have been killed by some of the loose stones of the cave falling on me, he had been in the morning to see, but that I was then well.

"Cavini looked dissatisfied, and taking the man by the arm, led him out of the cave. When the party had passed by I had shifted my station to a small recess near the mouth of the cave, which entirely concealed me from sight; Cavini stopped close by me, and holding out a purse to Patrono, promised to give him the contents if he would rid him of all future anxiety respecting me by my death. Patrono eagerly took the purse, and promised to bring him the wished intelligence in the course of the next hour; and then, having first called out his comrade Lupoli to accompany him, set out on his dark mission.

"The party in the cave now departed from it, laden with various spoils, which I learnt from their conversation had been lately taken from a merchant-vessel, and they were carrying them to the boat with the intention of disposing of them in Sicily. Cavini was now left alone in the cavern, and I determined to seize that opportunity to revenge myself for the injuries I had received from him. I had observed a parcel of swords lying in a remote corner of the cave, and hastily rushing into it, seized one of them, and appeared before the astonished and terrified wretch, whose countenance grew of a deadly hue when in my emaciated features he recollected the man whom he had but a few moments before hired an assassin to destroy. Without speaking he drew his sword, and I rushed on him, determined, if it cost me my life, to deprive him of his.

"My impetuosity had nearly proved fatal; I received two wounds ere I could plunge my sword into his body; 'This,' said I, as I deeply sheathed the thirsty blade, 'is for Palmyra's wrongs; and this for my own.'

"The last thrust pierced his heart; he died instantly: and now that I had revenged myself as far as his death would permit me, I became solicitous for myself; my wounds were painful, and the loss of blood rendered me faint. With difficulty I left the cave, and the dawn assisting me with its rosy beams, I gained the abode of a peasant, where my wounds long detained me.

"During all my sufferings, the remembrance of your situation, lovely Agatha, was ever present to me; and the moment I was able I hasted to you, in order to carry into execution the plans I had formed for your emancipation.

"Thus have I amply accounted to you for my absence; and my pain-worn form is, I trust, a sufficient evidence of the truth of my relation."

Ferdinando thus concluded; and Agatha, who during the recital had forgot her sorrows in listening to his eventful tale, from his concluding words again hoped to enjoy the pleasures of the world.

CHAPTER XIII.

TIME at length mellowed the sorrows of Angelina, and the Conte was preparing to set in motion the design he had formed respecting her from the first moment when her beauties, though somewhat faded by sorrow, met his view. Her large estates had awakened his avaricious desires; her beauties had roused his passions; and he secretly resolved to possess himself of both. He therefore endeavoured to insinuate himself into her favor. His conduct was attention mingled with respect, before her he appeared all mild and gentle, and the unsuspecting Angelina thought herself happy in having a guardian who appeared to take so much interest in whatever could tend to soften the sorrows of her heart.

The Conte mistook the graceful looks of Angelina for the

gaze of affection; for his vanity would not permit him to take into consideration the great difference between his years and those of his lovely ward; and he therefore concluded that the wishes of his heart would be attended with success.

One morning he sent a message to Angelina requesting her presence in his apartment. She immediately complied; and entering the saloon, saw the Conte standing at the further end at one of the casements, apparently deeply involved in thought. He started when she was announced by the domestic who attended, and advancing toward her, led her to a sofa. He looked confused, and once or twice seemed going to speak to her, but stopped ere he had uttered any words. At length, however, he summoned resolution, and thus addressed the astonished Angelina:—

"I sent for you, lovely Angelina, to acquaint you with what 'tis likely my behaviour to you may have expressed. Need I add that love the most sincere, the most ardent, animates my breast for you. Yes, Angelina, Conte de Angelo solicits your hand, which will make him the happiest of men."

The surprize of Angelina at the speech of the Conte exceeded description. She, however, instantly determined that her answer should be such as would prevent further solicitation, and formed it in these words:—

"The Conte Angelo must not conceive me destitute of gratitude for the favorable opinion he has entertained of me, and also for his kind and attentive conduct during the long weary hours of sorrow which I have endured; but marriage is a subject which is far distant from my thoughts, and 'tis more than likely will never enter them."

As the yellow leaf of the autumnal blast, so fell the countenance of the Conte. He saw by her decided manner that he had no hopes, and all his air-formed visions vanished in a moment. Impatient of contradiction, he had almost hastily answered her; but recollecting himself, he thus replied:—

"Fair Angelina, in an unfavorable moment have I preferred my suit; suffer me, however, to hope that time and my attentions will cause a happy change in your resolution; at present I will not longer detain you."

Having said this he rose, and without giving Angelina an opportunity to reply, offered her his hand, and conducted her to the portal of the saloon; where bowing low he ordered the domestic who waited to attend her to her apartments, and then disappointed and vexed, returned to acquaint his confidential Lupo with his ill success.

In the retirement of her chamber Angelina reflected with pain on the occurrences of the morning. Rumour, with her many tongues, had not given to the Conte Angelo the best of characters; from his former conduct to her she was, however, inclined to disbelieve the prevailing reports, but now a suspicion not unmixed with fear crossed her mind, that he had sinister views respecting her, and that it was those which had induced him to attempt to veil his usual disposition, till his ends being served, it would no longer be requisite for him to wear the specious mask of hypocrisy.

She was much embarrassed when the hour of repast arrived; but, however, endeavouring to conceal the agitation of her mind, she entered the Hall.

Conte Angelo having noticed her approach, with his usual courtesy advanced to hand her to the table, and introduced her to his confessor, the father Hildargo, who had that morning arrived at the Castello.

Angelina instinctively shrunk from this man, whose appearance was such as might well account for her sudden dislike. A pair of ferret eyes glared from beneath his scowling brows; his nose was prominent and hooked; on his mouth seemed to sit a malicious smile whenever he gazed on the Signora Angelina; his height was far above the common size; and a stoop in his shoulders completed the uncouth figure.

Silent and unpleasant passed the time of the banquet; and when it was concluded, Angelina arose, and in the retirement of her chamber reflected on the occurrences of the day.

Her ruminations were interrupted by a knocking at the portal of her apartment. It was the father Hildargo. He came from the Conte Angelo to request that she would honor the evening banquet with her presence, and which he meant should be in a pavillion that was erected near the stream which meandered through the valley.

Angelina at first hesitated to comply with the wishes of the Conte, but at length, unwilling to incur the displeasure of a man in whose power the will of her father had unfortunately placed her, she requested the father to bear her compliance to the wishes of the Conte.

Pleased with the success of his mission he departed; and a short time after, Angelina, throwing a veil over her lovely features, left her chamber, and crossing the lawn approached the pavillion.

That building had been erected by the late Marchese de Carlentini, and in it he had passed many wistful hours with his beloved Louisa. Angelina had not visited the place since the death of those lamented parents, and the recollection of the happy hours she had there enjoyed with them overcame her, and the pearly drops of sorrow fell from her beauteous eyes as leaning on the arm of her attendant she surveyed the well-known spot.

Angelina was roused from her melancholy ruminations, by the approach of the Conte; he took her hand, and leading her to a couch in the pavillion, sat himself by her side, and expressed his sense of her goodness in acceding to his request. A table was spread with wines of various sorts and the delicious fruits of the season, at which sat the father Hildargo, who seemed to have partaken freely of the ruby vintage; and as Angelina once glanced her eyes on the countenance of the Conte, she observed with great concern that it was flushed with wine. He was profuse in his attentions and compliments, at which Angelina felt both confused and offended.

The band of musicians, who were stationed at such a distance from the pavillion that the dulcet sounds of their instruments mellowed by distance should appear to be the effect of enchantment, now sweetly filled the air with their harmonious cadences, which floated gently on its fragrant bosom, impregnated with the rising odors of aromatic shrubs and flowers. Those insinuating sounds filled the bosom of Angelina with an emotion of pleasure; for a moment she forgot her situation; but when the measure which had so much pleased her concluded, and a Sicilian piece was performed which she well recollected to have heard in the presence of her regretted parents, her bosom was the abode of sorrow, and the pearly drops of anguish started from her eyes.

The Conte immediately ordered the music to cease; and when Hildargo had retired for that purpose, he threw himself at the feet of the sighing maid.

"Empress of my soul," said he, "can you who are so feelingly alive to sensibility behold me at your feet? me, who so sincerely adore you; and who must be for ever miserable unless you compassionate my sufferings, and make me, by a blessed acquiescence with my wishes, the happiest of mortals!"

His speech, spoke in the hurry of affected passion, and the warmth which was caused by the wine he had drank, made Angelina immediately forget her sorrow; and regarding the Conte with a serious gaze, she replied:—

"I thought, Signor, that the conversation we had this morning would have prevented you from again bringing forward a subject displeasing to my ears."

"Oh! say not so," replied the Conte, evidently struggling to conceal the passion which was rising in his bosom, "do not condemn me to black despair; but by giving me your hand, cause joy and delight to visit my heart."

"From your years, Conte," said the offended Angelina, striving to disengage herself from his grasp, "I should have expected a far different conduct. I fully perceive your design in requesting my presence here this evening was to insult me; I shall now go, and take this as a lesson not to expose myself again to such unlicensed behaviour."

"By heavens, Angelina, you wrong me;" said the Conte passionately, "there is some minion whom you have favored with your affections, and is the cause of your present contemptuous conduct; but should I ever find him, dearly shall he rue the day."

Angelina haughtily arose from her seat. "When wine ceases to influence your conduct, Conte," she replied "you will recollect how much you have wandered from the path from which a man of honor never deviates."

The Conte Angelo started up; his countenance glowed with

rage; he again caught hold of the hand of Angelina, which she had with difficulty snatched from him, and in a furious tone exclaimed:—

"'Tis well, Angelina. What persuasions cannot effect, other means may; you now deride my power, but you shall dread it."

This said he loosed her hand; and Angelina, trembling at his words, and without courage to reply, left the pavillion, and entered the Castello. Scarcely conscious of her actions, she proceeded to her apartments, and gave vent to her grief by a flood of tears. She reflected on the words of the Conte, and the revengeful dark looks which accompanied them; she recalled to her mind all the unfavorable reports which had reached her concerning him; and a dread of his threats, since she had but too much reason to believe that he would endeavour to put them in execution, banished all comfort from her breast.

Sadly ruminating on her present afflictions, the pensive Angelina beheld the nocturnal vapour slowly arise from the valley, and the sable banner of night unfurled from the heavens. Her apartment was enveloped in gloomy obscurity, for neither did the moon or stars illumine the hemisphere; she for a time looked at the dark clouds as they sailed on the bosom of the blast, and often wished herself in those regions where she might survey them rolling thousands of leagues below her; regions where the blessed reside, where the virtues of her parents insured their reception, and where she hoped to join them, for her mind was unknowing of evil, and her bosom was the seat of virtue.

From such thoughts hasty paces in the corridore suddenly disturbed her; the door of her apartment was rudely thrown open, and Conte Angelo entered, followed by Lupo bearing a torch.

From his irregular steps Angelina, who had started from her seat, immediately concluded that he was still more inflamed with wine than when she had last seen him; and though trembling from apprehensions of brutal treatment, she collected sufficient fortitude to demand the cause of his intrusion.

"Sweet girl," said he, approaching her, while a malicious smile of settled revenge distorted his countenance, "I forget the unkind expressions which you used toward me; I love you, and the pious father Hildargo is now awaiting us in the chapel, to witness my vows of adoration."

Cold drops of water stood on the countenance of the trembling Angelina on listening to the insolent address and daring intentions of the Conte. To escape was impossible; the ruffian form of Lupo, who seemed to watch the countenance of his master, ready to execute his commands, was between her and the door of the apartment, while the Conte had seized her hand, which she in vain endeavoured to release from his firm hold.

"Your intentions, Conte Angelo," said she, "are such as I cannot fathom. I am willing to impute the rudeness of your conduct to the influence of wine, and hope you will show me that you are sorry for your behaviour by instantly quitting my apartment."

"To do that," said Angelo, "I will not refuse; but you, fair maid, must bear me company. Come," said he, dragging her along toward the portal of the chamber, "we waste the precious moments."

Angelina, the distracted Angelina, screamed with affright and horror; but the cautious Conte had removed the attendants out of the hearing of her exclamations, and no succor appeared to preserve her from the base intentions of the malicious designing Angelo.

Passing through an unfrequented part of the Castello, the Conte stopped at an iron gate, while Lupo drew aside the bolts which fastened it: heavily it creaked on the massy hinges as he forced it back; when overcome with the horrors of her situation, Angelina sank on the pavement, alike unconscious of her past sorrows and the anticipation of her approaching misery.

Lupo, taking her up in his arms while the Conte held the torch, bore her through the gateway into the chapel. At the altar stood the father Hildargo, who was to perform the ceremony that was to seal the misery of Angelina. Lupo deposited his insensible lovely burthen on the steps of the altar, and assisted by Hildargo, (for the Conte Angelo was too much intoxicated to afford her any help,) at length recalled her fleeting senses.

The father Hildargo first attracted her gaze. "Save me!" she exclaimed, "oh! preserve me from the unprincipled Conte; per-

Angelina sinking on the pavement at the iron gate.

form not a ceremony which my soul shrinks from with horrors indescribable, as you hope for happiness beyond this life."

Hildargo replied not. Hardened as was his heart yet he was not quite callous to the miserable situation of Angelina, and he silently returned to the altar, awaiting the further intentions of Angelo.

The Conte at the sound of her voice hastily advanced, and raising her from the steps of the altar, desired the father to pronounce the marriage ceremony.

Angelina rent the air with her screams; they re-echoed

through the chapel. The Conte paused; he was fearful that they would alarm the household; and should any other but those devoted to his interest witness the forced marriage, he was well convinced that it would be of no avail.

"Promise me," said he, "that on the third night from this you will voluntarily accompany me to the altar, or this moment witnesses the completion of my wishes. Answer me directly, or a few minutes sees you by force my bride."

The hope of escaping from a fate so dreadful made Angelina, after some hesitation, faintly promise to be the wife of the Conte on the day he mentioned. His stern savage features relaxed into a smile as he thanked her for her kind acquiescence; and he led her back to the door of her chamber, attended by Lupo, where bowing low, he departed with his trusty agent.

Angelina sunk nearly insensible into a seat. The agitations she had experienced throughout the whole of that day were more than her tender frame could support; and had not a flood of tears relieved her bursting brain, her intellectual faculties must have deserted her, and a horrible delirium have succeeded.

The early beam of the morning beheld the lovely maid pale, drenched in the flood of woe, her beauteous tresses all disordered, while the hectic glow which at times appeared in her cheeks announced the fever which tormented her trembling frame.

The chaos of miserable ideas which tortured her had not left her a moment's time to reflect on any other circumstance. She had given the Conte a promise to be united to him, which his agent would prove beyond the power of disbelief; an immediate flight was therefore the only resource by which she could hope to avoid the detested nuptials; but even that appeared impossible, as the Conte would doubtless watch her conduct with a wary eye till he had gained his vile ends.

Oppressed with such a weight of misery as these reflections brought to her panting bosom, she retired to a small chamber, which was set apart for the purpose of private devotion; she there threw herself on her knees before the altar, and besought the All-powerful to release her from her unjust persecutions, or to strengthen her to encounter whatever evils His wisdom thought fit to inflict on her.

From the clouds of dazzling lustre which veiled the Omnipotent, who from his empyrean throne high raised above myriads of celestial thrones, beheld the most secret actions, the most hidden thoughts of mortals, proceeded Hope and Confidence, sent by him to comfort the sorrowing Angelina. In an instant darting down from their celestial abode unseen, they hovered round the imploring maid, and infused in her breast their animating attributes; and having thus fulfilled their heavenly mission, again bent before the footstool of the Almighty.

Angelina arose from her prayers with a heart teeming with thankfulness for the internal composure which now resided in her breast; even a languid smile dimpled her beauteous cheeks as she gazed on the blue expanse of Heaven, while the grateful tear trembled on its lovely brink.

Some time was thus passed, and Angelina with a light pace now opened the door of her oratory, and passing through the apartment where she usually sat, endeavoured to open the outer portal which led to the corridore that communicated with the other part of the Castello; but the Conte, fearing that some sinister event might take place which would deprive him of his intended lovely prize, and well knowing how forced was her consent to be united to him, had taken the best precaution to secure her till the period of the nuptials, by making her a prisoner.

The countenance of Angelina fell when she found that the door was fastened, as it precluded all hopes of her being able to effect her escape; she, however, did not give way to despair, but waited with resignation the event.

She was deeply ruminating on her parents, when the noise occasioned by unfastening the portal made her cast her eyes on it. The unwelcome figure of Lupo entering as it unclosed, met her view.

"The Conte, Signora, has ordered me to inquire which of your domestics you would wish to attend you."

"I would have you ask of Conte Angelo," replied Angelina

firmly, "why, since I have acquiesced in his request, I am made a prisoner in my own residence."

"Signora," said the artful and trusty Lupo, "you know how passionate the Conte is, and were I to be the bearer of any message which brings his orders in question, 'tis like he would wreak his anger on me. I trust, therefore, you will excuse my not complying with your wish."

Angelina disdained to make any reply, and on his repeating his first question, desired that Annetta might be sent to her; on which he departed the chamber, carefully fastening the door after him.

Annetta was her favorite domestic; she greatly loved her mistress; and when she was admitted to her presence could not refrain her tears at seeing her treated in a manner so harsh and so unbecoming her rank. She had brought with her a basket filled with provisions; and Angelina, who had passed many hours without the strengthening aid of nourishment, partook, though sparingly, of the morning repast.

Angelina confided in Annetta her intention of escaping, if it was possible, from the power of the Conte; and the morning was passed in consultations on the way in which that desirable event could be brought about.

The suit of apartments which she occupied were very extensive, and formed a principal part of the Western Tower. Many of the chambers, as being useless, Angelina had ordered to be fastened up; and in the hope that from some of them there might be a communication, either with the courts below or the turrets above, she determined to examine them minutely.

In some of the chambers were doors, but they were either fastened on the outside or the keys were wanting which fitted the locks, and Angelina began to fear that no outlet could be obtained. She now entered the last of the apartments; in which there was also a door deep-seated in an obscure arch; it was also fastened, but on Annetta's trying the keys, one was found that fitting the wards of the lock drew back the bolts, and the door flew open.

Angelina hastily passed on to discover whither it led, and found herself in a passage, the roof of which was arched; long

narrow casements, whose panes were darkened by the labour of
the spider, afforded so gloomy and uncertain a light, that, half
afraid to venture in the unknown place, she drew back; she was,
however, somewhat encouraged by the presence of Annetta, and
leaning on her arm, silently proceeded, softly treading the dusty
pavement, lest the noise occasioned by their footsteps might unfortunately be heard, and frustrate her new-formed hopes.

The passage was of great length, and was terminated by an
arched recess in which was a door: this Annetta opened; it led
into a gallery, which Angelina on entering discovered to be in the
extensive chapel, which was in the south wing of the Castello. At
one end a flight of marble steps led down to the altar, and communicated with the lofty aisles of the chapel. To descend them at
that time would be attended with danger of a discovery of her intentions, and she resolved to wait for the friendly gloom of night,
which would shroud her actions from observation.

She then returned as quickly as possible through the tedious passage to her apartments, for she trembled lest the Conte or
Lupo might have been there in her absence; her fears, however,
were groundless; and now she long looked with anxiety at the
Heavens, where glowed in meridian splendor the bright luminary
of day; she watched his declining beams, and as he seemed to dip
into the tremulous waves of the western ocean, hailed the approach of the grey cincture of evening which began to skirt the
horizon.

The pallid face of the moon appeared in the east slowly gathering its borrowed lustre; its silver rays brightened the walls of
the Castello; the dim twinkling stars began to peep forth, and at
length the firmament glowed with myriads of nocturnal lamps.

The busy hum of animated creation now faintly reached the
ear; soon it died away, and night and silence commenced their
somnific reign.

Angelina tremblingly arose, and Annetta having lit the lamp
preceded her to the chamber from which was the passage to the
chapel; for she determined to accompany her mistress in her
flight, and to share her dangers and fatigues.

Angelina trembled when passing through the long-drawn

aisles of the chapel at the echoes which accompanied her footsteps. Timidly she viewed the recumbent effigies of her ancestors, which the feeble efforts of the sculptor had placed on their
tombs to convey to future times their decaying memory.

At length she left the chapel and entered the South Hall.
From that place Angelina knew there was a communication with
the northern part of the building, which if they could discover, it
would then be easy to leave the Castello.

Fortune favored her researches; she found the passage, and
passed hastily through it. In proportion as she advanced nearer
the north wing her fears increased, for there the Conte resided,
and his domestics, who perhaps might not have retired from the
hall. She often stopped to listen, but no sound met her ear; while
Annetta would endeavour to encourage her to continue on their
way.

She had almost arrived at the entrance to the North Hall,
when she observed from a door which was half open, a stream
of light; terrified she stopped, for to pass it was attended with the
utmost danger; and yet there was no other way to enter the hall.
Thus irresolute she leaned on Annetta, trembling with her fears;
when the door opened, and Lupo, carrying a lamp, entered the
passage.

He, however, proceeded toward the hall without turning
round; which if he had done Angelina must have been discovered.
Her terror, however, was so great, that Annetta for some time
could scarcely keep her from sinking on the pavement. That faithful attendant at length succeeded in some measure in composing
the agitation of her mistress, and they now cautiously advanced
to the hall.

Silence reigned in the dusky interior. Opposite to them was
the portals and to which the steps of the fugitives were directed.
They soon reached them; and as they were passing through the
gates that opened to the road from the courtyard in front of the
hall, Angelina looking up beheld the Conte Angelo slowly pacing
the walls in converse with Lupo.

Fear winged her steps, she instantly darted toward the grove
accompanied by Annetta, in the hopes that its dark recesses

would skreen them from the search of her persecutor, who had witnessed her flight from the battlements.

The light of the moon guided her steps in the grove, and without ever stopping to listen if she was pursued, Angelina gained the road: and unknowing which way she should turn, fortunately took that which leading over a hilly tract brought her out of the valley.

Angelina well knowing that if the Conte should overtake her, her destiny was certain, continued her journey, though almost fainting with fatigue, when the noise of horses' feet advancing toward them made her stop.

A moment's reflection convinced her that it could not be the Conte or any of his people, and her fears were therefore quieted on that head; but it might be a party of banditti; and should she fall into the power of lawless freebooters, her situation would be more dreadful than even the one she was endeavouring to fly from.

She looked despairingly around her for some place where she might hide till they passed by, but no such friendly covert appeared; the place they were passing over was an extensive heath, and the bright beams of the moon made all objects visible at a great distance.

Composing her agitation as much as she was able, she determined to meet what she could not avoid with all the fortitude she was able. She now could easily discover the horsemen, who were quickly advancing, when a noise of voices in the direction she had travelled made her turn round, and she saw the well-known forms of Conte Angelo and Lupo, with two of the domestics of the Castello. They were on foot, but by the speed which they used in their approach, fatigued as she was, to hope to escape by flight was useless.

Of two evils Angelina determined to choose the least. Her fate was certain if she was again in the power of the Conte; and the travellers, who were now at hand, even should they be banditti, might be prevailed upon by her entreaties and promises of reward, to protect her from her bitter enemy.

"Whoever ye are," said she, "have pity, I beseech you, and pro-

tect me from the unprincipled Conte Angelo, who is now advancing, and who would compel me to what is worse than death—a
union with him."

The party, consisting of a cavalier and two domestics, instantly stopped; and the cavalier leaving his horse advanced to
Angelina.

"Signora," said he, "you have fortunately met with friends; I
will dispute the road with the Conte, meanwhile do you and your
attendant mount my horses, and pursue your way to the convent
of Santa Maria, which is not more than a league hence."

The moments were precious; the servants of the cavalier assisted Annetta on one of their horses, while the cavalier placed the
trembling Angelina on his, and then bidding her a respectful adieu
said, "To-morrow, Signora, I shall hope to see you in safety."

Angelina breathed a prayer for his preservation; and turning
her horse's head, pursued the track he had pointed out.

She proceeded as fast as she was able, often turning round to
look at the party, who seemed to be awaiting the Conte Angelo;
distance now obscured them from her view; but once she stopped
her steed, for a faint clash of arms broke on the silence of night.
She listened some time, but those sounds of hostile import were
heard no more.

The lofty walls of the convent were now made perceptible
by the beams of the moon shining full on them; and Angelina,
after some stay at the gates, was admitted to the chamber of the
porteress, till the abbess should be informed of her arrival.

Conte Angelo, the moment he had beheld Angelina, descended instantly from the battlements with Lupo, in order to bring her
back. In their way from the battlements they passed through the
North Hall, and Lupo summoned two of the domestics to attend
them in the search. During this time the friendly grove had afforded a shelter to the Signora Angelina; and when the Conte entered
it, he employed some time in searching about for the fair fugitive,
supposing she had concealed herself in some of the umbrageous
recesses.

Thus unknowingly he afforded time to his intended victim
to gain the road; and when at length he became convinced that

she must have passed through the wood, he left it, and soon after beheld at some distance her white garments waving in the air, as she passed over the rising boundary of the valley.

His rage and vexation when he saw that she had met with protection and assistance from the horsemen was excessive, and he determined to punish them for it.

Furiously he advanced, and drawing his sword, threatened to sheath it in the breast of the cavalier if he did not permit one of his people to mount the remaining horse, in order to bring back the fugitives, one of whom, he added, was his affianced wife.

"As the speech of the Signora whom I had the happiness to assist did not imply such relationship, I hold myself bound in honor, Conte, to resist your attempt to follow her. If your pretensions were just, why should she fly you?"

"Who can account for the follies of women?" said the Conte hastily. "In one word, are you disposed to let me have the horse; or will you dare to oppose my progress?"

"The horse," said the cavalier, "I certainly shall refuse; and I dare oppose any one who endeavours to oppress a female."

"Enough," said the Conte, furiously attacking him; "you now seek your own destruction."

The cavalier defended himself with undaunted resolution; his servants were also engaged with Lupo and the two domestics; and Death clapped his skeleton hands, delighted with the pleasing prospect of glutting his rapacious maw with fresh victims.

The cavalier disarmed the Conte: a well-aimed blow divided his sword; and Lupo, seeing the situation of his master, attacked the cavalier. Short, however, was the contest: Lupo fell; and falling, died; his gigantic form was pierced with the sword of his opponent, and his life flowed out at the aperture.

The domestics fled, and the Conte remained with the cavalier, who thus addressed him:

"Learn from the fortune of this night, Conte Angelo, that the votaries of oppression should be thrice cloathed in complete armour ere with even greater numbers they dare to face those who are the defenders of innocence."

This said, he turned indignantly aside, and mounting the remaining horse, left the spot ensanguined by the yet warm stream which had flowed from Lupo's pallid corse.

Gloomily Angelo, cursing his ill fortune, retired. Angelina, the lovely Angelina, had escaped him. Concluding, however, that she could not have proceeded far, he hastened back to the Castello de Carlentini, where he immediately ordered a large party of his people to mount the fleetest horses, and to pursue the lovely fugitive; with a promise of a large reward if they should succeed.

Lorenzo de Montalto was the name of the cavalier who had so fortunately protected Angelina from the designs of Conte Angelo; he was the only son of the venerable Marchese de Montalto, a nobleman highly respected by his country and beloved by his monarch. His son walked in those paths of rectitude and honor in which his father had already trod; few indeed were there that did not love him; few who did not bless the hour that gave Lorenzo to the world.

Nature had been prodigal in her favors to him; his form was as graceful as his mind; and in his face were those beauties which would have graced the statue of an Apollo or a Ganymede. Of his courage a sufficient proof has been given in the preceding pages; and perhaps Sicily could not produce a more accomplished man than himself.

When he left the enraged Conte Angelo he struck across the heath, and reaching a small hamlet passed the night there, intending as soon as the morning dawned to visit the convent, which he doubted not the Signora he had rescued had reached in safety, as the distance she had to travel when she left him was but trifling. Still however fearful that she might have missed her path, or perhaps be exposed to dangers which her unprotected situation would leave her without the means of avoiding or escaping from, he changed his intention, and desiring his people to remain at the village till he returned, he crossed the heath, and arriving at the convent, had the pleasure of learning that the object of his solicitude was safe within its protecting walls. He then returned back to his people, delighted beyond measure at the events of the night, which had given him an opportunity of rescuing the oppressed.

The party which had been sent in search of Angelina returned without the wished success; they could not even gain the smallest intelligence whither she had directed her flight. They brought away the body of Lupo to the Castello, and the Conte had to mourn not only the loss of Angelina, but also that of his trusty and ready agent in his dark and nefarious plans.

The next morning Angelina was ushered into the presence of the abbess of the convent. She briefly related the circumstances which had induced her to seek a refuge within its holy walls till such time as her minority should cease, when the power vested in Conte Angelo would be no more.

The venerable abbess listened to her interesting detail with great attention. "You are not the first, fair daughter," said she, "of the family of Carlentini who has sought protection within these walls from tyrannical oppression. Well do I recollect the unfortunate Theodora de Carlentini, who fled from the power of her unprincipled Lord, who sought her life. Wounded and bleeding she arrived here; and if ever a soul went to Heaven, hers did. Fervently she prayed the Saints to forgive her sinful husband, and in blessing him and her child, the late Marchese, your father, Signora, she expired."

Tears stood in the dim eyes of the abbess as she recalled to her memory the mournful scene; and her sighs were echoed back by Angelina, who well recollected to have often heard her father express in the tender terms of filial affection his deep regret at not being able to learn the fate of his mother.

A silence of some minutes now ensued. Angelina wished not to interrupt it, for her thoughts at that moment were so melancholy that the frequent tears rolled down her cheeks, and her sighs made fragrant the zephyr of morning.

The abbess at length interrupted the mournful silence; she embraced the sorrowing Angelina, and assured her of her protection and friendship. "Here, fair daughter," said she, "you can remain unmolested till you wish to adorn the world with your presence."

A nun now entered the parlour, and informed Angelina that

the Signor who had protected her from the Conte was at the gate, and requested to speak to her.

Angelina having mentioned to the abbess her obligations to him, followed the nun, who conducted her to the apartment where he was. Lorenzo started when he beheld her approaching; till then his eyes had never beheld such united perfection.

The gentle Deity of Love for once entered the forbidding walls of a convent, he took from his golden quiver two arrows, with these he pierced the tender panting hearts of Angelina and Lorenzo, then well pleased he spread his little pinions, and sailed on the bosom of the rose-scented zephyr, which wafted him to the Idalian groves.

Both felt the influence of the tender passion, but it was their souls that sought to leave their abodes and be united; no gross particle of sensual ideas entered their minds, which, pure and un-sullied, shunned all thoughts repugnant to virtue.

For a few moments they were silent; Angelina, however, at length recovered from the confusion into which she had been thrown by the first emotions of love, and with blushing cheeks and downcast eyes falteringly expressed her gratitude to Lorenzo.

De Montalto surveyed with the gaze of the enthusiast her graceful form, the winning gentleness of her manner, her beauteous features; he conceived himself transported to those abodes where the angelic choirs tune their golden harps in heavenly melody, while listening to the dulcet tones of her voice.

How often did his bosom glow with delight at the recollection that he had rendered a service to so beauteous, so interesting a female; how often did he start with horror at the idea that if he had not succoured her she would perhaps ere then have been the wife of Conte Angelo.

"'Tis I, Signora," said he warmly, in answer to her speech, "who ought for ever to bless my good fortune in having preserved from the base intentions of a villain the fairest model of earthly excellence."

Lorenzo stopped; he feared he had said too much, for the deepest tint of the rose mantled on the cheeks of Angelina. A pause ensued for a few moments, when that lovely maid, without raising her eyes, ventured to ask if the Conte's party had not attacked him.

Concealing the act of bravery he had performed in sparing the life of Angelo when he had him in his power, he gave a general relation of the meeting; adding, that he feared one of the Conte's followers was mortally wounded.

From the description of his person Angelina knew that it must be Lupo; and she sighed to think how unfit was his soul to be disrobed of its mortal coil, and appear before the seat of judgment, to answer the stern interrogatories of an avenging Deity.

On the wings of rapture swiftly passed the fleeting moments, and at length Lorenzo with evident reluctance took his leave, for life he sadly sighing found would be to him a wretched blank, unless passed with Angelina. He requested ere he departed permission to call again at the convent; a request which Angelina could not refuse.

When he was gone Angelina retired to her apartment, where the busy powers of recollection brought to her ideal view the graceful Lorenzo; his words, his actions, the sighs which now and then escaped him, lived in her remembrance. She had passed some time in these ruminations, when she was struck with the impropriety of them. These, thought she, are not the sensations of gratitude, they are caused by a much more potent influence, or else the absence of Lorenzo would not appear so distressing to me. But the signal service he has performed me surely deserves more than common gratitude; and while my bosom still trembles at the recollection of the danger which through him I have escaped, surely more than common sensations must exist in my heart. What pleasure would it give me again to repeat my thanks to him; it would tend to calm all these emotions, so new, so pleasing, and yet so painful.

Such were the thoughts which existed in the bosom of the beauteous Angelina when her heart first throbbed with the wound occasioned by the shaft of Love. At one moment she feared it was that tender passion, at another hoped it was only gratitude; thus Lorenzo entirely occupied her thoughts, while each moment strengthened the golden fetters of that pure exalted affection which was dawning in her bosom, each moment lengthened the chain which began to wind round her heart, inclosing it in that delicious bondage which, to a bosom of such exquisite sensibility as Angelina possessed, at once was a source both of pleasure and grief. Her nature seemed to have undergone a change. Lorenzo now alone existed in her thoughts; and wherever she turned her eyes, in fancy she beheld his graceful form. She took up a book, and endeavoured to divest her thoughts by reading; but while her eyes wandered over the page, her thoughts were on Lorenzo, and in her ears still sounded the pleasing cadences of his voice.

She at length left the chamber, and walked in the gardens of the convent, which were of considerable extent; but the beauties of Nature could not tranquillize the emotions which her bosom now felt, and in order to divert them she sought the society of the Abbess.

Requesting to know the particulars of the escape and death of Theodora she turned the conversation on her; but the Abbess declined conversing on the subject which always made her melancholy.

She however opened a cabinet of polished steel, and taking from thence a small roll of papers, presented them to Angelina.

"These characters," said she, "were traced by her hand while it trembled beneath the emotions of pain and grief. She desired I would send them to her husband when she was no more. This I promised to perform, but on inquiry learnt that he was murdered by some of his debauched companions. I then deposited the packet in the place from which you saw me take it, and never have I had courage to touch it till now. There you will doubtless find every circumstance respecting that unfortunate Signora fully related."

Angelina took the papers, and after a short conversation with the Abbess retired to her chamber to peruse them; but her mind was in that perturbed state, that hardly had she cast her eyes over the first lines than she was obliged to lay them aside, for the idea of what the hapless writer must have endured, and the recollection of the words of the Abbess concerning her, made her unable to peruse them; and her eyes became dim with the frequent tear of commiseration.

Lorenzo long wandered in sight of the walls of the convent which contained the rich jewel that his soul panted to call its own. He envied the walls their fancied felicity in containing the lovely Angelina, whose beauties and mental accomplishments had so greatly fascinated him.

On the verdant margin of a stream which rolled its silver waves within sight of the convent Lorenzo passed the day. Absorbed in thought he heeded not the beams of the sun till declining they laced with streaks of gold the venerable walls of the religious pile. He watched them as they faded to the view, lost in the gradual approach of twilight. The mists of evening now veiled from his sight the abode of Angelina, till the moon gliding from the covert of a cloud darted through the darksome scene her silver streams of light, and brightly tinted its grey walls.

The cool and refreshing breeze gently curled the surface of the stream; the song of the grove was long past, and a stilly silence reigned around. Lorenzo arose from the flower-decked bank where he had passed so many hours, and almost unconscious of his steps, approached the convent, when a chorus of harmonious voices broke on the silence of the midnight air. It was the nuns chaunting the vespers; the swelling tones slowly ascended on the breeze, and Lorenzo, delighted, long listened to the sounds which seemed to waft his soul to Heaven. Deep sighs escaped his bosom, and a tear slowly bedewed his cheek as he pensively brought to his memory the love-formed image of Angelina.

At length the voices ceased, and Lorenzo retired to the hamlet where his domestics awaited him. It now verged to morning, and as he had not rested the past night, he threw himself on a couch, and soon after a gentle slumber stole over his eyes bringing with it airy dreams in which in fancy he beheld his Angelina.

He thought he held her up in his arms and resisted for a time the attempts of a being of tremendous form who essayed to tear her from him. Suddenly he found himself alone, and long wandered about in the shades of night distracted with his loss. The gloom now dispersed, and he saw his Angelina pale and dying laying on a couch surrounded by a number of people. With difficulty he forced his way through them, and flew into her arms; when immediately she opened her eyes, the color visited her cheeks, and she instantly arose, and returned his embrace. The scene then was changed; he thought he was standing at an altar by the side of Angelina; he turned round to speak to a priest who was there, but beheld in his stead the Conte Angelo; and when he looked for Angelina, found she was gone.

Here his imagination acted so strongly as to awake him, and he lay ruminating on his extraordinary dream, which he could not help thinking was something more than common; there was a consistency throughout the whole, which made it appear a foreboding vision, and as such he carefully treasured it in his memory.

When Angelina arose in the morning she felt refreshed by the tranquil repose she had enjoyed; she too had beheld Lorenzo in her slumbers, and when she joined in the matin service, gratefully recollected her obligations to him, and while she prayed for his happiness in life, secretly wished it might be connected with her own.

Assured of her safety from the base designs of the Conte Angelo, her mind became more at ease; and perhaps the idea that she should see Lorenzo the next day contributed not a little to her internal composure; and feeling a strong desire to peruse the manuscript of Theodora as soon as she was able, she retired to her chamber, where, while her eyes traced the characters, the deep sigh and frequent tear showed how much her sensibility was excited by them.

The contents were as follows:

———

The Narrative of Theodora.

"My hand, trembling with my mental as well as corporeal pangs, is almost unable to guide my pen. Slowly it traces the characters which describe my sufferings. While tears of misery dim my eyes, still, however, when the heart is unconscious of ill the mind has a comfort remaining among the accumulating evils. Such happily is the situation of Theodora: my conscience is unaccusing; in no instance have I acted to merit the smallest reproach, either in the sacred characters of a wife or a mother. Why then, cruel Marchese de Carlentini, why hast thou sought to terminate my existence? But I forbear reproach; my life has been spared long enough to enable me to petition Heaven for thy pardon; and from the inmost recesses of my heart do I forgive thee.

"Could it be possible that the tide of my mortal existence should continue to flow for ages to come, my sensations when I saw Grimaldi enter my prison with the bright instrument of death in his hand, and the determined dark looks which he cast at me, can never be effaced from my recollection.

"His hand, however, trembled, and its point missed my heart. I fell; and Grimaldi rushed from the chamber. In his haste he neglected to fasten the door. Horror-struck and faint as I was with the loss of blood, yet I had sufficient resolution to arise, and endeavour to effect my escape while the ability to do it remained.

"The tender longings of a mother to see her beloved child inspired me with fortitude. I wish to live for thy sake, my Ricardo; but never more shall I imprint on thy lovely smiling face my kisses, nevermore shall I fold thee in my arms, for Death is advancing toward me with rapid strides, and his eager eyes, like those of the deadly basilisk, chill the current of life, which now glides feebly in my veins.

"I left the apartment soon after Grimaldi had fled from it. I could hear the echo of his paces across the Southern Hall. Terror seemed to attend him; perhaps he thought my disembodied spirit would appear before him, or that some soul-appalling form would punish him for his guilty deeds.

"Unseen I traversed the passages of the Castello; no door opposed my progress, for Grimaldi staid not to close them. I listened ere I entered the North Hall, but all was silent; I advanced, and at that moment the tall figure of Grimaldi passed me. I was almost sinking on the marble pavement with fear when I saw him turn round and fix his eyes on me.

The Assassination of Theodora.

"Doubtless he conceived it was a visionary form which he saw, for he precipitately retired, and thus freed me from my apprehensions.

"I repaired to the cottage of a peasant and his wife; their terrors were great at seeing me, whom they believed to have long been an inhabitant of the silent tomb. At length I satisfied them that the life still lingered in my hapless breast; and having purchased their silence respecting what they knew of me, was conveyed by them to the convent of Santa Maria.

"Such were the means by which I effected my escape; but the

wound made by Grimaldi's dagger, and the sorrows of my heart, tell me that my Ricardo will be soon without a mother.

"O merciful Creator of the Universe! I beseech thee, if ever the actions of my life were such as were beheld by thee with pleasure, to guard from all evils, and protect the infantine years of my darling child.

"Carlentini! again I repeat that I do from my soul forgive thee and the unfortunate agent of thy designs against thy affectionate Theodora. Let repentance visit thy bosom, and recollect that there is an hereafter.

"My dissolution approaches—a cold chill creeps through my limbs, and the damps of death are settling on my face—my recollection fails—I hardly know what I have written—But of this be assured, I forgive thee, and shall pray to Heaven with my latest breath to do so too. Dying I subscribe myself, your constant affectionate wife,

"THEODORA DE CARLENTINI."

CHAPTER XIV.

ANGELINA dropped the tear of commiseration as she folded up the packet which contained the characters traced by the dying hand of the unfortunate Theodora. The sluices of grief once opened long flowed, for she thought of her departed parents, of her present unmerited wrongs; and perhaps some of the sighs which swelled her bosom might proceed from the remembrances which she tenderly fostered in her breast of the fascinating Lorenzo. Had he been there, it is likely the duration of her sorrow would have been but short; in his converse she would have found a charm that would have dispelled the tear, the sigh, and the melancholy pensive look which now sadly marked her lovely features.

She gazed on the glowing regent of day, while impatience was visible in her countenance; the sun seemed no longer to pursue his daily course, but to rest in his meridian altitude. Nature to Angelina seemed to have paused in all her works, and to have seized on the rapid pinions of Time.

Thus slowly wore away the lengthening hours of the tedious day. Evening then came with all its deepening shades; perched on the lofty branches of the grove the nightingale tuned her amorous descant, lulling the feathered race to sweet repose. The mystic lamp of night now rose brightly on the sable scene from the waving summit of the woods which grew on the eastern hills; the prominent features of creation and the walls of the convent were decked with her silvery tints, and her beams trembled on the glassy surface of the stream that gently glided on its devious course.

Night had now reigned some time over her silent empire, and her cool breath warned Angelina to quit the casement, where she had stood to contemplate the lovely scenes of sleeping Nature, when suddenly the soft tones of a lute floated in the air, accompanied by a voice.

The sounds of the lute were sweet and delightful; and produced by the finger of harmony, but the voice was to Angelina far more sweet, for it was the voice of Lorenzo.

She feared to breathe, lest she might disturb the wind that conveyed to her ear the loved cadences of his voice, and long did she endeavour, but in vain, to discover where sat the nocturnal harmonist.

At length the air was no longer impregnated with the dulcet melody, and Angelina, closing the casement, courted repose on her couch; and her slumbers giving birth to the airy visions of fancy, she listened in imagination to the strains of Lorenzo.

She arose early the next morning, and as she disposed with more than ordinary attention the luxuriant ringlets which sported on her bosom, the blush of expectation mantled on her lovely cheeks, and her heart fluttered with the emotions caused by the gentle Deity of Love.

When Lorenzo's arrival was announced, a still deeper crimson tinged her downy features. How was her countenance animated with the radiant glow of hope, while all the soft ideas of his soul beamed through his eyes.

The gentle spirits of love and sympathy, who inspire all the soft affections, who instil in the minds of mortals all that is beautiful in feeling and elevated in thought, who awake such thrilling harmony from that sweet instrument the soul, alone are able to tell what fine, what exquisitely fine cement unites congenial natures, what magnetic principles operate on them.

The day was far advanced ere Lorenzo could prevail on himself to quit the fascinating converse of Angelina; he at length departed, having first obtained permission from that lovely female to renew his visit.

Meantime Conte Angelo was informed by the people he had employed for that purpose of the retreat of his intended victim, and he immediately repaired to the convent, and demanded of the Abbess that she would give up Angelina, alledging as his right for such request the responsible situation of guardian, in which he was placed by virtue of her father's will.

The abbess listened somewhat impatiently to his well-framed discourse, and then signified her determination not to comply with his wishes, as his conduct toward his ward had been influenced by the most unwarrantable designs against her person and fortune.

The Conte, seeing that whatever he could say, was of no effect, determined on another method of getting the unfortunate Angelina again in his power; he sent father Hildargo to the Pope's Legate in order to represent to his holiness that the abbess of the convent of Santa Maria forcibly detained Signora Angelina, his ward, who had before the altar given her free consent to be united to him; but that influenced by the arts of the abbess and a certain cavalier, she had left the Castello de Carlentini in company with him; and had taken her abode at the convent, where the abbess allowed the cavalier to visit her.

This specious tale delivered to the Legate by Hildargo, who solemnly asserted the truth of it, had the desired effect; and he was immediately invested with powers to demand the Signora Angelina.

Exulting in his success, the Conte Angelo appeared before the gates of the convent attended by father Hildargo and a train of domestics, to conduct the hapless Signora back to her Castello.

No sooner did she receive from the abbess intimation of

the arrival of the Conte, and the authority with which he was invested, than she threw herself at her feet, and with many tears besought her not to deliver her up to his power. Affected at her tears, though the abbess did not dare disobey the order, yet she determined to oblige the Conte to make a solemn promise not to use any force in order to carry into effect his plans respecting Angelina; and to this end she sent to desire his attendance in the parlour of the convent, whither she repaired herself.

When the Conte entered, she thus addressed him:—

"The order you have produced concerning the lady Angelina I cannot but suppose was gained by artifice, and by unjust representations. That Signora has related to me the whole of your treatment to her, which was the reason of her flying to the protection of this convent; you must therefore, Conte, before I can give her up to you, solemnly promise not to confine her, or bias her inclinations. This if you do not instantly do, I shall, notwithstanding the Legate's order, hold myself justified in protecting her from your persecutions."

The firm and determined manner in which the abbess spoke these words convinced the Conte that he had no other resource than to make the promise she required, for he trembled lest the Legate should be informed of the truth of his conduct to the Signora, and allow her the sure protection of the church, which would entirely baffle all his deep designs.

Without any apparent hesitation he conducted himself according to her wishes, and took the oath required, which was administered to him by the Confessor of the convent, in the presence of the abbess and some of the elder sisters. She then proceeded to the trembling Angelina, and informing her what had passed endeavoured to comfort her under the pressure of the distressful moment.

The thought that in the Castello she should not be able to see the fascinating Lorenzo was not the least of Angelina's affliction; and in leaving the convent she felt that she left a place which was endeared to her by the remembrance of the happy moments she had passed in it when listening to his interesting and animated converse.

She now followed the abbess into the parlor, where the Conte with much apparent respect expressed his sorrow for the past, and repeated his promise that the future should behold her perfect mistress of her actions.

Angelina wished to believe his words founded in sincerity, and began to entertain hopes from his public professions that he would no longer attempt to persecute her with his addresses; now rendered, if possible, a thousand times more odious by the pleasing recollection of Lorenzo.

The thoughts of parting with him caused the frequent sigh; and she conceived that in acquainting him with the reasons of her leaving the convent, and also with the lasting sense she entertained of the services he had performed for her, she did not overstep the bounds of propriety. Hastily, therefore, she penned a few lines expressive of her thoughts, and then tremblingly prepared to accompany the Conte Angelo.

His conduct was as polite and respectful as when he first arrived to take on him the authority with which the will of the late Marchese de Carlentini invested him. With respect to Angelina and her estates, she was allowed her liberty in every respect, and he seemed willing to atone for his former outrages by his present attentions.

The deep-plotting Conte by these means succeeded in lulling to sleep her fears, while he was watching for a fit opportunity both to revenge himself of Lorenzo de Montalto, and to secure to himself the hand and fortunes of the lovely Angelina.

The grief of Lorenzo when in perusing the billet left for him at the convent he learnt that the sweet angel of his affections was once more in the power of the Conte was great indeed, since he knew too much of the Conte's character to suppose that he had given up his designs respecting her. He immediately resolved to keep a wary eye on his conduct; a matter of some difficulty, as he was confident that Angelo, could he once get him in his power, would amply be revenged for the part he had taken in defeating him, and rescuing Angelina.

All difficulties vanish before the eye of the lover; he bent his steps toward the Castello de Carlentini, whose walls contained the beloved of his heart; and to his delighted gaze, as he surveyed the lofty towers and frowning battlements, appeared the fair form of his love seated at a casement.

The mists of evening had began to condense on the earth ere Lorenzo had approached the Castle; but his eyes, irradiated with the fire of love, pierced through their dusky shades, and he contemplated with delight the adored form of Angelina.

She too saw him, and trembled for his safety. Silently she waved her white arm, and motioned him to quit the place. Lorenzo understood her meaning, and retired from the walls. Winding round the broad base of the turret, a small postern attracted his attention; it was beneath that part where, from her being seated at the casement, he concluded Angelina resided. He looked around him for some time, when no person meeting his view, he approached the postern, and perceived that the key was in the lock. Carefully he forced back the rusty bolts, which shot deep into the massy stone-work, and pushed the postern open. All was dark within; he entered, and by the dim light which slowly proceeded from the open door found himself in a narrow passage.

Though undetermined whether to proceed or not, still he moved forward till his feet struck against some steps. Darkness reigned around, and he did not think it prudent to ascend them, he therefore contented himself with returning to the postern and securing the key of it, since he doubted not but the passage had a communication with the apartments of Angelina, and that in consequence the key might at some future period be of use; then casting a long lingering look toward the Castello, he bent his steps toward his present residence.

Some days now passed, and Conte Angelo perceiving that the mind of Angelina had recovered its natural serenity, endeavoured to carry into effect his deep-concerted plans, which were the constant employment of his thought and conversation with Hildargo. He was determined that in his next attempt no consideration should prevent him from being united at the altar to his beauteous victim, for in friar Hildargo he had an agent who would not scruple to perform the blackest acts.

Recent events made it still necessary to act in a reserved and cautious manner, as he doubted not that he had the eyes of many on him, and particularly those of Lorenzo de Montalto, who he since had learnt was the name of her champion.

Black revenge had fixed its deadly root deep in the bosom of Angelo; and whenever he thought of Lorenzo a pallid hue sat on his features, his lips quivered, and his eyes rolled with the distempered thoughts of his soul. At such times the hilt of his sword was firmly grasped, and he felt eager to plunge the shining steel into his bosom, but he shrunk from the idea of the equal contest, and wished to perform the deadly deed either when the night had rolled its sable mists over the earth, or that sleep had sealed up the eyes of his unsuspecting victim. Such was the character of Angelo. No generous sentiment fired his breast, where lurked dissimulation, pride, envy, and every dastard, base-born idea.

He was musing on the best means of effecting the dark intents of his soul one evening, while leaning over the battlements of the Castello. Night in her sable empire was gloomily advancing, when the eyes of Angelo were attracted by the figure of a man gliding under the walls. He looked at him with some attention, and as he passed beneath the place where he stood, recognized the person of Lorenzo; he started from the place, and hastening to the hall, ordered some of his own domestics to follow him well armed, and then leaving the Castello, proceeded with them in the direction that Lorenzo had taken.

The Conte proceeded along the base of the walls for some time, till arriving at the postern beneath the Eastern Tower he found that it was open. Immediately conjecturing that Lorenzo had entered there to see Angelina, his bosom boiled with rage, and as he cautiously listened, he heard the steps of his hated adversary. Fearful of encountering his conquering arm, he sent forward his domestics, who after some difficulty succeeded; for aided as they were by the darkness of the place, Lorenzo in vain exerted his strength and courage.

Disarmed and in chains he was brought before Conte Angelo, who, in order to give his proceedings a show of justice, had returned to the North Hall, where he had seated himself in a chair of state, with the friar Hildargo by his side, and attended by the principal officers of the Castello.

"Who art thou," said he in a haughty voice, "who hast dared to attempt an entrance into the Castello at this dark and silent hour? and what were thy intents?"

"Conte Angelo," replied Lorenzo in an undaunted tone, "may, 'tis like, recollect that he owes his life to the lenity of this arm, when he attempted to act basely and dishonourably; and 'twas with a view to learn whether he had attended to his oath that Lorenzo de Montalto entered the Castello de Carlentini. Thou hast thy answer."

"Insolent intruder!" roared the Conte in a voice rendered almost inarticulate with rage, "thou shalt rue thy contemptuous conduct. Away with him," continued he to the people, "away with that fellow to the deepest, darkest dungeon of the Castello."

"Base, unmanly wretch!" said Lorenzo, "let me be free, restore me my sword, and then see if thou wouldst dare to utter a reproachful word, or to look on me for a moment."

"'Tis not likely," replied Angelo, "that I should put myself on an equality with a midnight robber, who has assumed a name in order to escape the punishment he merits. But why do I hold further converse with such a character? Lead him to the dungeon."

Lorenzo disdained to reply, and followed the attendants, first casting a look of the highest contempt and disdain on the Conte Angelo, who evidently shrunk fearful from it, and retired with Hildargo from the hall.

Lorenzo meanwhile was conducted to one of the prisons which were constructed in the frowning walls of the ramparts. A small grating which opened into a court admitted air and light, and the unfortunate Montalto became its gloomy resident.

His own sufferings were almost unthought of, while he considered the helpless situation of his adored Angelina; for the black traits of the Conte's character were too evident; and he doubted not but that he would instantly, unmindful of his oath, force her, now unprotected, to yield to his infernal schemes.

Such were the melancholy ruminations of Lorenzo, while the

Conte, shut up with Hildargo, held a long consultation as to what would be the best mode of carrying his schemes into effect.

Lorenzo he had got into his power, and in such a manner as gave a colour to his harsh proceedings, he therefore was no longer an object of fear.

The next morning, as Angelina was preparing to walk in the extensive gardens of the Castello, Annetta rushed almost breathless into the chamber, and her countenance was pale and agitated.

"Good Heavens!" said Angelina, starting, "what is the matter, Annetta?"

"O my dear lady! the cavalier, the Signor Lorenzo."

"What of him?" said Angelina, turning as pale as her attendant.

"Oh! Carlo says that the Conte will murder him."

"Murder him!" faintly replied Angelina. "I beseech you to explain yourself. What is the tale of horror you are charged with?"

"Why, my lady," replied the trembling attendant, "as I was crossing the North Hall I met Carlo. We were both brought up together, my lady, and Carlo—Carlo is—is always glad to see me, my lady."

"Well, well," said Angelino impatiently, "go on."

"Yes, my lady, I will; but I must tell it all in my own way. So says Carlo, 'Ah, Annetta, is that you? I have some news to tell you.' Ah, said I, you are always making me laugh, Carlo. 'No,' said he, 'what I am going to acquaint you with will not make you or your lady laugh.' Indeed! said I, what is it, dear Carlo! I said *dear,* my lady, to induce him to tell me."

"Good Heavens, Annetta, you are insupportable," said Angelina.

"Well, my lady, now I am come to the story. 'Well, what do you think?' said Carlo, who was quite grave. 'Late last night the Signor Lorenzo was found in the Castello by the Conte, and he is now loaded with chains, and confined in one of the prison chambers.'"

Angelina heard no more; but sunk on the ground, insensible

to her misery, and Annetta for a long time in vain endeavoured to restore her to existence.

When at length she recovered, she asked Annetta what further conversation had passed between her and Carlo.

"Why, my lady, to be sure I was indeed sorry about the Signor, because he was so handsome, and fought so bravely for you; so I said to Carlo, and do you think that the Conte will hurt him? 'Hush!' said Carlo, looking round, 'walls have ears; don't speak so loud. From what I heard last night,' said he softly, 'I am afraid it will go hard with him,' So I staid no longer, my lady, but hastened to acquaint you with the sad story."

The senses of Angelina were involved in a stupor of grief; her tears quickly followed each other down her pale cheeks. The dangerous situation of Lorenzo had awakened all the agonizing sensations which her bosom, full of love for him, could feel. Annetta said all she could to comfort her, but to no purpose. At length, however, a thought seemed to have arisen in her breast, which, by inspiring it with hope, made her somewhat composed, and this was to see Carlo, who, being the lover of Annetta, she thought might be prevailed on, in hopes of a future reward, to attempt the dangerous undertaking of restoring to liberty Lorenzo de Montalto, whose existence and happiness Angelina now found was far dearer to her than her own. She then desired Annetta to seek Carlo, and tell him to attend her immediately.

Annetta flew to obey the commands of her lady; and having communicated to Carlo her wish to see him, added thereto her own conjectures concerning what it was her mistress wanted to speak to him about. Carlo, though somewhat alarmed at hazarding the Conte's anger, yet being requested by Annetta, whom he had long loved, did not hesitate to accompany her to Angelina's apartments, before whom he bowed low, while he begged to know her commands.

"Carlo," said Angelina, "your love for Annetta I have long been acquainted with, and I will give my consent to your union, and a handsome present to you both on the day of your marriage, on one condition."

Carlo and Annetta blushed; she fixed her eyes impatiently on him while Angelina proceeded:—

"You know the situation of the Signor Lorenzo; you know that he was my preserver at the hazard of his own life. Common gratitude obliges me to exert myself for his present safety, which if you can secure by opening the doors of his prison, the heiress of Carlentini will make you independent."

"Signora," said Carlo, "if my ability was as great as my inclination to serve you, the Signor would soon be at liberty. I will, however, do all in my power. At midnight it will, I believe, be my turn to guard his prison, and if I have an opportunity to release him, I will do it; but, lady, I must leave the Castello, or well you know to-morrow will not see me alive."

"The Signor Lorenzo will doubtless protect his preserver," replied Angelina; "and the moment you are settled Annetta shall be yours. Meanwhile these jewels," she continued, presenting him with some, "will secure you against want."

The honest Carlo for a long time refused the valuable present, but Angelina at length prevailed, and she dismissed him in the fond hope that he would succeed in his important undertaking.

The morning was now far spent; the sun had long declined from his meridian altitude, and soon the gay scenes of midday splendor grew dim to the view; his last beams now faintly tinged the western horizon, till at length the clouds again resumed their fleecy hue, and the sober mantle of evening hung on the distant hills.

Angelina was too much absorbed in melancholy to meet the Conte at the hour of repast; she had sent an excuse to him, which served still more to irritate him against Lorenzo, who he determined should not long be his rival, for he easily perceived that she had been informed of the situation of that Signor, and which had so much afflicted her as to render her unable to attend the banquet.

Angelina passed some time in her oratory; on her knees she prayed for the success of her endeavours to release Lorenzo from the power of the Conte. Her eyes were suffused in tears as she raised them toward the bright abodes of the celestial host; but hope soon dried up the sources of grief, and Angelina arose from her suppliant posture, relieved from the pressure of her sorrows in proportion as her confidence in the All-powerful increased.

Some time remained ere the Castle bell would sound the long-tolling hour of midnight; and in order to divert the tedious moments Angelina took up a volume of old tales, having first sent Annetta to watch at a casement which looked into the inner Court, in order to bring the earliest intelligence of the success of Carlo. Meantime turning over the leaves of the book, her attention was caught by the following Fragment:—

THEODORA AND CELESTINA,

A FRAGMENT.

Chill blew the blast of night; it whistled through the umbrageous tenants of the forest; it howled through the caverns; it roared over the mountain; it raised the rough billows of the ocean, and dashed them against the sounding rocks of Calabria's shores: the white foam of the sea sailed on the blast; the Demon of Storms rode well pleased in the midst, or sported on the curled ridges of the black waves. Now deep sunk between two aqueous mountains, now elevated on the summit of a wave, appeared a bark. She bent before the rushing gale, her sails were torn and fluttering in the air, her cordage was broken, and her mast nearly destroyed. Impelled by the waves, and urged by the wind, she approached the Black Rocks.

Pale were the faces of the voyagers, distended with horror were their eyes. Death sat on the rocks awaiting his prey; they saw him on the sharp crags. The vessel bounded on the shelving shore, the waves rushed over her, she rolled from side to side; at last her timbers floated wide on the ridgy bosom of the deep, a dreadful cry was borne on the rushing blast.

No noise, save that of the storm, was heard: the flashes of electric fire from the low-hung clouds gleamed at times through the murky gloom, while the loud pealing thunder awoke the ech-

oes of the caves. At length the morning came. Sullenly the dark
vapours retired; the grey mist grew thin, a streak of crimson dye
faintly glimmered in the east; the mist, the surcumbent fogs that
hung over the vallies, faded away, when the sun beheld them from
the chariot of day as he urged on his immortal coursers.

Worn with the weight of years, slowly advanced from his
lonely cave an aged hermit. He paced the boundary of the ocean,
and sighing viewed the ravages of the storms; he started; the
body of a female lay before him, pale, lifeless; drenched with the
briny wave. He raised it up, and exerting the feeble remains of the
vigour of other days, brought it to his cell; there he laid it on his
humble pallet, and long endeavoured to call back the warm tide
of life.

The female at length opened her mild blue eyes. The suspended powers of recollection slowly returned; she gazed wildly
around the rocky sides of her present abode; and the venerable
preserver of her life, whose silver beard descended to his girdle,
at times caught her attention.

"Where," said she at length, "where has fate cast the miserable Celestina? Old man, tell me, I beseech you, where too are the
companions of my voyage? In thy countenance, stranger, dwells
the semblance of truth; unfold to me the tale."

"Lady," said the full of years, "my eyes did not seek for thy
friends; the cold winds blew; my frame trembles with age, and
I hesitated not a moment in performing toward thee the offices
of humanity. Compose your spirits; I will direct my steps to the
shores of the ocean."

This said, resting on his staff he tottered to the rocky boundary of the coast; he looked around; his eyes dim with age could just
distinguish vast fragments of the wreck trembling on the heaving
billows, but no human being did he see; no sound of mortal voice
reached his ear; silent and sad he returned and stood before his
agitated guest.

"In the womb of the ocean lie thy friends. To thee Providence
has been kind; be grateful for his favors, nor pass thy hours in
unavailing lamentations."

Wildly the female shrieked; her grief stole away her languid senses, and she fell on the ground, like the lily cut down by the careless sickle of the reaper.

Skilled in the knowledge of the various properties of herbs, the recluse hastily prepared a reviving medicine, which he poured into her mouth, and Celestina awoke from the torpor into which her grief had enwrapt her senses.

"Daughter," said the ancient man, "repine not at the inscrutable decrees of Providence, who heaps on us no more than he enables us to bear."

But the words of the sage to the distracted Celestina were like the wind among the reeds of the lake; they bend to the breeze, but the moment it is gone they raise their heads.

She heard his sayings, and listened to the matured advice of the collected experience of years; but her despair was the same. She smote her bosom, tore her lovely tresses that rivalled the feathers of the raven, bedewed her pallid cheeks with the scalding flood of sorrow, while in distracted accents she exclaimed: "My Theodore, then, is gone. No more shall I view his manly charms. The relentless waves of the ocean roll over his loved form; or perhaps, cast on some deserted coast, it lays to moulder in the scorching sun-beam. But I will seek it from the summit of some tall rock; I will behold the bed of the ocean, I will see if his grave be there; or if the shore bears his pale corse, I will entomb it in my arms."

Wildly she rushed out of the cave; the recluse sadly followed her steps, but he soon beheld her far before him, and the mist that dimmed his aged eyes obscured her from his view.

———

Clinging to a plank, a hapless sufferer, when the black waves tore asunder the beams of the vessel. One while an immense wave buried him in its briny bosom; another moment beheld him on the summit of a foaming ridge of the tempestuous element. As man naturally clings to life, so clung to the plank, his only hope, the unfortunate man. All was dark; the dreadful storm was thickly clad in sable horrors; at times the gleaming lightnings that made visible the tenebrous shades swiftly darted along the black tumbling waters, whose curled summit trembled at the peals of thunder which burst from the bosom of the low-hung clouds.

A long rolling wave advanced; the strong body of water, impelled by the violent gale, separated the unfortunate from the plank; forward it drove him with resistless force; it dashed him on a rock, and instantly receding, left him on it; he crawled slowly up the craggy side, and when the waves returned, held fast for fear of being washed into the deep.

The grey mists of morning beheld him fearfully hanging on the rocks, his body bruized, and his strength decreasing: below him rolled the dark waves.

Other thoughts besides his dangerous situation occupied his mind; a lovely maid was the precious freightage of the faithless vessel; his soul adored her, his heart was hers; she gave him her own in return. Sweet interchange! How bitter were now his thoughts.

It was Celestina whose death he lamented; and he was that Theodore whom Celestina grieved for; but no pitying angel was at hand to save two faithful lovers from black despair.

The morning came with its faint beams; Theodore still clung to the rock, but the animating powers of life were receding; his arms trembled; he could no longer retain his hold. Sighing out the name of Celestina he fell into the waves below. The rushing waters drove out his soul.

Celestina, the miserable Celestina, as fast as her trembling limbs could carry her, approached the rocks that hung over the ocean. She ascended their rugged steeps. The storm had partly subsided; the waves began to resume their cerulean colour, and the dark sand raised by the furious blasts sunk to the bed of the ocean.

Celestina gazed on the wide bosom of the waters; she looked on the dark rocks, but no Theodore met her view. Tearless were her eyes; her lovely locks streamed in the wind.

Thrice she called on the name of Theodore, and thrice

did Echo return the silver tones of her voice; but the voice of Theodore answered not.

She gazed on the waves below; she hung over the foaming precipice; she started, for plainly she beheld the waves rolling thinly over the body of her lover. Steadfastly for a time she surveyed the soul-harrowing sight, then she looked on the heavens with a rapturous gaze, a heavenly smile illumined her countenance.

"The soul of my Theodore," said she, "is now winging its rapid flight through the vast aerial expanse to regions of celestial joys. Wait a few short moments, beloved of my heart, and thy Celestina will bear thee company."

This said, she loosed her hold of the rock, and precipitated herself into the ocean: the waters divided over the body of Theodore, and she closed her lovely eyes for ever by the side of his pale corse.

At a distance the recluse sadly saw the deed of death. He waited till the tide had rolled the waves to other shores. He found the lovers on the pebbly beach; he viewed their inanimate remains with lively sensations of gratitude, while the tear of commiseration rolled down the furrows of his aged cheeks.

"Death, sweet pair," said he, "shall not divide you; one grave shall contain ye who had but one heart. These aged hands shall construct your simple tomb; the turf which covers you shall be moistened by my tears; sweet flowers shall unfold their varied beauties, and shed their fragrance round your silent abode; and when my soul, that is now lingering on the brink of eternity, meets yours in regions of joy, ye will thank me for this last act of friendship."

Mournfully the ancient solitary man began the fatiguing employment. Under the shade of a rock he raised the turf inclosure; in it he placed, side by side, the remains of the fond pair. He knelt down, and offered up a fervent petition to Heaven for the repose of their souls. The Angel of Death saw him; his moments were numbered; he sunk down, opprest with the immortalizing pangs of dissolution, and the tomb he had formed for the hapless Theodore and Celestina became also his own.

Her own sad situation, and the melancholy inspired by this pathetic tale, overcame the sorrowful Angelina. She dropt the volume, and deeply sighing, paid the tribute of a tear to the memory of Theodore and Celestina.

Her sorrowful ruminations were, however, soon changed into sensations of terror, for she plainly heard the paces of some people along the corridore that led to her apartments. Presently after the Conte Angelo entered, and closing the door after him, advanced toward the fear-struck Angelina, who trembled lest her attempt to liberate the Signor Lorenzo were discovered, and that he came to upbraid her with the part she had acted, and to put his former designs into execution.

END OF VOLUME THREE.

THE
DEMON OF SICILY.

CHAPTER XV.

THE morning sunbeams now began to disperse the misty nocturnal vapours, when Ferdinando concluded his narrative, and their mutual safety rendered it necessary that they should separate. Ferdinando promised to be with Agatha the next night, and then tenderly embracing her, withdrew.

That day beheld the remains of Marianne again consigned to the silent abode of death. The emotions of Agatha, though great and terrible, were not so poignant as what she had felt on a former occasion. She was at last secure from all fears of discovery; but that security, how dearly was it purchased; with the life of an innocent, unoffending fellow-creature.

According to his promise, Ferdinando met her again that night; and in order that they might pass the hours with more comfort than the gloomy chapel afforded, she led him to her apartment; which, from its being at some distance from those belonging to the nuns, was attended with little more danger than their meeting in the chapel.

This, then, was the night when the Padre Bernardo first beheld the handsome Agatha, whose beauties, tho' they raised the turbulent agitations which had so long slept in his bosom, yet could not drive away the love-formed image of the Signora whom he had seen in the pavilion.

With the method he made use of to separate the pair when he saw them embracing each other, the reader is already informed; and also of the promise given by Agatha to meet him the next night in the cemetery of the convent.

At that moment she reflected not on the spot fixed for their meeting, being much terrified by the cloud-formed appearance of the abbess, raised by the Demon purposely to separate them.

It was, however, now too late to alter it; and she was too fearful of offending the monk to break her promise. Although she had seemingly acquiesced with the monk's desire that she should not see Ferdinando any more, yet secretly she determined to admit him as often as she could with safety, till the festival, when she hoped to be able to effect her escape.

Can the feelings of Agatha be described when holding a lamp in her trembling hand she entered at the solitary hour of midnight the dreary abode of the dead, where lay the mortal remains of the murdered Marianne! that restless monitor which reigns in the bosom of the guilty—a self accusing conscience harrowed up every other sensation of her breast, save fear and remorse for her deeds of darkness.

The hollow echoes of her paces as she trod the vaulted cemetery made her stop; resting against one of the rude columns that supported the roof, she awaited the arrival of the monk.

Her eyes wandered round the place, whose cheerless gloom struck with melancholy on her soul, while in the dark masses of impenetrable shade her fear-struck gaze would oft depict some soul-appalling form.

A deep sigh apparently from that part of the cemetery where Marianne was buried now made Agatha start with the most horrible imaginings. Shuddering with fear, she bent forward to survey the place, expecting every moment to see the pale form of the nun striking through the gloom.

Dreadful were her sensations, and unknowingly she uttered aloud the thoughts that arose in her perturbed bosom:

"Sure my senses did not deceive me, for it must have been a sound from a human being which now assailed my ears. Will not the grave contain thee, Marianne? wilt thou again revisit the earth? has the supernatural being deceived me? or is it thy spirit, which, hovering over thy cold remains, sighs to reanimate them again?" A low hollow groan was heard; it appeared to proceed from mental, rather than corporeal agony. Cold drops of water stood trembling on the forehead of Agatha; the lamp dropped from her nerveless hand, and the light was extinguished by the fall. Opaque shades enveloped her; and now the long hour of midnight was told in harsh sullen notes by the abbey clock.

When Echo with her responsive train had resigned her short-lived reign to the mystic dominion of Silence, Agatha heard these words:—

"The murderess of Marianne is discovered."

A light now gleamed from the remote extremity of the cemetery; and as Agatha was sinking on the earth, her eyes glanced on the figure of the monk. "Save, oh! save me!" she exclaimed; "the spirit of Marianne is coming to punish me for having murdered her."

Bernardo hastened toward her; and supporting her in his arms, endeavoured to recal her fleeting senses. Somewhat comforted by his presence, she slowly revived, while the monk frequently kissed her pallid lips.

Greatly did the Demon rejoice at this scene. Invisible to mortal sight, he reared his dark form before them, and viewed the effect of his arts, which gratified his restless, malicious, and revengeful spirit.

The embraces of the monk and the nun continued. Seated on the steps that led down from the chapel into the cemetery, they kissed each other with increasing fervor, when a distant pace was heard in the cemetery, and the eyes of the guilty pair were instantly directed to where the sounds proceeded.

At length the object that had caused their fears came in sight. It was a nun; and Agatha soon recognized in the wan features the sorrowing Claudina, who had that night descended to the grave of her friend to lament over her cold remains, and had thus from her own mouth discovered the murderess of Marianne.

Unable longer to survey the guilty acts of Agatha, and fearing worse scenes, she left the grave of her lost friend, and was going to depart the cemetery in order to acquaint the abbess with the transactions of that night; but ere she ascended the steps, standing before their abashed sight she thus addressed them:

"Foul votaries of vice! at length Providence has ordained that ye should be discovered, and receive the just rewards of your horrible deeds of guilt. This night, Agatha, shall the abbess know the

vile cause of the death of the sainted Marianne, and the profanation of these sacred walls by your shameful conduct with a
monk."

This said, she was departing on her terrible mission, when
Bernardo starting up, seized her by the arm, and dragged her
back.

"You go not," said he, "to bear such a message to the abbess;
'twas well you told us your intents."

"Unhand me, father," said Claudina, "or my screams shall disturb the inhabitants of the convent." The cowl that covered the
face of Bernardo falling back discovered his features; pale with
fear, and distorted by rage, he looked steadfastly at the nun, while
in a hollow voice, he thus spoke:

"Swear," said he, "that you will never reveal to mortal the occurrences of this night, or else dread my terrible purposes."

"I fear not thy threats, father; nor will I yield to thy request,"
replied the resolute Claudina. "I am resolved to unveil the sinful
transactions which this night has witnessed."

Hardly had these words escaped her, when the monk instantly
seized her by the throat, and dashed her on the earth. The unfortunate nun struggled hard to release herself from his firm grasp,
but in vain. She lay beneath his strong hold gasping for breath,
while her quivering limbs shewed the agony she endured.

Agatha turned with horror from the terrible sight, and hiding
her face with her hands, awaited the result.

The efforts of Claudina now became every moment more
faint, and at length the breath of life ceased to animate her form,
and her soul flew to meet the kindred spirit of Marianne in realms
of peace and joy.

The monk started with horror from the body, and as he lifted
up his eyes beheld the gigantic figure of the Demon, who now
rendered himself visible, gazing with looks of satisfaction on the
murdered corse.

"Fear not, Bernardo," said his harsh voice, "thou seest me
here. My friend, this deed, which necessity alone prompted thee
to do, must be concealed from the world. Lay the body on the
grave of Marianne. The well-known attachment Claudina had for

The Demon of Sicily appearing to Bernardo.

that nun will account for her being there, and her decease will be
ascribed to her continual grief. To-morrow at midnight thou mayest again expect to see me."

As these words proceeded from him the abbey clock told the
commencement of another day. The figure of the Demon then
dissolved from the view, and the earth no longer supported his
blasted form. Deep in the bowels of chaos was his dread abode,
where he reigned the supreme monarch over myriads of wicked
spirits excelled only by himself.

The monk, following the counsel of the Demon, took the yet

warm body of Claudina in his arms, and carried it to the hillock which rose over the mouldering remains of Marianne, on which having laid it, he retired, deeply struck with pale horror at the dreadful crime he had committed.

Agatha remained on the steps. The last gasps of the nun, the appearance of the dark form of the Demon, and her own sensations, had nearly hurled reason from her seat; and but that the words of the arch fiend consoled her in some degree, it is probable that the fever of delirium would have raged in her frame.

When the monk returned from the grave of Marianne he took the passive hand of Agatha in his: both trembled, their eyes met; not as before, sparkling with sensations of pleasure, but languid and full of horror.

"We are safe," said the monk, in a low tremulous tone, "Death has sealed up those lips which would have betrayed us; that mysterious supernatural being is our friend; give not way, then, to useless terrors, sweet Agatha."

"Both our victims are indeed silent," said the ruminating nun. "How horrible were their deaths. Would that memory was no more; for the recollection makes my soul tremble."

The monk started while he recalled to his mind the various circumstances respecting Marianne. She too, thought he, has the dread weight of blood upon her; but what could cause her to perpetrate that dark deed?

For a while he too was lost in thought. Suddenly, however, pale fears visited his breast. "Let us haste from this place," said he, "for the spirits of the murdered are now, perhaps, hovering round us."

He then assisted Agatha to arise, and supported her to the steps of the altar, where she seated herself; but the Almighty, who from his throne beheld the deeds of the monk, expressed his anger in loud and awful peals of thunder, which shook the deep foundations of the consecrated pile; blue lightnings played around them, the stormy hail dashed against the casements of the chapel, the spirits of the tempest shrieked aloud, the gale roared between the echoing bursts of thunder.

The monk started with affright at the elemental war; aghast, he surveyed the blazes of vivid fire which illumined the chapel; thickly clustered the clouds in all their dark and gloomy horror, the magazines of Heaven's loud warfare.

The senses of Agatha, unable to bear up against the various horrors that lived unceasing in her remembrance, now deserted her, and she lay motionless and inanimate on the steps of the altar.

The monk's terrors were too great to permit him to afford her any assistance; he shook as the lonely thistle on the ruined tower to the restless gale of night.

Then it was that the murdered form of the nun appeared to his imagination. Slow and airy she seemed to glide past him; her eyes were fixed, no motion was in her distorted countenance.

Such was the fear-formed idea of his guilty soul, as he stood beneath one of the chapel casements, overwhelmed with horror and dismay.

Thus wore heavily the fearful lengthening hours of that dreadful night. Agatha at length revived; and as soon as she was able, sadly and slowly retired to her chamber; and the monk returned to the cemetery, which he hastily passed through, hardly daring to raise his eyes, lest he should see the breathless body of Claudina.

The absence of that unfortunate nun was taken notice of by the abbess at the matin service, and one of the sisters was sent to her chamber. It appeared, however, that she had not slept there; and search being made in the cemetery, her remains were discovered. Great was the confusion caused in the convent by her death. From the torn garments of Claudina, the marks of violence about her throat, and other circumstances, it appeared that some foul means had been made use of toward her. The singular circumstances respecting the death of Marianne, were now recollected afresh, and the abbess began to have thoughts arise in her breast that those nuns came unfairly by their death. On this subject she held a long conversation with the abbot; and as the suspicions of the abbess could not attach themselves to any particular person, the abbot advised her not to make any inquiry at the present moment, but to wait till time or accident should unfold the perpetrators of the horrid act; and in the meantime to appear to think that in despair for the loss of her friend, Claudina laid violent hands on herself.

Her remains were buried by the side of Marianne, and the Padre Bernardo and Agatha consoled themselves with the hopes that their deeds of darkness would never be unveiled to mortal sight.

The monk, on the succeeding night after the murder of Claudina did not forget the promise of the Demon to see him. The purport of his coming he was not able to conceive; and his curiosity being roused, he awaited with impatience the silent hour of midnight.

At length it came with all its attendant shades of murky darkness. The waning moon no longer illumined the hours of night; the stars too were hid by the collected nocturnal vapours; the comfortless blast of the east howled cheerless among the shady tenants of the forest; the bird of night from the time-worn turret or hollow of the knotted oak gave its discordant hootings to the ready echoes; no nightingale with her song of peace and love was heard; but Nature was wrapt in gloomy horror, while the lightning darted from the low-hung clouds, and the distant rolling thunder was at times heard.

The Demon was now visible to the monk. The sable monastic habit which he had formerly worn when he had appeared to him was laid aside; his form, moulded by the Divinity, was such as far excelled worldly perfection. Wings of the whiteness of the wave-washed swan shaded his lineaments. To have beheld him without the searching eye of the physiognomist, one would have conceived him a messenger from Heaven; but his features were marked with all the raging passions which war in the bosoms of the wicked; such as revenge, malice, pale ire, envy, and despair; and which bespoke him the prince of infernal horrors.

The monk gazed on him with astonishment; he felt awe-struck in his presence. How different would have been his sensations had virtue been his constant guide, how different would have been the conduct of the Demon had he been standing before a steady adherent to the rule of right. With servile adulation he would have bent before him; but now that that he beheld a being whose soul owned him for his master, and which he looked on as almost irrecoverably his own, his countenance betrayed the secret satisfaction which dwelt in his heart, while he gazed on the victim of his deep and well-concerted plans.

"Padre," said the Demon, "have the charms of Agatha obliterated from thy mind the lovely Signora whom I showed to thee in the pavilion? wilt thou then tamely resign her to the lover whom thou sawest with her? and hast thou forgotten that I promised her to thy power? Thou seest how prompt I am to serve thee, and how, in the exigency of thy distress the past night, I counselled thee how to proceed. Look on me as thy trusty friend, and banish from thy mind all vain fears which prevent thy thoughts from rolling in their accustomed channel."

"Since the moment that unwilling I was taken from her presence," replied the monk, "my whole soul has been wrapt up in the remembrance of her charms. Sleeping or waking my imagination has dwelt unceasing on her. Me resign her to the arms of her lover? Perish the thought. Be thou my friend, he not long shall be an obstacle to my wishes. When I think on her, I feel my nature changed; to possess her unrivalled beauties, methinks I could dare all perils, encounter all toils, so that she was to be my sweet, luxurious reward."

"Enough," said the Demon, drawing from beneath his plumy wing a scroll; "if such be thy resolve, thou wilt enroll thyself amongst these, my friends, whom I serve. That done, thou shalt find thyself in her presence, thou shalt be alone with her in the silent retirement of her chamber of repose."

Tired with the longings of his bosom, the monk hesitated not to comply with the request of the Demon; who, unfolding the fatal scroll, and taking thence a pen of bright steel, touched the swelling veins of the monk, when the obedient blood started into it; he then presented it to the monk, whose hand, notwithstanding the lovely prize that was to be the reward of concession, trembled with the emotions of a sudden inborn dread.

The storm had increased; the thunder rolled over the monastery; the flashes of electric matter that were lodged in the dark

The Monk signing his soul to the Devil.

caverns of the low-hung clouds darted frequent around; and as the monk received the pen from the hand of the Demon, attracted by the polished metal the lightning struck it from his hold, and by the sudden shock his arm hung nerveless by his side. The monk nearly insensible fell back in his seat, the Demon looked aghast; suddenly he snatched up the scroll and the pen, and with confusion and disappointment legible in his features, dissolved from the view of Bernardo, who remained in his recumbent posture for a long time, till his corporeal powers returning, he raised himself up, and paced his chamber, a prey to a dreadful chaos of half-formed ideas.

CHAPTER XVI.

THE Conte Angelo now determined no longer to wait for the accomplishment of his designs against Angelina. Struck with the manly graces of Lorenzo, and recollecting at the same time his visits to his beauteous ward when she resided at the convent, he easily conceived that she looked on him with a favorable eye. A thought occurred to him of the means which he now possessed to frighten her into compliance with his wishes, and he hastily left his chamber to consult with the friar Hildargo on the subject.

It was near midnight when the plotting, restless Conte appeared at the side of the confessor's couch, and communicated to him his resolutions. Hildargo then arose; and the Conte having summoned two chosen domestics to attend him, passed on to Angelina's chamber.

He found her sitting pensively by the side of a table, on which lay the volume she had been perusing; she started on seeing him enter, and arose from her seat.

"Your domestic, Signora," said he in a well-feigned tone of respect, "informed me you were unwell. My solicitude to hear of your recovery will, I trust, excuse the lateness of this visit."

"Most certainly, my Lord," replied Angelina, endeavouring to compose the agitations of her bosom, "I feel myself better now than in the morning."

"Can you account for your sudden indisposition?" said the Conte, looking at her with a scrutinizing glance; "was it occasioned by any unpleasant intelligence; or merely the effect of some sudden discomposure of the frame? for if I rightly recollect me, you were perfectly well last night."

Angelina was somewhat confused by this unexpected question. In the looks of the Conte she read that some dark and deep designs were lurking in his breast. She hesitated to answer; and the Conte passionately proceeded:

"Yes, Signora, I know the cause; it was the situation of Lorenzo de Montalto, your favored lover, who now inhabits a prison chamber beneath the east ramparts."

Angelina trembled; the next words she expected to hear the Conte utter was to upbraid her with her endeavour to free Lorenzo from his bonds, and she remained still silent.

"Your silence, Signora, confirms all my suspicions; and ere another hour has passed Lorenzo ceases to exist."

All the tender, grateful recollections of that Signor crowded to the heart of Angelina, the blood forsook her cheeks, a trembling seized her frame, and but for the support of Angelo she would have sunk on the floor. It was, however, not a moment to yield to the impulse of her distressed feelings; she endeavoured to collect all her fortitude, and disengaging herself from the arm of the Conte, thus addressed him:

"And what, my Lord, has been the crime of the Signor Lorenzo, that you entertain against him such a deadly design?"

"In brief, Angelina," replied the Conte, "I will answer your question. Did he not attack me? and shall that be unrevenged? Shall I too forget that you look on him with the eye of affection? and did I not find him concealed in the Castello? into which you doubtless had given him the means of effecting his entrance for purposes I blush to think of."

"Me, my Lord," said Angelina, rouzed by the base insinuations of her persecutor, "me connive at the Signor's entrance, Conte Angelo? You either forget yourself, or forget that you are addressing the daughter of the Marchese de Carlentini and the virtuous Louisa."

The Conte smiled contemptuously. "Virtues, Signora, do not descend in lineal succession; but I am willing to forget your imprudent conduct with Lorenzo, and even to save his forfeit life, on one condition."

"Name it," said Angelina in a faltering voice.

"Consent to bestow on me your hand, and the moment that sees us united breaks the chains of Lorenzo."

"No, my Lord," replied the hapless maid in a firm voice, "never shall Angelina be united to Conte Angelo. You dare not touch the life of Lorenzo without hazarding your own."

"Dare not!" vociferated the Conte, "this moment shall show you what I dare do."

This said, he stamped his foot, and the door of the chamber was opened by his trusty domestics.

"Now, lady, take your choice; either come quietly to the chapel, or my people shall bear you thither."

In the determined looks of the Conte Angelina saw her fate, yet she still thought that the life of Lorenzo was not dependent on her acquiescence; for desperate as the Conte was, yet such an act would be revenged by the state, and she resolutely determined to resist his present attempts.

"Have you so soon, my Lord," she replied, "forgot the solemn oath which you took at the altar of the convent chapel, that you would cease your unjust persecutions? Reflect on the dreadful consequences of breaking that solemn promise, and leave my chamber."

"Idle talk," exclaimed the Conte; "'tis true I said a few unmeaning words to quiet the old abbess, but they are now erased from my remembrance, and this hour shall be propitious to my wishes."

So saying he advanced to Angelina, and seizing her hand, drew her toward the portal.

She endeavoured to resist his efforts, but in vain.

"Stephano," said the Conte, "conduct the Signora to the chapel."

"Oh! Heaven have mercy on me!" said the hapless maid, as falling on her knees she raised her clasped hands toward the abode of the all-seeing Creator of the Universe, "look down on me, I beseech you, and guard me in the moment of horror."

The ruffian grasp of Stephano raising her from the floor interrupted her prayer, he quickly bore her from the chamber, and followed the Conte Angelo toward the chapel.

The tears, the exclamations of Angelina were of no avail; the inhabitants of the Castello were buried in sleep; but even had they been roused by her cries, it would have been of little avail, as the Conte's power was absolute, and no one dared to dispute his will.

The portals of the chapel were open, and a light at the altar attracted the tearful gaze of Angelina, when standing by it, ready to perform the detested ceremony, stood the gloomy figure of Hildargo.

Stephano now released his hapless burthen from his strong hold; and the Conte starting forward took her arm, and dragged her up the steps that led to the altar, and desired the confessor to begin the ceremony.

"Oh! father," said Angelina, "do not, I conjure you by Him who died for us, do not commit so great a sin."

"Lady," said the hypocritical monk, "you see I am not allowed to act according to my own wishes; the Conte will be obeyed."

Hope fled the bosom of Angelina, with hope also fled her senses; and pale as the lily which sweetens the zephyr that glides along the vale, she fell lifeless on the steps of the altar.

The Conte raised her up; and while he long endeavoured to call back the breath of life we will return to Lorenzo, who was confined to a dreary dungeon, which he paced with a disordered step while he reflected that the treasure of his soul, his adored Angelina, was now without a friend to protect her against the schemes of her bitter enemy.

Amid such distracting ruminations as his fears produced, the hours rolled heavily on; the ruddy streaks of morn now tinted the casements of the Castello, and Lorenzo from the grate of his prison examined the objects before him.

A court yard of some extent appeared to his view, surrounded with the different buildings that belonged to the edifice: on one side was a large gallery, which served as a communication from the ramparts to a structure of some extent, which from its appearance, Lorenzo concluded was the chapel of the Castello.

A noise at the door of his dungeon made him turn round; it was occasioned by the entrance of a man with some provisions. He silently placed them on a table, while at the door stood an armed guard leaning on his battle-spear.

He surveyed the men in gloomy silence, while they appeared

awed by his fierce undaunted looks, and hastened from his presence. The paces of a centinal before the door of the dungeon now broke on the silence which before was undisturbed. From this circumstance the fears of the Conte lest he should escape were evident, and Lorenzo passed some time in melancholy anticipations of what would be the result of Angelo's designs respecting him.

At length the mists of evening entering the grate of his dungeon slowly began to shade the objects it contained from his view, and as the gloom deepened around him, so sadly increased the gloomy thoughts of Lorenzo.

Thus rolled away the time; and now midnight lowered heavily in all its dark horrors over the earth, when Lorenzo, as he sat at the grate of his dungeon, beheld a light flash on the casement of the chapel; and looking through them, saw a monk approaching the altar, on which he placed a lamp.

Supposing that an act of devotion had drawn the father there at that silent hour, he again returned to the train of hapless thoughts which filled his soul; when soon after, by the light of a torch which glared at the further end of the chapel, he saw the Conte Angelo enter with two domestics, one of whom carried a female.

Her cries and lamentations shook him with horror, for he recognized in her the beloved of his bosom, his adored Angelina.

His disturbed eye-balls glared unceasingly on the objects that harrowed up his other senses; he saw her placed at the altar, and the detested Conte seize her hand. The priest then opened his missal, when Angelina sunk on the marble steps of the altar.

Loudly he raised his voice. "Fiend of hell!" he exclaimed, "may curses eternal wither thy soul! Execrable monster, would I had thee in my hold, the world should not long contain so great a villain."

But his words became indistinct ere they reached the ears of the Conte or his domestics, who were busily employed in endeavouring to recal Angelina to life.

It was at this moment that Carlo, faithful to the promise he made to the Signora Angelina, silently unbarred the door of the dungeon; and entering, beheld the distracted Lorenzo raving with the horrific pangs of despair and fury which raged in his bosom.

Carlo, ignorant of the cause of his sorrows, unseen approached him. "Signor," said he, "the door of your prison is open." As the lightning from the dark bosom of the clouds, so darted away Lorenzo; having first seized Carlo's sword from the sheath in which it hung by his side, he flew along the passages, and fortune favouring him, at length found out the gallery which led to the chapel.

Carlo, terrified at the wild behaviour of Lorenzo, snatched up his battle-spear and followed his hasty steps, deeply involved in fear and wonder.

Lorenzo at length reached the portals of the chapel; they were closed, but he burst them open, and rushed to the altar.

Angelina had recovered. Hildargo had already begun the ceremony, when Lorenzo deep sheathed his sword in the breast of the fear-struck Conte Angelo.

His blood dyed the marble steps; he fell; Angelina clung to the altar, horror struck; for as Lorenzo was hastening to her the sword of Stephano revenged the wound he had given his Lord.

He was at the point of repeating it, when Carlo thrust his spear through his body, and there leaving it, snatched up the fainting Lorenzo in his arms, and bore him from the chapel.

The domestic who remained with Hildargo hastened to the assistance of the Conte, who lay insensible on the steps, still bleeding. Opening his garments, Hildargo bound up the gaping wound, and without paying any attention to the distracted Angelina, was conveying him to his apartment, when she, beholding the ghastly corpse of Stephano, who lay at her feet with the spear deep planted in his body, exerted all her powers, and tremblingly tottered out of the chapel; and fortunately being observed by Annetta, who was returning to acquaint her with the escape of Lorenzo, she hastened forward, and caught her as she was sinking on the earth.

With some difficulty Annetta conducted her to her chamber, for the senses of her beloved mistress were disturbed, and she raved continually about Lorenzo; and frequently struggled to disengage herself from the supporting arms of her faithful domestic.

Meantime the honest Carlo, faithful to his trust, bore along the wounded Lorenzo; he left the Castello, and as quickly as he was able conveyed him to the forest, where he laid him down, and procuring assistance from the cabin of a wood-cutter, staunched the blood; while his afflicted patient, anxious only for his adored Angelina, repeatedly entreated Carlo to convey him back to the Castello, that he might be certain of her safety.

"Signor," replied Carlo, "you may make yourself easy. In all probability the Conte Angelo is no more; at any rate, he is so dreadfully wounded that he cannot now disturb the quiet of the Signora Angelina. Your fate and mine is therefore certain if we are taken, and the Signora will then be left without a friend."

Lorenzo suffered himself at length to be persuaded; and Carlo having procured a mule, he mounted it with his assistance, and attended by him, slowly proceeded to the village, where his attendants were awaiting his coming, greatly distressed at his long absence. A friar from a neighbouring monastery soon attended him, and having examined the wound, gave him the pleasing intelligence that it was by no means dangerous, and that rest was all that was required to heal it.

But the situation of Conte Angelo was far different. Lorenzo's sword had pierced some of his noble parts, and it was doubtful whether he would ever raise his long-closed eyelids.

A faint pulsation at the heart feebly told that the breath of life yet lingered in his frame; and at length, by the assistance of powerful medicines, a groan announced the increase of animation.

Slowly the Conte opened his eyes; but it was not till near the close of the next day that he could give distinct utterance to his words. His first inquiry was whether Angelina had escaped.

"No, my Lord," replied Hildargo, "she is confined to her couch."

"Where is Lorenzo?" demanded the Conte in a hollow voice.

"Doubtless he is scarcely alive, for he received a terrible wound from Stephano the moment after you fell. Carlo, who it seems had released him from the dungeon where he was confined, carried him out of the hall, and neither of them have since been seen."

The Conte seemed pleased to find that his adversary had not escaped unhurt, and was going to give orders for an armed party to go in search of him and Carlo, when reflecting on the time that had elapsed since they had left the Castello, he desisted, knowing how fruitless it would be.

The hapless Angelina, who feared that Lorenzo had fallen a victim to his exertions in her favor, was inconsolable, her eyes became two constant sluices to the torrent of tears which flowed down her pallid cheeks. Hope, that sweet soother of the woe-fraught mind, did not however quite desert her; and that it was which alone enabled her to exist.

Lorenzo quickly recovered from his wound; he rewarded Carlo far beyond his most sanguine expectations, and took him into his service; and the honest domestic would have been completely happy if Annetta could have shared his good fortune.

Lorenzo was anxious to gain intelligence of his adored Angelina; and having sent for Carlo, requested his advice in what manner he should act; when to his great surprise Carlo offered to be the bearer of a letter to that Signora.

Lorenzo was for a long time deaf to the intreaties of Carlo to allow him to endanger his life; but at length he suffered himself to be persuaded, and writing a billet to Angelina, delivered it to the care of the adventurous Carlo.

Perhaps it was as much the wish to see Annetta as to be serviceable to his new master that made Carlo resolve to approach the walls of the Castello. Love sees no difficulties, no dangers, it dares hazard every thing to meet the object of its affections.

The mists of evening were whitening around when Carlo departed from the village and shaped his course for the Castello. His features were concealed from observation by a large cloak. He soon entered on the Carlentini estate, where he learnt from the friendly woodcutter that the Conte Angelo still lingered in an uncertain state, and that fresh medical assistance had been procured.

Carlo knew that at a certain hour when the domestics were

engaged at the evening repast his obtaining admission into the Castello would not be attended with much danger; he waited beneath the walls till that time, when he cautiously passed through the gates, and traversing the most retired passages, at length arrived at the portal of Angelina's apartments, where as he listened the voice of Annetta sweetly sounded in his ears as she was talking to her mistress and endeavouring to console her.

He tapped gently at the door, which Annetta soon after opened; and Carlo, letting fall his cloak, became known to the delighted damsel.

"Oh holy Mother! it is Carlo, my dear Carlo, who"———

"Hush!" said Carlo, "recollect yourself, or you will cause me to be discovered. First give this letter to your mistress, and then come again to me."

Annetta flew with the billet to Angelina. "Here, my lady, here it is; the Signor has sent Carlo."

"What do you say?" replied Angelina, her countenance one moment bearing a crimson tint, at the next turning to a deadly hue; "Carlo here! and this letter."——

"Is from the Signor Lorenzo," replied the delighted Annetta.

Angelina tearing open the cover, while her hand trembled with the motions of her bosom, read the following lines:—

"The kind Deity who guards the innocent has twice blessed me, by putting it in my power to be of service to the truly lovely Angelina de Carlentini. Condescend to favor me with an interview. I may perhaps be of use if your enemy yet lives. The wound I received in my successful attempt to prevent the base Angelo from carrying his schemes into effect has been a great consolation to me; for was it not received in the cause of beauty and innocence when it trembled beneath the grasp of the oppressor?"

"Lorenzo de Montalto."

Angelina perused the hasty billet of Lorenzo while Annetta was engaged in conversation with Carlo; she blushed at his requesting an interview, but how could she refuse him to whom she was under so many obligations? who had twice risked his life in her defence? such a thought could not find admittance in her grateful heart; love, too, forbid it; she therefore took her pen and wrote as follows:—

"Signor,
    "In order to prove my gratitude, I will not refuse your request. In the evening of to-morrow I shall be in a pavilion at the extremity of the gardens of the Castello.
                            "ANGELINA DE CARLENTINI."

She now desired Annetta to tell Carlo to enter her apartment; and having learnt from him the particulars of their escape, forced him to accept of a valuable jewel, and giving him the billet, dismissed him, after having once more assured him of her intentions of providing liberally for his future days when time should put her in possession of her estates.

Carlo then departed, and Angelina that night tasted the sweets of repose. In her dreams she saw the gallant Lorenzo; and when she awoke her countenance had lost the gloom which had overcast it, for she anticipated the happiness of seeing him in the evening.

CHAPTER XVII.

BUT the Demon was not to be so easily foiled in his designs respecting the Padre Bernardo. True it was that he was shocked when he beheld the electric spark from Heaven strike the pen from the hands of the monk, and unable to remain in his presence thus defeated, he slunk away to his horrific abode.

The next night, however, he again appeared to the monk, whom he found seated in his cell, perusing the ancient manuscript of Bartolo, of which mention is made in the first volume of these imperfect records. The monk started at beholding him; pale horror was seated on his brow, his mind had been occupied by the pages before him, and some sentences which he had then read struck to his soul. The story he was perusing related to some deeds which had been perpetrated in the walls of the ancient Castello, on whose wide-extending ruins the monastery was erected. The tale was as follows:—

———

Rodolph and Felippo were brothers. Rodolph was the first-born, and possessed the estates belonging to the Castello; both loved the handsome Laurina; both loved, but Rodolph only was beloved.

In the murky recess of a wood the furious Felippo vented the swelling torments of his soul. "Thus," said he, "am I doomed to be for ever accursed; the possessions of Rodolph have gained him the love of Laurina; he will marry her, he will possess those charms, and I must behold her his."

Dark grew his features. "Rather," he exclaimed, "may the rolling waves of the ocean pass over my inanimate corse; rather may mountains overwhelm me; rather may chaos see me banded about for ever in his pregnant abodes of unformed nature where the confused materials of which worlds are formed rage in constant furious warfare, than behold Laurina united to Rodolph."

Settled were his dark resolutions; but first he saw Laurina.

"Lovely fair, listen to my suit; listen to the voice of the enamoured Felippo; 'tis he who truly, sincerely loves you; your frown kills him, your smile would make him the most envied of men."

"Signor Felippo well knows," replied the blue-eyed maid, "that Rodolph has the love of Laurina, Felippo her friendship; nor can Time in all his revolving years alter the firm affection of my heart; thou hast therefore heard for the last time my resolves."

"'Tis well," said the furious Felippo, "Laurina has known how great my love, she has now to experience my hate." This said, brooding dark plans of horrible revenge and cruelty, he strode away.

Laurina shuddered at the black expression of his features. How unlike, thought she, are the dispositions of the two brothers; Rodolph resembles the placid evening of Summer, and Felippo the stormy nights of gloomy Winter. Strange, that scions from the same branch should be of such opposite natures.

———

A huge mountain, whose summit in dreadful threatenings far overhangs its base, rises in the Val di Demone. Trees old and horrid thickly beset the ground; lonely is the place, and silent, save when the blast roars through the aged larches and pines, or rustles amongst the tall waving grass which covers its rugged sides. Beneath, a dark chasm yawns dreadful to the sight; the entrance to a cave, the dimensions of which the eyes cannot discover, for the light of a thousand torches could not extend to the far distant confines. The sun never entered there with his beams, nor does the pale moon visit it by night; the raging wind glides slow and mournful through the vast regions of night and horror, and frequent bears on its bosom dreadful shrieks and howlings of fearful import.

In the legends of years that are past this cave is mentioned to be the abode of diabolical spirits, who nightly there assemble to forge vain illusions, phantasms, and dreams, with which to mislead unwary mortals. Strange and dreadful are the tales of other days, full of vast and dismal horrors. We doubt not of the truth of them; for what is impossible?

It was to this place that the gloomy Felippo bent his steps. Deeds of horror rolled in his thoughts; he folded his arms, and entered the cave.

He was unobserved by man, for the shepherd never led his flock there, nor the herdsman his hungry oxen; industriously they avoided the place, and even the gale that howled over the gloomy forest, lest it should be infected with the exhalement of evil beings.

The air stilly breathed; no sound was heard through the vast caverns. Felippo gloomily walked forward. Suddenly a rushing blast passed him; it bore along a deep groan, which soon died silently away. Felippo fearful stopped: a sudden trembling seized his joints; low notes of harmony floated above; now they swell sweetly to the ear, echo repeats them; suddenly all is again silent.

Felippo proceeded; the tuneful notes recomposed him, they vibrated gently on his soul.

An enormous bell, as the deep tones which proceeded from it proved it to be, now tolled. Felippo started as echo replied to the brazen sound in harsh, discordant murmurs. Something rustled close by him; he laid his hand on his sword; he drew, and waved it around him. It, however, only cleaved the air; no resistance met its edge; veiled in flaky darkness was all around.

Again the bell tolled. Its sonorous sounds struck coldly on his heart, his knees stiffened, the sword dropped from his hand, erect was the hair on his head, he tried to return, but was not able.

The bell tolled a third time. "He comes!" said a voice, harsh and loud as the roaring of waves in a storm when they beat against the craggy black rocks of Calabria's shores.

In the tenebrous gloom now suddenly appeared before the astonished Felippo a bright form, borne in a luminous cloud. It was the Demon of Sicily. He smiled complacent.

"Brave indeed art thou, mortal," said the Demon, "to penetrate into these, our mundane abodes. Doubtless thy reasons for so doing were of no trifling import: impart them to me; and if I in ought can serve you, depend on my strength and power."

"Great is the grief which disturbs my bosom," replied the trembling Felippo. "I loved Laurina, but she loves Rodolph; she despised my love, and now my breast burns with emotions of deep hatred, and thirsts for revenge."

"Rodolph too smiles in security at thy sighs, he rejoices in the grief of thy heart, and anticipates with pleasure the miseries that will be thine when thou seest Laurina in his arms," returned the crafty Demon.

A volume of distempered ideas rolled dreadful in the mind of Felippo; his countenance grew black as the shades of night, when storms rage and ghosts arise on the earth.

"And does Rodolph smile?" said he, "is Felippo become the sport of others? shall they live? Being of awful horrors, I come to request thy assistance."

"And thou shalt not sue in vain. Yes, thou shalt be revenged. This wand is possessed of great power; wave it over the eyes of whom thou wilt, a slumber deep, and silent as the grave will seize the senses; thou mayest then do whatever thou shalt please."

This said, the Demon reached to the astonished Felippo a small wand, on which was engraven various talismanic figures; it was of gold, and of exquisite workmanship.

Suddenly all around grew dark; Felippo lifted up his eyes, but the form of the Demon was no longer to be seen. Presently a light arose as if from the earth, at a distance.

"Felippo, that lambent flame will conduct thee thence," said a voice.

Holding the wand he advanced toward it; it receded from him with a gentle motion, and after walking some time, he found himself at the entrance of the cave. The flame disappeared, the breath of morning was fresh on the earth, and Felippo bent his steps to the Castello, revolving in his mind how best he should be revenged of Rodolph and Laurina.

———

Stormo, the ruthless Stormo, was hired by the gold of Felippo: little recked he what crime he perpetrated, so long as he reaped a reward for it.

In the dead of the night he conferred with this, his ready agent; in two days the detested marriage was to take place.

A smile distorted the countenances of the consulters as they pitched on a scheme which would plant the sharp and rankling dart of misery deep in the heart of the fond pair.

The morning of the nuptials arrived with all its bright beams. Rodolph led Laurina to the altar; Felippo with composed features beheld the ceremony performed; his revengeful intents appeared not in his countenance.

The feast of mirth and joy made the long tables groan. Sounds of merry import floated in the air; and now the shades of evening descended, and the lamps and torches dispelled the gloom in the lofty hall.

Rodolph looked with the gaze of love on Laurina, who returned his enamoured glances. The fever of rage burnt in the heart of Felippo; sudden he waved the mystic wand.

As when the blast of autumn shakes the leafy tenants of the forest, and scatters their decayed burden to the ground, so fell the eye-lids of the numerous guests; each sunk back in his seat, oppressed with the imposed slumber, and a sudden silence reigned around. The minstrel's ready fingers stopped on the vibrating chords, the singer's harmonious cadence died away, the cup that was just lifted to the lips dropped from the inactive hand, and its ruby-coloured contents stained the floor.

Rodolph had sunk back on his superb couch, and Laurina slept with her head reclined on her lovely arm, which rested on the table.

On a signal from Felippo, Stormo entered the hall, and bore away the sleeping Laurina to the place agreed on; he then returned, and Rodolph shared the same fate.

Felippo did not quit his seat; but rejoicing in his well-concerted schemes, closed his eyes, and appeared to be alike influenced by the somniferous deity as the others.

When the shrill harbinger of morn crowed in the castle courts the charm ceased; each of the guests started up, surprised and fearful to be found sleeping on such a festival; each looked surprised at his neighbour, and for some time no words were uttered.

The absence of Rodolph and Laurina was not thought strange, they were supposed to have sought the retirement of the nuptial chamber; but the attendants of Laurina coming to conduct their mistress to her apartments proved their ideas wrong formed.

Felippo with the guests was active in the search; but the objects of their inquiry remained undiscovered. A superstitious dread, of which the fell contriver seemed greatly to partake, seized the whole assembly, and each returned to his abode with pallid fear depicted on his countenance.

Felippo beheld their departure with delight; and as soon as safely he could, sought for his trusty Stormo to know what he had done with the hapless objects of his deep and deadly wrath. Him he found in the gloomy retirement of a ruined turret chamber, where far from every eye he had taken his secret abode.

When Rodolph awoke from his slumbers he started with horror and amazement; massy fetters encircled his legs and arms, and an iron hoop to which a chain was attached that was fastened to a column, was about his waist, and prevented his leaving the place. By the light of a lamp that was set on a stone table he saw the form of his Laurina reclining against the wall bound in a similar manner with himself. She had not yet awoke, but the voice of Rodolph soon made her open her lovely eyes.

She screamed with affright; horror-struck she beheld the fetters. "Good Heavens! what mean these cruel bands of iron? Rodolph! my love, you too there? Ah! what bitter enemy has worked for us this woe?"

Sadly ruminating, they passed the melancholy hours. Laurina mentioned her suspicions of Felippo having thus revenged himself for her disregard of his professions of attachment; but the noble-minded Rodolph could not conceive his brother guilty of so black an act. "Rather," said he, "expect him to restore us to freedom."

Laurina sighed, for she remembered his dreadful threatenings, and the dark expressions of his features.

The place they were in was a gloomy cavern, far removed from the cheering light of day, and situated in the damp bowels of the earth. It was of great magnitude, and part of the roof was supported by stone columns of rude sculpture. The astonished Rodolph well recollected the immense dungeon; it was beneath the lofty walls of his Castello!

A heavy pace was now heard, and soon the gloomy form of Felippo was seen through the gathered mist. Rodolph was silent; the truth of the surmises of Laurina broke on his tortured soul.

"Now," said he in a voice of thunder, "now, Rodolph, laugh at the miseries of Felippo if thou canst. 'Tis my turn now; and you, Laurina, who treated my love with contempt, you may now sue in vain; look at these walls, they are those of your tomb."

Laurina's senses fled. Rudolph started; horror-struck he looked to Felippo.

"Heap on me thy revenge; but spare, oh! spare that sweet angel of my affections."

Felippo disdained to reply. A smile of exultation gleamed on his features as he regarded his hapless captives.

Soon he strode away; and enjoyed in the silent halls of the Castello his deep and deadly revenge.

Long and mournful were the hours of that day to the tearful Laurina and sadly sighing Rodolph. The next day came, but they were unconscious of its approach, for the beams of the morning reached not their gloomy abode; night, in all her sable horrors, had there taken up her residence.

The calls of nature were unsatisfied; no friendly step approached with life-sustaining food. Laurina sunk beneath the rage of fever; her mouth grew dry and parched; feebly she called on Rodolph, who unceasing gazed on her.

"Rodolph, my beloved, the cruel Felippo will be revenged: I feel the lamp of life expiring. Oh! that I could die in thy arms; 'twould be some consolation."

"My Laurina! soul of my existence, have patience; perhaps he will relent. Even now I think I hear the sound of approaching footsteps. Hark! it is so. Pray Heaven it may the bearer of food."

The paces approached; but the hopes of Rodolph were gone when the feebly gleaming lamp shone on the gloomy Felippo, and the gigantic figure of his attendant Stormo.

He leaned against the nearest column, and beheld the victims of his wrath; he was dumb to the entreaties of Rodolph, and the groans of the dying Laurina were as music to his ears.

Well pleased he retired from the sad scene. Stormo, the savage Stormo, whose bosom never before felt the smallest emotion of pity, was now melted by the dreadful sufferings of Rodolph and his Laurina, and he determined in the dead of the night to release them.

But the piercing eyes of the suspicious Felippo rested not; he watched the countenance of Stormo, he saw there the sensations of his soul, and blackly rolled the current of his thoughts toward him.

———

Night had now darkly descended from the lofty battlements of Heaven; the rushing blast sighed through the Castello; the roarings of the storm was heard without; the dashing of water increased; and the lofty trees of the forest waved with the blast.

Stormo took up his lamp, he drew his cloak around it, and descended from the ruined turret. The lightning gleamed silent and awful; the thunder rolled above.

Stormo crossed the extensive courts and entered the lofty hall of the Castello; he stopped, and uncovering his lamp held it high up, while with a scrutinizing look he examined the dusky interior.

No object met his view. Night and sleep held their silent dominion over the world; he strode forward; and entering a narrow passage, at the extremity raised a trap-door, and descended a flight of steps. They conducted him to a long subterranean passage; the walls were green and mouldered; humid was the air, the lamp burnt with a trembling, uncertain flame. He advanced to a large door, and took down the massy bars; and drawing back the huge bolts, entered a gloomy and extensive dungeon. A lamp at the farther extremity directed his steps, and he soon stood before the astonished and hapless objects of Felippo's cruelty.

"I come," said he, "to restore you to liberty. My soul is shocked at the cruelty of Felippo; I will free you from those weighty chains."

Stormo advanced. A hasty step was heard; Felippo plunged his dagger twice in the bosom of his agent ere he could avoid the death-dealing blow.

"Vile slave," said he, "take the reward of thy villany."

Stormo fell, a torrent of blood rolled out his soul. Laurina shrieked, and unable to hinder the approach of death, hastened by the horrid act of Felippo, resigned her soul with a deep groan.

Rodolph in all the madness of rage strove to disengage himself from his fetters, but in vain; Felippo beheld his fruitless exertions, while a ghastly smile played on his visage.

He dashed himself on the earth, the blood flowed from his lacerated limbs, curses deep and soul-breathed escaped him, still the savage Felippo smiled horribly.

Stormo rescuing Laurina and Rodolph, is assassinated by Felippo.

His groans, his exclamations echoed through the subterraneous regions. Felippo started, for he feared lest they should be
borne to the ears of the domestics of the Castello, and thereby
disclose the true reason of the absence of its lawful master.

It was now midnight; the castle clock in hollow tones had just
told that silent hour, which however was disturbed by the wild
ravings of the miserably dying Rodolph.

Hastily he rushed forward, and the dagger that had terminated the wicked career of Stormo deeply drank a brother's blood.
Nature started aghast at the horrid deed; but the Demon stretch-

ing on high his gigantic form, stood over the bleeding Rodolph, looking at the convulsed body and the pallid Felippo with savage exultation.

The groans of Rodolph had disturbed the inhabitants of the Castello. Directed by them they entered the dungeon, and witnessed the horrid scene of murder; they rushed on the blood-stained Felippo; for awhile he defended himself with the fatal dagger, but numbers prevailed.

Felippo by the justly incensed laws of his country was doomed to perish by the rack; loaded with chains, he was confined in a loathsome cell, the abode of the toad and poisonous adder, and the next morning was to witness his execution.

Conscience with her sharp sting goaded his bosom. Tearful and melancholy he sat by the stone table, on which was placed a glittering lamp; he rested his arm on it, and his head was reclined on his hand. The midnight bell had tolled, and the knell of death sounded in his ears; he lifted up his eyes toward Heaven, but he had no friend there to give him consolation; he cast them down again, full of despair.

The Demon stood before him. "Save me," said Felippo, "save me, and I am thine."

"Swear," said the Demon, "call thy saints to witness thy words, I will then preserve thee from the rack; to-morrow shall not witness thy dissolution."

Felippo swore; he resigned his soul to the service of the Demon. Instantly sharp and excruciating pains seized his body, his soul trembled on his lips; a fiend, commissioned by the Demon, seized it, and in his sharp talons tightly grasped it; and darting through the earth thousands of fathoms, at length hovered over the burning lake, where he released his burthen, which falling plunged deeply into the horrid flood, and then rising, rolled on with the flaming billows, to join myriads of unfortunate wretches in the same torturous state.

The lifeless body of Felippo was found the next morning in the dungeon.

————

Such was the tale which the monk perused in the manuscript of Bartolo. No wonder that he should look pale and confused when the Demon appeared before him, for he thought that in the latter lines he had read his own fate, if fortunately he had not been prevented from signing the scroll.

"Well, Padre," said the Demon, "art thou ready to accompany me to the pavilion?"

Irresolute what to answer, the monk was silent; and the Demon well knowing what he was revolving in his mind, and fearful lest by his refusal some of his dark plans should be frustrated, he thus continued:

"You are irresolute, Bernardo; reflect; my moments are precious, nor will I waste them by endeavouring to minister to the pleasures of those who are undeserving my attentions. The possession of the person of that lovely woman you beheld no longer excites your wishes. Padre, adieu; you leave her then to the embraces of the cavalier."

"No," said the monk starting up, all his passions roused to their full extent by the wily speech of the Demon, and the other sensations excited by the tale of Bartolo lulled to sleep; "no, I never will resign that heavenly maid; never while life glows in my bosom. Conduct me to her; let me again behold her lovely charms."

Instantly the Demon complied with his request; and darting through the regions of air, hovered over the battlements of a large Castello. The roof divided to let them pass, they entered an elegant apartment, where the Demon thus addressed the monk: "In the chamber, Padre, to which that opposite portal leads, you will find in the soft embrace of sleep, the lovely woman you adore. I leave you to advantage yourself of the favorable moment. The inhabitants of the Castello dwell in another part; they likewise are resting after the toils of the day. I must go hence on business of moment; but I will be with you ere the bell has tolled the next hour."

This said, he darted through the roof of the chamber, which closed after his huge form had passed through; and the monk, whose heart palpitated with the various emotions excited by the speech of the Demon and his present situation, was for a few moments motionless with astonishment. At length he moved toward the portal, which with the greatest caution he gently opened. He stopped for a moment to listen; no sound, however, caught his ear. He advanced: a taper was burning on a marble table which was placed near an elegant couch, the hangings of which were blue satin, richly fringed with gold. Again the monk stopped; a low noise, like some one breathing, now awoke all the turbulent emotions of his breast, and using all his caution lest the beauteous prize should awake, and escape his fell intentions, he slowly approached the couch, and drew aside the curtains.

But the Deity who guards the innocent was watching the slumbers of the Signora; he saw the monk approach, and hasted to disappoint him in his infernal project.

The monk, when he had drawn aside the curtain, gazed with rapture on the sleeping beauty; her head was reclined on her arm, whose whiteness far exceeded the Parian stone; taper fingers, delicately turned, each joint resembling an opening rose bud, and the nails beautifully tinged with a roseate hue. Part of her glossy tresses had wandered from their confinement, and sported over her bosom, which was exposed to the view of the monk. He watched the gentle features alternately; her dark eyebrows and long silken eye-lashes, the glow of health which dwelt in her cheeks; and her lips, which invited the kiss, contributed to rage the monk to the completion of the horrible design for which the Demon had conveyed him there.

He bent forward and inhaled her balmy breath; sweet as the zephyr when it passes over beds of eastern roses, impregnated with the fragrance of violet.

In that motion he displaced her missal, which was laying on her pillow; it fell on the floor. Fearful lest the noise should awake his intended victim, he hastily started aside, and replaced the curtains; she, however, still slept. After a minute's pause the monk again looked on her. A smile played on her lips, the dimples became visible in her downy cheeks, her dreams were dreams of peace and love, for her bosom was the abode of virtue.

The monk now resolved to make no further delay, and was with that intent approaching the couch, when on a sudden he was struck motionless with horror, for a shadowy form stood between him and the couch, and with an outstretched arm prevented him from coming nearer to it.

It was the venerable form of a nun enveloped in the habiliments of the grave; the countenance was pale and full of horror, the eyes were steadfastly fixed on the monk, who trembling shrunk from its gaze, and slunk into the next apartment; where, unable to stand, he fell into a seat, overwhelmed with the terrors excited by the supernatural appearance.

In this situation he was found by the Demon, who well knowing what had passed spoke not, but silently seizing his arm, bore him back to his cell in the monastery.

The terror of the monk subsided when he found himself far removed from the sepulchral form which had so greatly affrighted him, and the Demon observing it, thus addressed him:—

"I little thought, Padre, that you, who in so many instances have given such ample proofs of a firm and undaunted mind, should fly from a cloud-formed vision at the moment when such a favorable opportunity offered for the accomplishment of your wishes. My time has been thrown away on one who when the cup of bliss has been held to his lips refused to taste of its delicious contents."

The monk looked abashed at the speech of the Demon; he now, when it was too late, repented of his fears; and had he then been in the apartment of the Signora, no visionary form would have hindered his fell purposes.

The solitary toll of the clock warned the Demon to depart, and like the vapour of night before the beams of the morning, he vanished from the view of the monk.

Dissatisfied with himself, the monk for some time continued to pace the limits of his apartment, cursing his fears, that had prevented him from the commission of one of the most horrible crimes that the arch enemy of man delights in exciting mortals to perpetrate.

CHAPTER XVIII.

LORENZO perused with heartfelt delight the billet of his adored Angelina. Carlo was not forgot for the adventurous part he had taken, and the Signor determined that he should attend him the next evening to the place of appointment; for though Conte Angelo was incapable of taking any active steps against him, yet he doubted not but that his emissaries were abroad seeking revenge.

How anxiously did he count the tardy hours; the pale luminary of night beheld him watching the return of the dawn, and the beams of the morning witnessed his impatient gaze: at length they ceased to illumine the horizon, and Lorenzo, attended by Carlo, proceeded swiftly toward the pavilion.

The lovely Angelina was there, awaiting his arrival. The fire of love animated his eyes, as with a rapturous gaze they dwelt on the beauteous form of his adored. A smile dimpled her lovely cheeks as she stretched out her hand to Lorenzo, who kneeling imprinted on its soft surface an ardent kiss.

His words, his looks, bespoke the adoration of his soul; he avowed his love to the blushing Angelina.

"Fair empress of my affections, behold prostrate before the adored idol of his heart the man who to make you happy would think his life but a small sacrifice. On you depends, too lovely Angelina, all my hopes of happiness; deign, oh! beauteous maid, to listen to my protestations of love, lasting as my existence, and pure as the stream that flows from the cleft rock."

With averted face Angelina heard the protestations of Lorenzo. A glow of pleasure darted through her bosom, and her heart beat in responsive unison with the sensations which occupied the breast of her lover.

"Oh! tell me, fair angel," continued Lorenzo, "tell me, I conjure you, if your affections bless some other happy mortal, or if I may hope that my unceasing assiduities may claim some small portion of your regard, would I dared to say love. Angelina, answer, I entreat, a question of so great importance to my happiness, to my existence itself."

"Rise, Signor Lorenzo," replied the blushing maid, "I have already assured you of the grateful sentiments of my heart; what more could you wish."

"Wish? oh! my Angelina, it is your love for which my soul longs, the possession of which will make me the most blest of men; but without it, where will there be so miserable a wretch as Lorenzo?"

Lorenzo raised his eyes, entreatingly he gazed on Angelina, till the dew of sensibility caused by the emotions of his swelling heart overflowed the brink, and rolled down his cheeks. Unable to view without sensations of deep concern his agitation, Angelina turned aside her face, a sigh escaped her unconsciously, she pressed his hand, the gentle motion thrilled with sensations of exquisite delight through the breast of Lorenzo; quick indeed was the transition from pain to pleasure, from anxiety to joy. The breadth of the most attenuated thread divides the extremes of lovers' hopes and fears; a single word exalts them to the highest pinnacle of delight, or precipitates them to the deepest abyss of despair.

"When more happy days arrive, Angelina may listen to Lorenzo's protestations; but now, beset by dangers, and surrounded by foes, her bosom is too much agitated to admit any other sensations than such as are necessary to support her during her persecutions."

These words, spoke in a low faltering voice, sounded in the ears of Lorenzo far sweeter than the most ravishing notes of the melting melodist; his eyes beaming with gratitude told the sensations of his breast, while he thus exclaimed:—

"Angelina, source of my soul's bliss, there is then hopes Angelina, the beauteous Angelina, looks not with the eye of disdain on her adoring Lorenzo. Dear idol of my heart, O! listen now to my vows, nor think of danger; while life flows in my veins, in such a cause I could resist the efforts of the world. Speak, fair enslaver of my affections, wilt thou incline a pitying ear to thy devoted lover?"

"To what purpose," replied the blushing Angelina, "is your present solicitation, knowing that my guardian is the ruthless Conte Angelo? Think you he would countenance your addresses? Oh! no; his dark intents are too obvious. My fortune is his aim, and, unhappily, the will of my parent has placed it too much in his power."

"He dares not withhold it," eagerly replied Lorenzo; "his treatment of you, lovely Angelina would influence the ears of royalty against him; the King would instantly appoint another guardian, more faithful and honorable to the trust reposed in him. Shall I to the court, and state your wrongs?"

"Oh no," returned Angelina; "by so doing the fair fame of a revered parent might be called in question, in choosing a man of Conte Angelo's character for my guardian. The Conte's wound, I am informed, has exhibited some alarming symptoms; should he recover, his behaviour to me may change; and should he fall a victim to his outrageous conduct, I shall be free. A short time will show me what course I ought to pursue to preserve myself from future persecution."

Such was the resolution of Angelina, and from which Lorenzo found he could not persuade her, so much did she revere the memory of her father, and so unwilling was she that the slightest opprobrium should rest on him for the ill-advised part he had acted in leaving Conte Angelo her guardian.

Lorenzo at length unwillingly forced himself away from the fascinating possessor of his heart, rich in hopes and joyous expectations, for he saw that the ardent declarations of his affection were received with pleasure by the dear object that caused them, and he hoped shortly to be able to do away the many objections that arose in her mind respecting the exposure of the Conte Angelo's conduct.

Angelina, at the urgent request of Lorenzo, had promised to see him again in three days at the same place, when the probable result of the Conte's wound would, in all likelihood, be determined. Sighing, the enamoured cavalier left the pavilion, and calling to Carlo, who in the company of Annetta thought the hours as short as his master, returned to his present abode.

Angelina pensively leaning on the arm of Annetta sought her chamber, where she recalled to her mind the love-fraught speeches of Lorenzo, the impressive tone of his voice, and his animated features while he addressed her. Such a recapitulation could not fail of increasing her love for him, and a sigh, occasioned by her fond and tender recollections, oft escaped her lovely bosom. The next morning, as soon as she had concluded the simple duties of the toilette, attended by Annetta she descended to the gardens, and scarcely conscious of her actions, seated herself in the pavilion, where the evening before she had met Lorenzo, which place seemed now to possess a secret charm before unknown. The seat which Lorenzo had occupied remained in the same situation as he had left it, and Angelina deeply regretted that his loved form was not now there; even a tear trembled on its lovely brink, and the swelling emotions of her bosom too greatly proved how much she loved. From these reveries the unwelcome appearance of the confessor Hildargo advancing along the avenue that led to the pavilion roused Angelina. She feared that he was the bearer of some unwelcome message from the Conte, and the result proved she was not mistaken.

Hildargo with a slow pace entered the pavilion, and having bowed to Angelina, thus addressed her:

"Fair daughter, I have words for your private audience; will it please you to order your attendant to retire?"

Angelina having motioned to Annetta to leave the pavilion, Hildargo continued:

"Conte Angelo's situation is such that 'tis likely the number of his days will be short, indeed. He is conscious of his approaching dissolution, and is truly penitent. Deeply does he regret his unprincipled conduct toward you; and much injured as you are, you would indeed pity him. He has sent me to implore your forgiveness; which will in a great measure serve to compose his last agonizing moments."

Much as she had cause to detest the memory of the Conte,

Angelina could not hear of his present situation without emotion. She no longer remembered his conduct to her, and thought of him only as a fellow-creature whose last moments were tortured with remorse for his deeds of life, and which she fortunately had it in her power to allay the poignancy of. She wept to think of the manner by which he had met the deadly blow of retribution; and as soon as she was able, thus replied to the confessor:

"If my sincere forgiveness and prayers for his soul's happiness can give comfort to the Conte, I beg, father, you will instantly assure him of both. Tell him, too, how much, how deeply I regret having in some measure been the cause of his present situation; and assure him too the past will never be thought of by me."

The features of the monk brightened as Angelina spoke these words.

"Those assurances, fair daughter, from your own mouth would calm the anguish of the unhappy Conte. Will you, who seem to possess so good, so tender a heart, condescend to repeat them yourself to him? 'tis his last request."

Angelina could not refuse what in some measure her religion prompted her to do, and she replied:

"If, father, it would indeed make Conte Angelo happy, I would not for a moment hesitate."

"Indeed, daughter, I am so well convinced it would, that to withhold so good and charitable an act would be a sin of no small magnitude. Permit me then to attend you to the Conte's apartment; who perhaps is now accusing me for staying so long from him in his departing hours."

Angelina immediately arose; and anxious to quiet the emotions of the penitent Conte, accompanied Hildargo to the door of his chamber; where the father requested her to wait till he should prepare him for her presence.

Angelina, whose susceptible heart felt the deepest pity for the Conte, now that he was no longer her enemy, felt her emotions increase; when the door of the chamber being opened by Hildargo, who in a low voice desired her to enter, she beheld the form of the Conte laying on a couch. The chamber was much darkened, and she was some time in it before the surrounding objects became visible. The face of the Conte was pale and wan, and his speech faint and tremulous.

"Much-wronged Angelina," said he, "is it true what the father Hildargo has but now told me? Can you then forgive me; you, whom, alas! I have attempted so greatly to injure?"

"Most sincerely I do," replied Angelina. "Think not, I entreat you, of it; consider only the important business of preparation for an immortal existence; my prayers shall be unceasingly offered up for your soul's repose." Here Angelina's swelling emotions stopped the faculty of speech. The Conte seemed affected, and was for some moments silent; at length he replied:

"In the opinion of my attendants I am not likely to breathe the breath of life at this hour to-morrow; but my own sensations tell me that the resistless enemy, even at this moment, is laying on me his chilling hand. Yet, though comforted and happy by your forgiveness, still there remains a duty to be performed by me toward you, and which will be some recompense for the sorrows I have made you suffer."

Here the Conte paused, and seemed unable to speak; from the increase of his pains he groaned deeply, and Angelina began to fear that his last moments were indeed come.

Hildargo then administered to him some cordial, which appeared to allay the violence of his sufferings; and after waiting some time, he thus continued:

"You know, Angelina, that by the disgraceful conduct of my daughter she has forfeited irrevocably her title to my large estates; and by virtue of the will of my father they will now go out of the family, the Comptessa being dead. This fortune will be yours, if you will only condescend to accept the cold hand of a man who perhaps ere the sun is set will have departed to a better world. To me what once would have been the summit of happiness is now only of importance as it will serve to convince you how much I desire to show my deep repentance, and sincere wish to make you some recompense. As my widow alone can you possess those estates; and when you consider, Angelina, of the vast means it will afford you of exercising the benevolent principles of your heart, you will not, I am sure, refuse."

Angelina, the Friar Hildargo, and the Conte Angelo.

Angelina started at the idea of becoming the wife of the Conte, even in his departing moments. She glanced her eyes at the confessor, and saw his deep piercing regards fixed on her with an expression that bespoke anxiety to know her resolves. Some sudden ideas crossed her, and she was on the point of replying, when the Conte said,

"Your silence, Angelina, avows your consent; let then the holy father perform the ceremony, that I may die in peace."

"No my Lord," replied Angelina, "my own possessions are

already sufficiently ample; nor will I by a proceeding somewhat unjust deprive the next legal inheritor of your estates."

Saying this she again looked at Hildargo, whose eyes were now fixed on the Conte with a meaning which she did not find it difficult to divine. The Conte was silent for a long time; and as she endeavoured to observe his features, she could easily perceive that they were flushed with anger. Her stay in the chamber now became unpleasant, and she arose from her seat.

"And you entirely refuse to grant a request which will so greatly increase your possessions? a request too made in the hour of death?" said the Conte.

"My acquiescence," replied Angelina, "or my refusal cannot be of any import. I am fully satisfied of your desire to make amends for your past conduct, without desiring such a mark of it. You wished my forgiveness, Conte, you have it in its fullest extent. I shall now, with your permission, retire."

This said, she proceeded to the portal of the chamber, leaving the Conte with his confessor; and as she opened it, she plainly heard an execration pass the lips of Angelo, which immediately disclosed to her the deep scheme that the Conte had planned, in conjunction with Hildargo, to draw her into a marriage. That snare she had, however, happily escaped.

Her conjectures were right; Conte Angelo, finding that he was recovering from his wound, determined to employ the present moment in working on the feelings of Angelina; indulging a hope that, supposing he was dying, she, in order to possess his estates, would allow the monk to perform the nuptial ceremony; but he was still doomed to be disappointed in his deep-concerted plans.

Angelina now began to be tormented with her worst fears. She saw too plainly that Angelo was determined either by force or stratagem to carry his designs respecting her into effect; as, however, he seemed incapable of using coercion for the present, she hoped that the kind Providence that had hitherto protected her, would not withdraw his all-powerful aid. On Lorenzo she thought with increasing fondness, and the anticipation of the pleasure of seeing him allayed in a great measure the perturbations of her mind. The whole of the next day passed without her hearing any further from Conte Angelo; nor did his confidential confessor make his appearance. Foiled in their deep schemes, they were now consulting what other means they should pursue to effect their dark purposes.

The third day now beamed from the heavens, and Angelina hailed its coming with delight, for in the evening she would again see Lorenzo; again see him whose soul adored her, and for whom she cherished a kindred flame.

When the welcome shades of evening descended mistily on the earth, she, with Annetta, who was equally delighted with the idea of again seeing Carlo, proceeded to the pavilion. Lorenzo was already there. What delight beamed in his expressive features as he saw her approach. On his knees he expressed his thanks; and again in that suppliant posture avowed his love.

"The name of Angelina, so dear to me, has been echoed in those solitary haunts so favorable to lovers, which the adjacent forests and deeply seated vallies afford; there unseen have I poured forth the love-fraught sentiments of my soul till my sighs have increased the surrounding zephyrs, and my tears the chrystal stream that murmured at my feet. Oh! Angelina, if haply in your bosom there dwells for your Lorenzo a sentiment beyond pity for my sufferings, bless my ears with the dear confession; but if it is cold and insensate to the voice of love, never more shall Lorenzo again gaze on your heavenly beauties; his eyes shall no more open to the beams of day, his lips no more express the tender sentiment of love; his senses will no more exist, and beneath some given hillock his form shall moulder away; but his soul shall hover over the angel it adores, and offer up fervent orisons for her happiness."

Lorenzo stopped; deeply affected he gazed on Angelina. A pearly drop stood trembling in her beauteous eyes, and her speech faltered while she faintly replied:—

"Indulge not such melancholy thoughts, Lorenzo; if Angelina's love is worth your acceptance, 'tis yours; live then for her."

"Delightful ecstatic sounds! Oh! words imparting bliss. Indeed Angelina loves, loves Lorenzo; did she not say so? yes, even now the heavenly tones of her voice vibrate on my soul."

Lorenzo's feelings forbade him the power of further utterance; he embraced the hand which deeply blushing Angelina presented to him; and for some time both were silent, for their sensations cannot be expressed.

At length, however, the wild delirium of joy began to subside, and Lorenzo found utterance for his tender gratitude and vows of lasting attachment. Words which conveyed to the bosom of Angelina that pleasure which they only can ever form an idea of who truly and sincerely love.

She now informed him of the further attempts of Angelo to obtain her hand, and of her fears respecting him. Lorenzo heard her in silence, while the varying colour of his cheeks betrayed the emotions of his heart.

"And why, lovely Angelina, why will you not permit me to represent your situation to the King; when at once you will be freed from your present fears? Can any consideration be of sufficient importance to prevent your acquiescence? Only consider, dear possessor of my heart, that in an unguarded moment, when Lorenzo's arm is wanting, you may be made for ever miserable, and me—God of Heaven! what will be my situation?"

"For the present, Lorenzo, there can be no real danger. I will yet wait. From you I shall not withhold the knowledge of his future conduct to me. To-morrow evening I shall again see you."

This said, she smiled on Lorenzo, held out to him her lovely hand, and departed.

Many days now elapsed, during which the fond lovers frequently met in the pavilion; each interview increased their love and mutual confidence. The Conte had not taken further notice of her; but from Annetta she learnt that he was fast recovering, and even well enough to walk about his chamber. This intelligence filled her with sensations of fear; the continued silence he had preserved toward her for so long a time, and the distant behaviour of the confessor Hildargo whenever she accidentally met him, made her conclude that some new dispositions were making, which, when the Conte was well enough would be put in execution; and all her fears were at length confirmed by the following circumstance. It was Angelina's custom on the anniversary of the death of her beloved parents to pass a great part of that lamented day beside the tomb which inclosed their dear remains; there she invoked the gentle spirits to direct her in the course she ought to pursue through life's toilsome journey, and there she prayed for the repose of their souls.

That day had arrived and Angelina was employed in her devotional duties, when she heard some people enter the chapel; and raising her eyes, beheld the Conte and father Hildargo pacing the centre isle. They were deeply engaged in conversation; and some words which were borne to the ears of Angelina made her anxiously listen to them, for it was concerning her they were talking. By them she could not be discovered, for the tomb she was kneeling at completely shrouded her from view. As they approached nearer to her, their words became distinct.

"You have already witnessed, father, how cautious she is," said the Conte. "It boots us to be wary. I have even now a thousand fears she will escape before the time that my returning strength will allow me to complete my designs; and if I again confine her, no doubt it will be discovered by Lorenzo. You know, father, should my conduct come to the ears of the Court, we shall be ruined; and even now I tremble lest he should be already there."

"I like not procrastination, my Lord," replied the confessor; "why will you wait till the mandate arrives which will take from you the authority of guardian? Certain of the present moment, instantly advantage yourself of it."

"In your haste to serve me, my friend," returned the Conte, "you forget the weakness of my frame, and how necessary it is for me to recruit my exhausted strength. I will, however, think of your advice, and perhaps in a few days"—

Here their discourse died away in distance, but Angelina had heard sufficient to apprize her of the dangerous situation she was in. The Conte and Hildargo soon after left the chapel; and Angelina, unable from the distress of her mind to continue the devotional duties of that day, arose from her suppliant posture, and sought the privacy of her apartments.

She now saw that to preserve herself she must immediately come to some resolution. She could not think of injuring the memory of her parent by letting the world know how imprudent he had conducted himself in choosing such a guardian for her as Conte Angelo, and she had no other alternative than in confiding her future destiny to Lorenzo. Such a hasty step would, no doubt, meet the censure of the world; but she felt herself more equal to bear that than any reflections on her departed parents. She had, however, by no means formed her resolution, and waited till the evening, when she could consult with Lorenzo.

Won by his ardent protestations, she at length consented to be irrevocably his; and as the festival of the Santa Catherina was near at hand, it offered a good opportunity for them to travel without danger of discovery; for in the disguise of pilgrims they might safely pursue the road that led to the monastery, where at the altar Angelina's fears, as well as Lorenzo's, would be terminated.

The second night was appointed for the commencement of the journey, and Lorenzo, with Carlo, was to be in waiting at the gate of the gardens which led to the hilly boundaries of the valley. Annetta was to follow the fortunes of her mistress, and as soon as with safety it could be effected, was to become the wife of Carlo.

When Angelina returned to the apartment, and at leisure reflected on the important scene that was now before her, she could not help blaming her too hasty promise. Still, however, when she reflected on the crafty and designing Angelo, and that by her marriage with Lorenzo she would not only be out of his power, but also happy with the man she adored, she became more composed, and awaited the hour of her departure with anxious expectation.

Midnight was the time agreed on for Lorenzo to be at the garden gate; and when at length slowly the hour was proclaimed, attended by Annetta she descended from her apartments, and silently crossing the North Hall, entered on the passage which led to the garden. Angelina trembled as Annetta was unbarring the door, and earnestly directed a mental prayer to Heaven to direct her in her actions.

The door being opened Angelina continued for some time close under the walls of the Castello, fearful of being perceived if she passed along the grand avenue; till at length striking into a side path, she reached the gate, where the loved voice of Lorenzo greeted her pleased ears.

He assisted her to mount a mule; Carlo was equally attentive to Annetta; and they were soon ascending the mountain before them. The night was such as favoured their undertaking; the moon lent them her silver beams, and myriads of scintillating stars combined to illumine the hemisphere. Lorenzo, all raptures, could talk of nothing but his love and gratitude, and his tender discourse soothed the anxiety that resided in the bosom of Angelina.

As soon as they had arrived at a convenient spot the whole party alighted, and having arrayed themselves in pilgrims' garments, which Lorenzo had provided, they again set forward; and as soon as they entered on the road that led to the monastic pile dedicated to the Santa Catherina, they mingled in the crowds of devotees who were hastening to the same spot. They now conversed but seldom; and as their hoods concealed their faces, little fear was entertained of the possibility of their being discovered.

At length the venerable and far-extending structure met their view; and as they approached its grey walls Lorenzo's features spoke all the joy that reigned in his heart, while Angelina became somewhat pensive, and often invoked the Saints to direct her, in what was right. As soon as they arrived, Carlo and Annetta stopped at the porch that led to the chapel, while Lorenzo and Angelina advanced in order to seek a monk to perform the ceremony that would make the lovely maid irrevocably his.

CHAPTER XIX.

ON the night preceding that on which the Demon had conveyed the monk to the chamber of the lovely female he again appeared to him.

"Bernardo, an opportunity is now on the eve of offering itself for the secure accomplishment of your wishes. In two days the festival of Santa Catherina will arrive. Thou mayest recollect that the lovers in the pavilion named that as the period when they were to be made happy in the possession of each other. In order to avoid suspicion they will be habited as pilgrims. At one hour after vespers be standing beneath the chapel porch; thou wilt behold them approaching, they will request of thee to perform the marriage ceremony; conduct them to a private altar, and seeking a fit opportunity, let the hand of death descend quickly on the Signor; then bear away the lovely female to thy cell."

Here the Demon paused, and the monk, who had listened attentively to his speech, thus gloomily returned:

"Difficult, and almost impossible, will be the performance of what thou hast portioned out to me. Not that I fear to do the deed of death, for my bosom warms with revengeful fury when I recollect the tender kisses he imprinted on the coral lips of the beauteous fair, and I then darkly swore that he should die; nay, I would even then have rushed on him, but was restrained by you. But how shall such a deed be performed with safety to myself? and how is a female to be confined in my cell without being discovered?"

"I was prepared for thy questions," replied the Demon; "thou knowest that the altar of penance is far remote from observation, being in a retired chamber, the portal of which thou mayest make fast; it is also contiguous to this cell, and thou mayest smile in security with respect to the female, for know that at the extremity of this chamber is a sliding pannel, unknown to any of the present residents of the monastery, that opens to a winding staircase, leading to numerous dungeons and subterranean abodes which belonged to an ancient castello, on the site of whose ruins this pile was raised; there thou mayest secure thy lovely prize, there reap the reward of thy watchful hours."

The gleaming eyes of the monk well showed the satisfaction that reigned in his soul; a smile sat darkly on his features, while he brooded over anticipated delights; lost in reverie, he heeded not the departure of the Demon, who silently winged his horrific flight to where his restless, infernal projects required his presence.

Bernardo now arose from his seat, and taking up his lamp proceeded to the further extremity of his chamber, in order to find out the sliding pannel mentioned by the Demon. With some difficulty he discovered it, and succeeded in forcing it back, for the grooves were filled with the accumulating dust of years, and for a time resisted his efforts. He now trimmed his lamp, and stepping through, beheld the winding staircase described by the Demon.

He paused ere he attempted to descend, for the dilapidated state of the steps rendered it a matter of difficulty, if not danger. When, however, he called to his recollection the words of the Demon, and reflected that the only hope he had of carrying his designs respecting the lovely Signora was the dark concealment of the dungeon below, he gathered resolution, and cautiously treading on the loose stones, began to wind down the steps.

The remembrance of Bartolo's melancholy tale of the fair Isabella and the savage Leonardi di Vicensio now crowded in his memory, and in imagination he beheld Ugo de Tracy, following the sepulchral form of his beloved Isabella as it glided down the same steps which now tremblingly supported him. At length he reached the bottom of the long winding descent, and found himself in a rocky passage, which led to many dungeons, the doors of which were either just deserting their hinges or laying on the moist earth. Superstitious fears crossed the soul of the monk, he listened to the gale as it sighing poured through the gratings which gave light and air to the dungeons, one of which he entered, but started back, for the objects within forcibly recalled to his mind Bartolo's tale.

In the centre of the dungeon was a hillock of earth, and near it lay a heap of rusty armour covering the mouldering form of a skeleton. The helmet had fallen off, the chapless skull, and the apertures where once glared the revengeful blood-shot eyes of Leonardi di Vicensio opened horribly and ghastly to the view of the pallid monk, who hastily retreated from the spot.

For awhile the terrors of his mind rendered him unable to proceed further than the rock-hewn corridore, and tremblingly he leaned against the ragged wall to support his form; his eyes wandered around, but the light of his lamp threw its faint rays but a short distance from him, and only served to show the black horrors of the place.

At length, however, the monk's sensations of terror became less, and he then proceeded on the object of his search. He entered several subterraneous apartments, but none of them suited his purposes; that indeed which was the tomb of the hapless Isabella and her persecutor appeared to have suffered the least from the ravages of time; the door was yet entire, and the large bolts, though incrusted with rust, promised security, at least from the weak attempts of a female. The moments were now precious, the morning would soon dawn, and it was necessary that whatever was requisite to be done for the accomplishment of Bernardo's dark purposes should not be delayed.

Again he entered with a slow and cautious step the sepulchral vault, and for some time timidly surveyed the heap of rusty armour. At length he gathered courage, and lifted up the pieces, which no longer were united to each other as the leather thongs had for years past been destroyed; he bore them to another cell, and having collected the scattered disjointed bones in the breastplate, he also deposited them there. The object of his terror being thus removed, he next closed the door, and after some difficulty succeeded in making the bolts move.

Bernardo now hastily ascended the steps, for he conjectured that the dawn must be fast approaching, which would bring with it the long-expected festival held in honor of the Santa Catherina, the religious ceremonies of which would render it impossible for him to be absent without the cause of it being minutely inquired into.

Winding up the steps he entered his cell, and looking at the casement, beheld Aurora just beginning to streak the eastern horizon with a roseate hue, which increased every moment, till at length the glowing regent of day threw his gladsome beams over the face of Nature.

The circumstance of the festival in honor of the Santa Catherina taking place only twice in a century, was sufficient to attract multitudes to her shrine, from motives of curiosity, as well as devotion; as the monastery and convent were richly endowed, no cost was spared in the splendid preparation; and in addition to the usual solemnities, a nun was on that day to make her vows of seclusion, previous to her taking the veil.

At an early hour in the morning, the porches and cloisters of the edifice were thronged with spectators, consisting of the Sicilian nobility, and innumerable groupes of pilgrims of both sexes waiting with impatience till the portals of the grand chapel should be thrown open to admit them.

At length the tolling of the bell announced the arrival of the hour on which the ceremonies should commence, and the doors of the church were opened, the spectators soon filled the extensive side-aisles and galleries, the centre aisle being kept free for the procession. The marble pavement of that aisle was covered with crimson velvet, as also was the balustrades of the galleries, and an altar of massy silver rose at the further extremity of the chapel, on which was to be placed the statue of the Saint.

The procession now entered the chapel, preceded by a group of the most handsome youths that could be procured, bearing golden censers, in which burnt the costly odours of the East, whose rich perfume impregnated the air with a delicious fragrance. These boys were cloathed in scarlet robes, confined to the waist by gold bands, they were bare-headed, and wore wreaths of artificial flowers round their hair. Padre Ignazio, the abbot of the monastery, then advanced most sumptuously habited, supported by two friars, bare-headed, and followed by others carrying a crimson cushion on which lay a missal richly adorned with precious stones.

The statue of the Saint, of solid silver, borne by the monks, next entered the chapel. It was adorned with a profusion of the richest jewels; which, as the beams of the sun shone on them, sparkled with a dazzling lustre. The Saint was borne under a canopy of azure velvet, fringed with gold, which was carried by a select party of the nuns. The abbess next followed, walking under a canopy similar to that which covered the Saint: trains of the nuns and monks next followed, and these were succeeded by many of the principal nobility, bearing wax tapers.

As soon as the procession reached the grand altar, the youths with the censers ranged themselves on each side of it, and the abbot with a slow pace ascended the silver steps. The statue of the Santa Catherina was then placed on it, and the abbess took her station on the left, opposite the abbot. The whole train then fell on their knees before the altar, and the melodious voices of the nuns and the deep bass tones of the monks swelled in full and solemn strains.

The spectators were likewise on their knees, scarcely daring to breathe lest they should disturb the soul-awakening harmony which floated on the perfumed air. At length the hymn being concluded, the assembly arose from their knees, and the abbot from the steps of the altar made a most sumptuous oration in praise of the virtues of the Saint. A second hymn was then chaunted, and the abbess descending from the altar, advanced toward Agatha, who, superbly dressed, was standing at a short distance, supported by the nuns; for notwithstanding she hoped to be emancipated from the dreary seclusion of the convent that night yet the ceremony that was now going to be performed struck with terror to her soul. Encouraged by the presence of Ferdinando, who had taken his station not far from her, she advanced, and kneeling at the altar, repeated in a tremulous voice the vows of seclusion. Her beautiful locks were then submitted to the fatal scissars, and Agatha returned amidst the plaudits and sighs of the assembly.

The abbess at the head of the nuns now passed through the gilded skreen, the door of which was closed after them, and the abbot with his train of monks at the same time entered the monastery, leaving the altar free to the crowds of pilgrims of both sexes who thronged to pay their adoration to the Saint.

Thus passed the morning hours; and now evening duskly lowered on the earth, the chapel was illuminated with a lustre exceeding that of day's meridian beam. A curtain of crimson purple hung before the skreen, and the monks, with the abbot, again entered the grand aisle.

The shrine of the Saint, and the pillars of marble which rose on each side, appeared as one blaze of light, and suspended to the rafters that supported the lofty roof, large silver lamps dispelled the smallest shade of night.

As soon as the abbot and his train had taken their stations, the crimson curtain being raised discovered the abbess seated on a superb throne; at her feet were the elder nuns, surrounding Agatha, who had now thrown off her rich habiliments, and put on the habit of the profession. The rest of the nuns and lay sisters were ranged at the right of the abbess, and the boarders, of which there were many belonging to the powerful Sicilian families, were placed on her left.

Again the voice of harmony resounded through the lofty aisles of the chapel, raising the soul to heavenly raptures, while the splendor of the scene around enchanted the eye. At the close of the vesper service the curtain descended, and the chapel was left as before by the monks.

Bernardo had gone through the duties of the day with impatience; for though his eyes were incessantly roving on the beautiful features of the Sicilian women, yet no where did he behold such complete, such irresistible charms as the Signora he had seen in the pavilion possessed.

Often did he, while his quick-beating pulse told the emotions of his bosom, call to mind the promise of the Demon, nor did the idea of the horrid and bloody act he was to perform in the murder of the cavalier serve in the least to deter him from his resolutions.

At the time mentioned by the snareful spirit he took his station in the porch that led to the grand portals of the chapel, having carefully drawn his cowl over his face to prevent his features being seen.

He had not long been there when in an arched recess he beheld two people habited as pilgrims; his heart beat high, and he passed close by the place, when in the silver tones of one of them he recognised the voice of the lovely Signora.

Lorenzo de Montalto, (for he it was who disguised as a pilgrim was proceeding with the lovely Angelina to the chapel of the monastery of Santa Catherina,) now stepped forward, and thus addressed the well-pleased monk:

"Holy father, two persons who sincerely love desire your assistance to unite them in the holy bands of matrimony, for which good office their gratitude shall know no bounds."

"It rejoices me, son," said the wily monk, "to see two so well disposed; no doubt the immaculate Santa Catherina has influenced your hearts, nor shall I hinder for a moment her will taking place; but tell me, son, in the language of truth, is your situation such as requires privacy, or will ye be united at the grand altar, for to me somewhat of a desire for concealment appears in your actions."

"Thou hast rightly divined, father," returned Lorenzo, "the lovely maid who is with me is under the guardianship of a man who wishes to force her to marry him for the base purpose of possessing himself of her estates, and though I could by appealing to the King free her from the trammels imposed by her father's will, yet she holds the memory of a parent too dear to let his actions be the subject of censure now that his dwelling is the grave."

"Follow me," said the Padre Bernardo, "his sway shall cease, for the Signora shall soon be beyond his power."

This said, he unlocked a private postern that led into a long and narrow corridore, whose interior was dimly illumined by a few lamps, placed at unequal distances, continuing along this passage. The monk proceeded till he stopped and listened at a door which was just ajar, and started back somewhat confused. A groan, and the sound of several blows was heard.

"One of the brethren," said the monk in a low tone, "is now engaged in an act of penance, in which he must not be disturbed; we must wait awhile in this passage; perhaps he will soon depart; meantime, in order to shun observation, we will measure back some of our steps."

This said, he retired into the gloomy corridore, and Lorenzo and Angelina silently followed him. The air of the monk was disturbed; he paced the passage to and fro with his arms folded, and his head bent toward the ground; he now feared some disappointment would attend his present intents, for unless he could enter the chamber where the altar of penance was, he would not be able to reach his own cell with his lovely prize without hazarding a discovery, as he must then pass through some of the most frequented passages of the building; but in that chamber was a door which led through an unfrequented passage to the portal of his cell, and promised security to his fell designs. Patience was now his only resource, and in indulging the horrible anticipations of his black purposes he passed the present moments.

Lorenzo endeavoured to cheer the timid Angelina with the pleasing voice of love. "In a few moments, dear object of my adoration, will your fond Lorenzo claim you as his wife. Oh! dear word, ecstatic sound, when applied to the sweetest, the fairest of Nature's works."

The closing of a door and a faint sound of footsteps, which soon died away in silence, now made the monk raise his head. "The father is perhaps gone," said he in a low tone; "we may now venture; but be silent for fear of a discovery." This said, he proceeded toward the chamber, and listened some time before he opened the doors. No noise met his attentive ears, he lifted up the latch and looked in; the place was empty; a solitary lamp faintly burnt before an ebon crucifix, the wainscot was of dark oak, and in the large pannels were paintings representing the sufferings of souls in purgatory, and scriptural allusions of a gloomy and terrific nature.

Angelina, struck with the melancholy appearance of the chamber, hung on the arm of Lorenzo, and for a while hesitated to enter it, till cheered by his persuasive language, she slowly advanced to the altar.

The lamp gleamed feebly on the crucifix and a painting of the Virgin weeping over the body of the Saviour of the World, which was hung near the altar, a few paces from which the dusky shades of night rendered every object imperceptible. Angelina looked toward a Gothic casement which was near her, and saw the clouds swiftly sailing on the rough bosom of the nocturnal blast; a few stars were sometimes seen dimly, twinkling through the thin scud, but the waning moon was no longer visible to mortal sight; her monthly course, save a few more hours was concluded.

The monk having admitted his hapless victims, staid a few moments behind to secure the doors from intruders. He had armed his bosom with a ferocity which it was necessary for him to possess to do the damning deed of murder, and in his hand he now grasped the deadly instrument of his designs; his mind, however, in spite of his resolutions, was dreadfully perturbed; he felt as though in some hideous dream, and under the influence of horrible spirits his trembling hands for some time vainly attempted to force the bolt of the portal into the side beam, and while so doing the dagger fell on the floor. Guilt is ever fearful, and he watched with a scrutinizing glance de Montalto and Angelina, but they were too much occupied by the sweet anticipation of happiness to pay attention to the monk, who hastily picked up the thirsty blade, and with a haggard look advanced to the altar.

His close-drawn cowl, and the melancholy gloom of the chamber, prevented either his features or the agitation of his frame being perceived; but when Angelina saw his tall figure advancing through the dusky shades, an unaccountable apprehension crossed her bosom, and she leaned fearful on Lorenzo, who, throwing his arm round her waist to support her, conjured her not to give way to terrors which perhaps might prevent the performance of the nuptial ceremony; he then tenderly kissed her downy cheek, where the fading rose was giving place to the usurping lily.

The sight of the lovers, as leaning toward each other they embraced, roused to their highest pitch the fury of the monk; he advanced with a determined step, and as Lorenzo was gently loosing his hold of Angelina, starting forward he plunged his dagger in his side. The violence of the blow threw the unfortunate Lorenzo on the floor, and in falling he struck his head violently against the marble steps on which the altar was erected. A groan announced the agonies he felt, and Lorenzo soon ceased to breathe.

For a few moments horror-struck and motionless Angelina viewed the soul-harrowing scene. Her lover, her Lorenzo lay on the floor, drenched in the sanguine stream of life. Her visual orbs were distended, and her hands clasped together. At length a piercing shriek burst from her, and she fell on the lifeless body of the much-loved Lorenzo.

Her situation was favorable to the designs of the monk. Leaving the dagger in Montalto's side, he bore her in his arms to his cell, and having fastened the door, lit his lamp, when opening the sliding pannel, he carried Angelina, who was still insensible, down the steps, and laying her on a rude bench in the dungeon, anxiously waited till the breath of returning life should again animate her beauteous form; intending as soon as she was again sensible, to leave her, in order to dispose of the body of Lorenzo, which he could easily conceal in some of the subterraneous recesses of the dungeons.

Agatha, when the ceremony of her taking the veil was completed, retired to her cell. An hour after midnight was the time agreed on when Ferdinando would be waiting at the gate of the skreen in order to conduct her through the subterraneous passages that led to the ruined chapel in the forest, where he had provided the dresses of pilgrims, which would secure them from observation. Toward midnight the tapers and lamps were extinguished, and the devotees who still remained were obliged to retire, as the doors of the chapel were then closed; silence again reigned in the dark aisles, which had so lately echoed the hymns and prayers of those who had thronged their now empty spaces.

At length the hour of morning sounded solitary from the topmost turret of the monastic pile; pleasing was the vibration of the sonorous bell-metal to the ears of Agatha, who now arose, and hastened with a palpitating heart to the chapel.

Ferdinando, punctual to his promise, had repaired through the long passage which led from the forest to the monastery. As the door which opened into it grated heavily on its hinges he paused, for a slight sound of a human voice was borne on the air. Attentively he listened, but all was silent; he again pushed back the door, and entered the small chamber, which he crossed, and soon was in the extensive corridore which led to the chapel. A sound of a slow footstep made him hastily throw his cloak over his lamp, while he in vain stretched his eyes to their fullest extent to discover who it could be that at that silent hour had not retired to rest.

The night was dark and stormy, the thunder rolled awful in the heavens, and the clouds shot forth their angry lumens from their sable bosoms, the wind sighed through the embattled turrets of the pile, and murmured in the windings of the corridores; the lightning at times gleamed through the lofty casement that admitted light to the corridore, opposite to which Ferdinando now stood, irresolute whether to proceed or not, for the footsteps appeared to be approaching. A sudden tremor seized his frame as leaning against the wall he beheld slowly gliding past the casement the figure of a man. A low groan harrowed up his senses, he distinctly could hear the breathings of the form he saw, which to him appeared unlike those of a human being. A rolling peal of thunder which shook the pile to its deep foundations buried all other sounds in its dreadful roaring; a stream of fire burst from the clouds, and the hour of midnight was proclaimed by the long-sounding tolls of the clock of the monastery. Nature seemed still of dreadful wrath, and to rage in fierce elemental warfare.

The thunder continued rolling in stunning peals along the threatening blackened hemisphere; the wind roared mournfully, and with increasing fury; Ferdinando listened intently for the dreadful repetition of the dismal sounds he had heard, whilst the expectation of some terrible phenomenon distended every feature in wild affright. At length, however, the continued silence of all else but the storm began to compose his agitation, and he slowly moved along the vaulted corridore.

In his fears of being discovered he had extinguished his lamp, and he now was enveloped in the sable horrors of night, excepting when the lightning momentarily illumined the passage. Accustomed to the place, he however did not experience much difficulty in finding the portals of the chapel, into which he entered.

The long casements on each side of that extensive edifice shewed to Ferdinando the furious conflicts of the elements; the tempest was increasing in its tremendous uproar, and the rain descended in torrents; the reverberating thunders as they rolled gradually away in rumbling vollies stunned his ears; and the vivid flashings of the lightnings oppressed his sight: he now approached the skreen, and there waited with impatience till the first hour of morning should be proclaimed by the hollow bell.

At length it echoed drearily around, and in a few minutes after Agatha entered the chapel. Ferdinando greeted her in the tender terms of affection. "Dear lovely fair," said he, "the hour that gives you to love and liberty is at length arrived; in a short time we shall be far from these hated walls, where reside dark brooding Melancholy and Despair."

Agatha answered not; in her looks was visible the satisfaction she felt, and hastily she unlocked the skreen gate, and in the tender embrace she gave Ferdinando shewed her gratitude for his attempts to emancipate her from the gloom of a cloister.

Hand in hand they now hastened down the aisle, and passing through the chapel portals, entered the extensive corridore. They had not however proceeded more than half way when, amidst the pauses of the storm, a confused noise was heard in the galleries above; Agatha's lamp was instantly extinguished, and tremblingly they stopped to listen. Several footsteps passed along the galleries, and now a light streamed through the square hall at the extremity of the corridore, and the tall figures of some of the monks were observed passing across it.

Alarmed at their dangerous situation Ferdinando retreated with Agatha down a passage which they had discovered by the glare of the lights in the vestibule; there they wandered a time, unknowing whither they were going, and suffering the most dreadful fears lest they should be discovered. Stopping at length to listen, they felt comforted, for all was silent around them, and Ferdinando resolved to turn back to the corridore in order to see if the monks had retired to their cells, and if they could with safety leave the monastery.

Hardly had he entered the corridore when an opposite portal opened full upon them, and to their terrified vision appeared the Padre Ignazio, abbot of the monastery, attended by several of the monks, all of whom uttered an exclamation of astonishment, and instantly pursued the Signor Ferdinando, who fled precipitately with Agatha down the passage.

Fear winged their steps, and they soon were at some distance from their pursuers, when turning round a corner which they perceived as the lights the monks carried flashed on the walls, Ferdinando, who was foremost rushed unknowingly down a flight of steep steps.

His sudden exclamation, and the noise of his body as it

bounded down the steps stopped the further progress of the unfortunate Agatha. His groans struck to her soul; but soon her personal safety preceded every other thought, for she now felt herself in the firm grasp of the monks.

Viewing her with silent horror, they brought her down the passage to where the stern Superior was awaiting the arrival of the unknown fugitives. But when in Agatha he beheld the nun who had but a few hours before taken the solemn and awful oaths of seclusion, his countenance blackened, and he trembled with rage.

"Who," said he in a voice of thunder, "was thy companion? and, how didst thou contrive to leave the convent? and what were thy intents?"

The horrors of her situation bursting full upon her was more than Agatha could support, and she sunk on the floor for awhile insensible to the dark looks of the revengeful abbot, who ordered her to be taken into one of the adjoining apartments, and then sent some of the monks to seek her companion.

Him they found at the bottom of the stairs in a condition truly dreadful, covered with the blood which flowed from a deep wound in his head; he however still breathed, and when they had brought him up into the passage, the abbot sent for one of the brethren who was skilled in surgery, to endeavour to stop the stream of life which was ebbing fast away, determined to be acquainted with every circumstance relative to this mysterious affair.

Other events of a still more wonderful nature now called him away, and, attended by the monks, whose number had greatly increased, he left the passage.

When Agatha opened her eyes she fixed them on the monks who were standing round the seat on which they had laid her, and her recollection instantly returning, she closed them again in silent horror. Taken in the very act of attempting her escape, she well knew no mercy would be shown to her, and her punishment could not be less than death. It was now that her frame trembled beneath her mental terrors, while her too busy recollection long dwelt on the murders of the unfortunate Marianne and her friend Claudina.

The bell of the monastery now rung, and the monks starting, soon left the chamber; at the sound of their receding paces Agatha again looked up; a lamp which was placed on a distant table served to shew the gloomy extent of the apartment; and while her eyes wandered around the place, her ears were suddenly assailed by a deep groan of long continuance, which seemed to come from a remote corner of the chamber, where the rays of the lamp were unable to reach. Fearfully she fixed her eyes on the spot, expecting every moment to see some horrible, soul-appalling form start from the murky gloom.

Another groan and a faint exclamation, seemingly caused by acute pain, made Agatha start from her seat, and drag her feeble limbs to the deep recess; where she beheld stretched on a pallet the pale, blood-stained form of Ferdinando, her lover.

His wounds having been bound up, and the bleeding stopped, he was, though slowly, becoming sensible of the anguish of them; and when his languid eyes rested on Agatha, he attempted to speak, but was not able.

To describe the feelings of either were impossible; they silently gazed on each other, while disappointment and terror were visibly marked in their pale countenances. To escape was impracticable, for Agatha knew not the way to the subterraneous passage; and from Ferdinando she could obtain no information. Cursing her wayward fate in all the bitterness of accumulating grief, she now paced the chamber in a paroxysm of despair; and had the means of self-destruction offered, Agatha would speedily have avoided the pangs she was doomed to suffer.

After a lapse of some time the abbot entered the chamber; his countenance was pale and agitated.

"The holy abbess," said he, addressing himself to the trembling Agatha, "is informed of your horrible acts. Father Nicolo," continued he, addressing one of the monks, "conduct that nun to the parlour of the convent, that the abbess may have her in strict confinement till such time as I may resolve on the steps necessary to be taken in order to serve as a lasting warning, and to deter others from doing the like.

Agatha now threw herself at the feet of the abbot. "Oh! holy father!" said she, while bitter drops of terror rolled down her cheeks, "Oh! holy father! hear me, I beseech you, and have mercy on me. Obliged to enter these walls, and to make solemn promises of leading a secluded life, while my heart was full of worldly love, was too severe a task. Can forced oaths be binding? is a hard consent wrung from us to be treated as the voluntary vows of the heart?"

"Idle talk," replied the abbot, "the common cant of those whose irregular worldly passions predominate over the pious holy comforts of a religious life. Be assured, misguided female, no lenity can be shown to such an horrible offence. What! shall it be said that the convent of Santa Catherina, the sanctity of whose character never till this night of wonderful events was sullied; shall it be said that its members were permitted to exercise all acts of horror and depravity, while its superior withheld the just rod of punishment? No; the terrible officer of the holy Inquisition shall have due notice of your deeds."

This said, the abbot, disdaining further converse, turned aside, and father Nicolo assisted the miserable Agatha to arise, and then silently conducted her to the parlour of the convent, from whence, by the order of the angry abbess, she was conducted to a dismal, gloomy chamber, far removed from the comforts of light and air, and situated in the damp, unwholesome bowels of the earth. There, with a scanty portion of bread and water, she was left to meditate on all the horrors of her situation, and to anticipate the dreadful conclusion of a life marked with deeds of blackest hue; deeds that permitted not the smallest hope of mercy or forgiveness, either in this world or that which is to come; deeds which no repentance could hardly expiate.

CHAPTER XX.

THE monk paced the dungeon with impatience, he often looked on the pallid features of Angelina, her pilgrim's hood was thrown back and discovered her beautiful luxuriant tresses, dark eyebrows, and silken eye-lashes; her cheeks were pale, but still retained a lovely look, and her lips were slightly tinged with a roseate hue.

Bernardo, alarmed at her continued insensibility, raised her up from her recumbent posture, and putting his arm round her waist, laid his hand on her bosom, but not the least palpitation of her heart was perceptible; the grim king of terrors seemed to have laid his icy grasp for ever on the fair Angelina, and thus to have deprived the monk of the accomplishment of his horrific intents.

But a deep, long-drawn, convulsive sigh now announced returning animation in the form of Angelina; her lips trembled as her breath passed them, and the monk inhaled the balmy, fragrant zephyr with sensations of new-born delight, while his arm pressed yet more closely her slender waist.

The name of Lorenzo faintly was uttered by Angelina as slowly she unclosed her eyes, and the memory of the past entered her bosom; but when instead of his loved form she beheld herself in the arms of the murderous monk, she shrieked, and started from him.

The monk saw the wild emotions of her soul, and endeavoured to calm its perturbations, but in vain; she heard him not.

"Where am I?" she exclaimed. "O God! but now I thought I saw my beloved Lorenzo weltering in his blood, stabbed by thee, accursed monk. Was it but an horrible dream? Tell me quickly, ere my maddening brain bursts with my agonizing apprehensions."

"Love," said the monk, "dares any thing. It was thy beauteous form that made me commit the deed; thee for my bright reward, what dare I not do?"

The horrors of her situation were now unfolded to the hapless maid. "God of mercy!" said she, "is such a wretch permitted to breathe? do I yet exist; or have I passed the gates of life, and am in regions where fiends foul and horrible take their abode? for such a one is doubtless the form before me. Speak, monster, why am I immured in this horrible dungeon?"

"The precious moments," said Bernardo, "suit not with long parley; this however hear, 'tis some time since thy lovely form raised in my breast the unceasing flame of love. To get thee into my power have I committed dark and dreadful crimes; for thee have I bartered the eternal repose of my soul. Lorenzo is no more, and thou art now deeply concealed in the bowels of the earth, placed in my power by the arts of Hell's dreadful ruler. Thy cries and supplications are in vain; thou art far removed from all human aid, and I am protected by a supernatural power. Give then a loose to love, since it must be so, and no other source is left thee."

Angelina heard his speech, she answered not, her eyes told the wild workings of her bosom, distractedly she fell on her knees, and raising her lovely hands toward Heaven's awful throne, these words proceeded from her parched lips:

"God of all power and might, from whose searching gaze nothing is hid, who can penetrate the secret caves of the earth, and be as conscious of the deeds of horror there committed as if performed on the cloud-capt mountain, look down, I beseech thee, and in thy gracious goodness cut short the thread of my existence rather than let me fall into the power of this monster in human form. Pitying Angels protect me; shield, oh! shield me from this impending ruin."

The monk securely smiled at her ardent entreaties. "Fair maid," said he, "thy Saints hear thee not; the Demon has given thee to me, the pledge of a dreadful contract; dreadful indeed— No matter—away with reflection; the present moment is bliss, let what will come hereafter."

Thus saying, he advanced toward the trembling Angelina, and seizing her by her tender lovely hand, raised her from her suppliant posture, and putting his arms round her slender waist, attempted to kiss her. Angelina screamed unceasingly, and at length forced herself from his hold, and rushed to the furthest extremity of the dungeon.

The monk hastened after her, and again seized her, when the tolling of the abbey clock sounded drearily through the apertures made in the earth for the admission of air into those subterraneous abodes; and rattling bursts of thunder made him relinquish his hold, struck with sudden affright.

The waning moon had finished her monthly travel, and as the hour of midnight sounded, another supplied her place, but in that dungeon such a change was attended with a scene horrible indeed, such as human orbs had never before witnessed, but which was surmised to be the case, as the reader will find in Bartolo's tale of the fair Isabella de Tracy; and this was the monthly penance which the tortured soul of the savage Leonardi di Vicensio was doomed to suffer at her grave.

A second peal of thunder was heard, and now a third rolled with increasing fury along the vaulted arch of Heaven. The door of the dungeon was suddenly burst open, and the massy fastenings fell to the ground.

Bernardo stood trembling beside the terrified Angelina, looking with distended eyeballs at the opened portal.

Deep groans were now heard amidst the stunning peals of Heaven's warfare, loud shrieks rent the air, and the earth trembled as the pendent leaf to the autumnal blast.

A glaring light shone through the door-way, a rushing noise was heard in the passage, and presently after a spectre entered the dungeon. Pale and ghastly was the countenance, deep sunk and dreadful was the expression of the eyes as they fixed their horrible gaze on the rising earth which covered the form of the fair Isabella.

Furies followed the blood-stained form, and loudly exulting, with savage yells they pursued it three times round the grave, torturing the form with scorpion whips that gored the flesh from the sides, leaving the blood clotted ribs visible to the sight.

All this time the thunder roared, the red forked lightnings played around the dungeon, the groans of the tortured soul and the yells of the furies harrowed up the senses of the monk, and he fell lifeless on the earth, as had already done the unfortunate, persecuted Angelina, who now happily was for a time ignorant of the horrors of her situation.

———

Angelina first returned to her senses; she found herself lying on the damp earth, not far from the motionless body of the monk; the light of the lamp feebly gleaming around shewed her the horrors of the place, and having observed the door, which was thrown widely back, she immediately endeavoured to raise herself from the ground, in the hopes of being able to effect her escape before her persecutor should recover.

Her limbs, enfeebled by the late terrors of her mind, could scarcely bear her tottering form; at length she reached the lamp, and taking it up, left the dungeon.

Scarcely had she turned out of the deep archway in which the door was placed, when the monk groaned; convinced by this that his senses were returning, she hastened her footsteps, and soon after proceeded along the passage which led to the other dungeons and subterraneous cavities in which the place abounded.

The extremity of the passage opened into a large cavern whose rocky roof was supported by rough hewn columns; it was of great extent, for Angelina continued pacing it for some time without being able to discover the opposite side.

Fearful of bewildering herself in the vast cavern, Angelina paused; she looked anxiously at the lamp, the oil of which was nearly exhausted, and began to deliberate on what she should do, when the echoes of hasty footsteps broke unwelcome on the silence of those dreary regions of night and horror, and as she looked round saw her dreadful enemy the monk approaching her.

In the wild emotions caused by her deep terrors she dropped the lamp and fled; hastily the monk picked it up ere the light was extinguished, and pursued his trembling prey.

As the monk did not dare to exert his speed, lest by so doing he should extinguish the lamp, on which all his hopes of overtaking her rested; it was some time ere he again seized on the unfortunate Angelina.

The cavern re-echoed with her shrieks when she again felt his detested grasp, and saw his dark eyes glaring on her with all the fierceness of determined outrageous intentions.

She now tried to supplicate his mercy, but in vain; her eyes raised on him in urgent entreaty only fed the furious fires of his bosom, and uttering an oath deep and horrible, the dark purport of which was that nothing should now prevent his horrific intents, he strained the panting form of Angelina still closer to him, and stopped her cries with his detested kisses.

The poor remnant of Angelina's almost exhausted strength could now be but of little avail, and she was on the point of being made for ever miserable in this world, when a sudden glare of torches illumined the extremity of the cavern.

The monk aghast turned round, expecting again to behold the spirit of Leonardi, but instead of it the more unwelcome form of the abbot Ignatio advancing toward him burst forth on his tortured sight.

Leaving his hold of Angelina, he sought to avoid the monks, who, however, rushing forward, soon detained him, while their averted countenances bespoke how much they abhorred his vile, infernal deeds.

Angelina had sunk on the earth; the sovereign powers of reason had deserted her; she stared wildly around.

"My Lorenzo," said she, with a melancholy smile as she gazed around her, "dear Lorenzo where art thou? Oh I saw the blood flowing from his side; the monk stabbed him, and he fell; his soul has passed the gates of death, and is gone to Heaven: Oh! that mine could accompany it to those glad realms! Hark! what groan was that? See how the dreadful spirit stalks around!"

Here her eyes seemed to pursue some terrible vision of her disordered fancies. The abbot tried to comfort her, but she listened not to his words; her terrors and grief had deprived her of the use of her senses.

The countenance of the Padre Bernardo, thus discovered, and at such a moment, was gloomily dreadful; a thousand times did he shower curses on the Demon who had failed to protect him, while all the horrors of his situation rose in his mind: still however a hope existed that he would yet be his friend; and which in some measure enabled him to support the terrible anticipations of the severe punishment which he knew awaited him.

The abbot having directed that the Signora Angelina should be conducted to the chamber belonging to the porteress of the convent for that night, ordered Bernardo to be taken to the dungeon cell, where, chained to the floor, with a scanty truss of straw beneath him, he was left to reflect on the past.

Dreadful indeed and bitter were his reflections; he now saw the snare that had so successfully been laid for him by the eternal enemy of man, and into which he had so completely fallen. How much did he now repent of his too great confidence in his own virtue which had thus thrust him to the very verge of destruction. To supplicate for mercy was impossible; how could he hold up his hands crimsoned with murder toward the throne of the Almighty, without drawing on him the dreadful fury of insulted Heaven? How could he hope that his prayers, made in the moment of danger, and caused only by his fears, could meet with an audience?

All hope, thought he, from Heaven is lost; the murderer's prayers ascend not there, nor is heard the perjured sinner; I have forfeited all hopes of mercy; but still, is not the Demon possessed of power inferior only to the King of Heaven? To him will I look; through his arts I have fell, he may yet protect me.

Mistaken, hapless man, not to know that the angel of mercy is ever ready to receive the prayers, the vows of the penitent, and gladly to bear them before the radiant throne of Heaven. Plunged deep in guilt, Bernardo rather hastened to the very vortex of destruction than seek to court the assistance of the friendly plank which would have supported him to the shore.

To his sad reflections we leave him, while we relate to the reader the means which caused the double discovery which had taken place on that night teeming with events in the monastery of the Santa Catherina.

The blow which in falling Lorenzo de Montalto received against the step of the altar, instantly deprived him of his senses, and the blood flowing both from his head and the wound inflicted by the monk, continued for a long period to stagnate the pulse of life. At length, however, he opened his eyes; the lamp which still feebly glimmered before the ebon crucifix enabled him to discover that he was alone; distractedly he groaned out the name of Angelina, but her sweet voice answered not; again, in somewhat lower tones he repeated her name; echo alone faintly reverberated the sounds. It was then that he reflected on the conduct of the monk; my Angelina, thought he, is now in the power of that fiend of hell, who doubtless is some agent of the Conte Angelo. Oh! Heaven in mercy render me able to pursue the steps of the monster, and rescue my love.

This said, he raised himself, though with much pain and difficulty, on his feet; the dagger of the monk had fortunately glanced against a rib, which averted its progress to the mortal parts; the wound was however large, and the loss of blood considerable, but the situation of Lorenzo's mind, and his fears respecting Angelina, alone rendered him able to exert himself; he hastily endeavoured to stop the stream of life, and though almost fainting, left the altar, and slowly staggered toward the door.

The weak state of his frame rendered him unable for a long time to draw back the bolt, which secured the portal. At length he effected it, and passed into the passage; there he wandered for some time, unknowing whither he was going, for darkness reigned thickly around him.

At length he entered the large corridore that led to the chapel, and aided by the vivid streams of lightning which gleamed through the lofty casements, he directed his feeble steps toward the interior of the monastery.

The anguish of his wounds now caused those groans and convulsive sighs which were heard by the astonished Ferdinando when he was on his way to meet Agatha. The senses of Lorenzo were affected to such a degree from the violence of the agony he suffered, and the misery he endured respecting Angelina, that he neither saw nor heard that cavalier; but continuing his painful journey, arrived at the summit of the grand staircase which rose from the vestibule at the extremity of the corridore; where, with a deep and hollow groan, he sunk on the floor of the gallery.

Heaven, weary of the scenes of guilt which were passing within the walls of the monastery, had so ordered it, that the groans of Lorenzo reached the ears of one of the fathers, who immediately came out of his apartment to know the cause of them, and discovered the blood-stained form of the unfortunate cavalier.

Happily the monk was skilled in medical knowledge, and instantly, without seeking to know by what extraordinary means the person before him could have obtained entrance into the monastery, he bore him to his chamber, and laying him on his couch, staunched his bleeding wounds.

The moment that the faculty of speech returned to Lorenzo, he disclosed to the father the manner in which he was wounded, and the loss of Angelina, and entreated him immediately to make the superior acquainted with these circumstances, that his adored mistress might be sought for.

Such a tale, which at once so deeply implicated a monk and the high reputation of the monastery, was not to be passed over; and father Nicolo immediately repairing to the apartments of the abbot, related to him the extraordinary occurrence of the night.

The abbot immediately arose, and proceeding to the chamber where Lorenzo lay, questioned him concerning the monk who had endeavoured to assassinate him; but Lorenzo, who had not seen Bernardo's features, was unable to give him the smallest intelligence that could direct his suspicions toward any particular person.

Some of the monks whose chambers were contiguous to those of the superior and father Nicolo, awakened by the sound of their paces in the gallery, soon after joined them, and the abbot now determined to search the monastery, in order to find if the Signora Angelina was still within its walls, as from her he doubtless should obtain every information he wished. Leaving Lorenzo to pray for their success, the abbot, attended by the astonished father, descended to the vestibule, and attentively examined many of the chambers below, but without meeting the object of their search.

It was while they were thus employed that Agatha and Ferdinando were discovered, as is already related; an event which tended to raise to its highest pitch the anger of the haughty abbot, who foresaw the tottering reputation of the monastery which had been for many years far famed for the sanctity of its inhabitants. No wonder then that he doomed the pair to destruction. That event, however, did not long impede his search, but no where could he discover the least traces of the objects who caused it.

As there was little doubt that if the Signora had left the convent she would be accompanied by the monk, the abbot ordered the bell to be rung to assemble the community, when he might learn who it was that had been guilty of so outrageous a conduct. Padre Bernardo was alone absent, and a monk was sent to his cell to see if he was there; the father, however, soon returned with the information of the door being fastened, and that he had knocked and called some time without receiving any answer.

The abbot on hearing this immediately determined to force the door, and approaching it with some of the fathers, after some difficulty made it yield to their united efforts.

The chamber was empty, and they were on the point of quitting it when the open pannel in the wainscoting was discovered; this occasioned a further search, and the abbot instantly passed through the aperture.

Thus it was that the secret entrance to the dungeon was found out; and the abbot, determining to explore their subterranean recesses, whither it was evident the monk had retired, immediately descended the winding steps with the fathers.

When arrived at the bottom, the cries of Angelina were distinctly heard; and guided by them, he came just in time to rescue her from the black, horrible designs of Bernardo.

Thus did Heaven protect with its all-powerful arm the supplicating Angelina; and weary with the repeated crimes of the monk, Agatha, and Ferdinando, at length caused them to be discovered, at the very moment when they were going to reap the fruits of the deeds of darkness, delivering them to the avenging arm of jus-

tice in this world, in order to give a terrible warning to others, and
to deter them from following the like iniquitous paths. Heaven is
long-suffering, but it will be just, and sooner or later overwhelms
the guilty in confusion and horror, while to long-suffering virtue
it prepares a bright reward both in this world and in that which is
to come.

CHAPTER XXI.

THE distracted Agatha remained many hours in her gloomy dungeon, a prey to inexpressible horror, for each moment her disturbed imagination represented to her the wan, flitting shades of
Marianne and Claudina stalking before her, while her deeply accusing conscience tortured her unceasingly with its endless sting.
The morning came, but it came not to Agatha, for night held her
cheerless dominion in that dungeon.

At length the powers of animation became feeble, and Agatha
closed her eyes in a disturbed slumber, from which she was roused
by a noise occasioned by the removal of the bolts and chains of
the dungeon door, and to her terrified vision appeared three tall
figures, habited in sable flowing garments, with black visors on.
One of them bore a torch, which throwing gleams on the hapless
nun, discovered to them her pallid features, and her form reclined
on a scanty heap of straw. Unable to move, Agatha gazed on their
mysterious forms with silent dismay, while a deep voice uttered
slowly these words:—

"Agatha, arise; the holy Inquisition hath cognizance of thy offence; its officers await to conduct thee before its great and terrible judges; terrible indeed to thee, who art charged with so much
sin."

Such were the dreadful sentences which vibrated with terror
on the soul of Agatha. One of the gloomy looking officials now
silently advanced, and raised up her trembling and almost lifeless
form. Assisted by the others he carried her from the dungeon,
and traversing some dark passages, the man who bore the torch
unlocked a small postern, and having extinguished it, threw the

door open, when Agatha perceived a carriage waiting without, in which she was placed, and the three officials also entering it, they rolled away from the convent of Santa Catherina.

Padre Bernardo was also conducted from the monastery in like manner, and lodged in the silent horrific prisons of the Inquisition; but Ferdinando escaped the hand of worldly justice, for he breathed forth his last sigh ere the morning sun beamed on the hemisphere.

At midnight Agatha was summoned to attend the Judicial Court; a veil was thrown over her, and in that manner she was hurried along many passages, till at length she was ordered to kneel. The veil was then taken off, and she beheld before her a door. One of the officials having struck it with his staff three times, a voice from within demanded, "Who is there?"

"A miserable sinner," replied the official, "who comes to make confession of her crimes, and to receive such wholesome punishment for her offences as the holy tribunal shall be pleased to inflict on her, that her soul may be purged from all crimes, and be worthy of Heaven's mercy."

The voice then replied, "Enter; and may the pains here endured be an expiation of all worldly sins."

The portal then opened, and Agatha was raised from her knees and conducted into a large and gloomy chamber, illumined only by one lamp, which depended from the centre of the vaulted roof over a long table covered with black cloth, at which sat the judges of the Inquisition.

The conductors having placed Agatha at the extremity of the table, after making profound obedience to the inquisitors, retired. A silence for some moments was held, when the supreme inquisitor, looking at Agatha, who trembled beneath his piercing glance, demanded if she knew what crime she was charged with, and which had occasioned her being brought there.

Agatha tremblingly recapitulated the circumstances of her being obliged to enter the convent, and to take the vows from which her heart revolted; then mentioned her long attachment to the Signor Ferdinando, who had endeavoured to effect her escape, concluding with an earnest supplication to the grand inquisitor for mercy.

"We will be merciful, Agatha, if we find you deserving of it," replied the judge, who bidding a secretary note down the confession of the nun, thus continued: "You have now related the crime for which you suppose you were brought here; now tell me, Agatha, is thy conscience clear of other crimes of a more dark and deadly nature? Answer me as thou hopest for mercy from this tribunal."

The nun trembled. To confess the murder of Marianne would be to involve herself beyond all possibility of hope of being forgiven. She turned deadly pale, and hesitated in her answer. The inquisitor noticed it.

"You fear to confess, Agatha; recollect that no mercy will be shown you unless you strictly conform to the mandates of this court. We know full well your guilty deeds, but wish to see if there is yet any hope that our merciful intentions may be of service to your soul."

Still, however, Agatha, was irresolute, she had heard of the insidious wily arts used by the subtle officers of the Inquisition, and was divided in her ideas whether this was merely a scheme to draw from her what more she might have been guilty of, or whether they indeed were informed of the means by which Marianne met her death; yet a moment's reflection showed her the improbability of their having obtained such knowledge, and she determined to persist in her innocence of all other crimes; which she in a faltering, tremulous voice declared to the court.

The countenance of the grand inquisitor grew dark; he had minutely watched the varying tints of color in the face of Agatha; and though he had no real knowledge of her further guilt, (for his question was put to her at the request of the abbot and abbess of Santa Catherina, in order to find out if she was privy to the cause of the mysterious deaths of the two nuns, Marianne and Claudina,) yet he easily discovered by her confusion that she had more to unfold.

"Beware, Agatha," said he in an enraged tone, "how you seek to deceive this tribunal; know that the torturous rack awaits thee, which will force thee to confess thy guilty acts, which are so legibly impressed on thy countenance."

Agatha's fears increased, for at the mention of the rack her eyes glanced on that horrid engine of death, which was standing at no great distance from her. The sight of it palsied her frame, and for some moments she was going to make a full confession, but her resolution again returned, and she still persisted in avowing her innocence.

"Thy blood, then, Agatha," said the inquisitor, "be on thy own head, since thou art thus obstinately bent on concealing the truth."

This said, he struck the table violently with his clenched fist: the sudden noise echoing through the chamber affrighted Agatha, who looked round her with a dreadful expectancy.

Four demon-looking figures immediately rushed in, and seized hold of the arms of the terrified Agatha; their gigantic forms were covered with black serge, fitted close to the body, having two holes for the eyes, and the whole of their arms from the shoulders were naked.

Agatha shrieked aloud as the first of these monsters in human shape laid his hands upon her. Accustomed to scenes of horror, the pale countenances of the inquisitors betrayed not the smallest emotion while the officials were dragging her to the rack; nor did they heed her terrible screams; she was now on the point of being laid on the torturous engine, when no longer able to bear the dreadful anticipations of her sufferings, she faintly requested to be allowed to speak to the Grand Inquisitor. The men instantly loosed their hold, and stood by her side, while in a tremulous voice she confessed the whole of her guilty acts, implicating at the same time the Padre Bernardo, who she was ignorant was at that time in the dungeon of the same inquisitional prison as herself.

The Inquisitor started with horror at her relation, while a smile of self-approbation marked the countenance of the Grand Judge on his having so successfully come to the knowledge of the mysterious fate of the two nuns.

"Thou hast done well, Agatha, to confess thy sins," said he, as soon as she had concluded, "and all the mercy this tribunal can show to such crimes as thine shall, according to our promise, be done. A holy Dominican father shall daily attend thee, to prepare thy soul for that awful eternity to which in a few days it will hasten; meantime, hope not for a change of this decree, but in fasting, penitence, and prayers, endeavour to make some atonement for thy dreadful deeds."

The last words came not to the ears of Agatha; she sunk senseless on the floor, and the officials were ordered to convey her to her dungeon.

Padre Bernardo then entered the hall; a profound silence reigned in its gloomy interior; the eyes of the inquisitors were steadfastly fixed on him; his countenance, however, underwent no change and when the usual question was put to him as to what crime he supposed he was accused of, and which was merely asked in hopes the culprit would name some other offence than that for which he was brought before the tribunal, and so implicate himself still deeper, the monk, to the astonishment of all around, replied, that he was innocent of any crime; that it was true he was found in the dungeons of the ancient Castello with a female, but it was at her own request that he had conducted her there, after she had murdered the Signor, and that her screams which the abbot heard were occasioned by her fears of being discovered and brought to justice.

Astonishment seized the inquisitors as they listened to so palpable a falsehood, but Bernardo remained composed. He had invented this tale, as being entirely ignorant of the existence of Lorenzo, and he thought he was as fully entitled to belief as the Signora; and he knew, as it could not be supposed he had ever seen the parties before, there was but little apparent reason to think that he would assassinate one of them.

The Grand Inquisitor, as soon as the monk's answer had been noted by the secretary, then demanded of him if in his breast there did not harbour a remembrance of any other crime than the one which he seemed to think he was accused of?

Bernardo confidently replied in the negative, while a pallid hue stole over his cheeks as he recalled to his memory the last moments of Claudina. Of that circumstance being divulged he knew he had but little reason to fear, since no one was acquainted with it but Agatha and she, from self-interested motives, would not betray her knowledge of it.

"Instantly confess your crimes, or the rack shall extort them from you," vociferated the judge in an angry tone, while his countenance grew gloomy and determined.

Bernardo knowing that in persisting in his innocence was his only hope, still denied his knowledge of having committed any crime which could draw on him the anger of the holy Inquisition.

Enraged at his obstinacy, the Judge gave the signal, and the officials immediately entered the chamber.

"Put the prisoner to the question," said he, "his corporeal sufferings may make him confess."

The officials, long accustomed to their duty, took off the habit of the monk, and tying cords round his wrists and ankles bound him to the rack; he was demanded if he would confess, which still refusing to do, his body was distended on the engine, and so severely did they apply the torture, that the monk, from the dreadful agonies he suffered became insensible, and was carried out from the hall to his cell, where a surgeon attended to recal his insensate form to animation.

On the third night he was judged sufficiently recovered to attend the second examination, and he was accordingly again conducted to the hall.

"Bernardo," said the judge, "the pains you have suffered will doubtless induce you to confess your crimes, in order to prevent a repetition of them."

"I know not," replied the monk, "what course to follow. You wish me to confess myself guilty of crimes of which I am ignorant. I have already asserted my innocence, and the tortures I suffered because I would not confess imaginary sins must convince you that I am wrongly suspected. But produce my accusers; let them tax me with my supposed guilt, I shall not be at a loss to answer them."

"I am your accuser," said a hollow female voice, which appeared close to the monk, who immediately turned about to see from whom it proceeded. No person, however, met his gaze; his visage grew of a ghastly, pallid hue; again he surveyed the chamber, the distant walls were obscured in the gloom, and there might, for ought he knew, be many people enveloped in the dark mantle of night which hung around.

The inquisitors marked in silence the varying hues of his countenance.

"Did not you hear a voice, Bernardo?" said the Grand Judge.

"I did," replied the monk, "but know not from whom or whence it proceeded. If indeed my accuser is here, why not let him be produced?"

The judge now made a sign to one of the inquisitors, who left the chamber. "You will presently see the person who has revealed your dark acts," said he, addressing himself to the monk; "we shall then determine whether your asseverations of your innocence be true or not."

A noise behind him of approaching paces now engaged the attention of the monk: three figures advanced through the gloom toward the table; two of them, who were officials, seemed supporting the third, who had the appearance of a female, but the form being enveloped in a long sable mantle, rendered the monk doubtful.

"Thy accuser is before thee, Bernardo," said the Judge; then turning to the person who stood between the officials, "Speak now, and inform the Court of the guilty deeds of the monk."

"I accuse him of the murder of Claudina, a nun of Santa Catherina;" replied the hollow-toned voice.

The monk trembled; his quivering lips for some moments denied him the power of speech.

"Why do you not answer, Bernardo, to this accusation?"

"I demand," said the monk, "to see my accuser."

After a short consultation the Judge directed the garment to be taken off the form of the person, when the glare of the lamp disclosed to the wretched monk the pale wan features of Agatha; who, unable to stand, was supported by the officials. Such an unexpected person, and one too who was an eye-witness of the murder of Claudina, entirely bereft him of his faculties. The powers of life seemed suspended; his eyes were steadfastly fixed with a dreadful expression of horror, surprize, and fear on the nun; his mouth was open, and his nostrils distorted.

"The knowledge of thy crimes harrow up thy senses," said the Judge to the monk. "Wilt thou now confess thy guilt?"

Agatha's situation at this moment attracted the attention of the inquisitors. She appeared to be in the agonies of death; for some time the convulsed state of her frame prevented her from speaking. At length she uttered these words:

"My hour is come, in a few moments my soul, disencumbered of this form that brought on me my undoing, will appear before its Creator. Dreadful anticipation! how dreadful to me is the remembrance of my crimes. Cavini, thou who seduced me from the paths of virtue, much hast thou in me to answer for. But oh! the horrible recollection of the murder of a fellow-creature weighs most heavy on my soul; it is, I fear, a damning weight. Bernardo, thou hast yet moments for repentance; do not thou delay, but endeavour while yet this world contains thee, to make some amends for the guilty deeds thou hast performed in it."

Here the nun paused, a second convulsive pang seized her; for some time her eyes were closed, but at length she languidly half raised them, and then in a still more faint voice continued:—

"'Tis done, Death's chilling grasp presses hard upon me. In order to avoid the horrible punishment which I well knew awaited me, I have taken poison; even now I feel the deadly potion stopping the vital current of my existence. What horrors, what despair, what torturous emotions pervade my bosom! Marianne, thou art revenged."

More words were spoken, but in so weak a tone as to be unintelligible, and now a groan announced the departure of the soul that animated her frail form. We hope that as she died repentant, the dread punishment awaiting crimes like hers was in some measure lessened.

A profound silence was observed during the last moments of Agatha, and when the breath of life had for ever fled her lips, the judge ordered her body to be taken away.

"After what has passed, Bernardo," said he, "you will doubtless no longer seek to assert your innocence. If, however, you are still obstinate, remember the rack, and yet more dreadful torments await you."

The monk, conscious that there was no hope, tremblingly confessed his sins, when the judge thus addressed him:

"Awful is the task of delivering the sentence of death; but how much more awful must it be to the ears of the guilty. Bernardo, thou hast but two days of life, employ them in repenting of thy crimes. Miserable man! as thou hopest for Heaven's mercy do not neglect this advice, for the knell of thy departing moment will soon toll."

The Grand Inquisitor here made a sign to the officials, who silently conducted the monk to his dungeon, where throwing himself on the straw that formed his bed, he long remained in a state of insensibility to every thing but the anticipation of the torments he should endure. The whole of that day he never raised his head, but when the shades of evening began to steal away the surrounding objects from the sight, he arose, and paced the narrow confines of his cell.

He now thought of the Demon. His power was sufficient to liberate him from his present dreary abode, and he determined to solicit his assistance at this important period.

Buoyed up with fallacious hopes, he waited with anxiety for the midnight hour, when he invoked the restless enemy of man to his aid.

In a moment the Demon stood before him: on his dark countenance was strongly marked the traits of anger and impatience. "What wouldest thou with me?" said he in a voice of thunder. "Speak; for on thee I have no more time to spare. Weak, pusillanimous mortal, whose ideal fears prevented the fruition of thy soul's wishes, even when in the silent bosom of the earth thou hadst in thy possession the fairest of Nature's works. Thou art now justly suffering for thy timidity."

The monk looked aghast at this unexpected speech, and falteringly replied, "All I now entreat of thee is my release. Through thy arts am I now condemned to die; preserve me but this once, and I will not again trouble thee."

"Mistaken mortal," said the Demon, "thou hast wrongly judged. As soon as thy soul became the abode of impure thoughts thou didst confess my sway, and seek to enrol thyself amongst the myriads whom I reign over; then, indeed, did I increase the hold I had on you, and made you subservient to my own purposes. Now, monk, thou art wholly mine; all Sicily will behold thy torturous exit from this world; and that thy horrors may be complete, know that the lovely maid whom you sought in order to gratify thy abandoned desires was—thy own sister."

This said, with a smile of exulting malice the Demon became invisible to the eyes of the monk, who groaned with horror at his concluding words, and raving with the dreadful sensations they excited, dashed himself against the walls of the dungeon, till at length overcome, with mental and corporeal agonies, he sunk almost lifeless on the ground.

The pale reflexes of the beams of the morning which slowly entered his dungeon beheld him in his recumbent posture; he rested his languid head on his arm, and looked at the grating which admitted the light, while the agonizing reflection crossed his mind that he viewed it for the last time.

Hasty indeed were the hours of that day in their approach. A Dominican father entered the cell, and exhorted him to repent, but Bernardo attended not to his words. Deep sighs convulsed his form, his heart beat heavily against his side, his countenance was pale and ghastly, dreadful indeed were his anticipations, for all hope in Heaven's mercy was gone; and though his sufferings in this world would be terrible indeed, yet he feared that what he was doomed to endure in the next would be far worse.

Such were the thoughts that occupied his bosom during that day. With consternation he beheld the reflexes of the sunbeams fade away and the shades of evening lower around his cell; to him they were the harbingers of his speedy sufferings, and as the mists increased, so increased the distraction of his mind.

At length but one hour was wanting to midnight; and now the heavy bell of San Dominico began to toll. Bernardo started at the sound as if it had conveyed to his form an electric spark;

302 THE DEMON OF SICILY

his breath grew short, his heart throbbed, and he trembled with inbred horrors.

A second toll gloomily echoed through his dungeon; to him it was the knell of his departure from this world; slow beating in his ears each dreaded toll increased the horror that raged in his mind, till his senses were wound up to the most excruciating acme of misery.

Foot paces now echoed along the passage that led to his cell, and the door being thrown open, the officers of the Inquisition entered, to conduct him to the place of execution. Arrived at the court-yard of the extensive edifice, they stopped, and Bernardo raising his eyes beheld a vast concourse of people assembled to behold his dreadful torturous exit. He did not long survey them, for his gaze was attracted by a coffin, which was drawn on a hurdle and placed just before him; in it was the once-beauteous form of Agatha, now exhibiting an horrible and loathsome appearance; those cheeks, where once the rose and lily united, now robbed of their firmness and bewitching dimples, were sunk and blackened with the effects of the poison; those love-beaming eyes closed for ever, the nostrils distorted, the lips black, and decaying damps fast seizing on the livid corse.

The monk turned away his eyes; the contrast between her sad remains and the remembrance of what Agatha had been sickened his very soul, and yet he envied her situation, for she had escaped the horrible tortures now awaiting him.

From that place Bernardo was conducted to the chapel of the monastery of San Dominico, whose ponderous bell's horrific sounds long hung on the nocturnal breeze, and vexed the attendant echoes which sullenly reverberated the knell of death.

The chapel was illumined with the torches borne by the terrific-clad officials. It was crowded with the Sicilian nobility of both sexes, from motives of religion as well as curiosity.

Bernardo was brought into the centre of the chapel; he was scarcely able to stand; he never raised his head, but remained trembling with the awful horrors inspired by his situation, while the secretary of the Inquisition read aloud the dark confessions of his crimes.

A burst of horror ran through the assembly when he had concluded. The monk was then formally excommunicated the church, and the attending officials taking off his habit, put on him the dreadful garment allotted to the incurables; thus delivered over to laical authority, his body was sentenced to be consumed by flames till his soul should desert its agonized abode.

The procession now began to move forward from the gates of the chapel to the place where the fatal stake was prepared.

First advanced the Grand Inquisitor, in his splendid robes of office, attended by some of his colleagues, and the superior of the monastery of San Dominica, the patron of that terrible society; next came the friars two and two, bearing the banners and other insignia of the Inquisition; then came the hurdle on which was the body of Agatha, drawn by persons who had incurred the displeasure of the holy office, and were sentenced to perform many acts of penance in extenuation of their crimes; to them was allotted the task of fixing the fatal stake and placing the faggots round it. Following the hurdle came the wretched Bernardo; after him the crucifix with its back toward him, was borne by other Dominican monks, with a long train of lay brethren, and many of the nobility, who on this occasion shewed their zeal by joining in the procession, and carrying wax tapers; the officers of the Inquisition walked on each side, bearing torches, whose flames cast a lurid glare over the solemn train.

During this time the bell of San Dominica still continued its deadly tolls, and excepting its melancholy sounds, notwithstanding the astonishing concourse of spectators who thronged to see the awful scene, scarcely a murmur disturbed the silence which prevailed.

The miserable Bernardo was now led forward and chained to the fatal stake, and the faggots placed around him. Near him was laid the body of Agatha, and now the torches were applied to the pile.

Deep sighs and groans were heard from the assembly as the crackling wood began to flame around the monk, who as the wind often drove the fire against him shrieked out with the pain.

At this moment what must have been his sensations? on the

very verge of an eternity to which the most excruciating corporeal tortures were quickly hastening him, and where he had every reason to suppose his sufferings would be far worse; for could *he* hope for mercy who had never shown it? who could coolly deliberate on the murder of a fellow-creature, who could behold the quivering limbs of the expiring Claudina, the convulsed heavings of her bosom, till her last breath escaped her, and who could plunge his dagger in the bosom of another before the very altar where was raised the crucified form of the Saviour of the World, who died to expiate the crimes of mankind?

The smoke and flames now obscured the form of the monk; his agonizing shrieks became more dreadful, till at length they ceased to harrow up the feelings of the surrounding multitude, who still looked on the flaming pile with sensations of horror more easily conceived than described.

Unseen by mortal vision the Demon stretched on high his gigantic form before the flames which were consuming the body of the monk; a malicious grin sat horribly on his features as he surveyed him writhing with agony; and when his soul fluttered on his half-burnt lips the Demon seized it in his piercing iron grasp, and darting through the cleft bosom of the globe, winged his rapid flight along the broad path made by sin and death through the regions of chaos and ancient night, and arriving at his horrible domains, dashed far from him into the burning lake his immortal burthen, and casting a look of defiance toward the abode of blissful spirits, strode over the burning billows, plotting fresh schemes to entrap unwary mortals, to show his irreconcileable and deadly hate.

Thus perished Agatha and Bernardo; the hapless nun, by becoming the instrument of her own dissolution, increased her heavy load of crimes. Such is too often the termination of the existence of the female who listens to the syren voice of seduction. Gay, unthinking man, you know not what you do when urged by momentary passion you deprive an unsuspecting, confiding woman of her honor; she then becomes avoided by her own sex, and despised by the other. No wonder then, abandoned by all that is good, she becomes herself the votary of vice, and advancing progressively from one sin to another, forgets that there is a Heaven, forgets that she has an immortal soul, and self-murdered dies, invoking curses on her seducer.

Here we will conclude this chapter, and though the pen has imperfectly endeavoured to show the miseries of vice, yet we trust that some moral may be gleaned from it.

Let the lovely female consider how miserable was Agatha from the first moment she yielded to Cavini; distress and horror attended her steps; one crime led to another, till murder crowned the end. Let her sad story arm her with resolution to steel her bosom against the soft advances of love and the empassioned language of the seducer.

Perhaps too the fate of Bernardo will be a lesson to unwary youth to guard well against the strong impulse of vice, and to resist its specious advances.—"Vice to be hated needs but to be seen."

CHAPTER XXII.

FROM such scenes of horror, and the painful reflections naturally produced by them, we will return to the monastery within whose walls Lorenzo and Angelina now resided.

The senses of that lovely woman were still wandering, nor were the nuns able to say or do any thing that could calm the mental agonies which had hurled reason from her seat. She raved about Lorenzo, then thought she saw the Conte Angelo, and shrunk from the ideal touch of the monk Bernardo. The sisters looked on in mournful silence, for the sight of an innocent creature labouring under such torturous sensations as did Angelina, was more than the most insensate could view without pity.

The abbot Ignazio, after he had given directions respecting the confinement of the nun and the monk, returned to the chamber, where Lorenzo impatiently awaited him; who when he heard the situation of Angelina started from his couch. "Oh! father," he exclaimed, "I entreat you to let me see her; the voice of love will recal her wandering senses; do not, I conjure you, refuse me this request."

"My son," replied the abbot, "your present weak state will incapacitate you for such a task; seek now repose, think that Angelina is safe from all persecution, wait till the morning is far advanced, and should she not then be any better, I shall permit you to see her."

This said, the abbot departed, and left Lorenzo with the good father Nicolo, who did all in his power to comfort his patient, and frequently went to see Angelina, in hopes of being able to administer some composing medicine. Sister Ursula was also unremitting in her attentions; but still their lovely patient was insensible to them, and alive only to recollections which harrowed up all her faculties to the wild pitch of delirium.

At length father Nicolo persuaded the abbot to give permission to Lorenzo to see Angelina; he supported his faint steps to the chamber belonging to the porteress, and when the nun had retired, was allowed to enter it. He there beheld his adored love seated on the side of the couch, her lovely hair all dishevelled, her features wild and convulsed, her gaze vacant and unsettled, and her hands clasped in each other.

When Lorenzo entered he started back, horror-struck at her appearance. She, however, took no notice of him, though her eyes evidently were at that moment turned toward the door. Deeply affected he advanced, and kneeling at her feet, took her passive hand, and conjured her to speak to him. At the sound of his voice Angelina started; she raised her hands, and covered her face.

"'Tis his voice—he calls me from the grave, and thinks me unkind to stay so long from him. There he lies cold and motionless, his soul now hovers round me. Oh! Lorenzo! I will soon be with thee."

"Angelina, you are now with your Lorenzo; look on me, recollect your fond lover."

Angelina let her hands fall from her face; she looked on Lorenzo. Some faint recollections returned, and she burst into tears.

Father Nicolo appeared much pleased with this favourable

symptom; he then, though with some difficulty, made her take the contents of a small phial.

"Her senses," said he to Lorenzo, "are now returning; this medicine will, I hope, give her some repose; meanwhile do you, my son, withdraw. I will watch her slumbers; for should she recollect you before she is prepared for such an event, the sudden transition from grief to joy may be more than her frame, enfeebled by her sufferings, will permit her to support."

Lorenzo saw the prudence of such a step; and, having kissed Angelina's hand, he slowly withdrew, in the sweet hope that in a short time she would recover. He now bethought himself of Carlo and Annetta; and, on inquiring of the porter of the monastery, learned that those faithful creatures were quite distracted with the intelligence they had received from him, and had on their knees begged to be admitted, a favour which however could not be allowed them, consistent with the rigid rules of the monastery.

Lorenzo immediately repaired to the grate, where he beheld them sitting sorrowfully on the steps of the portal; their joy on seeing him was great, but it was much increased by the hope he seemed to entertain of Angelina's recovery.

Father Nicolo meantime attentively watched over his lovely patient, who yielding to the influence of the medicine he had given her, sunk soon after into a profound slumber.

It was not till the evening that Angelina awoke. She started on seeing father Nicolo and Ursula by the side of the pallet; her recollection returned, and in a soft, tremulous voice she uttered the name of Lorenzo, while a long and painful sigh, issued from her bosom.

"Compose yourself, daughter," said Nicolo, "all may yet be well; do not give way to grief."

"Oh! father, how can all be well? how can I ever cease to grieve? for is not my Lorenzo lost to me for ever in this world?"

"How do you know that he is dead?" said the father, delighted to find that she was now sensible. "Your fears, Angelina, are premature."

"What do you say?" hastily she replied; "is then Lorenzo living? Ah! father, do not give me false hopes."

"The Saints forbid that I should seek to deceive you, daughter, when I tell you that Lorenzo de Montalto yet lives."

"Yet lives did you say? Ah! let me see him, let me attend his couch, and receive his last sighs, they will be breathed for his Angelina."

"Far distant be his last sighs," returned the monk; "long may he live to return your love; his wounds, Signora, are not dangerous, nor is he confined to his couch, he was in this room this morning, but you knew him not."

Thus did the Padre Nicolo cautiously acquaint Angelina with the existence of her lover. For awhile she was silent, but her clasped hands and uplifted eyes showed her engaged in mental thanksgiving to the Almighty disposer of events.

"And shall I see him, father?" said she at length, looking on the monk with an inquiring, supplicating gaze.

"If you will promise to be composed I will bring him to you," replied Nicolo; "but I almost fear to do it, lest your agitation should be the cause of delaying your recovery."

"Oh! no, father," replied Angelina, "believe me I will endeavour to restrain the tide of extreme joy which swells in my bosom."

Nicolo then left the chamber, and assisted Angelina to rise from the couch, and seat herself in a large chair. She was very weak, but the fever of delirium had entirely subsided, her eyes had assumed their natural sweetness of expression, and the red flushing on her cheeks had given way to the delicate lily-tinted rose.

Ursula acquainted her with the wonderful events which had taken place in the monastery and convent; and when she heard that her persecutor, the monk Bernardo, was in the relentless hands of the Inquisition, her forgiving spirit made her forget the dreadful wrongs he intended her, and she sighed at his situation.

The melancholy thoughts excited by the information of Ursula were, however, soon dissipated by the entrance of father Nicolo and Lorenzo.

To describe their meeting, to give but a faint idea of the rapturous sensations of their bosoms, exceed the pen. The good old sister Ursula and father Nicolo could not unmoved behold the tender scene that presented itself, a tear stole down their cheeks, and they breathed a fervent prayer for their happiness in this world.

Lorenzo, when at length he was able to leave Angelina, proceeded to the abbot Ignazio, whom he made acquainted with every circumstance relative to Angelina and himself, not forgetting to mention the Conte's violation of his oath, and base attempts against the peace of his ward; he then entreated that as Angelina would not permit him to make his conduct to her public, on account of her father's revered memory, he would take her under his protection and unite them; slightly hinting at the same time his fears that if Angelo knew where his ward was, the sanctity of the convent would not be a sufficient security against his attempts.

The haughty abbot, fired at this last idea, replied, "The Signora Angelina need not be under any apprehensions from laical power, for while within these walls I will protect her from the daring Angelo; who should he be presumptuous enough to appear before the gates with hostile intents, shall quickly find a residence in the dungeons of the Inquisition; and I further promise you, that as soon as the Signora is recovered, you shall be united to her."

Lorenzo was pleased to find that he had a powerful friend in the abbot, and having expressed his gratitude to him for his goodness, retired. And now did he again admit to his bosom a pleasing train of joyful anticipations of days of happiness and unalloyed delights, he retired to rest while visions of blissful import crowded to his ideal view, and the healing powers of sleep repaired his care and pain-worn frame.

The absence of Angelina and Annetta from the Castello de Carlentini was discovered early the next morning. To describe the rage of the Conte is impossible; for it was on that day that he had determined to force her into a marriage. Parties were sent out in every direction after them, but to no purpose; at length the clothes which they had left behind them in the wood being found, not only acquainted Angelo with their probable route, but also that the object of his persecution was under the protection of his hated rival, Lorenzo de Montalto.

He now determined to search after the fugitives himself; and attended by his people, took the road that led to the monastery of Santa Catherina. The confused reports which he collected from the peasantry who resided near the monastery of the late wonderful events which had taken place there induced him to make inquiries at it; and as he was approaching the gates he had a slight glimpse of the persons of Carlo and Annetta, who, terrified at his appearance, fled for protection into the chapel.

Angelo on inquiring at the gate learned that the object of his pursuit was within its walls, and instantly demanded to see the abbot.

If Ignazio had not been previously prejudiced against the Conte by the recital of Lorenzo, his present conduct was sufficient to stir up all his ready pride and indignation. He slowly entered the parlour whither the Conte had been conducted, and then in no very complacent terms demanded the purport of his visit.

His stern deportment somewhat confused the Conte, who began to fear that he should have some difficulty in persuading him to accede to his wishes in delivering up Angelina; and assuming a respectful tone, he thus replied:—"Holy father, I come to request you will deliver to me the Signora Angelina, whose guardian I am by the authority of her departed parent."

"Angelina," replied the abbot, "claims the protection of the Church against your persecutions, Conte; nor shall it be withheld from her. I am informed of the oath you took before the venerable abbess of the convent of Santa Maria, and I grieve to hear that you have, unmindful of that sacred promise, persisted in endeavouring to bring your vile plans into effect. Unless she wishes it, the Signora shall not again be in your power; nay more, I have given my promise to Lorenzo de Montalto to unite them."

The Conte, exasperated to the highest pitch at the speech of the abbot, could scarcely articulate his words.

"Beware," said he, "how you do such an act. Angelina is my

ward; her fortune is at my disposal if she marries without my consent; and I have also witnesses to prove that she made a solemn promise at the altar to be mine."

"A forced oath," said the abbot, "and from which the power of the Church releases her. Your conduct has proved how unfit you are to be the guardian of Angelina; and when it is represented to the King, her fortune doubtless will be restored to her."

The Conte bit his lips; he looked blackly at the abbot, who eyed him with a haughty look; and then rising from his seat, said:—

"I have no time, Conte, for further converse; you know my resolutions."

"And you will marry Angelina to that impostor Lorenzo?" hastily said the Conte.

The abbot slightly moved his head in token of his intentions to that effect.

"Then beware the consequences, which shall heavily revert on yourself, proud abbot," vociferated the enraged Angelo.

"How," said the abbot, "is it that you address me? Know that I smile at your threats; and to prove how little I heed them, be in the chapel an hour hence, and you shall witness the nuptial ceremony of Lorenzo and Angelina. Nor is that all, Conte. Tremble," added he, looking darkly at him, "lest the Inquisition take cognizance of your contemptuous and insulting conduct to a minister of the holy church, and within its sacred inclosures."

This said, he left the parlour, and the Conte to his own thoughts. He already began to fear that he had said too much, and the last words of the abbot did indeed make him tremble; he saw that all hopes of his getting Angelina in his power were now at an end; still, however, he determined to withhold her estates. This idea in some measure served to console him under his present fears and disappointments; and he left the monastery determined to repair to the Castello directly, and there await the result of the abbot's threats; for he was fearful of again seeing him, lest he should provoke him further, and make him put them in execution.

When the abbot left the parlour he immediately sent for

Lorenzo, who in his ruffled countenance and dark looks easily perceived something unusual had taken place.

"The Conte Angelo has been here," said he, "his comportment has been such as confirms your relation. Insolent, ignorant man, not to know the respect due to my dignified station, or the danger of insulting the ministers of the holy church; but I shall teach him that we are not to be insulted with impunity; and to show him the utter contempt in which I hold his threats, will instantly ratify my promise made to you, therefore be in the chapel at the expiration of an hour, and I will unite you to the Signora Angelina."

Lorenzo joyfully expressed his grateful thanks to the abbot, which he received with silent state, while his angry looks showed him what he was now going to do was from motives of revenge for insulted pride, more than any wish to hasten the happy termination of his cares respecting his adored Angelina.

He immediately hastened to her, and disclosed the joyful tidings, which she deeply blushing received, and Annetta being admitted to her, prepared for the ceremony.

At the appointed hour she descended to the corridore which communicated with the monastery; there she found the impatient Lorenzo waiting her approach. She had thrown off her pilgrim's weeds, and was habited in a robe of white, which was confined to her slender waist by a circlet of diamonds; her hair was fancifully braided, and curled over her polished forehead. Thus simply attired she shone forth in all her natural charms, added to which was the blissful possession of innocence and virtue. Lorenzo led her to the altar, when the abbot Ignazio performed the nuptial ceremony; while his eyes, which yet retained an indignant expression, were often raised in expectation of seeing Conte Angelo enter the chapel, a circumstance which would have gratified the haughty abbot, as it would have afforded him an opportunity of triumphing over the Conte.

Angelina, the lovely fascinating Angelina, was now irrevocably Lorenzo's, and he sealed the happy contract on her coral lips. The abbot condescendingly gave them his benediction, and apparently vexed that Angelo did not appear, retired to his apartments.

Lorenzo passed that day with his beloved Angelina. Still, however, his happiness was somewhat alloyed from his apprehensions of the vindictive Conte, who he concluded was laying in wait for him, and from the number of his followers, both himself and Angelina would become an easy prey. The soul of Lorenzo knew not fear but for his Angelina, and he secretly determined to put a stop to his inquietude on that head.

As it was necessary that Lorenzo should inform his father, the Marchese de Montalto, of his marriage with Angelina, he now quitted the monastery, leaving her in the care of the kind and attentive nuns. Attended by Carlo, he soon arrived at his father's palazio, and disclosed to him his marriage with the heiress of Carlentini. The venerable Marchese congratulated his son on such an acquisition, for the beauties and virtues of Angelina were not unknown to him. With respect to the Conte Angelo retaining her possessions, he determined to have a private audience of the Monarch, who he well knew would see justice done to the oppressed.

Lorenzo now attended by a numerous party of retainers suitable to his father's rank, unknown to the Marchese repaired to the Castello de Carlentini, where he openly challenged the Conte Angelo to single combat. This he however tremblingly refused to accept, alledging as an excuse the weak state of his frame from his late wounds.

Meantime the old Marchese had seen the King, who justly incensed at the present as well as former conduct of Angelo, condemned him to be banished, and the estates of Carlentini to be immediately restored to Angelina.

As Lorenzo was returning from the Castello he met with a party of the King's troops, who were charged with carrying his orders into effect, and Lorenzo had the pleasure of seeing the Conte shortly after conducted by them to the place of his destination, accompanied by his ready agent Hildargo.

The Castello was soon prepared for the reception of its rightful possessors, and Lorenzo hastened back to the convent of

Santa Catherina, where he disclosed to Angelina the events that had taken place.

She immediately accompanied him to their future peaceful residence. At the entrance of the valley the numerous peasantry in their best attire met them, and hailed their coming with acclamations of heartfelt joy. It was not without emotion that either Angelina or Lorenzo heard their honest declarations; and when they had arrived at the Castello, ordered ample refreshments to be provided for them.

Light and airy Sicilian measures floated on the air till a late hour, the moon lent her silver beams, and the tranquil nocturnal zephyrs were undisturbed by angry gales; all was peace and joy. Content, with all her smiling offspring, presided over the Val di Carlentini.

Annetta a few days after was united to Carlo, and an ample independence presented them by Lorenzo and his Angelina; but they preferred staying at the Castello, to enjoy the happiness which reigned undisturbed in its walls.

Here these eventful pages terminate.

Weak indeed have been the efforts of the pen to pourtray the dangers of giving way to vicious inclinations, and to impress the instructive moral. Fain would it endeavour to elevate the mind, to show vice in its true colours, how hateful, how deformed; to show the blessings ever attendant on the votaries of virtue, and how in every situation an all-seeing Providence watches over and protects his creatures, hurling destruction on their oppressors. Such was the aim with which they were written; if happily they should succeed, great will be the gratification; and should they fail, still there will be this consolation—that their intent was good.

THE END.

www.ingramcontent.com/pod-product-compliance
Lightning Source LLC
Chambersburg PA
CBHW072056020726
47501CB00003B/607